Fatal Storm

(Storm Series Book 5)

A. R. Vagnetti

Wicked Storm Publishing

Copyright © 2022 by Wicked Storm Publishing

ALL RIGHTS RESERVED.

No part of this publication may be reproduced, distributed, or transmitted in any form or by any means, including photocopying, recording, or other electronic or mechanical methods, without the prior written permission of the publisher, except in the case of brief quotations embodied in critical reviews and certain other noncommercial uses permitted by copyright law.

This is a work of fiction. Any characters, names, places, or likenesses are purely fictional. Resemblances to any of the items listed above are merely coincidental.

Edited by: Haley Willens

Cover Design: Les at German Creative

Content Warning: Violence, blood and gore, references to rape, consensual BDSM play with explicit sexual scenes, and graphic language. Everything my readers come to expect from me and more.

This book is dedicated to my greatest supporter: the ultimate griller, camper, cross country driver, wood chopping, rock piling fiend. You know who you are and what you mean to me.

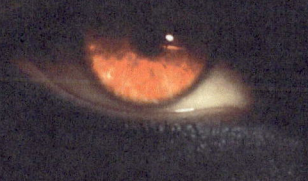

Chapter 1

Jagorach

"**A**ny changes, Andolf?"
"None, sire. Priestess Tanagra is as before."

It is the same damn conversation I have with my withered warlock every day. The fact his answer never changes ramps my barely controlled rage up to the surface, and I grip the arms of my iron throne to remain seated.

"Perhaps your presence would be beneficial, my Lord."

"Beneficial to whom, you pompous ass?" My brows furrow in irritation. "Do you imagine I enjoy staring at her lifeless body for moments on end, desperate for even a small twitch of life?"

The wizard has the sense to gulp in fear. "Nay, my lord."

I rise, my irises heating with a gathering storm. My personal Warriors, lining the room, never move. Instead, their watchful stares follow me as I prowl toward the one magical being I had high hopes would've had the answer to my growing dilemma.

Today was shit. Complete and utter shit. Moving the Demon Realm headquarters and my personal residence from Santa Fe, New Mexico to my new territory in Arizona was much more tedious and time-consuming than initially expected.

The second the vampire queen granted me the scalding region in our treaty, I could not wait to transplant our headquarters to the dry, scorching desert. It reminds me of a slightly more pleasant version of home down below.

But the transition cost me precious time which my little land nymph cannot spare. My anxiety at losing her forever to the power-hungry forces of purgatory is a lead weight crushing my chest.

I refocus on Andolf's trembling form. He's justified in his fear. "Is it beneficial to Priestess Tanagra that we have imprisoned her soul in Hell while you twirl your thumbs and present me with fucking platitudes?"

The inept witch cowers in alarm, igniting the darkness inherent in every molecule of my essence. If I could control the idiot's mind, I would command him to flay his own skin from his body for his failure. "I've exhausted every resource I possess, my lord," he whimpers. "What you solicit is far beyond my knowledge."

Fury claws to the surface, and my demon form roars for freedom, causing the skin on my back to itch with the compulsion to unfurl my wings. "Is that so?" I question quietly, even as my insides shriek to rip the scraggly white beard from his chin and to bask in his screams. "I seem to recall you assured me that what I had asked was well within your wheelhouse, Warlock. So please, inform me you have not wasted my time. Or hers."

When I gathered Kleora's lifeless body from the stone floor of the dark fae castle and into my embrace, the agony of losing another precious being I cared for nearly destroyed every piece of my precarious humanity. Frantic to keep her with me, I performed a binding spell as my beautiful nymph's bright spirit rose from her body. Before her dazzling light ascended to Heaven, I snatched her from my father's waiting grasp and entombed her soul inside my private chambers in Hell, linking her to me for all eternity. My one thought—keep her close until I could figure out a way to shove her essence back into her body. Her body now laying enshrouded in magic to preserve her flesh in a private room in my new Tucson home.

It was rash and forbidden, and one day I will pay the price for my willful disregard of God's rules. I bark out a laugh. Who am I kidding? Mr. All Knowing wrote my ending the second I attempted to overthrow him eons ago. I merely bide my time, pretending my place is on earth among the immortals while I wait for judgment day like the rest of the world.

In the meantime, while I selfishly ignore my duties down below, Hell falls into utter chaos. Well, more anarchy than usual. When I transported Kleora's soul, the level of destruction and turmoil astonished me. My disobedient soldiers overthrew my most trusted commanders, destroyed the throne room, and escalated torturing the souls trapped there forever.

The second the slimy abominations felt my presence, a tremor rippled through the burned wasteland. The cacophony of tormented screams and gnashing of teeth ceased in hushed terror. For about two damn seconds, then it was business as usual.

My absence created a shift, and I am not entirely certain how to regain the upper hand or if I even care. Right now, my chief priority is Kleora. The longer I keep her soul separated from her body, the odds of successfully binding them diminishes.

I rise to unleash my fury on the wizard at his utter failure when the oddest sensation tingles across my neck. I freeze mid-step.

"D-Darath?"

The soft voice I feared never to hear again floats over the room. I inhale sharply and spin toward the door. My heart stalls. My beautiful, petite nymph stands in the entryway. Her body, encased in the warrior outfit she died in, shimmers with translucence, the wall behind her clearly visible through her frame. The crazed glaze of her jade irises instills fear in my bones.

"Darath?" she repeats. "What did you do to me?"

"Andolf? What the fuck?" I mutter in astonishment, my eyes wide.

"I... I am uncertain how this can be," he stutters, his shock equaling my own.

I take a tentative step toward her. "Kleora?" At a loss for what else to say, I snap my jaw closed. How did she escape my chambers?

"I feel... strange," she sighs, a hand on her forehead.

Yeah, I bet. "Strange how?"

"Like... I'm no longer connected with nature." Her shimmering irises, painted the color of a brilliant rainforest, beseech me for answers. Yet, I have none to give. I'm damn confident this is not a gift from God, as anyone but me would wonder at this point. So how is it that her spirit is standing before me? When I checked on her last week, her translucent form hovered above my bed, unresponsive. Which is exactly how it has been for the last six months.

"Kleora..." I ease forward several steps. "Your body no longer walks the earth."

Well, that was real subtle, Jag. Way to break it to her gently.

She blinks several times. "What?"

"What is the last thing you remember, love?" I ask to distract her from the fact she's dead.

She hesitates, her regard searching the room as if for answers, but seeing none. "The dark fae castle," she blurts out, her confused stare finding mine. "I... I attempted to save Nicole from the witch, Abigail."

"Yes. That is correct."

"But this isn't the castle." Her silky chestnut locks sway behind her as she shakes her head. "Did I fail?"

I ignore her second question as I hold out my hand, beseeching her for understanding. "This is the Demon Headquarters in Arizona."

"How did you bring me here? Do my people know what's happened?"

Okay, this is where things could get a little tricky. Probably best if we do not have two dozen pairs of eyes and ears prying.

"Warriors," I bark, causing Kleora to jump. "Clear the room." The demons vanish in seconds, but my first lieutenant, Dzun remains, as I knew he would, leaving only the three of us to figure out how to deal with the baffled wraith.

"Viessa and Icarus's combined magic struck you. Do you remember that?"

She hesitates for a moment, scanning the floor for lost memories. "No, I..." Her image fluctuates drastically, her gaze widens in fear mere seconds before her scream pierces the silence.

"Kleora!" I lunge for her, but my hand passes right through her waist.

She grips the sides of her head, bowing forward in agony. Helplessness—a sensation I am not used to experiencing—saturates my being as I observe her torment.

"Goddamnit, Andolf. What is happening?"

"Her mind is catching up, sire."

As fast as it began, her screams cease abruptly. Slim fingers ease their death grip on her hair and drop to her sides as she slowly straightens. I stumble back at the rage boiling in her expression.

"You sent me to Hell!" she screams.

Christ.

"Please calm down and let me explain."

"I. Will. Kill. You. Demon."

For an insane moment, I glory in the magnificent beauty of her fury. Her petite, lithe body, encased in supple, brown leather, soars into the air. The stiff corset molds to her bosom, drawing my notice. Long chestnut tresses fly around her shoulders like the wings of an avenging angel, but it is the spark of pure rage shining with dazzling brilliance in the jade irises that captivates me, holding me immobile. What a magnificent creature my mate is. Beautiful as she is deadly.

When her spirit passes through me, instead of that luscious body plowing into mine, I relish the tingle and thrill of Kleora's ravenous anger filling my senses, becoming a part of me. As the Devil, I thrive on the turbulent emotions of others. Despair, rage, depression, lust. They energize and bring new life to my damaged soul, fuel it in a way nothing can.

I pivot to face her, but the succulent enjoyment of her passions invading my system dies a tragic death in the face of the land nymph ruler's murderous intent, showcased in every vibrating muscle of her translucent body.

"You will pay for what you've done, Darath." Her lethal hiss intensifies the dread bubbling in my gut.

"I am working on a solution, Kleora. Though unfortunately, I require a little more time."

"You not only robbed me of a chance to enter into Heaven, you son of a bitch, but you also cut off my connection to earth, which sealed my soul from being granted an eternity of peace."

What?

"Let us not fall into theatrics, love." I shoot my wizard a murderous glare before focusing back on the female fate blessed me with but ripped from my grasp before I could make her mine. "We will figure out a way to bring you back."

"There is no coming back for a land nymph once separated from nature, you sulfurous twit."

She stomps forward until her form is mere inches from my chest, her head barely reaching my sternum. A desperate urge to gather her in my arms and ease the suffering in her glower plows through me, despite her insult.

"Bury my body with my people, Darath," she demands.

"If I do that, love, I cannot restore you."

"How long have I been dead?"

"Not long," I evade.

"How long, Darath?" she insists, her tiny fists clenching.

"Six months." Her gasp rips at my heart. "But we are close to a solution," I lie.

"Bury me. Please." I swallow at the desperation in her plea. "Before it's too late."

"I cannot, Kleora. I refuse to lose you." Surely, a few more months should do no harm. "I vow to resolve this situation."

"Mark my words, Demon. You either bury me, or I will discover a way to kill you."

I smirk even as my heart breaks. "You are not even corporeal, little nymph. And have you not heard? I am Satan himself. No force on this earth can kill me."

She steps into me. Literally. Her spirit heats my chest, and my cock stirs.

Oh, for fuck's sake. Not now... I admonish my dick.

"Then I vow to haunt you for all eternity, Lucifer. You will never know peace again."

I can't help but chuckle at her words. "Ah, my beautiful female. I have not experienced peace in over two millennia." I lower my head, my lips hovering mere inches from hers. "Take your best shot."

Chapter 2

Kleora

Pain flares through every joint and muscle in my body. No, correction—Through my spirit. My actual body lies unscathed only King Jagorach Darath knows where. But does a ghost even feel pain? Is it because of where my spirit currently resides—In Hell?

After my threat, I shot several more barbed threats at the seven-foot demon as he attempted to calm my rage, until he finally snapped his fingers in irritation, and BAM—my ass landed back in the room I had woken up in mere moments ago.

Anxiety mixes with fury. My people believe a spirit will find no harmony until we lay the body to rest in our vibrant lands. Generations of land nymphs feed the earth, giving back all it has given to us.

Damn him. How could he do this to me?

I peer around at my confinement space. The walls are thick slabs of black rock that give the room a creepy, gothic feel. I would say it's appropriate. And for a chamber in Hell, it's pretty damn opulent, with an enormous bed to rival any kings and a lavish bathroom with a jacuzzi tub the size of some swimming pools. The hellish suite is more extravagant than my living quarters at the Land Nymph Domain in northern Georgia.

Our five-thousand-acre territory headquarters is home to the densest woodlands in the Chattahoochee National Forest. My people live in the trees and beneath the earth, where our connection to the elements fuels our needs. We commune with nature and the abundant wildlife which inhabits it, only taking life as a means of survival.

Land nymphs inhabit a simple existence, fueled by the sun and wind, fed by the earth's generosity. We rarely shop in malls or grocery stores, and only as a last resort, but rather we allow Mother Earth to supply our day-to-day requirements. Most of our people make their own clothes from the resources gifted to us. Although, as ruler of my people and a member of the Council of Unity, the governing body for the immortal races, my position forces me to utilize modern technology in order to keep up with current events. My residence has a state-of-the-art computer connected via a round dish on the roof so I can teleconference into council meetings and speak with other rulers when necessary, and I carry a smartphone. Although half the time I forget to charge it.

With a sigh, I close my eyes and rub my forehead. I suppose that's all gone now. I should refer to myself in the past tense, since I'm dead, my soul burning for all eternity in Hell. Thanks to the frustrating, sexy, red-eyed Devil with the most fantastic head of hair.

The long brown tresses lay in perfect waves down to his massive chest, and a part of me—the part once alive—craves to dive my fingers into those locks while his wicked tongue does naughty things between my thighs.

NO! What the hell is wrong with me? The fiend not only snatched me from the clutches of eternal paradise, but he refuses to bury my body. I must reconnect with the earth and escape the constant pain bombarding my spirit from the second I opened my eyes.

A pounding at the steel door startles me from my musings. One entity in this godforsaken place had visited me the second

I woke—Berkonnan, the vicious, cunning demon who rules the section where Darath's chamber resides. Lucky me.

"Open up, Priestess, if you wish to live." His nasal whine grates along my... well, I guess I don't possess skin at the moment, so through my spirit.

I ease closer, notching an arrow from the quiver at my back into my ever-faithful friend. I'm surprised at the strain of my muscles flexing against the natural strength of the longbow as I force the arrow back to my cheek. Every book I've ever read regarding ghosts depicted them as unfeeling entities. Clearly, that was wrong.

Thank God I died with my weapons. I never believed the rumors that said you lived forever in what you died in, but I do now. What I wouldn't give for a pair of shorts and a tank top in this furnace.

"Open the goddamn door, Tanagra, or I will have your head."

"Go snack on someone else's innards, Berkonnan. I've had my fill of demons today," I pronounce as I stretch the bow tighter, my anxious scrutiny on the thick entrance.

Please don't fail. I silently plead to the metal contraption.

"Is there a reason you stand at my door, Berkonnan?"

I'm startled by the deep, gravelly voice on the other side—the one I left mere moments ago. I have no clue how I materialized in his throne room to begin with, and no recollection of the last six months of my imprisonment. Was I comatose? Or was my spirit hovering between dimensions, unsure of where the heck it belonged?

To me, the battle at the dark fae castle transpired yesterday. The new bane in my departed existence must have kept me in some kind of stasis. Thank the gods. I shudder at the notion of living down here, awake and receptive, for six damn months.

I glower at my transparent form, easing my grip on the wood bow, and a recollection hits me like a nuclear blast through my brain. I remember the tremendous peace of the beckoning light when I died. The horror of my spirit being ripped from my body. The searing pain from Darath's enormous hands as he held on, refusing to let me go. And the fiery heat of the fatal storm engulfing me, trapping my essence in this lush suite in Hell.

An eternity in Heaven was within reach. Peace and tranquility at my fingertips. The erotic giant stole that from me, and I will never forget or forgive.

Wait. Did Jagorach declare this was his chamber? The wily fox. Did he place me in the lord and commander's private residence? It appears it's the one place the soldiers—even the high-ranking ones—can't enter.

A safety measure for his precious prisoner?

It doesn't lessen my rage toward him. Every chance I get, I will make him grieve tenfold.

"I was checking in on our guest, sire," Berk's annoying whimper snaps me back to my current predicament—Lucifer. The ruler over the fiery abyss locked my soul in his private chambers to suffer for all eternity or until he figures out a way to restore me. But if he hasn't come to a resolution after six months, my chances are slim to none of ever finding peace.

I raise the bow, my lethal contemplation zeroing in on the entrance. If my jailor dares walk through the door, my arrows will sink into his cold, selfish, black heart. Or at least I hope they will. If my weapons are as translucent as I am, then I might as well toss them in the trash for all the good they will do.

"My guest is no concern of yours, pathetic imp. If you attempt to speak with her again without permission, the lava pits will enjoy your cock for supper." I raise an eyebrow at Darath's threat. His menacing tone skitters down my shimmering frame. "On second thought, wait here. I wish to converse with you when I am done inside."

"Yes, my lord."

The second the barrier swings open, I release an arrow with a loud, pronounced cracking snap of the bowstring, quickly notching another in its place. I wait with bated breath to determine if it will pass right through or plunge into his chest. A mere inch from his chest, the bastard deftly snatches the projectile midair, snaps it in two before slamming the door with a resounding boom.

Well, at least now I know I'm not defenseless. Once the arrow leaves my touch, it becomes as real as the furniture in the room.

"Loose another, Kleora, and you will not enjoy the consequences."

He dares to threaten me? After everything he's done? Rage clouds my judgment, and I leap in the air. With quick precision, I mentally evaluate my target's range and distance, letting a barrage of arrows go at the object of my wrath. My muscles bulge and tremble from the tremendous amount of force that is required of me to shoot so rapidly.

Several sink deep into his flesh, but instead of piercing his heart as I'd planned, they plunge into his shoulder, waist, and thigh as the demon king ducks and rolls to evade the worst of my hits. For a big man, he moves with speed and stealth.

Satan's harrowing roar causes me to falter. My first mistake. The second was believing I could damage a former archangel. I leap for the tall dresser for added distance to shoot when Darath rips the bow and quiver from my grasp, flinging it on the ground.

The muscular arm attempting to wrap me up in a hold passes right through me. Apparently, only my weapons are corporeal. A quick tuck and roll puts me within reach of my armaments, but I sense the Devil hot on my heels.

For the first time since I lifted my lids, adrenaline and excitement course through my system. This is what I live for, combat. Even though I am… was… the ruler of my people, the warrior spirit of a Storm Walker still runs through my heart and always will.

When my fingers connect with the armament I died in, relief floods through me. I feared when Darath ripped it away, it would become untouchable to me, like everything else in this place.

My thighs bunch as I spring for the high dresser again, the last arrow notched and ready. My nerves settle as I hover above the edge and re-sight my target. The English oak of the bow creaks in protest under the enormous stress and pressure required to draw such a marvelous weapon back to its full potential. The bowstring bites into the fleshy part of my index, middle, and ring fingertips, but my vision narrows upon my target, now at eye level, the object of so many conflicting emotions boiling within me.

"Threaten me all you'd like, Darath. I'm not afraid. You've already delivered your worst by trapping my soul in this desolate dimension."

He yanks the first barrage of wooden missiles from his flesh, the red fire in his glare diminishing at my words. "Nay, love. This," he gestures to the luxury of my cell as his wounds heal, "is the finest Hell offers. What lies beyond that door, protected by the darkest of magic, might I add, is the stuff of nightmares."

"If I'm a ghost, why do I feel the agony of this place as if I am flesh and blood?"

"You are more than a ghost, love. You are a soul bound to Hell. Just because you do not belong does not mean your soul can escape the torment inherent here. My chamber dulls the effects somewhat."

"If you don't bury my body, what lives out there will be my new forever." Can't he see what he's doing by keeping me here?

"Give me a month, Kleora," he says as he holds out his hand, palm up, as if asking me to take it.

There was a time I would've laid my hand in his without a thought. Relished the tingle as our flesh connected. Now my flesh passes right through, since I'm nothing more than a trapped soul, thanks to him. Besides, Darath hurled my trust into the lava pits, as he called it, the second he denied my soul entry into Heaven.

Before the Lord of Hell takes another step, I let my last arrow fly and watch with horrified satisfaction as it streaks with blinding speed across the massive room before sinking deep into his chest, slicing right through the Devil's black heart.

.

Chapter 3

Jagorach

My petite land nymph is losing it. Suppose I cannot fuse her essence back into her body quick enough? In that case, the laws of nature will force me to do as she wishes—bury her corpse, hand her soul over to my father, and say goodbye forever. If given no choice, can I let her go?

"Is there a problem, sire?" Berkonnan inquires with a slight bow as I murmur the words to reseal my chamber door and slide the arrow from my heart with a wince.

The nymph is deadly, no doubt about it. If I were anyone but a son of God, I would be dead.

"Women." I shrug.

My skin crawls to escape this fucking place, but I hesitate. It's been centuries since I last made my rounds, and it appears a little reminder of who is actually in charge is in order. "You have one day to restore the throne room to its previous sinister glory, Berk. My children require a demonstration of who it is they serve."

The demon has the foresight to tremble in the face of my ire. "A day is not enough–"

I snatch the idiot by the throat and slam him into the unforgiving lava rock. "You dare question my command?" I lean in close and ignite the visage of my authentic form to float over my frame. Berk ceases his fruitless struggles and lowers his lids like a good little soldier. His red pecker stands at attention, ready and eager for punishment. I swallow my disgust.

Before Kleora, I would have relished offering Berk the sexual torture he preferred. She changed all of that. Changed me.

"Nay," he chokes around my squeezing fingers.

"One day or my earlier threat will become a reality for the next century." The red, muscular demon nods frantically. "In the meantime, you are responsible for the precious package in my chamber. Guard this door with your life."

"Yes, my lord."

At his agreement, I flick my wrist and send his powerful crimson body into the opposite wall with a satisfying crunch of bone. Little does Berkonnan realize, I am aware of every transgression he has manipulated during my absence, and he will pay a hefty price. But right now, I demand my most prized fighter.

"Don't leave me here, Jagorach!" I cringe at Kleora's muffled holler through the thick steel.

I step over Berk's broken body, contorting as it mends, and halt in front of the door. The demon snakes his claw-tipped hand around my calf, caressing it in thanks for his king's violent attention.

I ignore the vile beast and press my palm on the smooth, warm surface. "I am sorry, peach, but until I figure things out, this is the safest place for you right now."

"No. Please, Jag. The pain is unbearable."

My lids lower against the desperation in her voice. Shit. The last thing I ever wanted was to make her endure one iota of misery or distress. Yet, here I stand, inflicting the agony of my eternal damnation onto her soul, albeit muted while she's in my chamber.

"I know, love. Hang in there for a little while longer."

An acute pain pierces my mind. Like someone has shoved an icepick through my skull. Before I comprehend the cause, my body shimmers and teleports out of purgatory, landing with a bone-jarring thud smack dab in the middle of the vampire queen's private office.

"Damn, Viessa. Did you have to be so harsh?" Nicole asks with a grin that says she's not sorry in the least.

"My apologies, my lady. I'm still working on controlling my strength," the High Priest Oracle states with a vicious smile as she reaches for my hand to haul me to my feet.

"As much as I love rough play, especially with two beautiful women, what is the meaning of this abduction?" I brush ash off my smoking jeans and face the one vampire I trust with my life.

"We have a problem, Houston." The grin gives way to an ominous glare, the gray depths sparking with anger.

"When do we not?" I smirk.

Nicole Giordano gained my unwavering alliance the second she walked into my camp of one thousand demon soldiers, flanked only by her mate—the legendary Logan Moretti—his brother Sebastian, and the imposing shifter prince, now king, Kurtis Ruse. Hundreds of my warriors held ready to lay siege to her castle, but the powerful vampire in her own right offered a bargain. Few immortals had the cojones to face off with the infamous demon king.

She snorts at my comment and rises from behind her desk to stand before me, her slightly protruding belly on full display.

I'm stunned anew by the prophesied gift she carries in her womb—the future vampire king. The first vamp to be born of a Halfling. Half human, half vampire. Able to walk in the sun and eat regular food, this child will continue Nicole's legacy of peace among the immortals.

I glance up at Logan, who is set on watching me intently from the corner with those strange, iridescent green irises. The muscled warrior is shirtless, the black slashes and swirls of his

Moretti tattoo across his chest, shoulder, and bicep seeming to dance in the flickering glow of the fire.

"Are you still pissed I confiscated all your winnings on poker night, Logan?" I sneer at his stoic expression, stalling the inevitable showdown with Nicole.

Every month, the males in our weird little alliance get together for card night to let off steam and catch up. Unfortunately for my friends, Satan is the king of cards.

After the battle, the guys tried to offer their condolences for the death of Kleora, knowing I had been actively pursuing her for months. Instead of outright lying, I nodded with a mumbled thanks and said I no longer wished to talk about it. As males do, they gladly let it go.

Logan offers a lopsided grin in response to my jab. I peer over at Viessa dressed in her new Oracle uniform of leather pants and thigh-high boots. The backless halter top showcases the ever-expanding collection of sacred tattoos circling her back. What gives me pause is her livid expression. Her amber irises ablaze.

"Uh oh," I smirk at her. "It appears I have pissed off the ear of God. Whatever will I do?"

Not too long ago, the beautiful Tri-Bred, twin to Lucretia, had trouble determining past from present. Now she's able to snatch the Devil from Hell to her side. Quite Impressive. Viessa's irises glint, but she ignores my sarcasm.

"We've enjoyed a few months of relative peace after the battle with the fae." Nicole frowns, and dread burns through my gut. "Now it seems we are knee-deep in shit again, and you are the cause, my friend."

I work to keep my face passive even as shock charges through me. How the inferno did she discover the truth?

"As much as I love claiming dominion over all chaos, I am not sure to what you refer, Halfling."

"There's a rumor going around the Land Nymph Domain that Lucifer imprisoned their ruler's soul in Hell." Her forehead furrows. "Please tell me that's all it is, Darath. A rumor."

Son of a bitch.

"You should not place stock in stories, young queen," I evade without outright lying. The vampire ruler would sniff out a lie as quickly as any hellhound. Instead, I stroll to the two wing-back chairs facing the crackling fire to avoid her penetrating stare and that of the beautiful Oracle's.

Only one being I fear, and the big man upstairs would not give my antics a single glance unless it endangered his plans or his precious humans.

Nicole slides into the seat across from me, her hand resting protectively on her swollen abdomen. By my account, she's almost seven months along. The queen's determined expression elevates my trepidation even as I snicker at the words splattered on her hooded sweatshirt under an image of a set of fangs dripping blood. "Loving the monsters always ends badly for the humans. It's a rule." Laurell K. Hamilton.

"You know," she drawls as she leans back and rubs her belly. "I think it would hurt my feelings if you were dishonest to me, Darath."

By the arched brow and simmering glare, I seriously doubt that to be true. But I love word games as much as the next Devil. "You wound me, Nicole. As if I could lie to such a beauty as yourself."

"Hardy har har, Demon. Now cut the shit and tell me the damn truth before I let the furious Oracle have a piece of you. Did you hijack Kleora's soul and toss her into Hell?"

Since my wizard was useless and therefore dead, I might require the help of my friends. On a sigh, I respond, "Yes."

She swallows, her penetrating stare never deviating from mine. "What the fuck, Darath?"

Logan comes forward. "You lied to us. For months."

"I did not lie, per se. Merely omitted the whole truth," I mumble, slightly ashamed by my actions. I should go check on Kleora because I think Hell just froze over.

"Putting aside your dishonesty with your friends, do you have any idea of the turmoil you have placed Priestess Tanagra in? Not to mention the sheer agony her people are suffering at denying their ruler a final burial of earth and peace?"

I clamp my lips shut as the underlying fear of losing her morphs into anger. The last thing I desire at this point is to shoot my mouth off and alienate myself from my most trusted allies.

My glower follows Viessa as she moves into my line of sight. "By denying Priestess Tanagra entrance into Heaven, you crossed a line, my lord," she declares, her amber irises smoldering.

I bury my anxiety over her words and offer a bored expression. "I have crossed many lines in my centuries, Oracle. Mostly to my benefit. A few at the profit of others in exchange for their souls."

"I'm well aware, Lucifer, but your actions have drawn the attention of the Watchers... and your father."

Well, shit.

"You've instigated a war, Darath," Nicole states softly. She leans forward with her elbows on her thighs, her stomach drooping between her spread legs, her stare direct. "But right now, I need to know one thing, and one thing only."

I stiffen. My contemplation remains wary as Viessa moves to stand behind Nicole's chair. Dammit. I do not want to get on the wrong side of the Oracle. She's as unpredictable as a werewolf in heat on a full moon.

As far as the pathetic Watchers, they can go masturbate until their little peckers fall off for all I care. They do not have the power to destroy me. Only my father can blink my soul into oblivion, and I've been on his naughty list for millennia. The one reason I still live is because I have a purpose to fulfill. Without the Devil, there is no right and wrong. No good versus evil. No purgatory for those who deserve it. Humans and immortals alike would have no lasting consequences for their actions.

Pure fucking chaos.

Yeah. Keep telling yourself that, Jagorach. The reality is, we are all replaceable. Even me. Another power-hungry demon waits on the sidelines for me to screw up and take over as King of Hell. But not another Archangel, I remind myself.

"And what, pray tell, is that?" I mutter, dreading Nicole's answer.

"How can the Vampire Nation help?"

My eyebrows lift in surprise. Damn. Once again, her unwavering loyalty melts old Lucifer's heart.

Chapter 4

Kleora

Hell blows. I've spent hours sitting in the middle of Darath's massive bed with my legs crossed, working through every strategy to figure out how I escaped from this same prison last week. With a disgruntled sigh, I flop onto my back, arms outstretched. Although admittedly, hovering above the mattress loses a bit of the dramatic flair.

Above this literal, God-forsaken place, I am nothing but a wraith. Able to pass through walls and people. The only way I can connect with anyone is to merge with them. I must admit, when I conjoined myself with the Devil, it was a bit terrifying and illuminating at the same time.

The overwhelming emotion flowing through the malevolent beast was confidence. Darath is undeniably certain he did the right thing. And with the snap of his fingers, he would do it again. No doubt. No hesitation.

But layered under the thick levels of ego and arrogance, a niggling of fear mixed with anguish exists. Fear he won't be able to restore me before it's too late, and anguish that he is causing me even an iota of pain. Despite his doubts, his complex mind overrides the objections as weakness, concluding that my suffering is a necessary means to an end. Once he brings me back to life, all will be well, and I'll see reason.

Ha! See reason.

Never in a million years will I forgive the sexy demon. God punched my timecard. The hour had come to say goodbye. I could be resting peacefully in Heaven right now, my body replenishing the earth as it should if it weren't for Darath's selfish determination.

The big brute trapped my carcass in a magical hiatus and tossed my soul in hell. Hell. There isn't enough groveling in the entire universe to right that wrong. And now that I've remembered the 'why's and 'how's of my current predicament, my fevered intellect has conjured up some pretty brutal and creative ways to make him pay.

I nibble at my lip as the sensation of what lies below my righteous fury and well-placed resentment threatens to punch to the surface. Simmering deep under my ire is an ember of hopefulness that the Devil will succeed. A slim possibility exists I could have a second chance at life. And to be completely honest, if the bastard pulls it off, I'm uncertain how long I'll hold on to my anger when my mind cries out for his touch, and the warmth of his wicked embrace.

Before the fiasco at the castle, which resulted in my untimely death, I believed the erotic, sweet talker with a body I craved to lick and explore every inch of was my fated mate. The one being in the universe meant for me and no-one else. The male I've waited four centuries to find.

I cross my arms over my face with a groan. Mother Earth, give me patience with the devil. Why would the ancestors connect my soul to such an unworthy creature? He's the personification of evil. The enemy of humanity. The deceiver, and so much more.

His title alone is one of the primary reasons I refused to let myself fall into his embrace. No matter how desperately my traitorous body cried for those huge hands on my skin, to fulfill the promise in the crimson stare. Or how the deep gravelly voice whispering naughty fantasies produced flutters with the force of a tornado in my stomach. Simply being in the same room with the big male sent tingles over my flesh, caused my nipples to tighten, and for my long-neglected insides to clench in readiness.

I'm not even sure how sex with him would work. Darath is seven feet tall. I'm a mere five-foot-three. Believe me, I've had fun imagining every scenario and position out there. And since he's a large male, my overactive imagination concluded his manhood must be huge as well. Our first time together might require a certain finesse.

Whoa, wait a cotton pickin` minute! What the heck am I thinking? I hate him with a passion. If, or when, the day ever comes and I'm free of this horrible place, my one thought will be revenge. Period.

A soft knock startles me from my musings. "My lady?" inquires a familiar feminine voice from the other side. "Might I have a word with you?"

I leap from the bed, my heart ready to burst from my chest. My savior has finally arrived. "Viessa? Is that you?"

"Yes. Would you like company?"

"Boy, would I, but I can't open the door, it's...." Before I can finish the sentence, the beautiful vampire appears before me with a serene smile.

I'm so overjoyed to see her; I go to give her a big hug, forgetting for a moment, A) it's forbidden to touch an Oracle unless granted permission and, B) I'm a wraith. But instead of passing right through her, strong arms encircle my shoulders and offer me a brief squeeze before stepping back.

"Oh my," I exclaim, tears wavering my vision. "I-I can touch you." It's so weird. A simple touch from her brings me to tears.

"Yes," she smiles, the strange amber irises pulsing with her power. "I can't stay long. I'm breaking all kinds of rules simply by descending past the gates, but I wanted to offer a small gift to help you endure your interval here."

"You mean you're not here to rescue me?" Well, crap. This feels like the time I accidentally shot one of my arrows through a tree, and it wept. "Where is your father, Icarus?"

Tears shimmer in the amber depths and dread fires in my gut. "I'm sorry, my lady. Unfortunately, Icarus perished in the battle with the witch."

"Oh no," I whisper. My heart breaks for the sisters who never had a chance to know him and for Nicole. The priest's loss must have devastated her. "I'm so sorry, Viessa."

"We all feel his passing every day. None more so than the Queen."

"Are you still in training?"

She offers a proud smile, and it lifts the sadness somewhat. "I have completed my education, my lady." Viessa spins to showcase her accomplishments in the open-back halter.

Icarus stood no taller than five-seven, but his entire body, from his face to his feet, displayed his achievements in the form of sacred blue tattoos. The beautiful engravings would pulse with the power emanating from him, and it could make your hair stand on end.

It's clear Viessa is quite successful. The construct of amber and blue tattoos that span out in an ever-expanding tight circle over her entire back are beautiful and captivating.

"Wow, Viessa. You have completed so much in a short amount of time. Congrats."

The Oracle turns. "Thank you. I hope my gift helps." The tall deity offers a tender smile, touches the side of my face before disappearing.

"What gift?" I shout to the empty room, scanning around for anything out of the ordinary.

Good grief. And here I thought with all those accomplishments showcased on her back, the Oracle learned to master the disorder in her mind. Apparently not.

Icarus, the immortal world's High Priest Oracle and the seer of all things with the ability to commune with the gods, fathered Viessa and her twin Lucretia. But the higher deities denied him the opportunity to train Vi from a young age. As a result, the poor girl suffered her entire life, thinking all the voices and visions bombarding her mind labeled her psychologically disturbed.

Viessa, a Tri-bred—half panther shifter, vampire, and Oracle—could not differentiate between past, present, or future. Not until Icarus discovered her last year and started her training. Unfortunately, his untimely death may have hindered her abilities. Case in point. She broke all kinds of rules to come down here and then left without offering her gift. So, while it appears her powers have increased exponentially—she still struggles.

With a heavy sigh, I retreat once more to the bed. I'd love a long, fragrant soak in Darath's massive tub, but the damn water would pass right through me, so what's the point. My butt settles on the comforter, but it doesn't sink into the mattress, nor do I enjoy the silky softness of the sheets.

I glance up at the mirrored ceiling above me as an erotic image of riding King Darath fills my vision. The enormous hands cupping my breasts, heavy with desire. His irises glowing a beautiful ruby in his need, and my head thrown back in utter ecstasy.

In disgust, I yank my hair to one side and begin braiding sections as I work to slow my breathing. Who the heck puts a mirror above their bed? That's so 1970s. I wince at the constant burn in my joints and slow my frantic fingers. The pain eased in the Oracle's presence, but returned with a vengeance the second Viessa disappeared.

The breakdown in my body has begun. The longer I'm stuck down here—my connection to nature severed—the more difficult it becomes to separate from the agony inherent to this place. What I wouldn't give for Icarus to still be alive. No doubt the previous High Priest Oracle would get me out of here, no questions asked.

The notion that God never meant for my soul to go to the fiery pit offers little comfort in the face of actually being here. If the carnal demon figures out how to save me before I lose my mind, I'll rip his heart from his chest and stomp on the selfish organ with glee.

I will. I swear.

Our avoidance dance, or I guess I should say, my avoidance since Darath has pursued me relentlessly since our first meeting, was exhilarating, and even though my mind overflows with retribution, I can't help but remember my first encounter with the sexy brute. It was the night of Lucretia Bramen's trial at the Vampire Stronghold in the farthest regions of Canada.

Just recalling his scintillating words has me flopping back on the bed once more to settle in and replay that fateful night.

What else can a soul do in Hell but revisit the past.

Chapter 5

Kleora

"Thank you for transporting me to Lucretia's trial, commander Moretti. Sometimes, I envy your ability to trace."

"It was my pleasure, Priestess Tanagra. When you are ready to leave, let me know," Sebastian replies before disappearing once more.

The vampire set us down in an antechamber of the larger conference room where the tribunal will be held. An enormous bar occupies one wall with a stout, good-looking vampire serving drinks to the milling representatives. Although, it appears his sole focus is on the Succubus Queen, Jilaya Oresha, and who could blame him. Even knowing the repercussions of intimacy with the drop-dead—literally—gorgeous female, being in her presence now, I understand why so many succumb to her charms.

Intrigued, I wander over to the bar. "Queen Oresha," I nod before requesting a glass of cabernet from the handsome bartender for this solemn gathering. It's the only form of alcohol I've ever imbibed since my people cultivate a small vineyard for our own enjoyment.

Tonight is a pivotal point. We not only vote on Nicole's future as the vampire queen, but we are also swearing in the demon king—whom I've never met—as a council member. Lastly, and the most disturbing item on the docket, we decide the fate of the only female Guardian in the Vampire Nation. The discipline and fortitude it must have taken her to not only overcome the archaic patriarchy of vampire society but be allowed into the ranks of their elite warriors are beyond words. But tonight, the council will rip it to shreds. Her list of crimes is unsettling, and I can't imagine the hurt and betrayal Logan and Nicole must feel.

Queen Oresha's striking blue eyes swivel in my direction, taking several moments to peruse my body. I can't lie. I'm not unaffected by her allure, even though I'm not sexually attracted to women. I adore the beauty and sexuality of women, but I require the pure maleness of an Alpha male. And lots and lots of flesh slapping, sweat dripping male-dominated sex.

"Priestess Tanagra," Oresha purrs, turning to give me her full attention. "Please, call me Jilaya." Her sapphire regard traverses my body. "Aren't you a scrumptious little morsel?"

I chuckle even as my nipples tighten at the blatant sexual overtones in her comment. "And call me Kleora," I respond, reaching for the crystal goblet of dark red yumminess and taking a fortifying sip. "I'm surprised to see you here since you sided with King Grayflame against Nicole during the great battle."

"Yes, well..." she downs the amber liquid in her glass. "Everyone is allowed one mistake, are they not?"

I nod. "I'm a firm believer in second chances as long as the offense isn't unforgivable." I gently place my wineglass back on the bar. "And since it's rumored you never engaged in the battle directly, I understand why the vampire queen has agreed to an accord with you."

"Well, aren't you the forgiving type? I think I love you, Kleora."

Before I can stop it, a blush steals over my face. "I'll let you in on a little secret, Jilaya." I lean closer, and the succubus grins with interest before following suit until our faces are mere inches apart. "I bat for the other team," I breathe.

"Thank the levels of Hell for that," rumbles a deep voice from behind me. My spine straightens as tingles race down every vertebra, and my heart rate thumps into overdrive.

"Pity," Jilaya responds with a pout, giving whoever is behind me a saucy wink before turning back to the bartender, eager for her attention.

From the vibration of his tone alone, a hurricane of sensations swirls within me. I'm petrified to turn and discover who the rich, suggestive voice belongs to. But I've never shied away from anything, and I'm not about to start now.

I slowly pivot after a deep breath, coming face to face with a crisp white linen dress shirt and black tie. My observation travels up and up, encountering the broadest shoulders I've ever seen. Dark, luxurious hair brushes a massive chest that even the inky suit jacket, tailored perfectly, can't hide. Firm jaw and full kissable lips lifted in a smirk follow. But my heart nearly leaps out of my chest when I encounter ruby red irises.

Mother Earth. This is the legendary Jagorach Darath, the demon king being sworn in this evening. In my four hundred years, I've never encountered a demon. Are they all so tall and delicious? His mere presence commands the room and not simply because of his height. He exudes authority and draws every eye in the room.

The king watches me with mild curiosity, but it's the blatant ownership in his stare that causes my throat to spasm with the need to swallow the answering ache in my chest—the one screaming at me to submit. What the heck is happening to me? I'd never surrender to a male. As the ruler of my people, I must stay in control over every aspect of my life.

Get it together, Kleora.

"King Darath, I presume?" My tone is breathless as I work to ignore the internal conflict tearing me in opposite directions.

Instead of reaching for his shoulders and climbing this creature to relieve the inferno building in my core, I clutch the wine glass.

Damn the fates. Based on my body's reaction to the seven-foot demon, he's my fated mate. Seriously? After four hundred years, destiny gifts me with a notorious monster rumored to be a direct descendant of Lucifer himself? I am so screwed.

"You smell like a field of peach trees, little nymph. As it so happens, peaches are my favorite fruit."

"Well, like any good farmer, we spray our fields to keep the pests from eating our crops," I grin, enjoying the banter despite the wetness soaking my panties at his mere presence. Jilaya's chuckle behind me fortifies my resolve to fight this forbidden attraction, but still have a little fun.

The demon grins. "Oh, peach. It will take more than a mere pesticide to keep me from what I want."

"And what is that?" I dare to ask.

"My tongue diving into your soft, succulent flesh until your juices run down my chin."

A combined gasp permeates the room, every immortal ear tuned into our whispered conversation.

Mother earth. I'm in deep horse manure. Every fiber of my being craves those perfect lips, doing exactly what his words and eyes promise. Or his enormous hands exploring my body, his cock buried deep within me.

If King Darath were anyone but my mate, I might consider a naughty little rendezvous with the erotic-looking brute. But if I allowed myself such an indulgence, the mate bond would demand more, and my people will never accept a demon as their king.

"Well, King Darath." I lean closer, inhaling his intoxicating scent of sandalwood and fire, entranced by his sheer size. "You're old enough for your wants not to hurt you." I pick up my wineglass, turn my back on the deliciously enticing demon and make my way over to King Ruse and Queen Arra, conversing quietly in the corner, pretending not to listen.

The demon's dark laughter fills the room and shoots fear and excitement through my heart at the chase ahead.

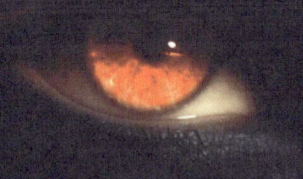

Chapter 6

Kleora

My fingers graze through his collection of outfits until a familiar suit halts me in my tracks. Laughter fills the closet. How ironic. I wonder if Darath is aware he owns several exclusive suits made by none other than my people.

I've remained Priestess for so long because I devised a plan to bring my people financial freedom. We have the most talented seamstresses in the world, but the land nymphs were the only ones benefiting from their brilliance. Through grit and determination, I forged a way to base our very economic foundation on our handmade clothing line. We limited our items to exclusive, high-end private auctions. The suits in Darath's closet range in price from $80,000 to $500,000. The demon business must be lucrative to afford even a viewing of our line.

What I find amusing is Darath has them arranged in color, with the shirts and ties already displayed on the same hanger—almost like how you'd see it done on mannequins from the plethora of stores humans frequent.

Interesting. I wonder if it's an ease-of-use thing—have the complete set ready to go—or if he is lazy and can't bother figuring out what goes best with what? Maybe the sexy demon is color blind.

Ha! A chink in his drool-worthy armor?

Yeah, right. I laugh at the concept and move on down the rack, startled to discover a dozen pairs of ripped jeans. Designer, of course, faded tees all in dark colors. A complete contrast to the bright polo shirts lined up next to them and frayed cut-off jean shorts.

What in the blazes?

An image of Darath in a pair of shorts, no shirt, sweat glistening on his sculpted chest imprints on my psyche. The thick muscles flex and bulge as he splits and stacks firewood outside my cottage while a cool breeze ruffles his gorgeous hair.

What would Darath think of my modest home? Even though our economy now thrives, we live simple, some would even say, archaic lives. The sun provides our electricity. The earth, our water. Trees provide warmth and housing. We hunt or raise our food supply. My people sustain massive farms, cotton fields, vineyards, and so much more that support our population. We are all happy to get our hands dirty to provide and protect our needs—myself included.

The vast majority of land nymphs have never seen a TV or have no idea what the Internet is, let alone a smartphone. Only my Storm Walkers—our elite fighting force—and I employ technology and magic. It's our responsibility to make sure we can protect our race against those who seek to destroy our lands. Humans, mostly. It's another reason our clothing line is in such high demand. I make sure the design name remains anonymous.

With a quick shake, I let go of my musings to refocus on my task at hand—poking around in Darath's possessions.

I pivot to the bathroom to see what insights I might discover there when a small box—obviously shoved in the corner in a hurry because the contents lay scattered across the carpet behind his massive shoe collection—catches my eye. My heart skips as I pass through clothes and expensive shoes to gape at the colorful images.

When I plop—well hover—over the carpet, guilt nibbles at my conscience as I examine the photos. Lots and lots of them scattered about in disarray. I attempt to snatch a picture from the pinnacle, but my fingers pass right through. So instead, I stare at it in stunned disbelief. The striking image embeds in my brain.

My current jailor—the Devil incarnate—has his arm draped around a woman's shoulders. He's holding a beautiful, dark-haired little girl with big red eyes on his other hip.

It's not the stunning beauty of the crimson-eyed woman or child that catches my breath. It's the utter joy and bliss radiating from Darath's warm smile and laughing eyes that says it all. His entire world rests in his embrace. I've seen no one exude such peace and happiness in a single expression frozen forever in time.

This must be Darath's wife and daughter. If memory serves correctly, King Giordano, Nicole's late father, slaughtered them years ago. My heart bleeds for the carefree male in this photo. How long after they snapped this image did the malevolent being, hell-bent on controlling the immortal race, rip Jagorach's purpose in life from his grasp.

How does one recover from losing not only their mate but also their child? I can't imagine the utter devastation and agony he endured. No wonder revenge against a Giordano ruled him. First Dimitri, and when Nicole stole the kill from him by ending her father herself, he turned his rage on the Halfling for a brief time. Eventually, the prophesied one convinced him to exact his revenge on Zacharia, Dimitri's first-born son and a total asswipe.

Did the former vampire king realize Darath's connection to this woman and child when he murdered them? And if so, did he have any idea who King Darath truly was? My guess would be no. No person in their right mind would double-cross Lucifer.

Absently, my fingers hover over my mate's image, imagining it is me sheltered in his embrace—happy and loved.

"I never took you for a snoop, peach."

My body jerks. My concentration was so caught up in my stupid fantasies, Darath's deep, angry voice startled me. I duck my head as guilt fuses my lungs.

"Well, Demon," I mutter, glancing at him over my shoulder. "What did you expect I would do while trapped alone in this suite for days on end? Twiddle my thumbs and stare at myself in the mirrored ceiling until you graced me with your presence?" Even to my own ears, my tone is petulant as I stand to face his scorn.

Truth be told, I'm rankled by my embarrassment at being caught sifting through his belongings. But why should I feel guilty about anything? This brute deserves whatever I dish out and more.

When he doesn't respond, I peer at him under my lashes, and my heart stops. The red-eyed sexy beast leans against the entrance, his hands resting casually in the pockets of his jeans, the spectacular expanse of his sculpted chest and abdomen on full display.

Oh my! The sight of his exposed flesh covered in a light smattering of dark hair is better than any fantasy I imagined. Taut abdominal muscles stretch and retract with each breath, disappearing into the waistband slung low across his hips. Bare feet finish the sensual—wet my translucent panties and stiffen my nipples—appearance.

The crimson irises drop to the front of my shirt, and I follow his gaze. Yup. The ladies are standing at full attention. I cross my arms over the two traitors and glare back at him. "What do you want, Darath? Unless you're here to let me go, please leave."

His head tilts as he analyzes me, his expression unreadable. "I will never let you go, Kleora. Not until my task is complete." His observation bounces to the scattered pictures in front of me. "Did you discover anything useful?"

The irritation in his tone tightens my insides, and I frown. Sarcasm has never been attractive to me, but here I sit, craving to ease the frown between his brows.

Mother Earth, get a grip, Kleora.

"I'm not your servant, Darath. Do not take that tone with me." Wow. How brave am I? But I'm dead. What else could he do to me?

When he prowls into the closet, kicks the box farther into the corner as if it holds no importance, causing more pictures to scatter across the carpet, I'm speechless. Then, in the next heartbeat, he flips me over his shoulder, strides to the bed before tossing me on the mattress and settling his hips between my thighs.

"You will learn my moods and submit, love." His growl is intimidating as his lips hover above mine.

I swallow. Wrong, Kleora. Darath could do more damage—like setting my sex on fire. "Never," I hiss, meaning it. Sort of.

"You should not challenge the Devil, peach. I never lose."

Oh, God. The press of his massive girth pressing against my throbbing middle causes my lids to lower and my eyes to roll back in my head at the sheer bliss.

Wait a tick.

I gape at him. "I can feel you," I exclaim.

"Kleora, you are going to feel me on every inch of your body for days to come." The wicked gleam in his stare forces all thought right out of my brain.

Yes. I crave to experience everything the demon offers and more. I've wanted him since the first moment I beheld the big male. No doubt he understands how to please a woman. After all, he's had two millennia to perfect his technique.

"But how am I sentient?" I inquire through a fog of lust.

"I believe you had a visit from the Oracle, did you not?"

"That was her parting gift? Sentience?"

"Yes. Much to my delight. And soon yours."

I gape at his roguish smile. Oh, Lordy. I'm in deep doodoo.

Chapter 7

Jagorach

The sensation of my petite nymph beneath me, the aroma of her arousal, and her jade eyes sparking with equal amounts of anger and lust nearly snap my control. This delicate female led me on a merry chase for several months before her untimely death. I finally have her at my mercy and right where she belongs—in my arms.

"I have waited a long time to have you beneath me, Kleora. Everything about you sets my blood on fire."

"You're the Devil, I'm sure that's a normal occurrence for you." Her sarcastic tone opposes her panting breath and heated regard.

The Priestess is not as immune as she would want me to believe, even though she holds on to her anger like a shield maiden in battle. My beauty's ire, smart mouth, and lust for revenge only add fuel to my already escalating fervor.

"Denial is not pretty, love," I taunt, running my lips along the side of her neck until I reach her delightful, pointed ears. "Especially when the beautiful bouquet of your desire fills my senses."

I hold back a grin when the tip twitches at the caress of my breath. The action causes her to press against my hardened length, which aches to be buried deep inside her sweet flesh.

Small but strong hands shove against my chest, even as an ankle hooks over my calf, keeping me in place. "Get off me, you brute."

Ah. I love this foreplay. I glide my erection along the seam of her crotch, hating the thick leather between us. Her fists no longer push. Instead, they flatten against my pecs, her blunt fingernails digging into my muscles.

"Are you sure that is what you want, Kleora?" I pump my hips again. Her lids lower, and her head tips back. Such an elegant expanse of vulnerable flesh exposed for my enjoyment.

The notion of sinking my fangs into her jugular, marking her as mine while in my authentic form, sears my brain. I brace myself. This beautiful creature would run screaming if she beheld me as Satan. My father was not kind in his anger.

I shove the fear aside and concentrate on the delicious delicacy before me, sweeping my tongue along the point of her ear. She shudders, the aroma of peaches blooming, infusing my soul.

"I am addicted to your scent. It makes me crave to rip your clothes from your body, bury my face in your sweet cunt, and enjoy the fuck out of you for hours on end."

"Jag," she breathes, her palms gliding down my torso before slipping between the waistband of my jeans to grip my ass. "Stop talking."

I chuckle at her wanton behavior. Based on her past innuendos, I always suspected the petite land nymph had an active libido. Good thing too, because my appetite is insatiable. "As you wish," I chuckle, sitting on my heels and hauling her with me to straddle my hips.

My beautiful female takes full advantage of the new position, gripping fistfuls of my hair and grinding against my throbbing length. I seize her head in both palms and swoop down to devour her lush lips.

I adore the low mewling sounds she makes as I delve my tongue in to duel with hers before sucking gently. Kleora's soft hands roam as far as they can reach, leaving a trail of fire in their wake.

Within seconds, I have the laces of her thick corset ripped open and tossed on the floor, my scrutiny bouncing to the scattered pictures in the closet. When I discovered her fussing around in my most prized possessions, anger sparked and I wanted to punish her.

The box is a reminder of all I lost. My charming wife, Zazzoth, and daughter, Kagar, were the light of my life. And while my spouse was not my bonded mate, my love for her ran deep, and there was never a more beautiful child than my precocious little girl. She was ten years old when Dimitri snuffed out her existence.

"Hey." Soft fingers caress my face. "Are you with me?"

Kleora's gentle question jars my mind back to the beauty straddling my lap, and my heart stutters. My primordial response to the land nymph astounds me. I have bedded and cared for many women in my lifetime, and yes, a few men, but without doubt, I adored my wife. When she died, I mourned her for years, vowing to seek revenge, but the Earth continued to revolve. Life moved on at a snail's pace.

If I were to lose Kleora, my black soul would shrivel and die. As a result, humanity, along with the immortal species, would experience the destruction of my wrath. This beautiful female is elemental to not only my survival, but that of the world.

"There is no other place I would rather be than right here with you in my arms," I state with an honesty I should not, holding her closer. "I only wish it was under different circumstances. Perhaps on a tropical beach somewhere."

Kleora stiffens at the reminder. "Why did you do it?" Her hands clutch my shoulders, ready to bolt in a heartbeat if I allow it.

I tuck a lock of hair behind her pointed ear and smile when it twitches. "You are my mate, peach," I confess, granting her more power than she realizes.

"No," she says, attempting to get off my lap. "I thought your wife was your mate?"

My arms tighten, refusing her escape. "I loved Zazzoth, yes, but we never bonded. You are my true other half. Without your light in the world, nothing would matter." My instincts balk at revealing such a vulnerability, but I can't deny them freedom as I rub my hands down her back, grip her succulent ass and pull her harder against me. "Fate linked our lives together."

"No, it did not," she insists. "We barely know each other."

"True, peach." I bend, kissing the frantic pulse in her neck. "But I can damn sure remedy that problem right now."

"But I–"

Before she finishes the sentence, my eager mouth latches onto a nipple, biting and sucking, while rolling the other between my fingers.

"Oh, Heavens above," Kleora gasps, arching her neck and clutching my head to her breast.

Damn, the softness and scent of her skin sends a thrill straight to my groin, like the succulent ripe peach her pet name implies. I wrap my arms around her tiny waist, drawing her closer. The slight weight of her frame on my lap, in my embrace, and the taste and aroma of her surrounding, invading, and heating my veins is all I dreamed about from the moment I regarded this incredible female.

Guilt should consume me for what I did, but I do not tolerate such an emotion. And if the result is Kleora in my arms, her heart rate rapid, her panting breaths caressing my shoulders, and her fingers tangled in my hair, silently begging for more, then fuck guilt. I would do it all over again if I got to enjoy this very moment.

"I need to taste you. Your fragrance is driving me insane."

Before she can protest, I settle her back on the bed, taking a minute to observe the simple beauty of my mate. Her skin is smooth and sun-kissed, her breasts incredibly full for someone so petite. Long, thick strands of chestnut hair fan out from her head across the silk sheets. I burn the image of her into my memory for all time. No matter what happens, I will always have this vision to keep me company.

"Jag, please."

Her begging pleases me. "What is it you desire, love?"

"You," she responds, attempting to reach for the button on my jeans.

I grip her wrists until those pretty jade irises, darkened with lust, lift to mine. "Be more specific, Kleora," I demand, pinning her arms above her head with one hand while the other skims along the swell of her breasts, avoiding the puckered points. She wiggles, and I bite back a grin.

"Jag," she frowns prettily. "Touch me."

"I am touching you."

"No. Give me what you promised."

"And what is that, my dear peach?" I ask, knowing the answer but craving to hear the words from my defiant prisoner.

Muscular legs come up and grip my waist. Determination and excitement fire in her gaze. "Your mouth on my pussy, licking, sucking, and biting it until I skyrocket."

"I would destroy the world for a taste of your sweet cunt." I let go of her wrists with an order. "Keep your hands where I put them. If you move, your backside will suffer the consequences."

"Oh, kinky," she giggles, and the sound is pure ambrosia settling in my veins. "Tell me, Demon, do you like it rough? To be in control?"

My lips curve. "Devil, remember? I like it every way."

I am perplexed when my comment chases away the smile. "You've lived a long time... Lucifer." My brows draw together at the name—a reminder of my origins. "No doubt you've bedded thousands. Men and women."

Ah. Is my little peach jealous? How sublime. My chest warms at her angry glare.

"Legions, my love," I tease, fanning the flames. She attempts to unwrap her thighs from around my waist, but I hold her in place, continuing my exploration of the tantalizing flesh pinned beneath me.

"Stop it, Darath!" She swats my hand away, but I simply pin them back above her head.

"Why does that bother you?" I ask, bending to suckle a nipple. "You will soon reap the benefit of my eons of experience."

"I—it doesn't," she gasps, her spine arching at the pressure of my teeth.

"Liar," I taunt as I work the stiff zipper of her leather pants, kissing my way down her quivering belly.

"It's... it's true," she insists. "Your sexual pro...." Her breath halts when I slip my fingers into her pants, slide beneath the gauzy material of her lace to find her sex slick with desire. "Oh, God."

"He has nothing to do with this, peach." I churn her swollen bud, watching in delight as her belly tightens and she lifts her hips, pressing tighter against my palm. "But you are about to feel the wonders of Heaven itself."

In a swift move, I rip off her boots and slide her leathers down her hips and thighs, tossing them over my shoulder, not caring where they land. I drop to my knees, bringing her ass to the edge of the mattress.

Tattooed low on her right hip is a circle with the symbols for the four elements inside. Each image shares the color of its origin. Red fire. Blue water. Green earth. Gray air. The design is beautiful and perfect, matching the nymph's earthly heritage.

I run my tongue across each one, causing her abs to ripple and tighten before ripping the silky thong covering what I crave. The second my lips latch onto her pussy, I close my lids in bliss and moan at her succulent flavor. A hunger builds and my fangs descend as I devour her essence with fervor, licking, sucking, and biting—just as she requested.

Fuck me. Her taste is the sweetest ambrosia. Dark, tantalizing, and addictive.

I spread her folds, capture her clit between two fingers, rotating it back and forth while my tongue dives into her core, savoring the pureness unique to Kleora.

"Jag!" Kleora shrieks. Strong thighs clamp down on the sides of my head even as her heels dig into my shoulders to gain purchase so she can grind against my mouth.

I fasten my lips over her swollen bundle once more, twirling and flicking it. The second her muscles stiffen in readiness, I plunge two fingers into her wetness, keeping a steady rhythm with my tongue until she shatters.

Observing her come apart from my position between her thighs is a beautiful sight. Her breasts thrust toward the ceiling, her small fists white knuckle the sheets, and her frantic, incoherent cries soothe the beast.

I have serviced many females in my time, but knowing my woman flies apart with such abandon because of me is a marvelous occurrence. Little does the land nymph realize how much authority she welds over the Devil.

Dark thoughts intrude. If I were foolish enough to complete the bond with Kleora, she would possess an inconceivable amount of influence over me. I will never allow another individual total control over the ruler of Hell.

Chapter 8

Kleora

Wow. The Devil made me orgasm harder with that dangerous mouth than I have in centuries. The male is talented, wicked, and an unselfish lover. Not something I would've imagined from the creator of despair.

Nor should I have allowed it.

As the earth-shattering sensations dissipate, Darath continues to suck and lick at his leisure, as if he refuses to abandon a favorite spot. With slow increments, my body recovers and the reality of my situation sinks into my brain like a needle through fabric. I permitted my jailor to give me sexual release... What in the world is wrong with me, and why can't I say no to this creature?

My instincts shriek to kill him for what he's done, but another part craves to have the impressive bulge in his pants impale me in any position he desires. Let's chalk this insanity up to the bond. That's it. The reason I'm flat on my back with my legs spread like an eager whore at a succubus convention is the biological link.

I'm a warrior, a Priestess, and the ruler of my people. I've not had many opportunities to enjoy sexual rendezvous outside of our domain. Within our species, female nymphs outnumber males five to one. Most of whom seem intimidated by their queen and avoid any intimate situations. Go figure. I've bedded a few shifters in my time. It was rough and wild, and I found sexual gratification. But when it was over, I felt as hollow as an old willow tree.

My heart stutters as the powerful being kisses his way up my belly. As much as I'd love to throw caution to the wind and experience life-altering sex with this demon, I must rein in my raging hormones. For the sake of my sanity.

I squeeze my lids and concentrate on calming my raging lust. Though it's pretty freaking difficult to focus with Darath's lips and hands roaming my body. When my pulse slows to the beat of a runner, I tuck my legs in and roll off the end of the bed. The second our flesh is no longer in contact—I transform into a shimmering specter. Darath's eyes snap to mine.

Holy crap. The raging lust rolling through this male's regard catches my breath.

"Come back here, minx," the king snarls, his frustration evident in the deep frown marring his forehead. "We are far from done."

Now that we are not in contact, it's easy to remain translucent, but goddess, that commanding tone tethers my pussy to him a little more. The possessive attitude he throws around somehow does it for me. Outside a sexual situation, I would loathe his arrogance, but in the bedroom... my soul responds with glee.

"This should not have happened at all," I say, holding my ground as Darath prowls toward me, the crimson irises glowing like hot embers. I may be butt-ass naked, but I refuse to back down. "Not until you either restore my life or do as I ask. Bury my body. Let me go."

"I do not respond well to ultimatums, Kleora." The hard edge in his tone has me biting my lip.

"Too bad, Darath. You created this mess. Undo it."

"What in purgatory do you think I have been doing for the last six months, woman?" He rakes his fingers through his dark locks.

Well, well, well. The mighty King Darath, Satan himself, is not as confident as he wishes everyone to believe. He made a rash call that night, and now he's peddling against a hurricane to figure out how to fix it.

I grit my teeth against the sympathy working its way into my brain. No. Darath does not deserve my compassion. What he did was wrong and the worst grievance a creature could perform on another—denying their soul entrance into Heaven.

"Either you undo this before it becomes a major catastrophe, or I will destroy you." I'm bluffing, of course. Darath stated he's unkillable, but it won't stop me from discovering a way to hurt him. Besides, what else is there to do in this horrendous place for days on end but devise a plan?

"Enough."

The deep demonic roar ramrods my spine and forces me back a step. This is the voice he uses to bring his minions to heel. It raises the hair on my nape, and I'm loathed to admit, scares me. Just a little. But I'm not one of his mindless minions.

"I refuse to explain myself a second longer. Were my actions thoughtless and selfish? Maybe. But I would do it again to keep you alive."

"That was not your choice to make, Jagorach. And I'm not alive!"

"Maybe so, but it is done," he shrugs. "Deal with it, Kleora, and help me discover a way to restore your life."

"How in the fuck do you envision me doing that while trapped in Hell, oh wise one?"

"I expect foul language from Nicole, but it is not becoming on you, love."

He makes a grab for my arm. I'm stunned when his fingers encircle my bicep, tugging me to him. With a quick mental command, I will my soul back to wraith form, but nothing happens. Instead, the inferno from his naked torso bleeds into mine, making me splendidly aware I'm nude.

"Let us put aside this unpleasantness and concentrate on the here and now. You in my arms."

My sex weeps for what he requests, but somehow, I dig deep and find the last ounce of fortitude to resist. "Unpleasantness?" I crane my neck to glare up at his handsome visage.

I can't believe he simplified this situation into a single word.

"Mayhap not the best word choice, peach." He grins before gliding his fingers into my hair while snaking his other arm under my butt to lift me against his torso. My feet dangle around his knees as I grip his broad shoulders. "I love how petite you are, and would fancy nothing more than to keep you glued to my hip forever."

"I'm not a child, Darath. Put me down," I grumble. I'd also never admit that I appreciate how towering and brawny his body is next to mine.

"Nay, peach. Wrap your thighs around my waist."

My brain betrays me because before I realize it, I'm doing exactly as he demanded.

Instead of taking me back to the bed, Darath grips the dresser and staggers as if in pain. The dark brow furrows and the massive shoulders bunch as he unwraps my legs, lowering my feet to the carpet.

"Goddamnit. Not again."

"Darath?" The discomfort in his expression is alarming. "What's happening?"

"Peach...." In the next instant, he vanishes.

As my body shimmers into translucency, conflicted emotions run rampant at his disappearance. On one hand, I'm relieved the decision to end our little foreplay didn't fall onto my shoulders. Pretty sure I didn't possess the fortitude to step away again. But on the other, my traitorous hormones screamed with disappointment, lamenting the fact his vanishing act denied us some action.

After several moments, the desire ebbs to a slow simmer, and concern over the way Darath departed takes its place. Who possesses the power to summon the Devil against his will? And what in Hell's lava pits will I do if my mate never returns?

I shake my head. Don't go nuclear with worry until presented with a genuine reason to stress. With shoulders back and chin lifted, I wander into Darath's closet to find something of his to wear. The thought of putting my leather outfit back on is depressing.

I crouch naked on the floor and take a second to scrutinize the images strewn about. If I believe Darath, then the woman in the photos, his deceased wife, was not his bonded female, but they had a child together. I don't understand a lot about the demon species, but I'm pretty sure they are gifted one mate. Similar to my people and the vampires.

I wonder if the rules are different for Satan? Can he acquire as many mates as he'd like and produce numerous offspring? Does the bastard have a harem of women eagerly waiting in the wings for his tantalizing attention? A low snarl fills the closet and I blink rapidly, realizing it's coming from me. Stupid mate bond.

I shake off the ridiculous misplaced jealousy and focus on the facts I know. If I remember rightly, Sebastian's malevolent mother wasn't his father's mate. Logan's mom was. And yet, she bore him a child. If I ever get out of this literal hell hole, maybe I'll ask Darath before I behead him.

If I can't touch anything, how on God's green earth will I put on clothes? I refuse to roam around the chamber naked, waiting for Darath's return. Determined, I eye the t-shirts with envy.

Since I'm a soul bound to Hell and not a regular ghost, I wonder if I can conjure garments? I close my lids and concentrate on visualizing my wardrobe back at home. It's too warm here for my leather outfits. I need something with ease of movement for fighting that is still breathable.

When the image formulates, I squeeze my lids harder and focus on the article of clothing encasing my body. Red yoga pants the color of my demon's eyes and a black tank top. Finally, after several minutes of intense mental commands, I peek one eye open and peer down.

Moon fucking stars. Still naked.

My gaze lifts with longing at Darath's assortment of shirts. Maybe the outfit must be in the vicinity for it to work. I hover my palm over a plain black t-shirt and close my eyes again, commanding the shirt onto my body.

A slight tingle spreads across my torso. I hold my non-existent breath before glancing down and... skin.

Son of a witch's tit.

I refuse to give up. I will not wait around in Hell, stark-naked. No way, no how. With a determined sigh, I slam my lids closed and call on mother earth for my powers.

"Please hear me," I whisper after nearly thirty minutes of intense concentration. Besides the one twinge, I haven't felt the reassuring presence of nature since I woke up; who knows how many thousands of feet below the surface? Is Hell even at earth's core, or am I in another dimension?

A warmth suffuses my abdomen. It's the barest hint, but discernable. My focus zeros in and visualize the shirt already in place. After several minutes, I glance down. My shout of glee echoes around the closet, and I grin like an idiot at the hanging suits. I did it!

The black t-shirt, falling to my knees, is a welcome sight even though I can't feel the soft cotton against my skin.

Because you don't possess skin, thanks to the red-eyed demon.

The shirt is huge, so I gather it around my waist in a knot and I march to the dresser, stepping over my discarded warrior outfit. Without hesitation, I jam my head into a drawer and pick out the only pair of boxer briefs, without a ridiculous lude comment, and repeat the process. Concentrate. Find the kernel of power. Visualize.

Armed in my outrageous attire, a strange fatigue sets in and I eye the bed with longing. I'd kill for a nice hot shower, then some much-needed sleep. But since I'm translucent again, the deluge of scalding water is out. Plus, I've been in stasis for six damn months. It's time for me to explore. There are several more doors I haven't investigated yet. Maybe I can find something to occupy my time. After everything, my brain requires a distraction far, far removed from my current troubles.

Chapter 9

Jagorach

"What the ever-living fuck, Nicole?" I bark, the red of my irises lighting up her gleeful stare roaming over my bare chest.

"Shit. We should've waited a few more minutes. I'd love to observe the mighty demon king butt ass naked." My eyebrow lifts at the rare sound of her giggle, which cools my ire somewhat.

Viessa summoned me to a small clearing amidst miles of towering woodlands. The Oracle stands with serenity next to the vampire queen, flanked by Logan and his brother Sebastian. I glance over my shoulder to observe Nox, Sebastian's second in command, standing front and center to a dozen or more Guardians.

"What transpires, Halfling?" I demand with a rumble.

"I suggest you summon your commander and a few of your Warriors to your side. We are about to meet with Sabrina Patraea, the current leader of the Storm Walkers and Kleora's replacement."

"A simple text would have sufficed," I grumble as I send out a mental command to Dzun.

"You would think," she responds, irritation replacing the dazzling smile. "Maybe if you responded to the zillion texts and mental calls, I wouldn't have to have Viessa drag your ass from God knows were, to my side."

"Are you cranky, or is it the pregnancy talking?"

She glowers at me for an entire minute, eyes hard as stone, and I lament my sarcasm. I lived with a pregnant demon. My former wife does not hold a candle to this vampire Halfling.

"You know what I am, Jag? I'm a happy bitch. A cheerful bitch full of joy." Based on the fire banking in the gray depths, she is none too happy. With me. "I will tell someone to fuck off while I skippity skip my way into a field of fucking flowers and enjoy the rest of my wonderful day." Her smile would rival any Prince of Hell.

"My apologies, Vampire," I growl back, still pissed at her for taking me from my mate at a crucial moment. "Cell phones and telepathy do not work in Hell."

Her mouth drops open. If irritation did not consume me, her stunned expression would have me laughing with glee. She places her palms over her abdomen, swollen with child, in a protective gesture.

I sneer at the action, taking a menacing step toward her. Does she honestly believe I would harm her or the child? Logan and Sebastian block my path.

"Calm down, Darath," Bastian says in a soothing voice, even though his sapphire irises glow with a warning. "We are in this mess because of your actions. So sack up and let us see if we can resolve it and avoid a war."

I inhale a deep, calming breath. The iridescent green of Logan's scowl shames me without words. Besides, the vampire commander is right. Dammit.

"Very well," I respond to my friend and allow the blaze behind my eyes to dissipate. As the Moretti brothers return to their positions flanking their queen, I refocus on Nicole. "It wounds me you think I would harm you or that precious bundle you carry."

She nods. "I know you wouldn't hurt me intentionally, big guy. And sometimes, rarely, like hardly ever, my mouth has a mind of its own," she says with a saucy grin. Her way of an apology.

"No," I respond in mock astonishment, playing along. "Not you?"

The smile fades. "Make me a promise. If something ever happens to me, do not drag my soul to your home. Are we clear?"

Before I can respond to the affirmative, Logan interrupts. "Do not take that vow, Darath."

Nicole swings a wide-eyed stare at her mate. "You'd let him drag me off to Hell? What the fuck, Logan?"

"If he pulls this off and brings Priestess Tanagra back, I want that option open for you."

"But Logan...."

"It is that, or I join you in perdition for all of eternity, my love."

The mighty warrior and Nicole's epic journey began the day she was born. Whether they realized it at the time, an ancient prophecy foretold their mating. And while their path has been a bumpy road, one thing always stood firm—Logan's devotion to Nicki. No doubt he would follow her into the farthest depths of my underworld.

Before the flabbergasted queen can respond, Dzun and two dozen of my Warriors materialize behind me. I pivot and lock forearms with my commander.

"What are your orders, my lord?" he asks, taking in my naked chest and the vampire Guardians at a single glance.

Dzun has been with me for almost a millennium now. The demon refused to conform to the human image we present to the world from the beginning. His long dark hair does nothing to hide the spiraled horns curving up over both sides of his head. Four deep black grooves slash from the top of his hairline down his forehead to above the black eyebrows, and three identical ones decorate his chin. The intricate tattoo of his tribe draws a pattern from above his right brow, down through his eyelid, continuing two inches below his eye. And of course, similar to all demons, he sports bright ruby irises, almost matching the hue of his lips.

When Dzun petitioned to become a Warrior, something about him snagged my interest. He more than proved his worth in many a battle over the years. Moreover, his loyalty and utter devotion to me set him apart from the other power-hungry demons clamoring for my seat. After a mere quarter century, I appointed him Commander, and he has never disappointed.

"I hope our Warriors' presence here is merely a show of strength and unity with the vampires, nothing more," I state, and receive a nod of acknowledgment from Nicole. "Keep all weapons hidden unless I verbalize otherwise." Dzun gives a brief signal of agreement before positioning the troops next to the Guardians. The two species eye each other with distrust. We may be at peace at the moment, but it is difficult to erase years of war and bloodshed.

The earthly demon Warriors, my elite fighting force, possess the ability to manifest weapons at will. With a single thought, they can conjure any armament of choice. Whether this negotiation ends in peace or conflict, my men are ready.

"Am I correct to assume we are deep in the wilds of Georgia?" I enquire of the vampire queen, turning with her to face the forest, the Warriors and Guardians at our backs.

"Yes." She does a once over of my torso. "Care to conjure a shirt?"

I grunt. "You summoned me, Halfling. You must suffer my beauty."

"There's no suffering going on here, big guy." Her smile teases, causing a soft rumble from her mate, and I cannot help but laugh at her pluck. She gives me another once over before turning to face the forest. "These woods remind me of every horror flick I've ever seen. It wouldn't surprise me if a thick fog started flowing across the moist ground."

The foliage is copious. Even with my superior eyesight and the brightness of the moon, it is difficult to penetrate the darkness more than a couple of feet.

Speaking of the moon... "Oracle," I smirk, still pissed at her ability to summon me at will. "Surprised to see you here on a peak lunar cycle. Liam must be beside himself." Viessa mated the werewolf king, another being I consider a friend.

Her grin is generous with sass. "King Scott patiently awaits my return, my lord."

Snort. "Must be a serious lock and key to hold the beast."

"His roar shook the rafters right before I left, but he's contained."

I laugh, willing to surrender an enormous amount of cash to witness Liam's beast hogtied and at Viessa's mercy. "Yes, I imagine you will have your hands full on your return. If you need help, I would be happy to lend aid."

"I'll keep that in mind, Demon, but I can handle my mate."

"Of that, I have no doubt, Oracle."

Among our group, it is not a secret Viessa is a Mistress that was trained by Sebastian, who owns several BDSM clubs around the world. Liam struggled with her dominant ways at first, which was delightful to observe, but in the end, they came to a compromise. On the night of the full moon, when Liam's beast lets loose, the powerful Oracle must submit to her king. The fact she chained him up and left him alone does not bode well—for her.

Few creatures can best a werewolf in beast form, myself included, of course.

With no warning or sound, a significant number of beautiful women, dressed like sexy Robin Hood and his merry men, emerge from the forest and I stiffen. The infamous Storm Walkers. Legend has it the females ranging in age and rank are swift and lethal with the bow and quivers strapped to their backs.

A striking blond with eyes the color of the summer sky steps forward. Her outfit is nothing more than a brown leather bikini decorated with intricate metal. Thick cowhide chaps with various buckles circling her thighs showcase a comprehensive display of daggers. A large copper hilt protrudes from the top of each knee-high boot.

What fascinates me the most is the icy, haunted, electric blue regard. This female must be Sabrina. Based on her posture and the swift, calculated assessment of our group, the new leader is a soldier through and through and has seen and doled out much death in her time.

"Queen Giordano," Sabrina nods briefly before zeroing in on me. And who could blame her? The Devil shirtless is a sight to see.

"I would congratulate you on your promotion, but under the circumstances, I doubt this is a proud moment," the Halfling responds.

The icy glare tracks to Nicole, and my eyes narrow. If the deadly creature takes one wrong move toward the Halfling, no matter the consequences, the Moretti brothers and I will engage to protect her.

Normally, I would sit back and relish watching the vampire queen rip the land nymph a new one. Now that she carries the prophesied child, the stakes have escalated.

Astutely, the warrior makes no sudden movements. She simply takes in the number of demons and vampires with a sneer, like she's amused by our show of force, until her observation stalls on Viessa.

"Why are you here, Oracle?" Sabrina asks, eyes narrowed. "Aren't emissaries of God impartial?"

The Tri-bred nods. "Yes, my lady. Unless called, not to be."

I grunt. Typical non-answer by a seer. My derision draws Sabrina's attention. Her expression transforms to stone. "You have something that belongs to us, Demon."

"I have acquired a great many things in my two millennia on earth, my dear. You need to be more specific."

"Goddammit, Darath," Nicole mutters under her breath, but I ignore her, keeping my focus on the blonde bombshell.

"Hand over Priestess Tanagra's body so we may bury her. I will not ask again."

Rage punches swift and brutal. I snarl, showcasing my enormous fangs and bright red irises. "You dare threaten me, female? I could annihilate your entire species without breaking a sweat."

Sabrina's laugh holds no humor. "I'd like to see you try, Demon. Do you expect your show of force here tonight intimates us? Hardly." She takes a step forward, the smile vanishing. "Storm Walkers are a lot like a pack of African lionesses. The ultimate pack hunters. You may think you have us figured out and, in your sights, until you discover too late, we are legion."

Nicole giggles. "I love that analogy."

I frown in confusion until a loud rustling emanates around the clearing. Vampires and demons trace to surround their leaders and face the expanding number of land nymphs emerging from the treetops, the dense foliage, and even underground hiding spots, their bows drawn tight.

"Well, well, well. The legends are true," I smirk, uncaring of their numbers. I will never part from Kleora.

"Enough!" Nicole barks, and with a wave of her hand, freezes every immortal within sight. Except, of course, the Oracle and I. We are immune to the vampire queen's power. Whether it is because we are both connected to God in different ways, I do not know, nor do I care at the moment.

"My pregnancy has shortened my patience. Not that I had much to begin with. Your numbers mean nothing to me, Sabrina." Pride fills my chest as the vampire queen reiterates my thoughts exactly. "And like King Darath, I don't take kindly to threats."

"I have no issue with you, Queen Giordano," the hardened warrior states with ease, even though she's frozen in place. "Or the Oracle."

"Look," Nicki sighs and rubs her belly. "Nobody wants war, commander. I understand your beef with King Darath, but we are here to find a resolution that will make everyone happy."

"We will accept only one outcome, my lady." Sabrina's direct stare pins mine, and I offer a wide, toothy grin. "The return of our leader's body."

"Your leader is my mate, Storm Walker." Oh, how her shocked gasp pleases me. "I will never give her up."

"You snatched her soul and willingly condemn your mate's soul into oblivion?" Sabrina asks. Her apparent astonishment gives me pause, and I reassess her comment.

"Elaborate," I demand.

"If Priestess Tanagra's body doesn't reconnect with the earth of her people before it rots, you won't have her soul to play with any longer, King Darath. It will blink out of existence."

Too stunned to respond for several minutes, I contemplate this new information. The warrior must be mistaken. A soul goes one way or the other unless struck down by a Watcher's sword.

"Her body is safe, surrounded by magic to preserve it while I figure out a way to reconnect her soul."

"You defy the laws of nature. You violated Priestess Kleora's eternal peace. There is no coming back from death."

Putting aside my uncertainty for later, one thing becomes crystal clear—the temporary land nymph ruler has no inkling of my origins or my power.

Delightful.

"You don't care that he could restore your ruler's life?" Nicole asks with a raised eyebrow.

"Whatever comes back is an abomination. Priestess Tanagra would agree," Sabrina states with a shrug and rage at her archaic and uncaring idealism infuses my chest.

"Seriously?" Nicole shakes her head, and it dawns on me. Nicole spat in death's face and, with the help of Icarus, escaped Hell to come back. The temporary nymph's words were an insult to the vampire queen.

"You realize the Vampire Nation, along with the Shifter Territory, the Werewolf Province, and the Valkyrie Regency, are all allies of the Demon Realm, right? You declare war with one; you declare war on all," Nicole asserts, her gray eyes gleaming in the moonlight.

The longer I know this Halfling, the more I adore her.

After the pronouncement, I expected the Storm Walker to back down, so I am flabbergasted when she offers a vicious smile. "So be it. You have a fortnight to produce Priestess Tanagra's body, Demon, or I will wipe your species from the map without breaking a sweat."

Dammit. I loathe when people use my words against me. This beautiful bitch does not know who she's challenging.

Chapter 10

Kleora

My search through Darath's nightstands was a real eye-opener. What does my malevolent mate need with what looked like leather paddles, actual silver handcuffs, and red rope?

Numerous other devices spiked my curiosity and my imagination. I've been around Sebastian long enough to realize the Devil is a sadist. What shocked me more was my response to said discovery. My body tingled with lust at the mere notion of being bound and at his mercy.

No. Bad Kleora. Very bad.

I shake off the erotic fantasies and pivot toward the closet to continue my search. My brain keeps reminding me I won't be able to hold a book, but I shrug it away when a light rapping on the door freezes me mid-step. Darath wouldn't knock. Did Viessa come back? God, I hope so. I could sure use a little company, even if it's the mysterious Oracle.

"My lady?"

Good grief. Berk again. What in blazes does he want now?

"Get lost, Demon." I say, easing closer, my bare feet soundless on the carpet.

"Please hear me out, Priestess. I can offer you a way out of here."

What? Does he take me for an idiot? This ruse is clearly to get me to open the door. Although I have no clue how to do that, and thank goodness, neither does the creepy-sounding fiend. Yet.

"Speak your mind, Demon," I demand, crossing my arms and glaring at the metal barrier.

"It would be best if we were face to face. No one needs to overhear our conversation, my lady."

Yeah, I bet. "Do not take me for a fool or waste my time, Berkonnan. State your purpose or leave me be."

"Very well." I almost snort at the irritation in his sniveling tone. "I may have a way to allow your spirit to escape to the surface."

My entire body stills. Oh, God. Dare I believe him? "What's the catch?" He hesitates so long, I'm afraid he changed his mind and left. "Berk?"

"The visits are temporary. Think of them as mini-vacations to a much cooler climate."

"How temporary?" If I'm on the surface long enough, maybe I can get word to Sabrina and find out who they elected as ruler. Or search for a witch who deals in dark magic to reverse what Darath did. And find my damn body before it disintegrates.

When the voice doesn't respond, I pose another obvious question. "And what is it you demand in return, Demon?"

"There is a simple artifact I desire you to retrieve." By the forced casualness in his tone, I suspect this artifact has a significant meaning. "Your sojourn to the surface cannot exceed sixty earth minutes. But do not worry, I will call your soul back before your time lapses. And unfortunately, I only have the basic coordinates of the object, not the exact location, so it may take you several trips to find the... item."

"And what is this item, Berk?" If I concoct a deal with a demon, I better make damn sure I know every facet of this arrangement.

"It is merely the tip of a sword, my lady."

Why would a blade tip be of such importance to a Hell demon? "The tip of what sword?" Silence greets my question once more. "Berk. What sword?"

"Tell me, Priestess, do you wish to be free from this place forever?"

"Of course," I respond, shifting my head so my ear is closer to the metal separating us.

"And would you like to enjoy vengeance against the one who imprisoned you? The being who denied your soul entrance into Heaven? The vile creature who preserves your body in his earthly bed chambers, doing hell only knows what with it at night?"

Holy Mother Earth!

Darath keeps my body in his bedroom on earth? That fact should creep me out, but strangely, it doesn't. What does he imagine when he observes my lifeless form? Does he envision me naked?

Stop it, Kleora. I admonish myself.

Darath's domain headquarters is now in Arizona. Is his personal residence there as well? If I found my corpse while on one of these brief vacations, could I merge with it? With a snort, I shake my head, clenching my fists at my stupidity. It took me an hour to conjure a damn t-shirt over my form, and I'd still need someone to bury me with my ancestors.

My toes curl, denied the pleasure of sinking into the carpet as I contemplate my options. This imp is petitioning me to aid him in eliminating his king. And I suspect the sword tip is more important than he's letting on, considering that he's willing to help me for such a mere object.

My brows furrow in confusion. I assumed it took God to destroy an angel, even the original fallen one. Has this creepy, power-hungry demon discovered a way to kill Lucifer?

I must warn him.

No. Wait. What am I saying? I've threatened to slay him myself. Numerous times. Now, this creature is offering me a means to not only escape this fiery death trap, but to exact my revenge.

Why am I hesitating? Sure, Jagorach is my true mate. The only one I will ever experience in my life. The chemistry between us is combustible, igniting with a mere look. But it's also more than biology. Before my death, I enjoyed his company. His quick wit and dark sense of humor, and for lack of a better word, his devil may care attitude. And maybe he held onto me for the same reasons, but that doesn't make what he did—is still doing—acceptable.

My mind flashes back to that night at Sebastian's villa in Italy. The Watchers, the self-appointed soldiers of God, carried swords with the ability to obliterate an immortal's soul. Like, blink it out of existence. No entry into Heaven or Hell.

Which is exactly what will happen to me if my soul doesn't reconnect with my body or my carcass rots above ground. Darath believes if he fails, my spirit should float back in its original direction. Ya know, the one he denied me. Unfortunately, he severed that pathway the second he held onto me with such selfish abandon and trapped me in Hell.

Now my only options are reconnection through magical means, or I cease to exist altogether.

I glare at the protective metal door. Is the artifact Berk wishes me to bring him the tip of a Watcher's sword? Mother earth. If that's true, he doesn't merely want to overthrow Darath and rule Hell—he craves to wipe my mate from existence entirely. Can I, in good conscience, be a part of something so vile, so permanent? Yes, I'm livid with him, but can I assist in such an abhorrent endeavor? Not sure the mate bond would even allow it. In all my years, I've never heard of an immortal killing their mate.

It's imperative I ascend to the surface, but let's think about the enormous elephant in the room, the one sitting on my chest.

Should I strike a bargain with the traitorous bastard on the other side of the barrier? It would allow me to get word to Sabrina while searching for a witch or warlock.

AS much as I hate Darath right now, I'll never bring Berk a weapon to destroy him. I'll simply claim I never found it. I shrug. What could the conniving demon beyond the door do to me that Darath hasn't already done? An image of bubbling hot lava pits burns through my brain and I cringe.

Darath's inner demon—meaning Satan—adheres to the same compulsions as me regarding the whole killing of your mate thing. Right? He could hurt me, as I've hurt him with my arrows. But condemning me to what's beyond this door, to a permanent death? I'm not sure it's possible.

Suppose I believe the magma pits are real and Satan could kill his mate. That the rules for the King of Hell are different. Besides the constant agony in my joints and muscles, my visit—I refuse to call it a permanent situation—has been rather mild. Although, the continuous muffled screams of suffering through the door are damn tangible and give me a severe case of anxiety.

I push aside my fear and concentrate on what I can control.

While I'm on the surface, pretending to search for the sword tip, I'll contact Sabrina and locate Troy Tenebris, the male witch who joined our task force to acquire the powerful Abigail Brevil. If anyone would know how to reconnect me with my body and either bury me or bring me back, it's him.

The mere idea of coming close to the dark magic Troy uses makes my skin crawl, if I had skin, but there is no way I'm destroying my mate. No matter how pissed I am at him. Unless he gives me no choice. Like a, me or him, type of situation.

"Where is the sword tip, Berk?"

"Underneath the Tree of Life."

Oh, come on!

"The Tree of Life perished in the great floods, as you are well aware. And even if it hadn't, God placed a powerful cherub with a flaming sword in front of the tree to protect it."

"Yes. You know your Bible, Priestess. It's the tip of the flaming sword I'm after. And while the tree no longer stands, I possess the general coordinates of where to unearth the tip."

So not the tip of a Watcher's sword, but that of an angelic cherub. It must be potent enough to bring down Satan if this idiot wants it so badly. "I'm translucent, remember? I cannot dig to retrieve anything."

"The how or why does not matter, my lady. All you need to know is if you assist me in this quest, I will restore your soul to your body."

Yeah, and do what to it? "You have a deal, Berkonnan. Get me out of here, and I'll find that sword tip so we can both be free of Jagorach Darath."

"One more thing, my lady."

Crap. I knew it.

"Once you locate the tip, you must not touch it."

"Well, since I can't dig it up, I don't foresee that as a problem."

"Pinpoint the location and I will take ownership."

"If you're able to go to the surface, then why not perform a search and retrieval yourself? Why come to me?" A nagging suspicion boils in my gut. This creature is omitting something vital.

"My trip topside is mere seconds, priestess, and requires a portal. Which would draw Dzun's, King Darath's commander's, attention." He pauses as if contemplating the consequences of that happening. "And trust me, my dear, you do not want to have a run-in with Dzun. If you get me the exact location, I can open the gateway, snatch the item and return to Hell before I'm detected. Hence why I've solicited your aid to locate it first."

"Uh-huh," I sneer. "Very well, Demon. You have a deal." I grit my teeth and pray I didn't make the biggest mistake of my life. I've bargained with high-ranking rulers across the globe for my people, but this arrangement gives me the heebie-jeebies.

"Excellent, my lady," he hisses with glee. "I will be back soon with the spell to release your soul temporarily and the coordinates, of course."

Goddess Mother Earth. What have I gotten myself into? I'm making a deal with an unsavory demon so I can attain temporary forays to the surface. Not merely to locate a witch of dark magic to restore my life or end it, but to recover a sword that will help annihilate my mate.

I peer around at my luxurious prison. Son of a goat fucker. This is all Darath's fault.

Chapter 11

Jagorach

"Does anyone else think Sabrina is off her rocker?" Nox asks, leaning against the wall in the converted garage at Alex's cottage in Newport, Oregon, with casual grace. We decided on a neutral spot for our strategy meeting, even though I offered the use of my new headquarters in Arizona. Apparently, no one wishes to step foot in demon territory.

Odd.

After the sexy land nymph's dominance play two nights ago, the petite but lethal Storm Walkers faded back into the forest. Their arrows trained on the bullseye in the center of my chest. Once we were alone, Nicole swiveled in my direction, pinning me with a furious glare.

"I've worked hard to bring the immortal world into a semblance of peace, Darath, and you've shot it all to shit."

"No need for theatrics, Halfling. One race exerting their control does not constitute war."

"Theatrics?" The pregnant vampire glowers with both fists placed on her hips, while Logan shakes his head at my stupidity. "I don't know about you, but I've heard and read about the Storm Walker legends, and they are not pretty. Nor do they bode well for our side. And don't downplay the seriousness of this situation or my fucking reaction, Jag."

Alrighty then. "My apologies, Nicole. I meant to express that if I do not develop a resolution in two weeks, I will handle Sabrina and the land nymphs. Alone."

"How dare you say that to me after everything we've been through?"

Actual tears shimmer in the—as a rule—unemotional vampire's stare. What in damnation? "I only meant...."

"I know precisely what you meant, Demon! You don't want or need our help."

"You better quit while you are ahead, Darath." Logan grins. "There is no arguing with a pregnant vampire."

"Apparently," I mumble as I reach down and clasp her cool fingers in mine. "I created this situation, and while I appreciate you having my back, I cannot, in good conscience, request the prophesied Halfling carrying the Daywalker vampire king to come to my rescue." When she opens her mouth to protest, I hold up a finger to stall the tirade brimming in her irises. "But, if I find myself in over my head, I promise to solicit your aid post-haste."

"I hate to break it to you, Darath, but you're already in over your head." When she steps closer and wraps her arms around my waist, I peer wide-eyed at both Morettis, grinning like fools.

"Enjoy it while it lasts, Darath. She will revert to her belligerent, mouthy self in no time," Sebastian snickers.

"Hey." Nicole glares over her shoulder at her brother-in-law and commander of her Guardians before turning back to me. "At least let us help you brainstorm regarding Kleora."

"It would honor me to pick your brain," I grin.

She glowers. "Are you pacifying the pregnant lady?"

"Yes," I chuckle. "I like my head attached to my body."

Dzun's deep baritone behind me refocuses my attention. "I found her extraordinary and striking—in a lethal way."

"Yeah," Nox laughs. "I'm sure she thought the same of you with the horns, tattoos, and creepy red irises checking her out."

I tune out their banter. Over the last two days, I've consulted with the dozens of different wizards and witches I summoned, on top of attempting every spell or incantation I could remember. Nothing. Not a goddamn twitch or tic of Kleora's body. Time is a ticking bomb, the seconds counting down to my mate's demise or redemption.

"Would Viessa intervene the way Icarus did with you, Nicole?" I ask, knowing what the previous Oracle did to bring Nicki back from Hell was forbidden and eventually cost the priest and her first unborn child their lives. If I could die—which I cannot—I would gladly sacrifice my existence for hers.

The image of her luscious breasts, the succulent taste of her sweet sex, and her cries as she came invade my mind, hardening me to stone in a second. I shift in my jeans to alleviate the discomfort.

"That option is off the table," Nicole states. "We only have one Oracle now, and I refuse to place her in a situation that could jeopardize her position or life."

"Agreed," Alex concurs, her bright red hair piled high on her head in a haphazard, messy bun, showcasing the petite, pointed ears which are akin to Kleora's.

"As much as we all want to restore Priestess Tanagra, I'm not willing to put my mate at risk," Liam declares, shooting a sympathetic expression down the table.

"Viessa is not the only Oracle on the planet, young wolf," I retort, snagging everyone's attention.

"Shut the fuck up," Nicki utters in astonishment. "There are others?"

"One other, to be exact. But he works solely with the dragon shifters. No one has seen or heard from him in centuries."

"Dragon shifters..." Nicole shakes her head. "That still fucking blows my mind. Is there a way to contact their ruler and maybe negotiate?"

"Unless you wish to be eaten alive or turned into a shish kebob, I suggest not. The Dragon Territory is in the harsh wilds of the Outback. Anyone who has ventured into their area never returns."

"I hate to ask this, but what about Troy Tenebris? That ancient bad boy could have the cojones to pull off such a complicated, dark spell," Alex interjects.

"I have reached out to him several times already," I inform the valkyrie. "He is either ignoring my calls or dealing with his own mate issues."

"What mate issues?" Nicole inquires, her inspection laser-focused on me. "If you're referring to Abigail, the bitch is dead."

"Yes. And so is Kleora, but here we are," I remind her.

Her deep sigh speaks volumes, and an uncomfortable sensation skitters across the back of my neck. "I hope to God you're wrong, Jag. If Abigail is still alive, we're all in jeopardy."

"I believe our best strategy at the moment is to locate Troy," Lucretia offers, and I notice she dressed in her sexy, leather warrior outfit, even though she is no longer a Guardian but rather the shifter queen. Once a soldier, always a soldier, I guess. "He agreed to help once before. If he refuses, at least we could glean information about Abigail."

"He only aided us because we were after something he coveted," Logan grumbles, his stare mesmerized by Nicole's palm caressing her abdomen with slow circles.

"It's worth a shot, and right now, our only play," Kurtis says. His chair groans as he leans back, testing its stability under his muscular frame. "Unless anyone else knows of a more formidable witch than Troy."

"Can I ask you a personal question, Darath?" Nicole asks, leaning forward, her elbows on the table.

"Ask away," I state with a wink.

"If you are Lucifer, aren't you more powerful than any witch?"

I regard her with curiosity. "You still distrust my identity."

"It's not that I doubt you." The beautiful, somber irises drop to her hands clasped on the wooden surface. "More like… can't comprehend, wish I hadn't found out about, type of doubt."

My deep sigh lifts her regard to mine. "I admit I have a long, sordid past filled with deeds and actions that most nightmares spawn from, and while my father wrote my future in stone, so to speak, you have my undying loyalty and trust. Until you break it, then all bets are off." I say the last in a teasing manner, but the lush lips never twitch.

"I've visited your home once, Darath, and while my time was brief, the agony seemed enduring." Her hushed comment obliterates my grin as silence reigns supreme among our group at the reminder. Logan eases next to his mate, placing a reassuring hand on her shoulder.

I lay my enormous palm over her white-knuckled grip, waiting until I gain her full attention. "I am uncertain as to why He marked your soul. Only my father can answer the question. But rest assured, if you are to become mine one day, Halfling, I will ensure your existence is as comfortable as possible. I vow it."

The vampire queen stares at me for several more minutes, offers a brief nod, and then it is back to business as usual, although Logan remains by her side.

"And as far as my abilities as Satan," I continue, "when it comes to reviving a soul marked by God, even my supremacy has limits.

Nicole's apprehension does not surprise me. She shares the same sentiment of many. My name evokes fear in most, a sick longing for power in others. I have earned my reputation tenfold. When I defied my father and decreed I should rule, I sealed my fate. Anyone who has read the Book of Revelation from the Bible knows I fail in the end. As will all the sinners in the world. Unless they pray for forgiveness, and mean it, they damn their souls to perdition after judgment day for eternity.

I am Lucifer. I enjoy tormenting the beings under my watch because they are there for a reason, deserving of whatever I dish out. The low and depraved. Killers, rapists, pedophiles, and so many more. But the moment I beheld my precious peach, my duties soured in my gut like rotten meat.

Do I still believe humans and immortals merit the suffering my second home offers? Yes. Do I entice them to commit carnal sins? Yes, and no. In the past, I played a bigger role. Now it is by my order and the control of my commanders. My demons put situations in individual's paths, but ultimately, it is their choice. Ah, free will.

"Why don't we send out those who can teleport in search of Troy," Nicole suggests, bringing me back to the discussion at hand—raising my mate from the dead. "The rest of you hit up every contact you possess in the witchery world. Troy didn't vanish into thin air. The fucker crawled under a rock somewhere, and we will kick over every stone until we find him."

The second we adjourn, the alluring succubus queen, who remained quiet during the meeting, steps in my path. "Hey sexy Devil, would you mind giving a girl a ride home?"

"Apologies, Jilaya, but I have urgent matters to attend to. Perhaps Sebastian can escort you?" I don't have time for Queen Oresha's seduction games.

She pouts her full, crimson-stained lips. "The little valkyrie put her foot down. She won't allow the erotic vampire to come out and play."

I glance over at Alex, glaring daggers at Jilaya. "Nox then," I insist and shift to move around her. She blocks me again, her red nails scraping down my forearm, which in turn causes goosebumps to sprout.

"He's already disappeared. Please, Jagorach, it will only take a minute of your time. I must get back to my duties."

"Very well," I concede with a sigh.

I reach to grab her wrist. The less contact with her, the better, but the troublesome minx wraps her arms around my waist. I peer down at her with irritation when a delicious tingle skates across my nape.

"You duplicitous bastard!"

Speechless, my arms frozen around Jilaya, I gape at the furious jade stare of my mate.

What the ever-living fuck?

When she charges, a silver blade materializes in her fist. I shove the succubus at an equally stunned Logan and confront my enraged female. Sebastian traces toward Kleora and attempts to grab her, but she passes right through him.

I raise my palms. "Kleora, wait. It's not–"

Her petite frame plows into me with such extraordinary force. I stagger back, losing my footing. My arms encircle her tiny waist as her dagger sinks to the hilt in my chest.

"Jag!" Nicole hollers.

Granted no time to subdue her, we both sink through the concrete floor into utter darkness.

Chapter 12

Kleora

How could he? I should've known better than to trust a demon to be faithful.

After a full day of lamenting my decision to bargain with the slimy Berk, I'd stiffened my spine and coerced my guilty conscious to step up or shut up.

It wasn't until the following night the demon returned with a spell. It not only opened the thick steel door, but would deliver me to the surface. The sights and sounds outside my protective chamber nearly had me fleeing back into my room and baring the door.

A boiling heat infused my frame through my leathers, which took me an hour to figure out how to get it back on, and I glanced down, expecting my skin to burst into flames. The ever-present ache in my joints intensified tenfold, and it was all I could do to remain upright and not curl into a ball of agony. What I wouldn't have given to be a mere ghost at that point instead of a soul bound to Hell, able to experience every nuance of this hideous place.

The walls were a thick rock that wept buckets of blood. Pits of various sizes lining the ground held either red hot lava or an inky substance that bubbled and reeked of sulfur. The screaming, wailing, and cries of help caused my vision to swim with tears.

My fated male, Lucifer himself, rules over this horrifying place. He inflicts the pain and suffering the souls endure. How could I have allowed him to touch me? To bring me such pleasure when so many have suffered right outside my door?

I worked to block the essence of perdition from my vision and turned to my rescuer. Berkonnan's appearance shocked me further, and I stiffened my shoulders to keep from turning my head away in disgust. Bile rose in my throat, but I swallowed it down and concentrated on my task at hand—getting the hell out of... Hell.

Berk had no skin. Instead, his body is comprised of exposed muscles and tendons, with bony protrusions jutting up from around his collarbone like a grotesque necklace. More bone protruded from his shoulders, elbows, and knees. His face was a distorted skull mask with large horns extending up from his forehead. Several rows of jagged yellow teeth consumed his mouth, slicing his bulbous lips when he spoke.

The demon reiterated our terms. He cautioned me that in sixty minutes, he would snatch my soul back into my chamber before it obliterated into nothingness. Great. I had to rely on a monster to keep his word. At least his consuming compulsion for the sword tip would ensure he kept me alive.

The trip to the surface was surprisingly smooth. I'd expected to endure severe discomfort. But, once above ground, instead of seeking Sabrina, my muddled brain focused on my mate, and I materialized in that garage in time to witness Darath embracing my best friend. I fixated on them through a scarlet haze of unbridled rage, surprised to discover a dagger in my hand.

When had conjuring weapons become a skill?

With no other thought than revenge, I plunged my knife into his chest, aiming for his double-crossing heart—without even being sure whether the Devil possessed one.

My body trembles when it connects with his enormous torso. Although Darath's frame is solid, the weight of his arms encircling my waist substantial, an extraordinary thing happens.

By touching the Devil, I become sentient, but at the moment we seem to be insentient to our surroundings—Hence us falling through the concrete floor and smothered by dirt, stone, roots, and bugs.

The oppression freaks me out, and I flail in Darath's hold. Nymphs are creatures of the earth, but I have no wish to suffocate hundreds of feet below the surface.

"Kleora!" Darath's furious bark snags my attention, and I cease my struggling. "Look at me," he orders.

I shake my head, afraid the oppressive soil will blind me the second I lift my lids. What the heck have I done? My instant rage swept aside all rational thought, and I doomed us both in seconds.

"Open your eyes, peach." The command, spoken in that deep seductive tone, has my lids lifting to meet the fiery red irises mere inches from mine.

Dirt moves all around us. Oh, God! We are still sinking. The stench of moist earth fills my lungs, and I grit my teeth to keep the panic at bay. Thank the heavens, branching between our faces is a pocket of air, like a protective bubble providing a meager amount of oxygen and we sink deeper into the earth.

"Are you doing this, Jag?" I ask, uncurling a finger from his shirt clutched in my fist to indicate the space.

"Yes, love, but I cannot trace us from here, or stop our descent without your help."

The foremost desire in my stupid brain should be escape, but for some odd reason, the scene from moments ago plays out in my mind. "Are you sleeping with Jilaya?" I blurt out before I allow myself to think it through fully, causing my face to flush.

Darath stills. The penetrating irises never deviate from my face. "You wish to discuss this now, while we are being crushed beneath the surface?" he asks quietly, and I can't tell if he's angry or curious.

And goddess, that wasn't a no.

A tingling sensation skates across my skin as forceful heat flashes through my body. Darath tenses beneath me, his arms around my waist a steel band, as if he senses the temperature change. His brows dip into a fierce frown.

"Kleora? What are you doing?"

I can't voice what is happening to me. It's like a wash of passionate fury saturates my frame and seizes rational thought. A vision of his tall, muscular physique wrapped in an ardent embrace with Jilaya's perfect form invades my brain, consuming everything else.

"Kleora! Stop this right now," Darath snarls through gritted teeth, and I realize my body has burst into flames, devouring us both.

"Did you fuck her?" I don't even recognize the guttural, angry voice as my own. Nor do I acknowledge the inferno engulfing us, sucking the oxygen from our minute bubble.

Darath's face contorts with agony as the fire turns the flesh on his cheeks a bright red, then a crispy black. His grip around my waist tightens, and his neck arches in pain, but I can't bring myself to care. Instead, my lips lift in a snarl of malevolent glee as I watch him suffer, not heeding my skin is crisping right along with his.

"No. Now stop this, Kleora." The demon grips my skull between his enormous palms, the crimson regard brightens. "As much as my body burns for you, this is a bit ridiculous."

"We've only begun, Lucifer." At my words, the flames burn brighter, hot enough to flay the charred skin from our bodies.

King Darath's roar of agony nudges something at the back of my brain to stop this insanity. I'm hurting my mate. And every instinct should recoil at the torture my insidious fury is inflicting, but the overshadowing rage is uncontrollable.

He betrayed me with my best friend. Denied me entry into Heaven. The bastard trapped me in Hell for his own selfish purposes. Those are my prevailing thoughts as I grip his skull and call upon the power of the earth to fuel the fire.

When Darath's visage shimmers and alters, the flames douse in seconds. Our clothes burned away with the first lick of fire, and our charred skin seared to ash, so I feel the explosion of his transformation in every muscle and tendon. The surrounding soil vibrates from the blast, taking the brunt of the detonation and halting our descent who knows how many hundreds of feet below the surface. The already bulky muscles beneath me expand, turning dark as night, and thick spikes protrude from his shoulders.

Fear swallows my anger.

The ground rumbles, and my heart hiccups as two large, black horns lengthen from the smooth, opaque skull. A low, raspy snarl showcases enormous fangs, and heavy, leathery wings stab out from his back, causing the dirt held in stasis by Darath's power to spill between us.

My scream pierces the space. Not only at the threat of suffocating to death, but at the ungodly transmutation of my mate. The crimson irises, filled with fury, zero in on mine, and terror grips me. He takes in my appearance, which, if I look anything like he did before he morphed into the Devil, must be appalling.

I'm so frozen by fear that I don't comprehend the immediate danger of the dirt covering my mouth and nose. Instead, my sole focus is on the creature before me. The deep rubies burn brighter with every second, holding me captive, sturdier than any chains.

When the powerful beast scoops the soil from my mouth and presses his hot lips to mine, I freeze. He exhales a harsh breath, forcing my lungs to expand. A part of my brain understands as long as Darath holds on to me, I am sentient, forced to breathe air like a living person.

I think the creature realizes this at the exact moment because he lifts my body away from his, pressing me into the packed earth. I panic as more dirt trickles between us and grip the massive shoulders tighter, not caring the sharp spikes slash my palms.

"No!" I screech, struggling in earnest. "Don't let go, Jag."

"I must, Kleora, or you will die." His growl is hellish as he shoves me deeper into the gritty earth. Chunks of dirt collapse, covering his body and building an impenetrable wall between us. "Let go," he orders.

"No!" I scream, clinging to the protrusions in his shoulders with every ounce of strength I possess. I kick my legs against the oppressive weight of tons of rock and soil to fight my way back to him. My efforts pull more dirt in until only his oddly beautiful face is visible.

"Please, Jag," I choke out, spitting muck. "Don't leave me."

"Never," he snarls, the red almost blinding in its intensity. "But you must release your hold, sweetness, so you can float to the surface. I will be right behind you."

I try to nod, but the weight on the back of my skull bears down on my head. When completely entombed, terror suffuses every synapse in my brain as the suffocating earth works its way into my mouth and down my throat. Still, my fingers refuse to release my mate.

The building burn in my lungs forces me to loosen my grip. Dizziness encroaches as thousands of grains of dirt and roots rip me from the creature I realize I'd die to be near.

Shit. There go my well-laid-out plans for revenge.

Chapter 13

Kleora

I take a second, or two hundred, to recover and comprehend where I landed. I had assumed I'd return to the garage the second I released my death grip on Darath. Instead, I'm flat on my back in the middle of a thick forest that somehow feels familiar.

Feels. Ha. I can't feel a darn thing. Which, in all honesty, is a significant improvement over the fire scalding my skin off, and dirt restricting my airway.

With a low grown, I roll over to my hands and knees, working to shove the image of Darath's authentic appearance from my mind. But no matter how hard I try—it's burned behind my retinas forever.

The king's human form is breathtaking. Seven feet of perfection. Not a tattoo blemishes his sculpted physique. And those gorgeous locks—every woman in the world would pay big bucks to achieve such abundant, soft waves. His demeanor is fun, flirtatious, and I'm drawn to him in a way I can't explain.

As the Devil, however, his visage was both terrifying and magnificent. The power in his body was unmeasurable. The inky flesh, bald head, and thick spikes stretching the skin, not to mention the enormous horns jutting up from his skull, magnified the spine-chilling scarlet irises and his purpose in this world.

I'm not a religious person. My people revere the earth above all else. We respect and honor the Oracles to guide us, trusting their visions and words as messages from God. Yes, we believe in God. So, I guess to trust in one, you must acknowledge the other. Good and evil. Right and wrong. Yin and yang.

Down through history, every race and species heard the fables of Satan, the original fallen angel. A powerful, intelligent, and beautiful angelic being, the chief among all angels. But Lucifer had free will, like the rest of us. He defied God and declared himself to be the 'Most High.'

Lucifer's beauty, wisdom, and might—all things created in him by God—led him to his rebellion and ultimate fall.

But the male I reluctantly care for, and I believe cares for me, doesn't jibe with that telling. Is Darath prideful? Absolutely. Does he relish all ideas sinful and deviant? I think he does. But the big question, and the one that burns doubt and anxiety in my gut... Is the Devil still after God's throne?

I couldn't live with myself if I sided with the bringer of destruction. In my heart of hearts, I could never turn my back on the creator. Not even for my fated male. I heard the screams of torment in the lower chambers. What I experienced was the tip of the fatal storm for others. A fate for all eternity.

"Priestess? Is that you?"

I allow the familiar voice to wash away my inner turmoil and rise to my feet to face the commander of my Storm Walkers. "Sabrina, it's wonderful to see you." As soon as I pivot to meet her, I realize I am naked from tip to toe—transparent—but naked nonetheless.

Without a hitch, the warrior whips off her dark cape and attempts to drape it over my shoulders, but it passes right through me to flutter to the ground.

"I... apologize, my lady," Sabrina blanches.

"No need, Brina. Allow me a second." I squeeze my eyes shut and envision the leather warrior outfit I died in, and within seconds, I'm fully clothed. Ha! My skills are improving.

"So, it's true. You have passed on?" my most trusted soldier asks as she retrieves her cape.

"That is an interesting way to put it," I murmur with scorn.

"Is King Darath responsible for your situation?"

"Yes."

"That son of a bitch," Brina grumbles, clenching her fists. "Has your soul been in Hell this entire time?"

"Yes, but do not fret, Patraea. I've been somewhat comfortable in Darath's luxurious chambers."

"How did you escape?"

"I bargained with a high-ranking Hell demon." I laugh at my lethal commander's horrified expression.

With a shudder, she refocuses on the situation at hand. "We stand at the ready to exact revenge, and your people work diligently to locate your body, my lady."

"Thank you, but I charge you to talk with the current ruler and convince them to hold off on war for now."

Sabrina lowers her lids as if in shame. "They elected me to rule in your place, Priestess."

I smile. "An excellent choice, my friend. No matter what happens, it eases my mind to know you will guard our people." I glance around in concern. "If you are the new ruler, why are you patrolling alone?"

"Old habits, my lady. Do you have an inkling of where he is keeping your remains?" Brina inhales a sharp breath before rubbing her forehead as if it aches. "It seems wrong to talk with you about your dead body."

I snort. "Imagine how I feel?"

"My apologies." She straightens her spine. "How would you like me to proceed, my queen?"

My teeth sink into my bottom lip, uncertain how much of my bargain with Berk to reveal to my ruthless commander turned ruler. I spoke the truth earlier. She will protect our race with her life. As for diplomacy, Sabrina has little patience or tact. And while it's an attribute I appreciate, and serves her well as the leader of the Storm Walkers, few tolerate her brashness.

"My corpse lies in King Darath's lair in Arizona. It's well-guarded, no doubt. But I'm working on a plan to reconnect with my body. I'll either restore my life or perish as I should have—with my soul in Heaven." I pin Brina with a commanding stare.

She is the ruler now and would be well within her rights to tell me to screw off and jump-start a war with the Demon Realm. We both know it wouldn't be with the demons alone. Nicole Giordano will spring to defend Darath, inciting the shifter, werewolves, and valkyries to join the fray.

"Do not implement your strategy against the Demon Realm just yet," I beseech Sabrina. I hold my breath as she scrutinizes me for several long seconds.

"As you wish, Priestess." She dutifully lowers her lids and offers a slight nod.

My shoulders ease. One less issue to fret about.

"What is the plan exactly?" she asks.

I place my well-earned trust in my commander and lay out everything I connived with Berk and what I discern so far. Sabrina listens with a quiet intensity, never interrupting, but no doubt her mind whirls with strategies and alternatives to save her ruler.

"Do you have faith in this, Berkonnan?" she questions when I finish.

"Not in the slightest," I snort. "But he's the reason I'm here now."

"The Oracle sides with the vampires, my lady, so any aid from her is unlikely."

"Her devotion to Nicole is as it should be, Brina. Send out feelers into the Witch and Seer realms. See if you can drum up any clues on how to solve my predicament and find the witch Troy Tenebris."

Darath alluded he was working on a plan, but I refuse to sit around twiddling my thumbs in hopes my mate will come through and save me. As I informed Sabrina, I'm not foolish enough to believe a word Berk says. That vile creature possesses his own greedy agenda, which I doubt includes restoring my life. The putrid male couldn't give two shits about me.

"I will contact you whenever I'm on the surface, so…" A blast plows through my spirit. Agony sweeps through me as I watch Sabrina fly across the clearing and crash into a nearby tree. The warrior lands nimbly on her feet as blood trickles from her lip.

"What was that?" she asks breathlessly, knocking an arrow into her bow and studying the terrain.

"I'm uncertain." Bent over, hands on knees, I catch my breath and wait for the pain to lessen. "I've experienced nothing like it before."

"Maybe you should head to the coordinates the demon gave you and at least show a pretense of compliance."

"Smart thinking." I straighten, the hairs on my arms not relaxing in the slightest. "I'll be in touch."

"Kleora," Brina interjects before I vanish. "Do not place your trust in King Darath, no matter the circumstance."

"I may be dead, but do not take me for a fool." She lowers her gaze without protest at the command and anger in my tone. "Jagorach will pay for what he's done. I vow it."

Before she can respond, I disappear. My destination? Mesopotamia, now known as Iraq.

Chapter 14

Kleora

The world spins. A sharp, throbbing pain takes hold, so much so, it causes bile to rise in my throat—meaning I'm ready to projectile vomit like a sick baby. I pray the suffering will spew out with it.

Don't panic, Kleora. Jagorach's chambers are around the next corner.

My little pep talk stopped working days ago. Or maybe it's been weeks. The agony fogs my brain until I no longer comprehend the passage of time, only the ebbing and flowing of suffering.

With every careful step, a way out of the torment seems more and more unrealistic. I press my fingers against my temples, urging my ears to close to the surrounding sounds, my vision to block out the atrocities through each level.

Darath's home is deep and desolate, with chamber after chamber of altered versions of Hell. In my current spot, flames continuously burn and rain from the sky. The temperature given off by the flares is hotter than any fire I've encountered on Earth. And to top it all off, noxious sulfuric gasses hang in the air, and rivers of molten metal flow freely.

I've never felt this thirsty or bone-weary tired. It is all I can do to not collapse and wither in misery on the sweltering ground. Sweat peppers my skin, the leather outfit intensifying the heat, but this situation will not snuff out my warrior spirit. I'm determined to either find Darath's room myself or locate Berk to help me, even as everything in me screams to give up. This horrendous place compels me to admit defeat.

Never.

I've pushed forward through narrow portals, vast gaping caverns with lava falls at the height of skyscrapers. Unfortunately, one doorway leads to another gloomy, horrifying world. Clouds of dust and ash fill the air. It stings my eyes and lungs. Sometimes it's so thick it obstructs my vision.

Danger hides around every corner, each turn. This underground leviathan reeks of sulfur and decay. Yet, with my goal in mind, I move forward, despite the fact I can't feel my legs anymore. Everything is going numb, and I'm not sure if it's a good thing—not being able to endure the constant pain—or a bad thing, meaning my soul is becoming one with this place.

Maybe I should rest. Yes, that would be best. I should save my energy. A deep breath follows another as I crouch behind a steaming boulder. A quick glance around the edge reveals two demons raping a female soul over and over again in her cell. Either simultaneously or taking turns. It's probably her greatest fear and now her eternal anguish. They bite and scratch her skin, so much so, I can't tell what race she is from all the blood and wounds covering every inch of her body.

My mind screams to help, to intervene, but even if I killed the two pale-skinned horned demons with razor-sharp teeth, others would replace them, and her torment would begin anew. I've witnessed it over and over throughout my journey in Hell.

Ride it out until they leave, Kleora, then sneak past.

Fire lances on the top of my shoulder. I gasp at the searing pain and look up. Lava dripped from the ceiling, landing with a sizzling plop on my flesh. Abrupt, eerie silence stops my heart, and I ease my head around the stone, dismissing the agony encompassing my shoulder. Two sets of blazing red eyeballs zero in on my position. My gasp compromised my hiding spot.

The demons materialize in front of me, and I rise to my feet, the numbness gone—entirely replaced by terror.

Crimson irises stare at me with malevolent fury. White horns on either side of their bare skulls extend. The smell of death escapes both creature's full nostrils set within an arched nose. The taller one rolls his gaunt head on his massive shoulders and ossified body, and I get my first glimpse of his pecker.

The skin covering their bodies may be pallid, but their pricks are pure ebony, with pale spikes protruding along the top of their extended shafts. I cringe at the mere notion of those stabbing inside my delicate flesh, and a fresh wave of rage at the added pain they inflict on their captives bolsters my courage.

How could fate tie me to a creature who rules such a place? Who commands these hideous abominations to torture the damned for all eternity? What crimes did the poor woman enact to deserve this sentence?

Shadowy curls coil around the tall one's torso like another being, and I refocus on my current dilemma. A powerful tail undulates behind it. Each movement scrapes the floor with a shower of sparks.

"What have we here, Vorgroth?" the tall one asks, saliva dripping from his bulbous lips. I nearly gag.

"Fresh meat, brother," Vorgroth replies with glee.

"Think again, dickwads." I leap over their heads, landing behind them with a swiftness that startles them. Before they can react, I clutch Tall One's razer-tipped tail, and with a wide arc, I slice one of his horns from his head with his own appendage.

Vorgroth bellows as he tackles me with the force of a linebacker. His bulky body crashes into mine as we impact the rock floor. Agony bursts through my spine and chest, making it difficult to breathe. I lament my inability to become translucent in this violent place.

I shove the pain away and use the idiot's forward momentum against him, flipping him over my head and straight into a lava pit.

Whoop! One down, one to go.

My elation is short-lived when his brother grabs a fist full of my hair and yanks me to my feet before slamming my cheek into the rock I so innocently hid behind. My frantic gaze locks with the woman in the cell. Her fingers grip the bars. A manic expression I can only define as excitement saturates her face. She's getting off on watching, and I can't determine if she is excited because I killed one of her tormentors or if she gets off on the pain of others. Maybe this psycho's sentence is justified.

"Fuck her in the ass, Dagaran!" she bellows.

Yup. The woman is a total bitch and deserves whatever punishments the demons dole out.

Egged on by her screaming, Dagaran rips my leather pants down the middle, keeping a constant pressure against my skull. The hotness of the rock sizzles my face, but I refuse to go down without a fight. The sick, deformed bastard will not stick his weird, tortuous shaft in my ass.

Terror ignites in my soul. Scalding fire suffuses my body. The second I feel his hardness against my bare ass cheek, my skin ignites with the same hotness as the surrounding fires. Fury gallops down my spine as I reach back and grip his disgusting prick, ignoring the fact the protrusion on the top punctures my skin. I viciously twist and pull until cold blood sizzles the fire dancing over my skin.

The pressure on my head eases with his bellow. I spin and shove the now flaccid cock into Dagaran's mouth, cutting off his roar of agony. One claw-tipped hand covers his empty groin squirting a vile smelling black ooze while the other tries to dislodge his willy from his throat.

Before he recovers, I scramble for his tail and slice open his neck, hacking away at muscle and bone until his head bounces into the lava pit to join his brother.

Completely bare from the waist down, except for my boots, I bend over, gripping my knees, and take several moments to catch my breath. If I don't find a way out of here, this type of encounter will become my new normal. Before long, my mind will fracture, and I'll be as insane as the woman chanting obscenities.

"I saved your dumb ass, so shut the fuck up!" I bellow and sacrifice precious minutes to conjure another pair of pants.

"You're gonna die. You're gonna die," she singsongs, shaking the bars like a deranged animal.

Before her big mouth produces more demons, I take off in a sprint around the next corner, realizing the next encounter might be my last.

Chapter 15

Jagorach

When Kleora let go, disappearing through rock and sand, I attempted to teleport to the surface, but my body refused to budge.

God damn it. Now what? Flitting from place to place above ground is as easy as breathing, but being crushed hundreds of feet below the surface negates my tracing ability? Good to know. Not that I plan to plunge deep into the earth ever again.

In my cursed but most potent form, I claw through the ground, tearing a path in the direction my mate's spirit drifted. Unfortunately, the furious nymph catapulted us so deep into the earth, it requires a tremendous amount of energy for me to move mere inches.

To distract myself from the suffocating weight working to pulverize bone and flesh, I replay the terror in Kleora's expression when she beheld my true appearance. The horrified stare did not perceive the full effect, since dirt covered most of my body.

I do not blame her. My form is repulsive to anyone but a Hell demon. Even my wife abhorred my Satan persona, demanding I never alter in front of her or our daughter. In all my centuries as king of the Demon Realm, I have only morphed into Lucifer a few times. The first couple of times were so long ago, I cannot remember why. My shifts typically occur with extreme emotion. Rage acted as the biggest catalyst.

When Dimitri slaughtered my wife and child, a frenzy of fury and grief consumed me, and I transformed. The occupants of Hell took the brunt of my despair for over a month. Lust imps relished the harrowing attention from their master. Others I ripped apart to assuage my misery.

Most recently, I shifted when Kleora lost her life during the battle with the witch Abigail. I would not have been able to grab her soul in human form, so I made a split-second decision. Regrettably, the occupants of the room took the brunt of my metamorphosis. The blast broke Liam's leg, dislocated Logan's shoulder, and shattered several of Sebastian's ribs.

But I do not regret my choice. Remorse is a wasted emotion. When I restore her life, and I will, my beautiful mate will come to realize my actions were more than justified, and her anger will be for naught.

My strength wanes. Fingers turn numb from being shredded and then healing over and over as I hack through tree roots and rocks. In between bouts of digging, I close my eyes and rest, replenishing my strength enough to start the process again. After what seems an eternity, I sense the surface. The oppressive weight of the earth eases. I burrow deep for added power and punch my fist through the last rough layers.

The cool air of the night caresses my neck as I ooze my massive body through the hole, expanding the opening. My wings snag at the breach, but I forge upward. With a violent shrug, I burst the tips through the last obstacle, digging the points into the ground to use as leverage, and yank myself up and over the lip, landing with a bone-jarring thud on my stomach.

"Fuck. Me. That's something you don't see every day."

Spitting dirt, I lift my aching head and peer up at a shirtless Nox. "I take it this is not Kansas anymore, Toto?"

"Idaho," he says, dropping the axe next to the pile of split wood.

What in Hades? How the inferno did I go from being buried under Alex's garage in Newport, Oregon, to who knows where Idaho? I must have teleported underground without even realizing it.

As I rise, I shed the demonic visage, spitting the last of the dirt from my mouth. Then, butt ass naked, I face the wide-eyed vampire.

"Oh, come on, Jag," he groans, pressing his fingers into his eye sockets. "Can't you conjure a pair of fucking pants?"

I bark out a laugh at his discomfort, knowing I am too depleted to even try at the moment. "Come now, young Nox. You know you have always wanted a glimpse of the Devil's prick."

"Not in any lifetime, Demon," he mumbles as he tosses his discarded sweatshirt at me without removing his hand over his eyes.

I observe the shirtless male with interest. Across his ribcage, on his right side, up over his chest and down his arm to his wrist, is Nox's family emblem. All male vampires who enter the elite ranks of the Guardians must tattoo their family crest on their bodies. The Moretti brothers chose opposite sides of their chests, shoulders, and arms.

Christoph's intricate tattoo swirls with ancient hieroglyphs depicting his lineage. Interesting. Nox's family line hails from a clan of long-forgotten but notoriously evil Vikings under the bloodline of Eric Bloodaxe, son of the first Norwegian King.

I chuckle at the Viking descendant, who is still busy covering his face as I knot the offered shirt around my waist. The fabric covers my groin, but the brisk night air strokes my bare bottom.

"You know you are going to sleep with this shirt and jack off to images of my cock, young vampire."

"I'm burning the damn thing, perv."

"Oh, come now, Nox. Secretly, you are dying to be dominated by the Devil."

"Where have you been, Jag?" Christoph ignores my taunting and I snicker. "Nicole has been frantic over your absence, and Logan is beyond pissed you've upset his mate."

I scratch a bare ass cheek and regard Christoph with a frown. "Whatever are you babbling about? I disappeared mere minutes ago."

"No, Darath. You and Kleora fell through the floor a week ago."

I blink rapidly, staring open-mouthed at the young vampire with striking mismatched irises. What the Hellfire is going on here? Did I dig in the wrong direction for days? And how could I not comprehend the passage of time? Maybe the times I rested were longer than I thought.

"I'm surprised Nicole did not have the Oracle summon me. It would have saved me days of digging."

"Maybe your sorry ass wasn't important enough for her to bother."

"Touché, Nox"

Since spewing from the earth, I take a moment to collect my scattered thoughts and peer at my surrounding. The terrain is rugged, but breathtaking. Enormous fir and cedar trees dominate the landscape, with a large river undulating a mere fifty feet to my left. Lush green undergrowth covers the area, making for a natural grassy backyard to the modest cabin on my right.

"A beautiful spot, Nox."

"Thanks," he replies with a smile. "It's been in my family for years."

"Is yours the only home?"

"No, but I own twenty acres on either side. Listen," he gestures to the log structure, "why don't you come inside, and we can contact Nicole and find out what the heck happened to you."

"Nice ass, King Darath."

The soft, feminine giggle has me whipping around to spy a blue-haired young werewolf strolling from the forest's edge. I peer at Nox over my shoulder with a lifted eyebrow. "Does Liam know you are consorting with his little sister?"

"What?" Christoph exclaims, his cheeks darkening. "Yes. I mean, no, nothing is going on between Cellica and I. She and Josh own the cabin on the next property over."

"Convenient," I sneer, making sure Nox's shirt is covering my girth. The last thing I need is an enraged werewolf king pissed because I flashed his sibling. "What became of Kleora?" I ask. "Did she return?"

"No clue," Christoph replies, his frown deepening the more Liam's little sister ogles my sculpted torso with avid interest. "Neither one of you surfaced."

What the hell? I watched her float upward. Where did she go?

"Jag," Nox barks. "Seriously, dude, conjure pants."

"Never took you for a prude, Vampire," Cellica smirks. Her hip juts out with her fingers splayed out over the denim covering her slight curves. "I'm more than fine if you want to drop the shirt, Demon."

Even as a low grumbling emanates from Christoph's chest, I raise an eyebrow at her saucy attitude.

"Go home, little girl." Nox's mismatched glare shoots daggers at the werewolf, and her grin vanishes. "Nobody wants you here."

Wow. Harsh. And deliciously revealing.

"One day, you will regret those words, fanger." Her tone is livid, but I perceive the hurt below the surface. This budding wolf, who has not yet transitioned into immortality, holds feelings for Christoph.

Before I can investigate further, an orange glow catches my eye mere seconds before a flaming bolt sinks deep into my shoulder. I roar, pain mingling with fury, my irises heating with retribution, until I spy Kleora at the tree line.

Wicked flames engulf her body, but do not seem to burn away the leather outfit. Her crazed look consumes her expression as she nocks another arrow, taking aim—At me.

"What the fuck?" Nox whispers in stunned disbelief, and I second the sentiment.

Based on the licking fires dancing over her body, the demented stone-cold regard, and the weapon aimed at my heart, pissed doesn't begin to cover the dead land nymph's emotions.

"Kleora," I attempt to reason while yanking the smoldering projectile from my shoulder. This feels all too familiar.

Nox snaps out of his shock and traces in front of Cellica, still standing frozen behind me. When the enraged priestess lets loose another missile, I trace to the side to avoid the hit. Sadly, the vampire did not, and the blazing arrow plunged into Nox's chest.

"Chris!" Cellica screams as the force of the blow knocks him off his feet and straight into the petite werewolf.

Before I can assist, she cradles him in her lap and yanks the shaft from his sternum. Heedless of the pain, she stamps out the fire spreading over his torso with her bare hands. "Nox. Are you alright?"

Lids flutter open. A duel-covered glow pins the young wolf holding him against her chest before shifting to Kleora. His focus brightens like a Christmas tree, and large fangs drop low in a vicious snarl.

Relieved he will recover; I turn my attention to the incensed nymph. How can she ignite into flames, and what, pray tell, pissed the wraith off now? Besides the whole 'I stole her soul and trapped it in Hell' thing. I open my mouth to question her further when she charges our trio—death in her blistering gaze.

Still in apparent agony from the hellfire, unable to trace, Nox rolls Cell beneath him, protecting her with his body. Before Kleora reaches the young couple, I trace to intercept, tackling her to the ground.

The sizzling boil of the flames is familiar, comforting in an odd way as I rip the bow from her stiff fingers and pin her to the grass with the weight of my body. "Stop this, Kleora!" I roar, not recognizing the woman beneath me. The maddened expression sends alarm spiraling through my gut.

My mate throws her head back. The agonized scream emanating from the depths nearly ruptures my eardrums. Small fists pummel my chest as she thrashes from side to side. My black heart fractures at her torment.

"Baby…" I mean to soothe her distress, but a buzzing fills my skull. The stark stench of sulfur permeates the woods. Pine needles and bits of bark from Nox's woodpile swirl in the air, and demonic power blankets our quartet.

I leap to my feet, conjure my battle armor to cover my frame, and yank my sobbing land nymph to stand behind me.

"What in God's name is going on, Darath?" Nox shouts above the buzzing, getting louder by the second. He's back on his feet, his jaw clenched tight against the pain of the scorch marks across his chest not healing. He keeps the little werewolf tucked against his spine, not daring to come closer.

"Get out of here, Nox," I command, still in disbelief at what is happening.

"Screw you," Christoph scowls. "I'm not leaving you here alone."

"I'm goddamn Satan, you idiot. Fully immortal, remember?" I turn my scrutiny from the dark swirling mass developing a mere twenty feet from me and pin my bright red irises on the vampire.

Before I get the chance to exert control over his mind and compel him to trace away, Cellica's slight frame convulses uncontrollably. Christoph spins to capture her shuddering body before she drops to the ground.

"Cel? What's wrong, baby girl?"

"Get Cellica inside the cabin, Nox," I command, confused by her sudden seizuring. "I will return as soon as I can." Fear pervades Nox's expression as he holds the twitching werewolf to his chest. "Keep her away from Nicole. Just in case. Do you understand?"

The vampire's eyes widen before he nods and disappears with his damaged package in tow.

Chapter 16

Jagorach

I eye the ever-expanding blackness while concentrating on my mate, who is now tucked behind me. The fires of purgatory still engulf her frame. I utter an ancient spell, dissipating the flames as if doused with water. Kleora's chest heaves with her panting breaths, causing delicious friction against my back.

"I knew you were hot for me, but this is ridiculous, peach."

"I hate you," she grates out between clenched teeth, her ire not diminishing in the slightest with my humor.

"We can discuss all the reasons you loathe me later. Right now, we have more pressing matters," I say, pointing to the dark tunnel before me.

Kleora clutches my bicep as she peers around my arm. "What is that?" she whispers.

"That, my love, is a portal."

"To where?"

"Not to where, from where," I answer grimly. "And it appears your presence on the surface has triggered it."

"Oh, God." Horror reveals itself in the worry lines on her forehead and the death grip on my arm. "Please tell me you can close it, Darath."

Even as deep in shit as we are, I cannot help the warmth spreading through my chest every time this beautiful creature says my name. Her touch kindles a longing I thought had been long gone. The melody of her voice soothes the monster inside and sends hope spiraling through my veins.

First things first. "How did you get to the surface, love?"

Silence greets my question, and dread ignites in my gut. She did not escape my chambers without help. My biggest concern is who deceived my warrior, and what did she offer in return?

"Answer me, Kleora." I twist to confront the more significant threat to my existence. If we mated, the petite beauty before me could bring the Devil to his knees, as my enemies well know.

When male demons bond fully, a powerful compulsion consumes them anytime their female demands something of them. The bond coerces them to fulfill their deepest wishes. It is why most high-ranking demons refuse to take a mate. Such power wielded over their heads is a link most avoid at all costs, even if it means the sacrifice of their happiness.

If Kleora and I mated—and that is a massive sized if at the moment—the elder imps could compel her to order me to do whatever they wished. I would have no choice but to obey. As much as I would love nothing more than to claim this exquisite creature, to bond her life force to my own, it can never be…

"Tell me, Kleora, or so help me, I will take you over my knee."

"You left me to burn in the fiery abyss for over a week, you vile creature. So don't you dare threaten me with a spanking," she snarls, shoving away from me.

I stumble back a step, pain heating my chest as if she plunged a dagger through my heart. "What are you going on about, woman? You were perfectly safe in my chambers."

"I couldn't get back in!" she shouts and dismay fills my chest at the tears glistening.

What in Purgatory?!

I ignore the expanding circle behind me, not afraid of anything that might leap through the darkness. My beautiful mate, on the other hand….

I grab her shoulders and haul her against my chest, needing to have her close. "You endured Hell for a week?" I question. No wonder she seems crazed. It astounds me she is even lucid.

"Yes, you sick, sadistic, demonic bastard. Don't act surprised. It was on your order." She tries to wriggle free, but all she accomplishes is rubbing that enticing body against mine.

Now is not the time, Darath.

"Kleora," I soothe. "You must know I would do nothing to hurt you."

Her escape attempts lessen. She eyes me with a new wariness I cannot tolerate. "Then, why? I've never suffered such torment."

Her words pierce my heart, and I crush her to my chest again. Her broken sob almost buckles my knees as I lay my cheek on top her head. Her fragrance reassures the beast she is well and safe in my arms. This female is fierce, resilient, and lethal. My domain brought her to her knees. Caused the tears fracturing my demented soul and her fingers to clutch my leathers in desperation.

"I thought you washed your hands of me and threw me to the demons, as if I was their newest toy."

"Listen to me." I kiss the top of her head before lifting her chin, needing her to witness the sincerity in my gaze. "I do not know how you escaped Hell, let alone my chamber. Or even how you have contained the hellfire on your body, but if the door refused to open for you, I vow it was not my doing." I brush a lock of hair from her cheek, relishing the sensation of my woman against me even as my inner demon paces with restless alarm in my skull. "Did anyone... touch you?"

Her muscles stiffen. "Oh, they tried," she hisses with feral purpose, and I almost feel sorry for the morons who faced off with my mate. "You're a few demons short."

"Good girl," I say, tucking a strand of hair behind her adorable, pointed ear.

It mollifies the beast Kleora eliminated those who dared to harm what belongs to me. Although I would have enjoyed a longer punishment session involving specific body parts and the lava pits.

"I would never intentionally hurt you, éros mou." My tenor deepens as my passion for this incredible creature grows, causing me to revert to ancient Greek momentarily.

Her breath hiccups. "How can you rule such a place?" A lone tear leaks from the corner of her eye, and my chest caves. "Your subjects torture souls in hideous ways for all of eternity."

I grind my teeth at the scorn and horror in her expression. "I am Satan." I shrug. "We all have our destinies to survive."

Her eyes soften. "No, Darath. You chose this path the second you defied your father."

"God wrote my course long before he created me, needing me to be here to tempt his precious creations." My tone is harsh, but my touch is gentle as I swipe my finger under her eye and dry the moisture leaking from their lush emerald depths. "Free will, love. Humans and immortals decide their own fate—love God and follow his laws or forsake him and earn a place in Hell with me."

"You stole the choice from me. What about my free will, King Darath?"

Fuck.

How do I explain my obsession with her? That I could not imagine an existence without her by my side. My selfishness seized an eternity in Heaven from her grasp. I do not blame Kleora for her loathing. And a part of me understands she can never forgive what I have done, but I do not give two shits right now. She is here with me to touch and hold, talk and fight, cherish and love. If I had it to do all over again, I would make the same choice, for I discovered I cannot live deprived of this graceful beauty in my life.

I open my mouth to lay my soul bare when something sharp and heavy plows into my back, knocking us both to the ground.

Chapter 17

Kleora

Jag's warmth burns hotter than the hellfire that ignited my flesh a moment ago. Instead of shying away from it and him, I seek his warmth.

The flames charred my skin during my week in purgatory, but inside lay an arctic wasteland, believing whole-heartedly he'd abandoned me. I'd watched in horror and agony as the inferno flaked off the outer layer of my skin repeatedly. It drifted through the air to mingle with the embers perpetually coating the atmosphere. Still, within, my emotions froze with despair and an ever-growing rage.

The second I popped down in the middle of Hades and not safe and sound inside Darath's suite, I panicked. The extreme heat and pain that riddled my body nearly brought me to my knees, and I launched myself into the fiery abyss, desperate to find an escape.

For several agonizing moments, my mind couldn't comprehend what was happening. I sprinted around corner after corner, but his door never appeared.

After days of fighting for my life and killing hideous demons, who lusted after my frame to either torture or hold me prisoner, I slid to the ground. Even in my despair, I avoided the bubbling vats, producing enough steam to thicken the air, and wrapped my arms around my knees. Every passing second, the terror of being stuck in this gruesome prison forever built, along with my rage. But I clenched my fists, pushed deep, and worked to forge an alternative plan.

I couldn't summon Darath to come to my rescue. He'd question how I got out of his chamber to begin with. The last thing I desired was to witness King Darath's fury when he discovered my duplicity with his lieutenant.

After an eternity, or at least it felt that way, Berkonnan appeared in all his demonic glory. "Did you find the sword tip?" he asked, not caring about the agony which suffused every inch of my body.

"Gee, Berk, I'm fine. How are you?" I whined and received a lifted, bony eyebrow in response. Stupid demons. "No. There wasn't enough time."

I'd floated, or traced, or whatever it is spirits do, to the coordinates in Iraq and actually found the location of the Tree of Life. Or the place it once resided, that is. In the Bible, the Garden of Eden had a physical location, not purely a mythical one. The four rivers: Euphrates, Tigris, Pison, and Gihon, were the birthplace of humankind. The Tigris and Euphrates are two well-known rivers that still flow through Iraq today and dump into the Persian Gulf.

I'd always pictured Iraq as a dry wasteland with parched, arid conditions, sustaining no plants other than the occasional hearty shrub. But where the Garden of Eden once lived at the headway of these tributaries was quite beautiful. Lush foliage thrived along the banks, but the terrain was still rugged and waterless, farther out.

"Your directions were off," I lied, staring into his crazed scrutiny to solidify my deceit. "I require more time to scout the area."

"Hmm. No doubt," he murmured, reaching down and gripping my biceps to haul me up and shove me against the scalding rock wall. "Why are you outside of the Master's chambers?" He asked with what I can only assume was a frown. Hard to tell with all the bony protrusions on his face. "You do realize every demon in this place is chomping at the bit to get control of you?"

"No shit." I lifted my chin, able to maintain a whimper as searing pain lanced through my joints. "I couldn't find it."

"Is that so?" Surprise flashed in the flaming depths, but he shrugged the massive jagged red shoulders. "The only one who could keep you out is Lucifer himself. But how fortuitous." His serrated grin sent terror spiraling down my spine.

"Get your meat cleavers off me, Berk," I command bravely, facing off with my worst nightmare. "If Lucifer—goddess, saying his name made me cringe—finds out you've touched me, he will fry your disgusting skin from your body inch by revolting inch." Not sure if that was true or not, but like the old saying goes—it's not what you know, but who you know. And in this case, it was the Devil I knew.

Berk's frame jerked at the notion, no doubt contemplating if raping me would be worth the consequences. "A small sample might be worth the delicious suffering Master inflicts," he muttered, and I braced myself for the fight of my life. The other demons I fought had nothing on Berkonnan.

I scrutinized his face for a smooth spot to punch that wouldn't fracture my hand, but instead of attacking me, Berk leaned in and sniffed my neck. A shudder ran through his physique, and a low rumble vibrated his chest.

"I understand why the Master is so infatuated with you—You smell scrumptious. I've never enjoyed females, but I crave a taste of you."

"I'm not tasty. At all. Trust me," I stammered. My stare darts around for any weapon I could use against this dangerous fiend. "Go find a male demon to slacken your sick desires."

I couldn't help it. The topic of conversation had me glancing down between us. Mother Earth. His phallus had sharp boney protrusions down the top, similar to the others', only more pronounced.

"Allow me to aid you, Priestess." I swallowed with relief when he traced us to the steel door I'd been searching for all week. Before he could attempt to open the door, the air shifted, becoming thick with an undulating gray smoke.

"Mother fucker," Berk muttered, shoving me back with such force my head slammed into the bleeding rock wall.

For a few seconds, blackness danced at the edges of my vision, and confusion clouded my mind. Did Berk turn against me after promising to help? I focused on the red jackass, but his back was to me. Clutched in each fist were large deadly looking swords, and his body was stiff in readiness.

That's when movement caught my eye, and a deafening roar filled the vast chamber, pursued by my piercing scream. What I could only describe as a giant smoke monster hovered twenty feet above us. The eye sockets glowed a fiery orange, as did the gaping jaw filled with huge, jagged teeth. Arms, the length of a high-rise building with wicked black claws, reached for me huddled on the ground.

I scrambled backward, my heart in my throat, my life flashed before my eyes. This was it. The hideous creature was about to tear me limb from limb.

A flash of silver blinded me for several seconds. One of Berk's swords slashed through the smokey appendage. The creature bellowed with rage as his arm separated before falling three feet from me with a loud thud, jarring me from my petrified state.

"A-rul shach kigon!" Berk bellowed before he charged the enormous... I didn't even know what to call it.

"Berk!" I leaped to my feet, unsure if my best course of action was to fight or flee, when Berkonnan soared through the air straight for the smoke creature's head. I stood frozen in place as the giant demon opened its mouth wide and swallowed my protector whole.

Good, God!

The creature took a ground-shaking step in my direction, his other arm outstretched, and my heart nearly sprang from my chest. I spun to take off around the corner, but a crushing force seized me around my middle, halting me in my tracks. Pressure crushed my ribs as it lifted me into the air.

I fought the hold, but it was useless, so I stared death in the face. The blazing, lethal mouth which swallowed Berk whole was about to do the same to me. The smoke demon halted abruptly and the stricture around my middle clamped with such force, I cried out as sharp pain radiated through my chest as more ribs fractured.

Through a searing haze of pain, I noticed its eye sockets expand, in what I can only assume was a look of surprise, before it careened sideways. I glanced down at the rough, unforgiving ground fifteen feet below, dotted with smoldering pits of death, rushing toward me with breathtaking speed and braced for impact.

The demon's cloud hand cushioned my fall, and I rolled out of his palm, clutching my ribs. I took several steps back and propped a hand against the scalding wall, taking in quick, shallow breaths.

What in damnation happened? Why did the smoke demon go down? I glanced around, expecting to be surrounded by a horde of monsters, but it was only the gigantic creature and myself.

I never imagined such beasts existed. One thing was certain—it wanted me, and Berk died trying to protect me. Oh, God. Now that Berk laid dead in the beast's belly, how on God's green earth was I supposed to get back inside Darath's chambers by myself?

I eased around the severed arm, still clutching my shattered ribs when movement caught my eye. The area I assumed was the creature's stomach expanded, and my eyes darted to its face.

Oh, Lord. Please be dead.

When an enormous sword ripped through its abdomen, opening it from stern to stem—from the inside—I stumbled backward. Relief replaced my confusion when the giant red demon, covered in black goo, stepped out. I nearly swooned.

What in the....

Berk wiped the inky grossness from his face. "Are you hurt?" he asked as the wicked swords disappeared into thin air.

"N... No," I stuttered, gazing at him with wide-eyed disbelief. So... he killed that creature from the inside out. I'm definitely in Hell. "You?" I asked, with a slight tremor in my voice.

"Never better." His massive shoulders shrugged, and a jagged grin split his lips.

Without another word, he strode to Darath's chamber door. Like this incident was merely an annoying interruption. In a shocked daze, I followed. Pretty sure this incident fractured my mind as thoroughly as my ribs. If I didn't get out of Hell soon, I'd go insane.

Chapter 18
Kleora

After several failed attempts to open the damn door, I nearly broke down in tears. How I kept the river at bay, I had no clue. Admitting defeat, Berk sent me to the surface once more, stating the Master must have locked me out. Here I am, days later, and instead of killing Darath for making me suffer, even though my body healed the second I hit the topside, I stupidly believed the words coming out of that oh so kissable mouth. The inferno and extreme torture scrambled my mind... It's the only explanation.

When Berk slammed into his king, Darath wrapped his arms around my body, twisting at the last minute so his enormous frame took the brunt of the unforgiving ground. Breath leaves my lungs in a whoosh as his hard chest knocks into mine. When his hold goes lax, I roll to a safe distance, becoming incorporeal the second I'm no longer touching the King of Hell.

I watch Berk falter as he comes face to face with his Master. His fearful gaze darts in my direction. It's evident he wasn't expecting to find Darath when he crossed over. In my crazed state, I'm fascinated by the fact Berk showed no fear in the face of the enormous smoke creature but standing toe to toe with King Darath… Lucifer… he's shaking in his boots.

My breath stalls as I observe my mate rise to his feet without the aid of his arms. The iridescent rubies brighten with rage, and his image blurs at the edges like his original form demands the right to surface.

The dark tresses swirl around his head from the gusting wind generated by the portal, and his fists clench and unclench as he works to control his fury. Darath's wrath is horrifying and intoxicating at the same time. My heart beats faster. My breath turns harsh, as if I've run a marathon, and dampness floods my panties.

Why am I not as terrified as Berk appears to be right now? Instead, I'm turned on. So much so, I want to launch myself at my mate and let the Devil have his wicked way with me. Not caring if the red-skinned demon observes. Or maybe because he does.

For Pete's sake, Kleora. Get a grip.

Darath's nostrils flare. His hypnotic irises find mine for a brief second, as if he smells my arousal. Crap. I should float the heck out of Dodge, but my translucent feet seem glued to the pine needles beneath them.

"Master," Berk whines and drops to one knee. "I did not intend to strike you."

"You defied my law, Berkonnan, by opening a gateway," Darath states with a calmness that's scarier than if he'd shouted.

"Nay, my lord," the grotesque demon pleads. "It was not I."

"Yet here you are." Darath takes a menacing step toward Berk.

"I attempted to remedy the problem when the force of the void sucked me in, sire."

"Is that so?"

It's clear Darath doesn't believe his lieutenant. Yeah, I wouldn't trust this idiot for a second either. Although, isn't that what I did in order to get to the surface? Despite his threats, Berk never touched me. He was a good boy and kept his hands to himself, even defending me against the other vile creature who wailed for a bite of me.

"Then enlighten me on who opened the portal before I take your head." Vicious black claws extend from Darath's fingertips, and I foresee Berk's horned skull bouncing into the dark forest.

Wait a tick. As much as I'd love to see the end of this scheming demon, if he dies, there goes my get out of Hell free card. Besides, he did save my ass. Darath said to trust him, that he was working on a means to revive me, but I've never been the type to sit around and expect a male to rescue me.

I depend on no one but myself and Sabrina.

With a trembling breath, I step in front of Berkonnan to face the towering being hellbent on keeping me for himself. As much as I loathe Berk and trust him about as far as I can toss him, I require his aid.

Are his plans for my benefit? No. Do they include overthrowing my mate and becoming the ruler of this dreadful place? Yes. But I'll worry about that later. One thing at a time.

"I opened the gateway," I state with a bravado not matching the anxiety trembling within me. My chin lifted. Berk's slight gasp at my blatant lie on his behalf fortifies my resolve.

Darath's massive body, encased in leather, goes motionless. His expression hardens. The blood-red irises pin me in place. "You conspired with my lieutenant behind my back?"

Oh Lordy.

"It's not like that." I stammer, petrified of his calm rage.

"No? Then please clarify, Kleora." He crowds my space, making it difficult to breathe.

The big demon at my back gains his feet. And between the inferno of Darath and Berk, it's like being trapped in a raging forest fire.

I'm already a spirit. What more could he do to me?

Images of damnation flit through my mind, but I shove them aside and shrug my shoulders as if I'm not quivering at his wrath. I survived a week in Hell and kind of figured out the numerous labyrinths and their traps. If forced, I could survive on my own. But damn it, I don't want to.

"I found an alternate means to escape Hell."

Darath raises his hand, and I flinch. His scowl widens at my response, but instead of striking me, he merely snaps his fingers. Berkonnan and the dark swirling portal disappear, leaving the two of us all alone. The quiet is deafening after the loud whirling gateway to Hell.

"I realize you do not trust me. Yet. But I will not tolerate you plotting with my demons. Especially the power-hungry Berk who would stab his own mother to get his hands on my throne. He would not hesitate to throw you into the lava pits if it served his purpose."

Strong fingers clasp my arm, and I'm instantly corporeal. His warmth sears my flesh, and electricity shoots down my spine. The next instant, we are back in his chambers, and I grind my teeth in frustration.

"It appears you require a firm hand." What the Mother Earth is he talking about? "Something to remind you there are consequences to betraying me."

"I didn't betray you, Jagorach," I assert, even as I struggle in his unrelenting grasp. On the surface, it may look like I did, but I had no intention of keeping my end of the bargain.

"Collaborating behind my back constitutes a betrayal, Kleora."

A hard edge enters Darath's tone, and my insides clench. Why do I find his commanding tenor so arousing? And the way he utters my name with panty-wetting authority sets me on fire.

When he strolls over to the high bed and points at the mattress, I gape at him in disbelief. Is he kidding me? Does he honestly think I'm going to submit to a spanking by lying prone across the bed like a meek little girl? Not for all the wealth in the world.

"You can't be serious?"

"When it comes to discipline, I never kid, Kleora. Remove your pants and lie across the comforter on your stomach." Though his face reads as serious, his eyes dance in amusement.

I snort. "In your dreams, Demon." My arms crisscross over my chest, challenging his authority. Probably not a brilliant move.

In all honesty, I conspired behind his back to help his lieutenant toss him from his throne. And maybe that does constitute a repercussion, but I'll be damned if I'm going to humiliate myself and eagerly submit to a spanking.

Darath's head tilts as he examines me. "Deep down, you want this," he has the audacity to state. "To feel the burn of my palm across your backside. I can smell the sweet, sweet aroma of your arousal from here." He holds out his hand with unnerving patience.

For some odd reason I can't explain, I take a step toward him, then halt in horror. What the ever-living hellfire am I doing? I can't deny my body is flush with desire, and my adventurous spirit is eager to experience what the demon demands. But the notion of walking to that bed, lowering my pants to my ankles, and lying prone, has my inner warrior balking in mortification.

"If you think I will willingly submit to such treatment, you don't know me very well, Darath."

"Kleora." God, I love when he says my name in that Alpha tone. "We can do this the hard way or the harder way. It is up to you." He crosses his arms over his massive chest encased in the leather of his combat gear. "In one fashion or another, you will receive a thorough thrashing for your betrayal." I nearly quiver at his words, but I don't allow myself to show it.

"Well, Demon," I hiss and drop into a fighting stance. "I guess it's the harder way."

Chapter 18

Kleora

After several failed attempts to open the damn door, I nearly broke down in tears. How I kept the river at bay, I had no clue. Admitting defeat, Berk sent me to the surface once more, stating the Master must have locked me out. Here I am, days later, and instead of killing Darath for making me suffer, even though my body healed the second I hit the topside, I stupidly believed the words coming out of that oh so kissable mouth. The inferno and extreme torture scrambled my mind... It's the only explanation.

When Berk slammed into his king, Darath wrapped his arms around my body, twisting at the last minute so his enormous frame took the brunt of the unforgiving ground. Breath leaves my lungs in a whoosh as his hard chest knocks into mine. When his hold goes lax, I roll to a safe distance, becoming incorporeal the second I'm no longer touching the King of Hell.

I watch Berk falter as he comes face to face with his Master. His fearful gaze darts in my direction. It's evident he wasn't expecting to find Darath when he crossed over. In my crazed state, I'm fascinated by the fact Berk showed no fear in the face of the enormous smoke creature but standing toe to toe with King Darath... Lucifer... he's shaking in his boots.

My breath stalls as I observe my mate rise to his feet without the aid of his arms. The iridescent rubies brighten with rage, and his image blurs at the edges like his original form demands the right to surface.

The dark tresses swirl around his head from the gusting wind generated by the portal, and his fists clench and unclench as he works to control his fury. Darath's wrath is horrifying and intoxicating at the same time. My heart beats faster. My breath turns harsh, as if I've run a marathon, and dampness floods my panties.

Why am I not as terrified as Berk appears to be right now? Instead, I'm turned on. So much so, I want to launch myself at my mate and let the Devil have his wicked way with me. Not caring if the red-skinned demon observes. Or maybe because he does.

For Pete's sake, Kleora. Get a grip.

Darath's nostrils flare. His hypnotic irises find mine for a brief second as if he smells my arousal. Crap. I should float the heck out of Dodge, but my translucent feet seem glued to the pine needles beneath them.

"Master," Berk whines and drops to one knee. "I did not intend to strike you."

"You defied my law, Berkonnan, by opening a gateway," Darath states with a calmness that's scarier than if he'd shouted.

"Nay, my lord," the grotesque demon pleads. "It was not I."

"Yet here you are." Darath takes a menacing step toward Berk.

"I attempted to remedy the problem when the force of the void sucked me in, sire."

"Is that so?"

It's clear Darath doesn't believe his lieutenant. Yeah, I wouldn't trust this idiot for a second either. Although, isn't that what I did in order to get to the surface? Despite his threats, Berk never touched me. He was a good boy and kept his hands to himself, even defending me against the other vile creature who wailed for a bite of me.

"Then enlighten me on who opened the portal before I take your head." Vicious black claws extend from Darath's fingertips, and I foresee Berk's horned skull bouncing into the dark forest.

Wait a tick. As much as I'd love to see the end of this scheming demon, if he dies, there goes my get out of Hell free card. Besides, he did save my ass. Darath said to trust him, that he was working on a means to revive me, but I've never been the type to sit around and expect a male to rescue me.

I depend on no one but myself and Sabrina.

With a trembling breath, I step in front of Berkonnan to face the towering being hellbent on keeping me for himself. As much as I loathe Berk and trust him about as far as I can toss him, I require his aid.

Are his plans for my benefit? No. Do they include overthrowing my mate and becoming the ruler of this dreadful place? Yes. But I'll worry about that later. One thing at a time.

"I opened the gateway," I state with a bravado not matching the anxiety trembling within me. My chin lifted. Berk's slight gasp at my blatant lie on his behalf fortifies my resolve.

Darath's massive body, encased in leather, goes motionless. His expression hardens. The blood-red irises pin me in place. "You conspired with my lieutenant behind my back?"

Oh Lordy.

"It's not like that." I stammer, petrified of his calm rage.

"No? Then please clarify, Kleora." He crowds my space, making it difficult to breathe.

The big demon at my back gains his feet. And between the inferno of Darath and Berk, it's like being trapped in a raging forest fire.

I'm already a spirit. What more could he do to me?

Images of damnation flit through my mind, but I shove them aside and shrug my shoulders as if I'm not quivering at his wrath. I survived a week in Hell and kind of figured out the numerous labyrinths and their traps. If forced, I could survive on my own. But damn it, I don't want to.

"I found an alternate means to escape Hell."

Darath raises his hand, and I flinch. His scowl widens at my response, but instead of striking me, he merely snaps his fingers. Berkonnan and the dark swirling portal disappear, leaving the two of us all alone. The quiet is deafening after the loud whirling gateway to Hell.

"I realize you do not trust me. Yet. But I will not tolerate you plotting with my demons. Especially the power-hungry Berk who would stab his own mother to get his hands on my throne. He would not hesitate to throw you into the lava pits if it served his purpose."

Strong fingers clasp my arm, and I'm instantly corporeal. His warmth sears my flesh, and electricity shoots down my spine. The next instant, we are back in his chambers, and I grind my teeth in frustration.

"It appears you require a firm hand." What the Mother Earth is he talking about? "Something to remind you there are consequences to betraying me."

"I didn't betray you, Jagorach," I assert, even as I struggle in his unrelenting grasp. On the surface, it may look like I did, but I had no intention of keeping my end of the bargain.

"Collaborating behind my back constitutes a betrayal, Kleora."

A hard edge enters Darath's tone, and my insides clench. Why do I find his commanding tenor so arousing? And the way he utters my name with panty-wetting authority sets me on fire.

When he strolls over to the high bed and points at the mattress, I gape at him in disbelief. Is he kidding me? Does he honestly think I'm going to submit to a spanking by lying prone across the bed like a meek little girl? Not for all the wealth in the world.

"You can't be serious?"

"When it comes to discipline, I never kid, Kleora. Remove your pants and lie across the comforter on your stomach." Though his face reads as serious, his eyes dance in amusement.

I snort. "In your dreams, Demon." My arms crisscross over my chest, challenging his authority. Probably not a brilliant move.

In all honesty, I conspired behind his back to help his lieutenant toss him from his throne. And maybe that does constitute a repercussion, but I'll be damned if I'm going to humiliate myself and eagerly submit to a spanking.

Darath's head tilts as he examines me. "Deep down, you want this," he has the audacity to state. "To feel the burn of my palm across your backside. I can smell the sweet, sweet aroma of your arousal from here." He holds out his hand with unnerving patience.

For some odd reason I can't explain, I take a step toward him, then halt in horror. What the ever-living hellfire am I doing? I can't deny my body is flush with desire, and my adventurous spirit is eager to experience what the demon demands. But the notion of walking to that bed, lowering my pants to my ankles, and lying prone, has my inner warrior balking in mortification.

"If you think I will willingly submit to such treatment, you don't know me very well, Darath."

"Kleora." God, I love when he says my name in that Alpha tone. "We can do this the hard way or the harder way. It is up to you." He crosses his arms over his massive chest encased in the leather of his combat gear. "In one fashion or another, you will receive a thorough thrashing for your betrayal." I nearly quiver at his words, but I don't allow myself to show it.

"Well, Demon," I hiss and drop into a fighting stance. "I guess it's the harder way."

Chapter 19

Kleora

Red fire ignites in Darath's irises at my challenge, and a smidgen of fear slithers up my translucent spine. Maybe I bit off more than I can handle, provoking the demon king.

In all honesty, this side of Darath makes my insides burn. A tiny, and I mean microscopic, part of me glows with curiosity to explore some downright dirty kinks with the Devil himself. I've always possessed an adventurous spirit regarding sex. And the few times I'd ventured toward the darker side, well, let's just state it was anything but climactic.

The rare partners I offered that kind of control over me were trustworthy, and a spark existed between us, but it wasn't anywhere near the explosive fireworks I experience when Darath touches me. Even dead—sort of—he sets me ablaze with a mere look. Crimson devours me in a manner I've never enjoyed with anyone else.

But the jerk-off kidnapped my soul and imprisoned me in Hell. There is no way I'm going to make things easy for him, no matter how much my mind screams for me to submit and feel the burn of his discipline.

"Why do you fight what you desire, peach?" Darath purrs, never moving an inch in my direction. I'm no fool. He may appear causal, but the towering frame and thick muscles are stiff in readiness. The second I pounce or try to escape—the Devil will snatch control and pin me in a heartbeat.

Why does that sound so appealing?

"I think you're projecting your own desires, Darath," I smirk. "If anyone deserves a thorough thrashing, it's you, Demon."

He blinks several times, noticeably surprised by my comment. "You wish to spank me, peach?"

Hmmm. I've never fantasized about a role reversal before. But now that he uttered the words, I clench at the delicious image of Lucifer at my mercy, ass reddened from a paddle. My palm wouldn't even do his flesh justice. I'd wind up hurting myself more than him.

"Would you enjoy that?" I blurt out, the controlled barrier between my brain and mouth disintegrating.

"With you, love, I would relish anything. As the Devil, there are no boundaries between us."

Okay. Wow. Good to know.

"As delicious as this conversation is, your stall tactic is not working. Before I leave this chamber, your beautiful ass will experience the blaze of your duplicity." His grin is pure sex. "And if you are a good girl, I will ensure the reward is… earth-shattering." He unfolds his arms, pointing to the bed once more. "No place to run, Kleora."

"I wouldn't run even if I could. I'm not a coward," I state with a defiant lift of my chin, although an exit strategy would be welcome.

"I am counting on it."

Options, Kleora. Think. My gaze darts around the room. I still have a few arrows left, but Darath's already demonstrated they have no effect on him. And hand-to-hand combat with a seven-foot Devil would be a joke.

The king studies me with a smirk as my mind struggles with how to get out of this predicament. Good Lord. Short of begging—and I'm a queen, we never beg—I'm out of options. Maybe... just maybe, it's time to take my medicine. How bad could it be? He said if I behaved, he'd reward me. The humiliation of being spanked might be worth a few orgasms.

"For the record," I mutter, shuffling closer. "This is getting added to the list of reasons I hate you."

"How does the saying go? This is going to hurt me more than it will hurt you," he says, his lips twitching with amusement.

A mere foot from the powerful demon, I halt, unable to take the last steps. How will I lower my pride enough to drop my pants and bend over the damn bed? I pluck at the boning in my corset. This is beyond insane. But a yawning, dark part of my psyche grins like a Cheshire cat at this alternate side of our male. To find a man worthy of a queen sexually is more challenging than you'd expect.

Darath reaches out and snags the back of my neck, tugging me against his hard body. The second his fingers connect with skin, my soul bursts into being, and all the delicious warmth I felt earlier rages out of control.

Solid and sure lips capture mine, and I can't stop the moan from escaping or the tingles from dancing across my flesh. In all my years, no other creature has set me on fire the way King Darath can with a single glance or caress.

I grip the powerful biceps as he continues to devour me, our tongues dueling for control. In Darath's massive arms, I feel petite, cherished, and protected. Yet, at the same time, my hormones spin with the force of a tornado, craving more, demanding more.

The demon doesn't disappoint. Both palms grasp my backside and hoist me up, putting me at a more advantageous level with his seeking lips. I wrap my thighs around his waist and clutch fistfuls of his luxurious hair as I nibble and bite at his commanding mouth.

The deep rumble from his chest sets my heart aflutter, and my insides melt, wetting my panties even more. If this was my last moment as a conscious being, I would leave this plane a lucky woman.

Well, that's if my vagina wasn't clamoring for a certain demon's thick anatomy. Yeah, once that box gets checked, then I can die a happy nymph.

"Fuck, your desire smells incredible," Darath groans as he shifts to lay me on the bed.

His words bolster my courage. Maybe if I can distract him enough, he'll forget all about the spanking. Or what I did.

The second my spine contacts the mattress, he eases back enough I'm forced to release my death grip on his waist. With a flick of his wrist, the leather pants and corset disappear, leaving me in my soaked red thong, panting with desperation for his touch.

"Jag," I gasp, my back arching at the feral look devouring me.

"Hush, peach. I will give you exactly what you need."

Before I can comprehend what *exactly* means, Darath sits on the edge of the bed, drapes my stomach over his lap with my face planted in the mattress.

"What the hell?" I demand, attempting to escape his hold. But that's like trying to move a mountain, so nothing happens.

"I am a demon of my word, Kleora," he snarls, and I freeze at his tone. He isn't screwing around. "You conspired behind my back. This punishment is more than deserved."

"Don't do it, Darath," I grate out between clenched teeth, my anger and lust warring with each other. Who will win out is anyone's guess?

When his massive palm connects with my bare ass, I gasp in shock. That wasn't an erotic teasing spank, meant to heighten my desire. Oh no. That was a full-on, you're a bad girl in need of punishment, kind of smack. It stung!

"Ow!" I howl, struggling harder.

"I do not tolerate betrayal of any kind," the fiend states calmly, right before he delivers another sharp smack on my other cheek.

Tears burn my eyes at the searing pain, but I refuse to let them fall. Hades will freeze over before I cry in front of the Devil. "You bastard," I shriek. "I will kill you for this."

His answer is an additional resounding slap. Mother Earth, that hurts. I reach behind me to cover my smarting butt, but Darath grabs my wrists in one hand, pinning them at the small of my back. Another whack and I'm kicking my legs to get free, but he merely covers them with his massive leg, holding me down with ease.

Son of a…. If my people could see me now, restrained, my bare butt receiving a thorough spanking from the King of Hell, I'd never regain my reputation as a badass queen again.

Every slap reverberates through my flesh and muscle until the sharp painful stings escalate into a surprisingly delightful burn. The heat spreads across my flesh and straight to my anus and clit. My sex pulses in time with my heartbeat, wetting my opening.

Am I getting off on the pain?

No. That can't be. This hurts. Why would I enjoy it? But there's no denying the effect the spanking is having on my body. My breath is harsh with yearning. The obvious evidence of my lust soaks my pussy, and my clit throbs with the demand to detonate.

I shift my hips to settle my pelvis against his hard thigh, seeking relief from the ache building like a crescendo. If Darath touched me right now, I'd ignite. A flame to dry tinder.

"Jag," I groan low, grinding on his leg.

"If you come without permission, it will extend the spanking," the Devil states harshly. Like that's a deterrent now? Although, I am satisfied to hear the gruffness in his tone which is an indication that he's not unaffected.

Several more slaps reign supreme on my sore ass, and I don't even try to contain my need—pushing against his thick leg muscle despite his warning. Sparks flare through my clit, spreading a delicious warmth and tightening my hollow core. I bite down on the comforter to muffle my moans in hopes the demon doesn't notice my body erupt in orgasm from his spanking while gyrating on his thigh.

"Tsk tsk, little peach."

Yeah, no such luck, apparently.

Darath runs his scalding palm over my inflamed skin, and I can't help but groan at the sting.

"So responsive," he moans low, continuing to graze his fingers over his handiwork.

"Please, Jag," I pant, not even sure why I'm begging or what I'm pleading for. Do I want him to continue the spanking or put me out of my misery and fuck me senseless? It's a win-win either way.

"Do you wish for more, Kleora?"

I hesitate. Enjoying it is one thing. Admitting it out loud is another. A sharp slap is my reward for not responding, and I can't stop the grinding of my hips.

"Answer me," he commands, and his tone gets my juices flowing even more.

"Yes," I admit in a muffled murmur, keeping my heated face buried in the blanket.

I tense, waiting for the blows to continue. Instead, he lifts me to stand between his widened legs, facing him. I cringe at being at eye level with the being who disciplined me into orgasm. It's unsettling. So I focus on his full lips as they move.

"Spread your thighs," he directs, and I obey, widening my stance.

When did that happen? How did I go from defying the arrogant brute at every turn, to submissively obeying his sexual commands in the hope he will continue this mind-boggling torture?

"Place your palms on my shoulders, love. Do not move them until I instruct otherwise."

What does this demon have up his sleeve now? Eager to find out, I do as he directed and grip the bulging muscles in anticipation, trying to ignore my panting breaths. My pulse throbs in my clit, erratic and out of control. This is beyond anything I've ever experienced, and I'm hooked.

Large rough fingers spread my sodden folds, and my knees nearly buckle at the exquisite touch.

"So wet. So beautiful," he murmurs, his bright stare zeroed in on mine. "How did you escape Hell, Kleora?"

Wait. What? My lust-filled mind is having difficulty following speech. All I can concentrate on is mentally urging his fingers left or right to find the golden spot. Why is the gorgeous creature even talking? He should use those lush lips for something more in the "oh God" realm.

A sharp slap to my slit jolts through my brain like a lightning bolt, frying all rational thought in an instant. What in holy goddess was that?

"Do not move," he barks out, and I stiffen my muscles to obey.

The resounding vibration and sting spread through my sex, constricting my insides, and causing brief spasms to erupt. "Jag?"

"What are you keeping from me, Kleora?"

"N-nothing," I lie. I'd hand over my soul right now to not interrupt whatever is about to take place. Oh, wait... He already possesses my soul—the fiend.

"Hang on, peach. I am about to blow your mind."

Arrogant much?

But when the giant hand sets in with sharp slaps to my drenched center, I realize he's not wrong. Sensation after life-altering sensation spiral through my sex, spreading to my anus. With desperation, I clutch at Darath's shoulders to remain standing, even widening my stance to give him better access as my body responds to his punishment with abandon.

"That's it, Kleora," he groans, increasing his pace, answering my unspoken demand for more. "Let go, baby."

At his entreaty, I arch my neck and allow the crescendo of tremors to burst. Fire ignites across my sex. My thighs tremble, and my nails dig into Darath's flesh, desperate to remain standing and not end this fantastic ride by falling flat on my face.

When he leans forward and latches onto a stiff nipple, a fresh wave of fervor consumes me. I cry his name as mini-explosions traverse every pleasure nerve in my body.

Before I can catch my breath, I'm on my back once more, and the lips I salivated for a second ago devour my pussy like a starved man. The possessive growls and grunts as he revels in the feast of me shoots my euphoria over the precipice once more. I clutch fistfuls of his hair, shamelessly gyrating my swollen center against his face, demanding more.

"Fuck, Kleora," he groans in a low voice, shoving my thighs apart to open me further. When a sharp sting penetrates my clit, I arch off the mattress at the perfect pleasure of pain. A large palm slams down on my stomach to hold me in place as he continues to bite, suck, and lick.

"It's too much," I whimper, my head thrashing from side to side at the impassioned reactions the Devil wrings from my body.

"More, Kleora." His command is all Alpha.

I writhe to obey, needing something beyond my reach. An unknown element to shoot me over the edge once more. I sob, craving the release but unsure how to get there.

I shouldn't have worried. My wonderous male instinctively knows what my body begs for, even when I do not. Darath eases back and delivers several harsh slaps right over the bundle he was lavishing with his mouth. Light explodes behind my lids as the most overwhelming, all-consuming blast rocks my frame. The magnificent man rides the wave by inserting two thick fingers.

"Jag!" I scream as he thrusts while his lips and tongue worship my clit until the tremors ease.

My bones are liquid. If all the demons of purgatory came barging in here right now, I wouldn't have the strength to care. I've experienced nothing so profound and powerful in all my life. And I want to do it again. Not having a care in the world that my ass is on fire or that my nether regions swelled from their spanking.

I groan with renewed passion as Darath continues to lick and suckle at my sex like he can't get enough of my taste.

"Was that a first for you, peach?" he asks, nuzzling my pussy. "Pain with pleasure?"

I blink, still working to jump-start my brain. "To that extent, yes," I admit freely. Pretty sure my reactions gave me away anyway.

"Told you I would blow your mind."

I feel his lips lift against my sensitive lips, and I lean up on my elbows to look down at the erotic beast between my thighs. "Arrogance isn't becoming."

He chuckles, rising to climb up my body. "Have you learned your lesson?" he questions, nipping at my waist before kissing his way to my aching breasts.

"You know," I sigh and flop down, unable to hold myself up a second longer. "You should really rethink your form of punishment."

"Oh?" he murmurs, before latching onto a turgid nipple with gusto.

"Ahhhh," I gasp and arch at the pleasure shooting from my aching point straight to my swollen sex. I could so go another round of discipline.

"Yes. The receiver shouldn't enjoy the punishment." I grasp his head and direct him to the other breast, craving attention.

"Should the retribution be harsher?" he asks, nipping at my neck now. "I do have a reputation to uphold."

Harsher? God, yes! More scalding spanks on my butt. More of the delicious fire on my core. God. I think I'm addicted to this now. Not that I would ever voice that to him.

"Admit it, female. You relished your spanking."

You bet I did. "It was okay." My dramatic sigh of disappointment causes Darath to lift his head and eye me with suspicion.

"Five orgasms was just, okay?" he asks with disbelief

"Yeah. I think you ought to up your performance, big boy, if you wish to keep me satisfied."

The Devil laughs. "Game on, peach."

Chapter 20

Jagorach

"I have pressing matters to attend, young Halfling," I snarl into the phone. "As much as I would relish becoming your beck and call demon, I cannot drop everything when you snap your fingers."

"I love how you referenced a line from Pretty Woman, Jag, but would those more pressing matters be figuring out how to restore Kleora?" Nicole persists. "That's your priority, right?"

The subtle threat grates along my nerves. As much as I worship and adore the vampire queen, my failure on Kleora's behalf eats away at me. "She is my only priority, Nicole," I reply with a low rumble.

"Good. Then get your ass over here because I may have a lead on Troy. I'd come to you, but pregnancy and teleporting are a risk, and I've met my quota for the week. According to my overprotective mate, anyway."

"Logan is correct. You should not take unnecessary risks with your precious bundle," I express absently as I walk down the dimly lit corridor of my home. Even though it is the first week of May, the temperatures have hit the low 100s already in Tucson, and I'm enjoying the dry heat immensely.

I have yet to kick on the central air. This is my first summer living in Southern Arizona, and I wish to experience every nuance of the desert climate. We will see how I will fair come August. Hell may be preferable.

"Give me ten minutes, vampire," I impart and disconnect as Dzun rounds the corner, and by the scowl on his face, we have problems.

"Report," I bark without preamble.

"It appears a Prince has escaped."

My commander is the recorder of all souls and demons. How he keeps track, I have no desire to know. I delegated those trivial details a long time ago. "A Prince? Are you sure?"

"Yes, sire," Dzun responds, worry etched deep between his brows. And with good reason.

"Which one?"

"Asmodeus, Sire."

Shit. Seven of us were the first to fall from grace after the great battle in Heaven. Each Prince represents one of the seven deadly sins: lust, gluttony, greed, sloth, wrath, envy, and pride—the last of which I represent.

"Ah, Asmodeus. He is one hellcat in the sack. His lust rivals my own." I grin at the memory but quickly sober. "How in curses did he break through, Dzun? A Prince hasn't gone missing in over a millennium." I made sure of that by locking the gates down tight to the most destructive and powerful—the six Princes of Hell.

"Through the portal Priestess Kleora and Berk opened, my lord."

Son of a bitch. "Do we have his location?"

"Not yet, but I'm working on it," he responds with a bow.

"Find him, Dzun. That demon could wreak serious damage in a short amount of time. We are talking priest and choirboy level of scandal."

"Yes, sire."

"In the meantime, I am off to the Vampire Stronghold for a meeting. Keep me posted."

"When I catch him, how would you like me to proceed?"

He's asking for permission to punish/torture the demon for daring to break my laws. "We will burn that bridge when we get to it, Dzun. Find him first. He may have possessed an innocent soul already."

"According to my intel, Troy went underground in Arkansas. Your territory, Darath," Logan claims, pointing to Little Rock on the map laid out across the conference table. It surprised me that Nicole assembled the entire task force for this meeting.

"What is the plan here, Nicole?" I question with a raised eyebrow. "Is this a recon mission, or are we converging on the witch en masse?"

"Since it's your territory, Jag, I'm hoping you and Viessa can do a little covert scouting to determine if the bitch Abigail is still alive and with him."

"And if she is?"

"Then we converge and get some fucking answers."

"As much as I enjoy your gun-toting, bullets flying attitude, in this case, caution might be prudent. Troy is not a witch to be trifled with, and if he sniffs an ambush...." I let the sentence trail off, knowing the others will fill in the blanks on their own.

"How is Kleora?" Nicki counters, eyes narrowed, her meaning plain as day. No doubt young Nox spilled the beans, but it is also a reminder of Sabrina's fast approaching timetable. If I do not hand over Kleora's body in the next few days, the Storm Walkers will declare war and attempt to take her by force, ending in a bloodbath on both sides. I lost a precious week clawing my way out from under the earth.

"In high spirits," I express as fire leaps through my veins at the remembered disciplinary action I doled out for her betrayal. The little land nymph not only enjoyed her spanking, she begged for more.

I shift in my seat, willing my erection to calm down.

Liam Scott, the werewolf king and one of my closest friends, glances at my crotch with a knowing grin. "No doubt you have her hog-tied to your bed, showing her the wonders of your dick," he laughs, and I cannot help but chuckle.

The rest of the males around the table grin, but Nicole's irises spark with gray fire. "You find this funny, bastards?"

I sober in the face of her anger. "No, my dear. Not at all. The sooner we can restore Kleora, the better for everyone."

"Sorry, Nic," King Scott interjects. "Just blowing off steam."

Nox comes barreling into the room, his mismatched eyes dilated in a frenzy, and Nicki leaps to her feet. Well, leap might be pushing it, considering her belly is filled with a child.

"We have a problem," Christoph announces with a harried glance at Liam.

"Now what?" Nicole demands with a frown, her palm landing on her stomach in a protective gesture.

"There is something seriously wrong with…" he pauses, his gaze darting to the werewolf.

"Spit it out, boy," I prod. I'd love nothing more than to delve into the young vampire's mind and flesh out the issue myself, but that would be rude.

After a fortifying breath, Nox turns to King Scott, his body braced. "Your sister is behaving… erratically."

"What does that mean? And how the hell would you know?" Liam demands in a low, dangerous rumble, the whisky irises laser-focused on the Guardian.

"She's..." Christoph runs his hand through his hair, spiking the locks into even more disarray. "She tried to seduce me," he blurts out. "I barely escaped."

Before anyone can react, Liam is out of his chair, pinning Nox to the wall with an elbow at his throat. "Did you touch my sister?" The beast is heavy in his tone, the irises sparking the blue of his wolf.

Christoph's regard brightens in response to the wolf's aggression. "What? I'm good enough to drink and play poker with, but I'm not good enough for your sister?" Nox's fangs descend, but he's smart enough to make no move against the king. "Why? Because I'm a vampire? Or is it because I'm a lowly Guardian?"

"Fuck you, Nox. This is my baby sister we're talking about."

"Boys!" Nicki barks. "Stow your shit."

Liam's chest rumbles with warning before releasing Christoph. "Where is she?"

"At my cabin." King Scott's growl permeates the room. "Nothing happened, bro, but I had to restrain her. She's not herself."

This piques my interest. "How so, Nox?"

"She's... she's aggressive," he answers, plainly uncomfortable with this discussion.

"Aggressive how?" I press, enjoying the soap opera drama taking place.

Nox shoots me a dirty glance, knowing I'm stirring the pot. I shrug. What? I cannot help it—I am the Devil. I enjoy watching him squirm his way out of this one. My money is on Liam.

"You're not helping, Darath," Kurtis mutters, hiding a smile behind his hand. Proof he is relishing this little scene as well.

"Sexually, okay," Christoph blurts out, swallowing at the flickering of Liam's irises. "I don't know what happened, but not long after the incident with Priestess Tanagra at my place, it was like a switch flipped." Nox runs his fingers through his hair again. "She turned into this sexy, wanton hellion coming at me with both barrels. I had no choice but to tie her up."

"Jesus," Liam mutters, turning his back on the vampire. No doubt afraid he will rip his throat out if he stares at him a second longer.

This is getting juicy. "Do you expect the first change is upon the little wolf, and you happened to be the only male around? Or do you surmise she has the hots for you specifically, Nox?"

"Dammit, Darath. Knock it off," Nicki chokes, spewing her coffee.

"What?" I utter with all the innocence the Devil can muster. "It's a legitimate question, the bitch could be in heat."

Christoph's fist slams into my jaw and I stagger back a step in surprise. Shit, the boy has a wicked right hook.

"Watch it, Darath," he snarls, irises bright and fangs low.

Well, well, well. The young Guardian has a protective instinct for Liam's little sibling. This gets better and better.

"Stop poking the hornet's nest, Jagorach," the petite valkyrie Alex, admonishes, much to her mate Sebastian's delight. Alex and I share a special bond. I have seen the inner workings of her mind up close and personal and tasted her passion. Albeit it was in a vision, but still.

"You have a thing for my sister, Christoph?" Liam asks with a quiet calm. His early wrath gone. Although, I suspect it simmers close to the surface, ready to burst forth at the slightest provocation.

"What?" Nox turns a stunned gaze on the werewolf king. "No. Of course not. I... he shouldn't talk about her like that. That's all."

"Uh-huh," Liam grunts, his mouth set in a hard line.

"Look, whatever is going on with her isn't normal. It's like she's possessed."

This snags my attention, and an image of her twitching body at the portal fills my mind. "Explain," I command, all humor gone.

"Don't get me wrong, Cellica flirts, but it's in an immature way. This is out of the ordinary. Forceful. Over the top sexual. She's almost a different person."

"Care to share your thoughts, Darath?" Nicole regards me with a direct stare.

Damn empath.

I run my tongue along my top teeth, prolonging the moment. "Before I arrived, Dzun informed me a demon escaped when Kleora accidentally opened a portal. Unfortunately—or fortunately, depending on how you look at it, Nox—the possessor in question, is the demon of lust, and it appears he's set his sights on you."

"Son of bitch. That explains a lot," the vampire mutters, running his fingers across his nape.

"So, get it out of my sister, Darath," Liam demands, his hands clenched into fists over his worry.

"It is not that simple, King Scott."

Actually, it kinda is, but I crave to let this play out for a bit longer, and allow Asmodeus a little fun with the playboy vampire. Now that I know where the wayward Prince scurried off to, Nox could use a rude awakening.

"I don't believe Cellica is in any danger. Our priority has to be getting Troy to assist with Kleora before the land nymphs attack or her body gives up the ghost. So to speak."

"You don't believe?" Nicole questions with an incredulous expression.

I ignore her disbelief and turn to Christoph with a severe expression. "We are on a timeline here. Can you keep her contained for now? Watch her, so she doesn't hurt herself?"

"I'll take care of my baby sister," Liam barks.

"Unless you want your sibling to attempt to have sex with you, wolf, I suggest you stay away from her." It takes everything not to bust out laughing at Liam's scandalous expression.

"So… what? I'm stuck with babysitting duty while the rest of you go on a mission?" Christoph questions, displeasure evident in the hard lines of his gaze.

"Your mission, if you choose to accept it, is to guard the little possessed werewolf, but to keep your hands to yourself no matter what she says or does. Think you can handle that, Guardian?" Geez, I'm brilliant.

Nox's loud swallow fills the room. "Yeah. Of course… No problem."

Oh, to be a fly on his cabin wall.

Chapter 21

Kleora

"My lady?" The thick steel muffles Berk's deep, grating tone. "I must speak with you."

Yeah, I bet. Lucifer caught him red-handed trying to escape Hell. Pretty sure his punishment is forthwith, and he wishes for me to intervene on his behalf.

I snort. Like I have any sway over Darath. He proved, most deliciously, I might add, how little control I possess. Who knew a spanking would thrill me? No, it was more than a thrill. I exploded with lust, begging the demon for more.

Goddess. Remembering the burn of pain and how it spread through my body in all the right places has heat pooling in my sex. So what else does the Devil have up his sleeve in the sex department? The creature has two millennia of experience, and I've become the beneficiary.

But for how long? Till my corpse, held in stasis, disintegrates and I cease to exist? And if by some miracle I'm brought back whole, what then? After what Darath did to me, my people will never accept him as a suitable mate for their queen, and in good conscience, how could I? No way I'll give up my kingdom for exceptional, out-of-this-world, soul-shattering sex. So not even entertaining that notion. At all...

"Priestess," Berk grates with annoyance. "We had a deal."

I approach the door. "My last foray above ground was uneventful, Berk. Are you telling me your latest intel is any better?" Not that I'd hand over the sword tip to this power-hungry demon. As furious as I am with Darath, I wouldn't give this idiot a weapon that could hurt or destroy my mate if my life depended on it.

What would King Darath do if he discovered the extent of my subterfuge? My stomach somersaults as dark fantasies fly through my mind. Me tied up. Flogged. Fucked in ways I can't even imagine. Taking that enormous length down my throat.

No. Keep your eye on the prize, Kleora. You are getting your soul out of Hell, one way or another.

"Yes, my lady. The new coordinates are accurate. I can assure you."

"Yeah, no offense, but you said that about the last ones, Demon." I can almost hear his teeth gnashing. "I'm not risking my hide again unless I have certain guarantees."

"Speaking of which. Thank you for taking the punishment for the portal. I heard your screams." I nearly choke on my spit. "I hope he wasn't too harsh."

Oh, for crying out loud, Kleora. Why must you be a screamer?

"Yes, well, it was pretty bad." The biggest lie of all time. It was fantastic. "So you must understand my reluctance to risk everything on a whim again." When did I become such a proficient liar? Purgatory is rubbing off on me.

A piece of cloth slips under the door. I bend to read it but rear back in disgust when I realize it's not material, but skin. Like literal skin with writing etched in blood. Gross.

"What is this, Berk?"

"Sorry," he responds, not sounding apologetic at all. "Paper doesn't last long in Hell, Priestess." Is it my imagination, or did he sneer at my title? "These are the directions to the exact location of the sword tip. Unfortunately, after the portal incident, Lucifer is having me constantly monitored, so my window of opportunity above is minute."

"Then how are you going to retrieve the artifact? Incorporeal, remember. I can't pick it up."

"Locate the tip. I will work out the logistics."

"You're not right in the head, are you, Berk?"

"I've never been clearer, my lady. Now," his tone changes. "Memorize the coordinates, and then I will destroy the message. If you, in fact, crave to escape my king and Hell, you will do as commanded."

"Destroy it how? I can't shove it back under the door." Man, this demon is thick. My mouth compresses, and my ire spikes at his insolent tone.

"Do you have it burned into your memory, or not?"

Sheesh. I quickly recite the directions out loud. I always remember things if I speak them. "Done," I grumble, hating conspiring with this bastard. But the enemy of my enemy and all that.

"Now do as ordered, Land Nymph."

My hackles rise. "Or what, Berkonnan?"

"Or I will reveal all to the master. How you conspired to rip his command from him, and dare I say, murder an archangel? You thought your punishment was severe before? That was a walk in the park."

"In doing so, you expose your betrayal, Berk."

"I am a demon, my lady. I've endured a millennium of pain every single day. You, on the other hand, wouldn't stand a chance."

Can't argue with that. One week out there, and I almost lost my mind. Would Darath cast me into everlasting punishment if he discovered my subterfuge? I'm his mate. I would bet my life he would never hurt me—crap, poor choice of words.

"Fine. How are you going to meet me in…" I glance at the paper… skin, whatever. "On the banks of the Euphrates?"

"I will not. Once you are in place, I will inform the master you escaped and give him your location. Once he touches you, hide the tip on your person before he drags you back."

"Oh, great. Essentially you'll be throwing me under the bus again, jerk."

"I'm not sure a bus is involved, but under, over, or in front of it, you will do as I've commanded."

"Berk," I purr, edging as close to the door as possible. "When this is over, I vow to send your soul into oblivion never to return, you slithering piece of slime."

His cackling laugh sends chills up my spine. The disgusting leathery skin bursts into flames within seconds until it is nothing but a pile of embers. A gust of wind, or maybe it was Berk blowing his putrid breath under the door, scatters the ash as if it never existed.

Who am I more afraid of? Berkonnan with his innuendos and roaming claws, or Darath, the most powerful immortal on this planet with the ability to torture my soul for all eternity?

Pretty sure Lucifer wins, hands down. Yes, I'm attracted to the beast, and our mate bond compels me to protect him. Still, I must remember he holds me prisoner in Hell, keeping my carcass in magical stasis. At the same time, he gallivants off to God knows where doing God knows what as my body rots and my soul becomes a permanent fixture in Hell.

A portion of me understands. The longer I'm stuck here, the more I lose a part of myself. One day soon, I could become Berk. Evil. Demented. Uncaring. My connection to nature severed. Will my spirit morph into the ghastly creatures I witnessed during my week in purgatory? I shudder at the thought.

With a heavy sigh, I wander over to the bed, despair a lead weight on my translucent shoulders. Put aside your doubts, Kleora. I scold myself. It's up to me to resolve this situation. My entire life, I've always only relied on myself. I fought hard to join the Storm Walkers' ranks and even harder to climb the ladder to command.

The crown was not an inheritance or birthright. I scraped and clawed my way to the top, earning my place as queen. My vision was to bring my people out of hiding. To devise an economic plan to sustain our way of life, and to join the hierarchies of the immortals and obtain a seat on the Council of Unity.

The land nymphs have survived for centuries in the shadows, concealed in the trees and underground, in order to live in peace. We stayed out of the immortal wars unless they forced our hand. And even then, they didn't witness the full impact of our deadly Storm Walkers. We've had hundreds of years to perfect our military. A legion of female warriors that no army in the paranormal world can hold a candle to in combat.

Our soldiers do not take our power lightly. Our priority is to always steer clear of conflict unless given no choice. By now, Sabrina has offered a small demonstration of our resilience in a bid to get my body back.

If I understand Nicole Giordano at all, there is no doubt that the Vampire Nation is backing Darath. This means the werewolves, shifters, and valkyries will as well.

We are looking at outright war with most of the immortal world. And while we are more than equipped and capable, is that what I want? To destroy the prophecy and decades of sacrifice for my own selfish needs so my soul can skip through the pearly gates and find peace?

Devine Goddess, my choices suck.

Chapter 22

Jagorach

"Fuck, I detest the humidity," I grumble in a low whisper, crouched in the damp pine needles between the Moretti brothers in the dense woodlands outside Little Rock, Arkansas. "Give me 100 degrees of dry heat over this suffocating moistness any day."

"Stop your bellyaching, Jag." Logan shoots me an irritated glance. "Can you sense Troy in the cabin or not?"

With a dramatic huff, which produces an eye-roll from Sebastian, I shut my lids and ease my energy toward the rustic building nestled among the towering trees. The meager moonlight penetrating the thick canopy dances over the eerie fog floating over the ground. The forest creatures are strangely quiet, which only adds to the spooky element of the setting.

My power travels through the mist, up the porch steps, and under the front door. I allow it to hover inside the entrance, taking in the pristine but run-down interior of the cabin. A shabby couch sits facing a fireplace with a rickety rocker off to the side. The floors are bare wood planks with throw rugs strewn about for added warmth.

The kitchen lies behind the sofa, along the far wall, and consists of a rustic gas stove, sink, and small fridge. A table for two butts up against the shuttered window. The place is quaint for a weekend getaway, but I wouldn't care to live in it for long.

Troy comes sauntering around the corner from a back room, and I exhale a sigh of relief. The formidable witch is here. Nicole's intel was correct. But where is Abigail? Is she alive? Maybe in the backroom he strolled from?

Dare I venture farther into the home? With Troy's arsenal of magic, he might detect my presence. The last thing we need is him disappearing again because I proved to be an idiot and got caught.

Still debating my next move, an apparition, as familiar as my own skin, flashes in the center of the room. Troy spins to the threat, his palms open, a ball of dark fire igniting between them.

"You have got to be kidding me…" I mutter back at my body.

"What do you see, Darath?" Logan murmurs low.

I ignore him for a minute to take in the breathtaking beauty of my mate, clothed in her brown leather, her high ponytail cascading down her spine, her bow and quivers firmly in place as she faces off with the most potent witch in existence.

What in hellfire is she doing here? And how did she escape? Again.

"Mr. Tenebris," she says, her voice strong and regal, like the powerful queen she was… is. "I mean no disrespect by barging in on your privacy, but I wish for a moment of your time."

"You're a wraith," states Mr. Obvious.

"Yes. Thanks to King Darath."

Dread boils in my gut, and my focus sharpens on Kleora. What are you up to, peach?

"You're the only witch powerful enough to reconnect my soul with my body."

"You lost your life attempting to kill Abigail. Why should I help you?"

"I died trying to protect the prophesied Halfling. Unfortunately, I got in the way of the Oracle's powerful magic, which, in turn, lessened the full impact on others."

"Fair enough, but reconnecting your soul and body is no guarantee you will live, Priestess."

"I understand. My spirit lifted for Heaven when King Darath snatched it, so I'm hoping if things go south, I'll head to my original destination. If not, my people must bury me, so I can find peace before it's too late. Alive or at last rest, my conclusion needs to take place as soon as possible. This situation has disconnected me from earth for far too long."

Oh no, you do not, little mate. Rage clouds my reasoning. She doesn't get to leave me. Not ever.

"What you solicit has never been done before," Troy continues with a deep, grating gravel like it has been centuries since he spoke. He contemplates the spirit before him with a blank expression. "Not to mention you're asking me to go against Lucifer. So, what's in it for me, Land Nymph?"

Kleora regards the witch for several seconds, her focus darting to the back room. "My people are powerful healers, the best in the world at cell regeneration. I could convince the current ruler to aid you in your... endeavors."

Endeavors? Is she speaking of Abigail? Would Kleora help save the bitch who tried to kill Nicole? Who slew Icarus, the High Priest Oracle? She has to comprehend that Abigail will come after Nicole again. If for no other reason than to thwart Icarus's prophecy.

My mate has spent too much time surrounded by the influence of Hell. The Kleora I know would never betray the vampire queen or mitigate circumstances that could damage the prophecy for her own needs.

I still have not figured out how she is escaping the confines of my chamber. I even implemented new wards on the door after her last breakout, and yet here she is, attempting to strike a similar bargain behind my back. Apparently, her previous punishment wasn't severe enough to halt her scheming. It appears my mate is due for an eye-opening revelation on what it means to betray Satan.

Troy glances at the door, and I sigh, realizing he senses my magic.

"I will be right back," I inform Logan and Sebastian before materializing in the cabin behind my rebellious female. Tenebris regards me with a smirk over Kleora's head.

The wraith spins, perceiving my presence. She stumbles back several steps, the shimmering stare wide with disbelief and... fear. Good. She should fear me.

"Does the king require aid in controlling his woman?" Troy chuckles, but my furious regard never deviates from my female.

"How did you find me?" she asks with a defiant lift of her chin.

Fuck, her fire ignites my lust unlike anyone I've ever known. "I did not. It appears you found me, little peach."

The lids with incredibly long lashes round to the size of saucers. "You... you are here to talk with Troy as well?"

Rage demands I keep my mouth shut, so I clench my jaw. If my mate would only trust me, she wouldn't have to conspire behind my back to do the same damn thing I am attempting. Kleora swallows at my quiet fury.

After several minutes, the beautiful nymph lowers her gaze, and I lift my regard to the witch, watching us with amusement. "I have a bargain to strike with you, Troy. I fear mine differs from Priestess Tanagra's."

"No doubt," he grins.

"What are you doing, Demon?" The priestess demands with fists perched at her waist.

"Quiet," I bark, and her eyes narrow with anger. "I will deal with you later." With a snap of my fingers, my mate's furious visage disappears, trapped in my chambers once more.

"That's cold, Jagorach. Real frosty. Trapping your woman's soul in Hell?"

I wave away his comments. "Can you bring her back or not, Troy?"

He shrugs. "You heard what I said to your captive. I have never performed such a spell before. Besides, it depends on what you're offering. The land nymph's bargain was enticing."

I snort. "I present more than simple cell regeneration."

Troy's black eyes spark. "You're gonna need to be more specific. I know you have a beef to pick with Abi, Demon, so your proposition could mean her death as far as I know."

So, she is alive.

Only a mind as devious as mine would understand I didn't actually offer anything. "What is it you seek? I am the master of deals. You stroke my dick, I will stroke yours."

Troy glances at my crotch with a raised eyebrow. "As enticing as that offer is, I'll leave the stroking to your female, Lucifer. Although I'd be careful exposing your sensitive parts to the livid nymph."

Logan and Sebastian come barreling through the door but halt inside the entrance. I shift my frame to block them from any dark magic the witch might decide to hurl their direction.

Troy continues as if the interruption meant nothing. "Why did you wait so long to seek me out, demon? Priestess Tanagra died months ago."

"You are a hard witch to track down, Tenebris, but you finally made the mistake of staying in one spot for too long." My grin is cold.

He nods. "Heal the damage to Abi's body. I've kept her mind in stasis, blocking the pain while I attempt to restore her flesh, but nothing seems to work."

"No fucking way," Logan snaps, but I raise a finger, indicating I need him to place faith in my bartering techniques for a minute. The warrior rumbles but remains quiet, trusting me—unlike my mate.

"Let us just say for shits and giggles, I have the power to fix the damage. What then? I cannot allow her to come after Nicole or any of my friends."

"The Devil claims friends?" he jeers and my ire sparks.

"Answer the question, Tenebris, or I will destroy you and everything in this cabin," I glance at the backroom to make my point, "with the snap of my fingers."

"Her revenge was against the Oracle Icarus," Troy shrugs. "He's dead."

"A fact the witch should pay dearly for," Sebastian rumbles, his icy regard lethal.

I ignore his comment. "Not sufficient, witch."

Troy's contemplation bounces between the three of us with quiet amusement. This male has no fear of us. Intriguing. "What guarantees do you require, Demon?"

"You restore Kleora's life, and I will heal Abigail's body...."

"The fuck you will."

"No fucking way."

Logan and Sebastian warn at the same time, and I hold up my hand to quiet them before I continue. "With the understanding, she never comes near Kleora, Nicole, the Moretti's, Alexandria, Lucretia, Nox, Kurtis, Viessa, or Liam. Ever. I will mark her soul with a tracker, just to be sure."

"Abi is a willful female. What happens if she is foolish enough to disregard our contract?"

"You better hope you can control your woman, Troy, or her essence will find an especially hideous place in the depths of purgatory. I vow it."

The bottomless stare regards me for several long seconds. "Anyone else you'd like to add to the list?" he finally asks with a smirk.

"Yeah, any of our future heirs or family as well," Logan contributes in a low, furious tone.

I nod to the warrior and turn back to Troy. "Do we have an accord?"

"What you're asking is not an easy endeavor, Demon. It requires extreme sorcery. The darkest of magic," he warns.

"I am the Devil, my boy. I thrive on it."

"Yes, but does your female? Her luminosity is already murky from her time spent in Hell. This could obliterate her light altogether. If it fails, her corpse will rot and her soul will fracture."

"What does that mean?" Bastian questions with a frown. His captivating sapphires burn with his hatred for Troy.

"The witch is melodramatic," I say with a dismissive shrug for Logan and Bastian's benefit. Inside, my heart stops, and dread simmers like the incredible geysers in Yellowstone Park, waiting to erupt at the first sign of trouble. Pain eats away at my insides. Not merely at the notion her stay in Hell has already affected Kleora, but at the dire consequences if this fails.

"If anything happens to her, witch, you will be my next resident in Hell."

"I'm willing to broker my soul. Give me a week with her body," Troy says, getting straight to the matter at hand, and I nod, revealing my Tucson address with his assurance that he will begin the necessary prep work at first light.

As the Morettis and I prepare to leave, I communicate telepathically with Troy, seeking one last favor. He nods his agreement.

Our trio steps away from the cabin, and the weight on my chest lifts. If anyone can pull this off, it's Troy. Soon, Kleora will live again. What that means for us, I have no clue. But one thing is certain: Alive or dead, I can never let her go. If I must dive into war with the entire world to keep the defiant spitfire by my side, so be it.

If the spell fails, I will hand over Kleora's body to her people and keep her soul safe in my chambers in Hell. It would not be the first time I defied the odds in order to get what I wanted.

Sadness fills my chest, recalling the unknown means she utilized to materialize at the cabin. Did she conspire with Berk again, or has her duplicity extended to other ranking members of Hell? Kleora's lack of faith in me dents my pride, but it also upsets my equilibrium because, well, can I blame her? What I did was unthinkable, especially to a creature so connected with the earth.

I shrug. I cannot bring myself to regret it. Regret is a wasted emotion. What I did was to ensure she lives a long full life, and I would do it again in a heartbeat. I have seven days to persuade my mate she belongs to me, living or deceased.

I rub my palms together, a wide grin lifting my lips as I anticipate every conceivable way to convince her the fates bound us for all eternity. Damn if my woman will not heel and beg for mercy before this week ends.

Chapter 23

Kleora

Mother Earth help me. I've never seen Darath so pissed. His rubies smoldered with fire. And for the first time since I've known the big, sexy brute, I fear for my life. Well, for my trapped soul, anyway.

What bargain did he strike with Troy? I guarantee it wasn't the same awful deal I bargained for before he showed up. I wring my fingers together, astonished I almost let down my friends, not to mention the God-given prophecy, so my body and spirit could reconnect with the earth.

I collapse back on the bed. What is wrong with me? Not only did I attempt to betray the individuals I love and care about, but I was finally able to locate the hideous weapon needed to bring down my mate.

With a heavy heart, I glide my fingers through the pillow, touching the cool exterior of the blade tip. Even now, I'm dumbfounded that I possessed the ability to pick it up.

My brief sojourn to the surface consisted of three stops. First, I met once more with Sabrina. Updated her on my plans and received a situation report from her end.

My second stop, and the one that still gives me the heebie-jeebies? The location Berkonnan gave me. As I stood on the banks of the Euphrates, I stared at the spot in the dirt for a full ten minutes, debating my next move.

No way would I allow Berk to tattle to his master and bring Darath to my side. First off, he'd see right through any lie I came up with, and second, I'm pretty certain I'm not stealthy enough to hold on to the Devil and pick up the weapon without him knowing. I couldn't even work the logistics out in my head.

So, my realistic options were to walk away, pretend I never found it, and trust Darath restores my soul before it is too late... Or take matters into my own hands.

None of the options sat well with me. Nonetheless, I had a decision to make. Anger and grief exploded in my heart at the path Darath forced me down because of his actions. So when my fingers plunged through the dirt and touched the sword tip, power flowed through my limbs. Miraculously, I grasped the blade and held on to it.

At that moment, I didn't require Darath to be sentient. I sat in shocked silence, gazing at the dull surface of the ancient weapon. A device powerful enough to bring down the first archangel, Lucifer. My mate.

If the gods permitted, maybe I wouldn't have to hand it over to Berk.

Yeah, and monkeys would fly out my translucent butt any second.

With my eventual stop in mind, I leaped to my feet, tucked the blade into the bodice of my corset, and set out for the address Sabrina discovered for Troy Tenebris.

We all know how that ended—with Darath discovering my duplicity, snapping me back to his chambers in a rage to sweat it out until he graces me with his malevolent presence.

As much as I relish a spanking, I sure hope he calms down first. Although, a good angry bout of sex from the Devil sounds... delightful. I laugh at my idiocy, even as my insides clench at the imagined invasion of his size pounding into me, his eyes blazing with retribution.

Dammit, Kleora. What in the bottomless pits of purgatory is wrong with you?

When several hours pass and Darath's still a no-show, my spirit crawls with dread. Maybe he's so pissed he can't bear to be near me.

I curl up in a ball, hovering inches above the mattress, and attempt to rest. Despite how warm the chamber is, coldness saturates my heart, and I toss and turn above the bed. At one point, my eyes burned with tears that never fell, which makes me even angrier because I can't allow my emotions to impede what I must do.

Yeah, Darath gave me life-altering orgasms… and introduced me to the joys of discipline. He was the first male I allowed myself to be vulnerable with in a long time. But I'd known from the first moment he snatched me down here—fate did not mean for us to last. It was the one constant in our weird relationship—my subconscious hammered in the back of my brain. So why am I taking this so hard?

Was it the idea that while I stewed and fretted all night down here in Hell, mourning my decisions, our destiny, he was staying away because my actions pissed him off or hurt him? Was I able to wound the Satan? Does he feel genuine emotions?

Like the soul-sucking emotions I'm currently marinating in?

With an irritated huff, I scramble off the bed and head to the bathroom. Determined to pretend to enjoy a nice warm bath and forget everything and everybody else, I glare at the faucets, daring them to disobey me. I flex my fingers like I'm about to enter a race, and they must limber up.

With hopeful concentration, I wrap them around the handle and twist. Nothing. Tears gather at the prospect of being denied something so mundane as a bath. Or a goddamn shower. Or hell, I'd jump for joy at the chance to pee at this point. Anything living people take for granted every day.

Instead, I'm left to fret about the awaited consequences of my actions. Like I'm a rebellious teenager who got caught cheating on a test or sneaking out to a party. As a grown female, centuries-old, it's galling. I vehemently dismiss the part of me tingling with excitement.

Darath appears in the doorway, his expression grim. He looks stupid-huge in his leather boots, jeans, and the red button-down that matches his irises. The long, dark locks shine under the recessed lighting, and I want to hate him for his beautiful hair. And the sexy bastard had probably already enjoyed a nice, hot shower.

In one step, he's in my space. I can't back up, or I'll end up planting butt-first into the tub. So I hold my breath, praying I don't cave to the desires swirling through my core. Easier said than done with his heated power caressing my skin and that spicy scent of sandalwood and fire invading my senses.

"Why does Hell have electricity and plumbing?" I blurt out in an attempt to delay his retribution.

"Magic."

"But I...."

"Kleora."

That one word, my name, used in that oh so pissed tone sets my blood boiling. My gaze drops to the crazy lushness of his lips, remembering the immense pleasure they gave.

Darath's arm snakes around my waist, bringing me smack bang into his scalding heat. I crave the sentience he grants me. It plows sensations through my body like a forest fire out of control.

With enticing slowness, he drags me up his solid muscles with one arm, demonstrating his strength. I force my expression to remain passive, even though my hormones perform a happy dance on the inside.

"Why?" he asks once my face is almost level with his, and my heart hiccups.

"Jag, I…" What? What excuse can you extend for not trusting him? For conspiring behind his back with Berk… My contemplation bounces to the pillow in the other room, a reminder of what lies beneath it. More proof of my duplicity. "I'm sorry," I offer with genuine remorse, pleased to see the flare of surprise in his expression.

"Thank you for your apology, but before this night is through," he says with a furious low rumble as he grips a fist full of my ponytail, yanks my head back, and forces me to peer into the determined glare of the Devil. "You will reveal every aspect of your betrayal." The threat burns through my veins like lava.

Darath leans down, running his nose along my throat and up my cheek. With his tight embrace, I'm forced to hold perfectly still. I wouldn't move, anyway. The last thing I desire is to antagonize the beast. Well, any further than I already have.

"Fate linked us, Kleora Tanagra," he rumbles against my skin. "A bond unbreakable by magic or death. One day you will learn to trust me."

It's what I crave to hear, but it means nothing. He still owns me. I'm his prisoner in Hell.

"It's not that I don't want to trust you. I do. But your actions make me question my sanity. I should loathe you for what you've done, but I don't. And is it because of the mate bond or something more?" Mother of pearl. Am I revealing too much? My cautious brain balks at the admission, while my heart begs me to reveal more.

Instead of answering, Darath's lips press against my throat, and I shove my misgivings and all the crap we find ourselves knee-deep in far away in an obscure corner in my mind and groan my surrender. I want this… whatever this is, one more time. I have no idea what deal he brokered with Troy, if any. Right now, I don't care that he undid my plans with the witch. Or the fact that my contract with Berk hangs over my head. Tonight is about my furious mate showing me what he's made of, pushing my sexual pleasure to soaring heights I can't imagine.

The rest of the world could damn well bugger off.

Darath drops me to my feet and steps back, forcing me into my translucent state and jarring my focus. What the….

"I think you put a spell on me," he growls close to my face.

"What?" I whisper in a daze, not understanding his words.

"I cannot even remember my life before you waltzed into it. The things that once brought me great pleasure sour my stomach. Every waking moment, my thoughts revolve around you."

Oh Lordy. I'm so turned on right now I don't have spit to swallow. I feel like my body is about to self-destruct if he doesn't touch me, bring me to life the way only he can.

Involuntarily, I move, pressing against him. The memory of our time together and the multiple orgasms are all my frazzled intellect can compute.

Darath laughs, a dark, seductive sound. "I plan on tying your naked ass to my bed and making you come a thousand times in a thousand ways." Before I go up in flames at his declarations, he steps back again, and I mourn the loss. Like my vagina is literally crying at this point. "But first, strip."

This time I don't hesitate. Instead of undressing the way a normal person does, without him touching me, I'm forced to concentrate on mentally willing my garments away. Concentrating on anything other than Darath's skilled hands on my body is tricky, and it takes longer than I would've liked.

I glare at the male's knowing smirk. Cheeky bastard.

Chapter 24

Jagorach

I watch my mate work to undress with her mind as deep-seated anxiety grabs hold of my gut. I meant what I said. She will lay bare all her secrets, but my balls tighten at discovering how bottomless the pit of her subterfuge goes or how profoundly she's embroiled with Berkonnan.

The second my devious lieutenant launched through that portal, I sensed Kleora's fear. Was it at the demon's grotesque appearance, or was she afraid her scheming would come to light? Since she spent a week in the fiery Netherworld witnessing all sorts of atrocities, no doubt it is the latter.

When my beauty stands before me, her nude image shimmering, the seductive jade stare eager for direction, my concerns disintegrate for the moment.

"You are beautiful," I breathe, my voice gruff and my dick hard as a rock behind my jeans.

My words seem to bolster her confidence as she straightens her shoulders and lifts her chin, allowing me time to devour every inch of her with my heated gaze. The fullness of her breasts entices me. As does the narrow waist and slight flare of her hips. Her frame shimmers, but it cannot hide the bronzed thighs with sleek muscles. My brows lift to discover the little land nymph has no tan lines. Does her heritage contribute to the golden complexion, or does the naughty female sunbathe in the nude?

An image of her stretched out naked on a lounge chair by my pool in Tucson, the sun caressing her skin as I sample her scrumptious cunt bounces through my mind. With a wicked grin, I push the future fantasy aside and concentrate on the here and now—breaking down my mate's defenses and persuading her to confess her sins. Unfortunately, Kleora is about to discover forgiveness is not my forte. A few Hail Marys will not redeem her. The Devil demands complete surrender and a pound of flesh.

"Follow me," I instruct and head into the bedroom, where I already laid out the tools of her discipline before I walked into the bathroom.

The lids widen when she spies the lengthy pieces of black rope attached to the four corner posts on the bed. They bounce to the flogger, slim paddle, nipple clamps, and my favorite device—a labia clamp, all displayed over dark felt on the nightstand.

Does she even understand the pleasure/pain these devices are to inflict? I do not know her sexual experience in this arena... It's best to start as if she's a virgin in the ways of BDSM.

"You will require a safe word, Kleora," I say, and her wide-eyed stare swivels to mine. "One easy to recall." I walk over and snap the rope, ensuring it is secure, hiding a grin when her fingers curl at the action. Anxious eyes follow my every move. "Think of it as your 'Get Out of Jail Free' card. Once you utter it, everything stops, so be absolutely certain it is what you want. Do you understand?"

"Yes," she breathes, her chest rising and falling rapidly. The addictive aroma of her arousal fills my senses. "I didn't think the Devil adhered to such rules."

"It is the one rule I follow. I would never betray your trust." This is not a torture session. It is about pleasure as much as pain and getting some damn answers. "Do you have a word or phrase in mind?" I ask.

"Beetlejuice."

I quirk an eyebrow, surprised she knows the reference. "Beetlejuice?"

"It's a classic, and if I'm forced to utter it three times, watch out."

I cannot help but laugh at my woman's sense of humor, even facing the challenge of the unknown. "You know the movie?"

"Jilaya is a big fan. Turned it into a drinking game one evening when we got together."

It still amazes me that my little nymph befriended the succubus queen. "Beetlejuice it is then, and I guarantee you will only have to utter it once." She smiles, and something catches in my chest.

I stride into her space, making her tilt her head back to look me in the eye. My brave woman holds her ground, and I adore her fearlessness and the way her body comes alive at my touch.

"Do you comprehend what the devices on the nightstand do?" I want to make sure she fathoms every step of this process. I do not desire to hurt her beyond what she wishes. Or damage our fragile trust. But I also relish her fear and uncertainty. My cock pulses with the compulsion to hear her scream my name. In pain and pleasure.

"I know what the thing with all the leather strips on it is—A flogger."

"Yes. It is similar to my palm, only to a greater extent. It heightens the pleasure/pain receptors wherever it strikes."

"I don't understand how that's possible. I reached Mount Everest with merely your hand," she confesses.

I grin. "Oh, baby, that was the first basecamp," I say, going with her mountaineer analogy. "Tonight, we hit the summit." The jade irises dilate, and she bites her bottom lip. I cannot tell if my statement turns her on or makes her apprehensive.

"And what are these for?" she asks in a breathy voice, her translucent fingers grazing over the clamps.

I pick up the nipple fasteners. "They tighten down on your nipples, but these beauties also vibrate, intensifying the experience. Especially when removed."

"Huh." She views them with growing interest before moving on to the next item. "And this?"

"The same concept but for your succulent pussy." Her eyes widen to saucers, and I bite the inside of my cheek to keep the evil grin at bay. Kleora will never forget this night. My centuries of experience at enacting pleasure with the perfect amount of pain ensure it.

"Now climb up onto the bed," I instruct, still caressing the nipple clamps in my palm. "Lie on your back in the center."

When she pivots and clambers up, the sight of her glistening folds nearly brings me to my knees. "Stop," I command, and she freezes on all fours, hovering above the mattress. I sidle up behind her and run my fingers over her ass, squeezing and needing the muscular flesh. Her hands and knees sink into the mattress and Kleora moans, dropping her chest to the comforter, giving me better access to her delicious center.

She comes alive under my touch, and a secret part of me thrills it is my touch that makes her sentient. Her skin changes from ethereal beauty to a healthy, vibrant golden brown, flushed with the desire for my stroke.

I bend and press my lips to each butt cheek, reaching for the bottle of lube appropriately placed on the nightstand. "Before the dawn breaks, I will spank, pleasure, and fuck this body to its brink. To test your endurance. Your limits." I run the pad of my thumb over her puckered anus. Kleora tenses, but does not draw away. "Were you ever pleasured back here, peach?"

"I've um... had anal sex before, if that's what you mean."

Excellent. Not virgin territory after all.

"But I wouldn't say it was pleasurable though," she admits, her face pink with embarrassment.

"Then the male was an inept fool. The anus is one of the most sensitive parts of the human body, with the densest concentrations of nerve endings. You can achieve extraordinary pleasure with merely external stimulation. But internal stimulus, done right, reaches the clitoris and the root of the penis from inside—adding another layer of decadence. With my size, let us start with something small to warm you up and go from there."

"Oh, okay," she replies. By her tone, she is nervous about experimenting in this area, but not entirely apprehensive.

"Do you trust me, Kleora?"

"In this area? Yes, sir."

Her ready admission, and the use of 'sir' without prompting, has me adjusting my rock-hard dick to a more comfortable position in my pants. It is not lost on me that she felt the urge to clarify the statement.

I let it go for now. "Good girl," I respond and drop a dollop of lube right over her pink puckered opening, swirling it around.

My mate moans, pressing against the pressure, seeking more. So damn responsive. I answer her demand, slipping my thumb past the stricture. "Relax," I order, and the vice eases, allowing me to glide my entire digit into her.

"Oh my, Jag," she pants.

"Easy, peach. Enjoy it. Don't rush into things." I reach down and begin circling her clit with my other hand, keeping up a steady pumping.

This evening, I intended to start with her punishment and then move on to carnality, but sometimes you have to go with the flow. So we will fill tonight with pleasure, followed by pain, and finish with gratification once more.

When her muscles tense and I sense she is close, I give her wetness several sharp slaps. She gasps, widening her knees, and with a smirk, I shift to the side for a better position. As I rain down punishment on her soaked pussy, driving into her anus, my mate writhes, keening low, and grips fistfuls of the comforter for leverage to push back.

"Do not come, Kleora," I bark.

"Jag... I... I need... it's too much." Sobs fracture her words, but she struggles to obey, even though the loud wet slaps to her clit or the thrusting of my thumb have not lessened.

The second I sense she is about to detonate, I halt all movement. Kleora cries out, shoving against my hands in an attempt to find release. "Hold still," I command, but she ignores the order, pumping her hips. I haul off and smack her a good one on her left butt cheek. The instant handprint is a satisfying sight.

The sharp pain grabs her attention, and her gyrations cease. "You will learn to obey. No matter what you are feeling." I spank the other side, my thumb still deep in her ass. She gasps, her anus clenching around my digit. "Do you understand?"

"Y-yes, Sir."

I reach for a small stainless steel butt plug decorated with a flat ruby at the end, douse it with fresh lube before easing from the tight stricture. "Relax, love," I say, and she complies, enabling me to replace my finger with the toy, with little resistance.

"What is that?" she asks, trying to glance over her shoulder.

"This is your one and only job this session, besides following my orders. Hold this in position until I remove it. Do you understand?"

"I..."

Whack. Right over the jewel.

"Do you understand?" I repeat.

"Oh, God. Yes, I understand."

"Keep my father's name out of our play, Kleora," I command in a harsh tone and strike her several more times to get my point across.

"Yes, sir," she whimpers, her cunt weeping for the release I denied it.

"Now lie on your back in the middle of the bed and spread your arms and legs." She crawls to the center, easing down onto her spine. I nearly grin at the concentration on her face to keep the plug inserted.

When she is in position, I use the ropes to restrain her ankles and wrists to each corner, spreading her wide, maintaining a connection to her flesh, so she stays corporeal.

Satisfied with my handiwork, I brush my fingers across her feet as I round the bed. The trick will be to ensure I touch her at all times, guaranteeing she experiences every strike, vibration, and pinch.

I grasp the clamps I'd pocketed earlier and bend over my mate to lick and suckle her rigid nipple, offering the other a light slap. She nearly levitates off the bed, the ropes keeping her in place.

"Oh G… goddess," she moans, remembering my prior command at the last minute.

I pinch and twist one hardened nipple as a reward while biting down on the other and teasing the tip with my tongue.

"Jagorach," she keens, pulling on the restraints. "What are you doing to me?"

"Whatever I want," I rumble in response. "You are at my mercy, little nymph. Mine to do with as I please. To fuck and torture to my heart's content."

The priestess regards me with equal parts lust and trepidation warring in her expression. She craves my ministrations like nothing she has ever hungered for before. Still, she is wary of gifting someone—namely the Devil, who she understands is livid with her—absolute control over her body. Her apprehension heightens my carnality.

"Do you enjoy it when I lick your breasts?" I ask, demonstrating by running my tongue up the side of her tit and across her puckered point.

"Yes," she groans, her neck arching.

"How about when I bite them?" I clamp down with my teeth.

"Oh, yes!"

"And if I spank them?" I employ a sideways smack to a nipple. "Do you like that?"

"Yes, sir." Her sexy toned body writhes on the mattress.

"Where else do you wish me to stroke, Kleora?" I ask, running the tips of my fingers down her neck and around her heaving breasts, soothing the pinkness from my slap.

"Between my legs," she answers. Her lids flutter. Lips tremble with need.

I caress the inside of her thigh. "Here?" I tease.

"Touch my pussy, Jag," she wails in frustration, and I chuckle, my shaft jerking at her directness.

"Like this?" I skim the glistening folds with the lightest of touches.

"Harder, sir."

So perfect. I slip a single finger into her dripping center, and her muscles clamp down like they desire me to never leave. "Is this what you want, peach?"

"More," she sighs, but instead of granting what she covets, I withdraw. Her lids pop open to glare at me when I move to the nightstand, keeping my fingers on her arm.

"As much as I adore giving you pleasure, this evening is also about punishment. You have conspired behind my back in the most dangerous place ever created." I frown down at her, my voice dripping with ice. "Tonight, you will declare everything you have hidden from me."

The beautiful land nymph watches me with unease, but her expression shuts down. A dark part of me thrills at the challenge, but a flare of disappointment sparks at her unwillingness to trust me with her crime.

"Anything you would like to confess before we begin?"

Her jaw hardens as she turns away to stare at her reflection above the bed. With a determined gleam, I reach for the flogger, run it along the leg and arm closest to me while keeping her fingers clasped in mine.

"Very well. Are you ready to begin, Kleora?"

"I won't submit."

"Oh, you will submit," I growl. "Before I am through, your luscious lips will sob every sin you have committed in your lifetime."

Before she responds, I flick my wrist and initiate the process of training my willful mate in the ways of discipline and the repercussions of betraying me.

Chapter 25

Kleora

Beetlejuice floats through my euphoric daze. Who am I kidding? It's rested on the tip of my tongue several times in the last hour. I opened my mouth to utter my safe word, but a fresh, thrilling sensation blasted through me, producing a mind-numbing orgasm causing me to swallow any notion of stopping my sexually deviant mate.

In between the flogging, Darath demanded answers. My stubbornness and fear refused to give him one iota of information. In response to my silence, he'd introduce another device before resuming whipping my chest, stomach, and legs.

The butt plug stretches my anus. Clamps pinch and vibrate both nipples and my clit pulses with vibrations, delivering me into rapture over and over again. I can't imagine there are any more ways to pleasure someone.

Wrong, Kleora.

Darath wraps black silk across my lids, and I panic as my sight vanishes. "Settle, Kleora," he commands, and my struggles cease. Mother Earth. The male has me as obedient as a well-trained monkey eager for its next treat.

When he eases back, making sure his fingers stay in contact with my body, I tense. What now?

"How are you feeling, peach?"

Before each new transition, the king asks me the same question. My answer is always, "I'm fine." Although, it's becoming more difficult to express any response at all.

"What deal did you make with Berk?" he questions seductively, trailing something soft yet firm along my inner thigh.

Oh, God. What is that? My limbs tremble. Sweat beads on my skin with the effort to keep another orgasm at bay as vibrations on my pussy and nipples increase.

"Jagorach, please," I beg, almost at a breaking point. Son of a witch's tit. He is relentless, and I suspect he could continue indefinitely until he draws my confession.

"Reveal your lies, and this will stop. A nice warm bath awaits."

I can't repress a sob. He's won. My ability to hold out a second longer disintegrates to ash. "He said... he would reconnect my soul... with my body."

"And what did he want in return, Kleora?"

My heart stutters at the hard edge of his tone, clenching my insides. Dammit. If I disclose that the weapon to kill him rests under my head, what fresh torture will he inflict? My threshold is cracking. Can I endure more, or will my mind and soul shut down?

"Answer me," he barks, and goosebumps spread over my flesh. Still, I grit my teeth, refusing to damage our microscopic bond any more than either one of us already has. Also, because my skin itches to experience more. Apparently, I'm a masochist.

Without another word, whatever he was caressing me with slips down my oscillating labia to nudge my soaked opening. "What is that?" I ask, uncertain I want his response.

"A vibrating cock," he breathes in my ear.

Oh my God. Does he plan to screw me with a dildo? "No. I need you, Jag. Please." I crave the real deal pounding into my flesh, not a rubber substitute.

"You wish me to fuck you, Kleora?" He inches the head into my eager opening. "That's a privilege you haven't earned. Reveal the truth to me, and I will bury my cock deep inside your aching cunt and fuck you senseless."

"I..." The dildo slips deeper, stretching muscles taunt from lack of use. "I... not like this." I'm terrified to expose my duplicity while I'm tied up and at his mercy. "Stop this. Please."

"You hold power to end this with one word."

His reminder jolts my heart. If I halt everything with my safe word, what then? Will he walk away? I... can't. As desperately as I wish to reveal all and break down the wall between us, I refuse to surrender, to confess my betrayal under duress. I'm glad the blindfold keeps me from seeing his striking face as I refuse to grant him the admission of my sins.

"Very well, love."

His whispered words, laced with disappointment, prick at my conscience. But Darath gives me no time to contemplate my inner turmoil, plunging the fake substitute deep. I cry out against the brutal invasion, but the pain skyrockets my rebellious body into a muscle-clenching orgasm I couldn't control if my life had depended on it. And it just might before the night is through.

Between the clamps, the plug, and now the vibrating dildo, it's like being taken by two men, with a third and fourth pinching each nipple. Each time Darath slams the fake phallus home, he somehow taps the toy in my ass. I've lost count of how many times his devices have sent me careening over the precipice. More than I have in years. All I'd require was his glorious cock in my mouth, and he'd have every orifice covered. Like a massive orgy, and I'm the sole focus.

My head thrashes from side to side. The skin on my wrists and ankles is raw from yanking on the ropes as I jerk and strain through multiple muscle tensing explosions.

"Tell me of your deal with Berk," he demands again, licking along my neck. "And I will take care of you. I promise."

The speed of his thrusts increases. My thighs quake with the desire to close them and put an end to this delicious torture. The control to finish this lies with me. While a tiny part cries to cease the torment, the more significant portion, the dark, twisted segment, wants to experience one more orgasm. Just one more has run through my mind for the past hour.

When the next climax hits, I scream, my body going taut as explosion after explosion rocks my soul, clamping down on the fake cock.

"Fuck, I love watching you fly apart," he admits gruffly.

Before the tremors in my sex ease, all stimulation terminates. Acute discomfort spikes through each nipple as Darath removes the clamps, and I sob at the pleasure/pain. It spreads across my breasts, and I yank at my bonds. It terrifies me how much I enjoy Darath's unique brand of torture.

The king leaves the butt plug in place but discards the dildo and vibrating labia clamp. I wince as fire spreads through my sex. Before I can contemplate what fresh torment Lucifer plans to put me through, a sharp slap strikes my aching pussy.

Hellfire! Between the inferno scattering from the clamp and the blow, my safe word almost slips out. He must have picked up the thin leather paddle. I wondered when he was going to employ it. I'd assumed it would be for my ass. Nope. The throbbing in my abused sex brings tears to my eyes.

"Care to spill your guts yet, Kleora?"

Oh no, mighty king. I want a pussy whipping. Just one more orgasm.

Darath snarls in irritation when I refuse to respond and sets in, slapping my slick, swollen folds with hard, fast blows that take my breath away. The blood flashes back to my throbbing sex like a rushing river of lava, and my insides clench, begging for my king's massive length to fill it.

"Oh fuck, yes!" I scream, arching my spine at the exquisite sensations blazing through my pussy. "More, Jag."

"Jesus, peach," he whispers, sounding awed by my deviant need. "You were born for the Devil, that's for sure."

The strikes increase and my hips gyrate, needing release. Just one more. When it hits, it destroys me. My muscles tremble as a blazing inferno spreads like tentacles from my groin, up across my quivering abdomen to my throbbing nipples.

"Jag," I whimper, my voice rough from screaming off and on for over an hour.

The spanking stops, and I sag into the mattress, delirious, spent, and nearly comatose. I've never had someone devote such time and energy to me before. Darath seemed to relish in doling out the punishments as much as I enjoyed receiving them.

I must admit, I'm proud of myself. I kept my lips sealed through days of torment. Okay, it wasn't days, merely an hour, maybe two, but still. And I wouldn't call it actual torture. Yes, sometimes it hurt, testing the limits of my pain threshold, but it was also mind-numbing, cosmic shattering bliss. I'm worn out. My body aches in all the right places, and if the world exploded, my head would stay nestled in the silky cloud of my pillow. I couldn't lift it even if I wanted to. My muscles are liquid.

Rough fingertips graze my ankles, removing the ropes before sliding along my side to reach my wrists. I wince as Jag grazes the raw, sensitive flesh, somewhat surprised when his lips caress the burns, as if to kiss away the hurt.

With the restraints gone, I still don't possess the strength to move, so I remain splayed out as Darath removes the blindfold. Firm, full lips brush against mine, and I moan, wanting to respond but too depleted.

"You amaze me, love," he murmurs, kissing each closed eyelid before licking the tears leaking from the corners. "Your level of endurance is remarkable." Warm fingers sweep the damp hair from my forehead and cheeks.

"I'm going to roll you over and remove the plug."

"Mmm," is my only answer.

My face should burn with embarrassment when the big male rolls me on my stomach, sliding an arm under my hips to lift them in the air, but I'm too exhausted to care. I don't even twitch as he grasps the toy, instructing me to relax. Relax? Shit, I'm putty in his hands.

Once I'm free of devices, Darath tucks a blanket over my nakedness, cradling me against his chest. I snuggle against his warmth, pleased he didn't let go. I wish to experience the aches and soreness for as long as possible, and if he were to release me, the effects of our session would vanish in a heartbeat and the burn and ache of Hell would return.

When the sound of water running penetrates the euphoric fog, I smile with relief. The king promised to take care of me, even though he never extracted the truth he wanted. It appears he's a demon of his word.

My confession would have meant nothing if he'd coerced it from me, using my body's reactions against me. So I knew when we started this session, I would do everything in my power not to reveal a damn thing. And while I exposed the primary context of my deal with Berk, I held the more crucial aspect behind clenched teeth. But I can't lie. I almost spilled the beans numerous times.

Deep down, I aspire to confess my sins to the all-powerful demon, but not under duress. Instead, on my terms, to demonstrate my trust.

As the bath fills, Darath holds me close, his lips in my hair, not uttering a word. A heaviness settles into my bones and heart. For the first time in my existence, I've discovered a male who not only brings out my innermost desires, but the more deviant they are, the more he seems to relish in them. If circumstances were different—meaning I wasn't dead—we would be a perfect match.

I lift heavy eyelids when Darath holds me with one arm while he undresses and removes the blanket. When he steps into the tub filled with steamy, fragrant water, lowering us both into the hot wonderfulness, I whimper. Magic tingles through me and I realize Darath spoke the truth. The delicious warmth spreading over my flesh, stinging the raw wounds on my wrists and ankles, doesn't hail from plumbing—it's truly delivered by magical means.

I shove aside the mysteries of Hell. For the first time since I woke as a wraith in Darath's bed in Hell, I'm experiencing what I craved with every fiber—a bath.

He positions me between his thighs with my spine to his chest. I want to turn in his embrace, explore the tantalizing expanse of fiery flesh warming me as much as the heated water, but my body refuses to cooperate.

All I can manage is a slight swishing of my hips, rubbing my low back against the massive hardness pressing into it.

"Do not tempt me, female. I prefer my sexual partners active and responsive when I fuck them," he growls and wraps his arm around my waist to hold me still. "Relax and let me take care of you."

Yeah, he doesn't have to ask me twice.

Darath massages and cleanses my body, whispering words of praise and encouragement into my ear. I realize this male, Lucifer himself, has become my happy place—my haven. Nothing else in the world matters but the here and now. Not even the fact my soul is in jeopardy interrupts this moment.

How could I have fallen for such a malevolent creature? And yet, he's not. Is he cruel and sadistic? Yes. Does he thrive on chaos? Absolutely. But he also lives life to the fullest. He's devoted to his friends. Would sacrifice anything for his mate in order to take care of her... me.

Satan knows I've conspired behind his back to betray him. Although he doesn't understand to what extent. But instead of actually torturing me, shoving me out the door and into the bowels of the underworld to capture answers, he provided me with the most intense sexual experience of my life. He killed me with the perfect amount of pleasureful pain to get me to talk. What does that say about him?

And now, he's cherishing me in the aftermath. Massaging my aching muscles, applying a soothing salve on my wrists and ankles. Even though the second he lets go, it will be like they never were. His long fingers wash the sweat and sticky wetness from between my thighs with a slow sensualness, with no thought of his own gratification.

My heart aches with the urge to spill my guts, to hand over my fears and concerns onto his capable shoulders, but my lids are so heavy they refuse to stay open. The lethargy in my limbs zaps my strength. Sleep sucks me under.

Later. I will confess all after a much-needed nap.

Chapter 26

Jagorach

"Sir, a dozen more demons have escaped Hell," Dzun informs me several hours later in my private home office in Tucson. Within minutes of sinking into the tub, Kleora zonked out. Her soft snores warmed my heart as I continued to massage her muscles until they were lax. She didn't even wake when I lifted us from the water and dried her tempting body with a fluffy bath towel.

The petite nymph is a wraith. Her skin healed the second she became incorporeal, but I enjoyed the aftercare. It has always been my favorite part after a session. And tonight was intense.

I have never come across a creature who could handle the intensity level I enjoy in all my thousands of years. Kleora not only handled it, she owned it, begging for more and more. Her enjoyment had my dick rock hard, and several times I had to stroke myself to relieve the painful ache.

I craved to plunge my length into her sopping pussy. Or to flip her over and give her beautiful ass a thorough fucking. But unfortunately, last night was about getting intel from the wily female. For over an hour, I teased, prodded, slapped, and whipped every inch of her, and those luscious lips refused to confess her sins.

"Any of concern, Dzun?" I ask, forcing my thoughts to the matter at hand and letting go of my disappointment in my mate's refusal to spill the beans. Her body craved my ministrations, but her mind declined to trust me. And that I cannot tolerate.

"Yes, lord, several," he answers, garnering my full attention.

"Have you found the portals?"

"One, and we took care of it, but I fear there are others. Every time your female ventures to the surface, she opens numerous gateways."

Damn it. "Lock Berk up. He's behind this somehow. Until I determine to what extent and repair the damage, I don't want him roaming around and having access to Priestess Tanagra. Is that clear?"

"Yes, sir. I will take care of Berk personally." The warrior's eyes sparkle with glee.

"Try not to kill him, Dzun. I need him alive."

"He will only wish for death, sir."

I shake my head at my lieutenant. "You are a scary son of a bitch, Dzun. Glad you are on my side."

"For eternity, my lord."

And with that, the demon disappears. No doubt heading straight for Berk. Those two have butted heads from the beginning, and I almost feel sorry for Berkonnan. But then I remember his influence over my mate, and I secretly wish to be present when Dzun tortures him.

'What the fuck is going on in Hell, Jag?' Nicole's angry voice penetrates my head. It still surprises me when she barrels past my defense. A defense I have spent a millennium erecting. Yet, she is the only creature in the universe with the ability to invade the Devil's mind. 'I have a dozen reports on my desk of demon possession. And not purely in immortals.'

'I am well aware, Halfling. I will notify you if I have anything to report,' I respond as calmly as I can, even though irritation rides my spine.

Her sigh filters through. 'I'm sorry, Luci. This pregnancy has turned me into a nervous nelly, worrying about every goddamn thing. It's pissing me off and making me cranky.'

'How are you feeling, physically?'

'Like dogshit. My ankles look like elephant feet. My lower back aches all the time, and I'm jonesing for a thorough spanking, but big bad Logan is too scared to touch me for fear of hurting the baby. Life fucking sucks right now.'

I chuckle, surprised by her candor. 'Well, good luck with that. Have Logan Google how to discipline a pregnant female and see if it helps. Or tap Sebastian's brain. He is the owner of several delicious clubs...'

'Fuck. Why didn't I think of that? Thanks, Luci. And bonus, Logan will blow a gasket when he discovers I talked to his brother about our sex life.' Her devious chuckle warms my heart with pride. 'Talk later. Call if anything changes with my girl.'

Before I can respond, she disconnects the mental link, leaving me sitting at my desk with a stupid grin on my face. No one but her would dare shorten my real name to Luci. I would burn down the world for that vampire and her unborn child.

Maybe I should go check on the "girl" in question instead of completing the paperwork in front of me. My mind is not on it, anyway. Instead, I have spent the day mentally hashing out another session to loosen her lips. This occasion will require my cock getting in on the game.

I rise to leave when Viessa materializes on the other side of my desk. "Oracle," I exclaim. "How can I help you?" Damn. I should ward my residences against unwanted intrusions.

"Time is running out, King Darath. Tanagra's body is deteriorating at a rapid pace. If you don't rejoin her soul soon, she won't have a vessel to jump back into and her soul will blink out of existence."

What the fuck?

I trace to the secret chamber holding Kleora's body, leaving the Oracle to follow or not. Her petite frame, clothed in her combat outfit, hovers about waist high in midair, encased in a magical sphere. Which is supposed to preserve her muscles, hair, and tendons for as long as I deem necessary.

At first glance, everything looks as it should. However, upon closer inspection, her chestnut tresses do not look as shiny. Her skin appears pale instead of the golden hue it usually holds.

No. This cannot be happening.

Viessa emerges next to me. "Any news from Troy?" I question, my anxious stare never leaving my mate's body.

"No."

I twist to the seer. "Do I succeed or fail, Viessa?" I probe quietly, my heart frozen.

"I do not know, King Darath. I'm blocked from Kleora's future. Not sure if it's because technically she's already dead or because her future is uncertain." She turns those bright amber irises in my direction, and I grit my teeth as power pulses from her body. "You never should have interfered in her death. If you weren't an archangel, albeit a fallen one, I would kill you where you stand for interfering in your father's plans for her."

Well, damn. If there was one creature, besides God, who could destroy me, it might be this tall, lethal beauty standing before me in leather—the sacred engravings on her back pulsing with fury.

"Tell me how you really feel, Oracle," I mutter, my tone dripping with sarcasm. I could not care less if I enrage her further. My concentration returns to the visual of my mate's body.

"I did," she mutters.

"How much time?"

"A few days, a week at the most."

I lower my lashes as panic swells. "Can you put a fire under Troy's butt?"

"If you mean, make sure he understands the urgency, then yes. He's my next stop."

"I cannot fail. Without Kleora's light, the darkness will consume me, and God help you all if that happens."

"We will never find out. I will end you before I allow that to occur," she states, her calmness unnerving.

"It's a date, Oracle," I utter before she disappears.

Part of me revels in the challenge. Another part fears my demise. What becomes of the Devil when he dies? I have spent thousands of years torturing the souls sent my way. Will they all get a piece of me if I no longer rule? Would my father be so cruel? Is it his plan to leave me pained for the rest of eternity without my mate?

Fuck. What have I done? My selfish weakness for my mate could condemn her soul. If that occurs, the Kleora I love and cherish will cease to exist. Her soul will become a mindless entity, searching every level and chamber for her next fix of pleasure. Or the opposite could be true for her.

Certain souls feel too much, and that is their eternal punishment—to endure every minutia of pain and agony. Others seek it but are forever denied even the softest of touches. Their emotions rage out of control. They attempt every lewd and sick behavior to achieve something they will never find. While others relive their worst nightmares over and over and over again.

My chest aches at any of those scenarios coming true for my beautiful land nymph. If I lost her forever, I would revert to the Satan of old. The fire and brimstone days would seem like a walk in the park. The earth will tremble at my feet. The gates of Hell will crash open, allowing my children free rein on the human and immortal populations. That's if the Oracle does not annihilate me first. God will end me in order to save his precious creations. And without the consequences of Hell, utter chaos will ensue.

"Do you hear me, father? Help me fix this, or your children will suffer my wrath."

I am not surprised when I receive no answer, although He damn sure heard me. God and I haven't spoken since he cast me out. So, for me to pray to Him now is monumental and not something I will repeat. Ever. But for Kleora, I swallowed my ego. Which is quite the feat for the demon of pride.

I turn my back on the empty shell of my mate with a heavy heart and seek Dzun. Maybe a little torture is what I crave to get my mind right.

Chapter 27

Kleora

A profound lethargy weighs me down as I stretch, working to eradicate the fog from my brain from the first sleep of my life. Hours spent dreaming of King Darath performing wicked, erotic things to my body.

Maybe I should stop the merry chase and give in, let the tall, sexy brute have his way with me.

After several minutes of stretching, I force my lids open and come face to face with my shimmering image on the ceiling.

What the hell?

I bolt upright, taking in the strange room with a glance. Where the heck am I? Pain spikes through my joints, and fire consumes my brain. Images flash by with the speed of a hurricane, and I clutch my skull to keep it from exploding.

Oh, God. That's right. I'm dead. In Hell. And those weren't dreams. Last night happened, and it was freaking amazing. And I enjoyed a bath! Actually fell asleep with the warm water caressing my skin and Darath's broad chest and arms cradling my body. The experience was out of this world magical. His gentleness, the way he massaged and cared for me after owning my body, was… beyond words.

I kept my secrets through it all, although I mentally promised to reveal my shame after a bit of a nap. I glance around the room. I'm not even sure what day or hour it is. With no windows to the upstairs world and no clocks, I could've zonked for hours or days. Hopefully not six months like the last time.

When I first awakened here in Hell, I didn't understand the reality of my current situation. Panic consumed me, unsure how I got here or where here was. Until my mind played out the battle at the dark fae castle and everything that transpired after.

Upon waking this time, last night obliterated everything else, and I smile. Boy, I never imagined I'd be the type of person to get off on such extreme play. Was that extreme? Since I have no frame of reference, I have no clue. But, if it wasn't, could I endure more? Maybe a whip or belt? Being restrained while Darath pounds into my eager vagina or ass? Maybe both?

The notion of those things has my fingers sliding down my body as my brain titillates me with different scenarios.

My demon tied up and at my mercy stalls at the forefront, and my fingers rotate over my sensitive clit. But, unfortunately, there's no electric sensation, no building tremors. Nothing.

I leap off the bed in disgust. It appears I can't find a sweet release unless the Devil is touching me. Figures.

I shut my lids and imagine cut-off shorts, a black tank top, and flip-flops. When a ripple cascades over my body, I glance down at my attire and am pleasantly pleased by my escalating abilities.

A few days ago, I discovered Darath's massive library behind a locked door. But, of course, locked doors mean nothing to a wraith. So with nothing else to occupy my time—no TV, no Internet, no cell phone—books are my only entertainment. Which is fine by me. I've always enjoyed the escapism of a good story. Especially a juicy romance. The naughtier, the better. The fact I can't touch it or open it doesn't deter my determination. At least I can read the spine covers and discover my mate's taste in books.

"Priestess Tanagra?" a strange male voice stops me halfway to the secret library, and I glance over my shoulder at the entrance to Hell with a frown. "My name is Mogrun. I am an associate of Berkonnan. He asked me to relay a message."

"Where's Berk?" I question as I edge closer to the door.

"He is currently indisposed, my lady."

"Indisposed how?"

"Commander Dzun and the King are torturing him for information."

Oh no! Why oh why didn't I confess when I had the opportunity? No doubt Berk will throw me under the bus to save his own skinless ass. I drag my hands down my face, my heart rate sprinting like a terrified rabbit. I may have screwed my one chance to confess.

When Darath discovers the extent of my betrayal... I shudder. He has not directed his rage at me yet. Although, I suspect that's about to change.

"Priestess? Are you still there?"

"Yes. What do you want, Mogrun?"

"Master Berk asked me to help you back to the surface to continue your search for the sword tip."

I roll my eyes and glance at the pillow. Another trip would grant me the opportunity to check in on Troy, to see how things are going with whatever deal Darath and he concocted. It also means I could touch base with Sabrina again to find out how my people are faring.

"He would also like you to mate with the king. A bond between you two would solidify Berk's plans."

"How so?" I question with a raised eyebrow.

"I'm not at liberty to discuss such information, Priestess, but if you open the door, I would be happy to assist you to the surface."

"I can't open the door, you nitwit," I huff with exacerbation. "Berk transferred me to the surface through the other side of the door."

"You are a wraith, my lady. Simply walk through the door."

What? There's no way it's that straightforward.

"I don't think I can," I admit, eyeing the steel barrier with trepidation.

"Yes, you can. Imagine the door isn't there and walk through it."

Okay, now the fiend is patronizing me. Like I'm a two-year-old in need of oversimplification. Reluctantly, I do as he instructs and concentrate on the door being invisible as I back up several feet to have a run at it. This will either be epic, or I'm about to bust my face wide open on solid steel. At least I'll heal in a millisecond.

One. God, please let this work.

Two. If not, don't let me lose any teeth when I go crashing into it.

Three. I leap at the doorway.

A shriek escapes when I go sailing through the metal only to land on who I can only assume is Mogrun. Red muscular arms encircle my waist as we both go flying toward the opposite wall from the force of my hit. The massive demon twists and takes the brunt of the impact.

"Goddess. I'm sorry," I mumble as he straightens and lowers me to my flip-flops. Within seconds, searing heat engulfs my feet, melting the rubber shoes. I leap back up into the demon's arms, holding on for dear life. This was not the appropriate clothing choice for venturing outside Darath's chambers.

"My lady. Please change your attire," the red-eyed, red-skinned creature states indignantly while cradling me in his arms.

"I... I will. Give me a second," I mutter, appalled by dependency for this rather handsome demon—if you're into the whole muscles outside of the body look—to keep me in his embrace.

Unlike Berk, Mogrun has no bony protrusions. Instead, his body is a mass of striated, well-defined muscles, minus skin, a smooth round skull with no horns, and softly glowing red eyes.

While I concentrate on changing my attire, Mogrun examines me with a strange gleam. "You are quite beautiful, female," he murmurs, and it finally penetrates my brain. The demon is holding me. Touching me. I'd almost forgotten—when in Hell, I become sentient. Feeling and experiencing every god-awful moment in this place.

"I'm touching you..." I express lamely, stating the obvious.

"Yes," he replies, the eerie regard dropping to my lips. "And it's delightful."

Uh oh. It appears my new friend is somewhat infatuated with me. Needing to get back on my feet ASAP, I imagine my immortal combat outfit, boots and all. As soon as everything is in place; I shift in his embrace. "You can put me down now."

When he doesn't respond, I push against his bulky shoulders. "Mogrun. Let me go."

"I think not," he states with a calm demeanor that alarms me more than if he'd bellowed. "My curse is to feel nothing. No matter how many diverse pleasures I seek, numbness consumes my body. But with you, my prick hardens with the need to fuck. That has not happened in centuries and only with the Master."

You've got to be kidding me? I've gone from the frying pan into the fire. Literally. At least with the ugly Berk, he was never too inappropriate. Cruel sometimes, but never overtly sexual. This dude needs a lesson in the word NO. No wonder he's in Hell.

"You remember Lucifer is my mate, right?" Yeah, maybe I'm name dropping, but whatever works, right?

"Yes, but you have not yet mated. Which makes your fragile body fair game."

"Not if I'm saying no, you imbecile." I push in earnest, sickened by the tip of his cock pushing against my butt. Geez, do they not believe in clothes in Hell?

His throaty laugh sends chills down my spine. And when he tosses me over his shoulder, striding through horrifying chamber after chamber, away from the haven, I was stupid enough to leave again—I panic.

"Listen, Mogrun. You don't want to do this. Lucifer will eviscerate you."

"You, my scrumptious cunt, might be worth it." His gigantic hand rubs my backside, and I feel the fever of his skin through my leather.

"No. No, I'm totally not worth it," I declare before slamming my boot into his groin.

He bellows, but instead of loosening his grip, he slams my spine into the unforgiving rock wall. Fire sears through my corset, and flashes of my week in Hell momentarily shut down my brain.

Mogrun pins my wrists above my head, pressing his erection into my pelvis. "You like Mogrun." His scalding forked tongue slimes my neck before his enormous claw-tipped hand rips my corset in half, leaving deep gouges and a trail of blood down my chest. I scream in agony and fight with everything I possess.

Unable to free my hands, I lean forward and sink my teeth into his neck, biting down hard. Bile threatens the back of my throat as thick, slimy muscle—smelling of death and decay—fills my mouth and nose. Before I vomit, I jerk my head back, ripping a chunk from his body.

My attack seems to inflame the asshole. "Oh, yes!" he shouts, his hips slamming my tailbone into the rock repeatedly as he pumps his engorged erection against my stomach. "I glory in your bite. You love Mogrun." Terror clogs my throat. I kick his shin, his knee, anywhere I can reach, but my struggles only add fuel to the fire.

When he lowers his head and bites my breast, drawing blood, my mind shrieks for Darath.

Jagorach! Help me!

The next thing I know, I'm crashing to the ground on my hands and knees. Sharp rocks slash my palms, and sobs break from my lips. I scramble to a corner. Where's Mogrun?

My frantic search stalls a mere fifty feet from me, and my heart leaps into my throat.

A terrifying creature clasps a dangling Mogrun by the throat with one hand.

The beast stands at least nine feet tall. His skin is inky as the night, enriching the rage-filled, blood-red irises. Thick horns fold over his head, and enormous black leathery wings expand from his back, nearly touching the walls on either side of the chamber. Large bony protrusions, a shade lighter than his skin, stick up from his shoulders, and each wingtip boasts sharp, curved daggers.

This isn't the Darath from last night. Instead, the hellish beast before me is the terrifying creature that was trapped in the dirt with me—Lucifer, in all his glory.

"You dare touch what belongs to me?" Even Darath's voice is deeper, the demonic sound booming off the walls.

"I did not know who she was, sire," the red-skinned bastard lies, wheezing around the constrictor of his king's fingers at its throat.

"Yes, he did," I choke out, and the spine-chilling, malevolent gaze pins me for a brief second. When he takes in the damage to my sternum and breast, Satan roars. I clasp my hands over my ears at the enraged bellow shaking the foundation of Hell.

Expecting Darath to snap the slimy bastard's neck and finish him, I'm frozen when the Devil slowly and methodically strips Mogrun's muscles from his body one by one. The red demon shrieks in agony but doesn't evade Satan's vengeance.

In wide-eyed horror, I watch as Mogrun's enormous scarlet pecker grows harder. It pulses with each new agony, like he's getting off on the excruciating pain his master inflicts. Pre-cum actually drips from the engorged tip, and his hips pump, fucking air, until the Devil grips his erection and yanks it from his body.

Bit by bit, the enraged beast dismantles the demon until he is nothing more than a pile of bone and chunks of muscle at the king's feet. Finally, when there's nothing left, the Devil bends down and picks up Mogrun's beating heart off the ground, and… oh shit… he eats it. Huge fangs sink into the organ, ripping hunks off before swallowing it down. Unable to hold the contents of my stomach at bay, I pivot and vomit the bile stewing in my gut.

With his meal finished, Lucifer extends his arms wide, tilts his head back and lets loose a deafening, diabolical roar of… satisfaction? Is the Devil pleased he avenged his mate? Or did he enjoy torturing and ending Mogrun? His big body shudders as if in pleasure, and his deep laugh, full of jubilation, echoes around the massive chamber.

Wiping my mouth on the back of my hand, I stare in horrified fascination. I've never witnessed something so grisly, so violent. Did Mogrun deserve punishment? No doubt. And maybe he deserved to die. The sicko was ready to rape and torture me for his own pleasure. But what the King of Hell did to the demon was… inhuman. Barbaric. Right out of one of those horrific slasher movies I've watched with Jilaya. Not only that, he got off on it. They both did.

Lucifer turns toward me, and I can't help but cower against the wall, my body trembling at the fire burning in his gaze. The malevolent creature saved my life, and a part of me warms at the idea of such a powerful being willing to do anything to protect me.

Give me a bad boy any day of the week. A hero will sacrifice those he loves to do the right thing for the greater good. A villain will sacrifice the world to protect what he craves. My heart does a tap dance at the notion my mate is the baddest of baddies, and I'm the one he will defend at all costs.

He halts, the leathery wings flutter, glowing rubies watch me intently as blood drips from his hands and mouth. Oh. My. God. His visage terrifies me, but the power emanating from him ignites my soul.

"Come to me, Kleora." His command is guttural, his expression wary as he extends an enormous claw-tipped hand dripping gore.

While his appearance is straight from a nightmare, I'm entranced by the lethal, malevolent beauty. Underneath the fiendish mien lies my mate. The male who defied God to hold on to me. To keep me.

Before I contemplate my reasoning further, I go with my gut and scramble to my feet. With a suppressed sob, I launch myself at my male while dismissing the images of his retribution toward Mogrun. His enjoyment of it. He did it for me. To avenge me.

Even though the reason the demon and I were together was an obvious betrayal, he did exactly what I informed Mogrun he would do—he eviscerated him.

And then ate his heart.

Yeah, okay, our romance is not the conventional sort, but I don't care. With Darath, I'd never have to fear anything or anyone. He is all-powerful. Invincible. At this moment, I realize how deeply I love this creature. In human form or Devil form, it doesn't matter.

Large, warm arms encircle my body as I grip his waist as hard as I can. Tears run freely down my cheeks in the aftermath. When the soft leathery wings encircle us, offering a dark, cool haven from the scalding wasteland and misery around us, sobs shake my body.

"Hush, baby. I have you."

I lean back and peer into the beautifully terrifying face of the Devil. I swallow my fear. This malevolent being saved me from a fate worse than death. He annihilated a being with a ferocity and violence unmatched in history. All because it dared to hurt his mate. Me.

"I... I can explain," I blurt out.

Silence greets my words. The crimson irises peer down at me with eerie concentration, and anxiety percolates in my gut.

"Let us get you back inside my chamber, so your wounds can heal."

The time to reveal all has come. What will the King of Hell do with me now?

Chapter 28

Kleora

The second we enter the room, Darath's visage reverts to the spectacularly gorgeous Demon King clothed in blue jeans, a faded black t-shirt, and no shoes. So sexy.

"Let me have a look at your chest," he says in a matter-of-fact tone. No warmth or kindness in his expression or voice.

Crap. Crap. Crap. I'm in seriously deep doo-doo now.

I turn my back, covering my bleeding wounds with my arms. "It's fine," I sniffle. "They are healing already."

It's so strange, but out there, in Hell, I'm corporeal, cursed to endure the torments right along with everyone else. In here, I'm still a soul but the effects are muted. And above ground, I'm merely a ghost, with intense emotions, unless Darath touches me. This rollercoaster is making me crazy.

I squeeze my lids shut, wiping the moisture from my cheeks but discovering no moisture as I conjure up my shorts and tank top from before, minus the flip-flops. I glance down and am pleased to see the gashes across my chest have vanished, including the deep bite mark on my breast. Even the blood has disappeared. I guess being a ghost has advantages.

Darath says nothing, but I feel the burn of his stare on my back. Okay, Kleora, put on your big girl panties. It's time to face the music.

"How did you know I was in trouble?" I think to ask, avoiding my ultimate confession for a brief moment.

"Your scream echoed through my brain. At a damn inconvenient time, I might add."

I duck my head in shame and stroll over to the bed to reach beneath the pillow. Like before, the sword tip allows me to pick it up. With the vile thing resting in my palm, I hold it out to my mate.

He glances at it briefly before pinning me with his furious glare. A muscle works in his jaw as he clenches his teeth. No doubt to keep his anger in check.

I clear my throat. "This is what Berk had me go to the surface to retrieve."

"A hunk of metal?" he questions with a lifted eyebrow. "For what purpose?"

"It's more than that," I say, surprised he didn't know what it was immediately. I take a tentative step closer. "According to Berk, this is the tip from...."

"From what?" he demands quietly, his stony regard sparking.

"The flaming sword tip from the cherub who guarded the Tree of Life."

The crimson stare hardens. "Is that so?" He crosses his arms over his chest. "And what did you plan to do with it, Kleora?"

This is where things could go sideways. I swallow my fear. "He..." I hesitate, dread tingling across my spirit. "I'm not exactly sure," I fib, needing to delay the fallout of the truth for a second longer. "But he said it would aid him in overthrowing you."

"Aid him how, my love," he questions with a sneer, the soft tone more frightening than if he'd shouted at me.

"To kill you," I whisper, panic threatening. "Berk wanted to kill you. But it's been in my possession for a while. I... I had no intention of giving it to him." I can feel my emotions welling up in my eyes, though my current state doesn't allow them to fall.

"No?" He finally steps closer. "And yet you brought it here." With my hand still outstretched between us, his stomach was mere inches from the blade. I tremble with the impulse to stride back. "If you did not hold up your end of the bargain, how would you achieve your goal?"

Good question. "Another way would've presented itself."

In all honesty, I relied, namely on myself and secondly on Darath, to produce a solution. Berk merely allowed me the time I needed on the surface.

"Where is Berkonnan?" I ask.

"Berk is no concern of yours any longer, Kleora." Before I can blink, Darath snatches the sword tip from my palm and flings it across the room. The end embeds in the rock so deep it almost disappears. "Did you honestly think a blade from an angelic cherub would kill me? Only my father has the power to smite me out of existence."

"What? Then why did he go to so much effort to have me retrieve it?" I ask, confused.

"It was never about the blade. You are the weapon."

My jaw drops, and I blink at him for several seconds, not comprehending what he means.

"How can I be the weapon? That doesn't even make sense."

"You really have no notion of demon sociology, do you?" By his incredulous expression, I'm thinking that's something I should know as a ruler. Or former ruler.

"I..." I shake my head, unable to articulate my ignorance in the ways of demons.

"Right now, all I care about is the fact you plotted my demise with my lieutenant. You assumed the blade would kill me. Did you not?"

"Yes, but I... I never planned to use it or give it to him. I would've found another way." Surely, he sees I would never murder him? Especially after the mind-numbing orgasms he gave me. A girl has to have her priorities in line... Besides, the bond would never allow it.

"And if you did not find an alternative?"

Yeah, Kleora? What then?

I stare at the floor, picking at the fabric of my shorts. "I intended on telling you everything last night," I state lamely. A total moot point now.

He snorts. "You expect me to believe that?"

"No, but it's the truth," I say, lifting my gaze to his, pleading with him to trust me, even though I've given him no reason to grant me such liberty. In reality, I'm hoping the mate thing will offer me some brownie points.

"I should have let you go when you died," he states with an extra layer of ice in his tone.

I gasp as pain explodes in my chest. Holy mother. That cut deep.

And yes, I've been berating him for his actions since the moment I confronted him the first time, but his words... they maim my soul. They dismember it the same way he dismembered Mogrun. Only instead of bit by bit, he destroyed me in a single sentence.

My brain can't comprehend his hatred, especially after last night. Maybe I'm naïve. Such sessions might be a common occurrence in the Devil's sexual life. The idea of him doing what he did to me with another female gets my blood boiling. What happened between us was amazing and special.

For only you, apparently.

I lift my chin, refusing to let him see how deep his comment cut, and call forth the ice of my Storm Walker training, encasing my heart in a thick wall. Never give the Devil an advantage or an insight into your weakness.

"Yes, King Darath, you should have. Instead, you trapped me in your chambers in Hell. Forced me to endure your vile touch. Your cruel torture. I'd be floating on a cloud in Heaven, or whatever happens up there, right now, if it weren't for you." I conjure my bow and quiver filled with arrows without concentrating and put some distance between the beast and me. Just in case.

The weight of my weapons has never felt so tremendous.

The Devil laughs, but no warmth exists in the sound. "I could kill you for conspiring to murder me and be well within my rights to do so."

"I'm already dead, you hateful bastard. So do your worst." In the next breath, I have an arrow notched and at the ready, but tears blur his image, and my arms tremble with the weight of this moment—the loss of my mate's warmth and tenderness. His dominance and sexual prowess. It's all gone. I see it in the chilly hatred of his crimson gaze, and the ice wall around my heart melts as the anguish forces its way in.

"You release that arrow, Kleora, and I will show you true punishment."

Instead of his threat sending fear down my spine, my traitorous soul betrays me. Desire flashes and my spirit grows brighter.

Jesus, Kleora. With the fury pulsing in his regard, his retribution would no doubt hurt like a mother. So why am I so hot and bothered by his warning?

Deep down, a part of me understands I deserve whatever retribution he's about to dish out. I conspired behind my mate's back to kill him. How screwed up is that? I should have trusted in him, in his promise to make things right. In our bond. No matter how fragile it was.

With no other options before me but to fight, I release the arrow aimed at his heart before leaping for the door in a bid to escape. The malevolent grin spreading across the Devil's lips as he yanks the projectile from his chest terrifies me. I'd rather take my chances in the depths of this literal God-forsaken place than face whatever reckoning Darath plans for my flesh.

Within an inch of freedom, a massive arm snatches me around my waist, rips the quiver from my back before seizing my bow from my fingers and snapping it in two. I let out a girly squeal when he throws me over his shoulder, striding toward the bed.

I pound my fists against the vast expanse of his back, but he doesn't even acknowledge the hits. "Put me down, you hateful bastard!" I holler, hitting harder.

A large palm comes down on the back of my bare thighs with such force, I freeze at the sharp pain and grip fistfuls of his t-shirt. I grind my teeth together to keep from screaming. I will not give him the satisfaction of making me cry out. No fucking way. No matter how much I deserve this, I'll be damned if I make it easy on him. This entire situation is his fault.

He dumps me on the mattress, and I twist to scramble to the other side, but his fist closes around my ankle and yanks me to him. I peer over my shoulder and kick out with my free leg. My bare foot connects with his jaw, sending pain shooting through my sole and jerking his head to the side, but his hold doesn't loosen. Instead, he flips me over, popping the button of my shorts before brutally ripping them down my hips and legs. Still not saying a word.

"No," I wail, struggling harder. I'm stunned and appalled. Would my mate use such brute force to teach me a lesson? The Devil he may be, but I didn't think rape was his style. My efforts are like fighting against a God. Useless. As much as my body craves his unique form of discipline, I can't bear it if it's given with such hatred. It shines bright in his gaze.

Instead of pinning me to the bed and forcing himself on me, I'm across his lap, my wrists pinned behind my back, and my kicking legs restrained beneath his thick thigh. Without a word, the sharp pain from his first hit steals the breath from my lungs.

Oh! Blessed be. He's not playing around. And while I'm relieved my instincts were spot on regarding his tendencies, his hit was not a little pleasure/pain foreplay. It's an actual punishment meant to hurt. I bury my face in the comforter and hold on for dear life as blow after blow punishes my poor backside. Fire spreads over my cheeks as silent tears soak the blanket.

Darath is rightfully angry with me, but deep down, I believe he's also filled with agony at my betrayal and lack of trust. As much as the spanking hurts, I mean, like really fucking hurts, he's not hitting as hard as he could or injuring me in any way—beyond the sharp sting of pain and humiliation of the moment.

A telltale sign he can't bring himself to cause me serious injury? Every few slaps, Darath hesitates and rubs his palm over the soreness as if to soothe the pain.

Soon the severe burn blooms into a delicious heat, contracting my sex, puckering my nipples, and wetting my opening. My clit pulses with each strike, shocking me with the level of suffering I crave to get my juices flowing.

The crazed king halts, running his fingers between my clenched legs. His body goes motionless when they encounter my soaked pussy, and for several heartbeats, neither one of us moves. Then he shoves my thighs apart and starts slapping my wet lips with such speed and intensity it takes my breath away and forces me to bite my lip until it bleeds to keep from crying out.

Within seconds, my muscles seize, ready to detonate, but he stops, and I groan in relief and frustration.

"No coming for you, Kleora. Bad girls do not get to come."

I'm still contemplating his revelation when he grips my waist and lifts me, forcing me to kneel on the floor between his spread thighs. I gulp at the tense aggression on his face. Now what?

In response, Darath yanks my tank top over my head before ripping it down the middle. Was that really necessary?

"It's my turn for you to pleasure me, little nymph," he commands, his irises burning with intent. "Swallow the cock you were so ready to annihilate."

My scrutiny drops to his crotch, revealing the impressive hardness beneath. The Devil got off on his harsh punishment of

Mogrun and me, and I should spit in his face and tell him to go to hell. But my inner whore demands I follow through and finally get a taste of the demon.

"Unbutton my jeans."

Without taking my scrutiny from the harsh glow of hatred, I reach out and unfasten his pants, slowly lowering the zipper. The flesh of his rigid shaft unveils, pointing at me as if it too demands my lips around it. Should have known the Devil went commando.

I shove the sides open and grip his length in my palm, amazed by his size. Not only is he long, but his girth is so thick my fingers don't wrap all the way around. But it doesn't stop me. Instead, I use both hands to stroke him from base to tip as I observe every nuance of his expression.

The muscle pulsing in his jaw is the only indication what I'm doing is affecting him at all. "Lick me, Kleora," he commands, and I perk up, eager for my first chance to savor him, to pleasure my mate with my mouth, like he's done for me numerous times. I shuffle closer, salivating for a taste.

He fists my hair. "After I fuck your lying, traitorous mouth, the Devil will glory in punishing your tight little cunt until you cry for mercy."

Oh, my. His harsh words have my core spasming. I truly am sick and depraved. My entire life, I never dared to utter or act out the dark fantasies that plagued my sleep for years. They were taboo and not worthy of a queen. I trusted no one with that wicked part of myself.

Now, I've discovered a male who not only revels in my naughtiness but demands more. Unfortunately, my devious actions sullied our relationship and tainted his sentiments for me. Darath is beyond pissed. Maybe even hating me a little right now. My heart screams I should stop this, shout my safe word and cease the disintegration of my self-esteem.

But I don't. I crave his dominance, his harsh control. I deserve his insults. So I disregard the fact I'm not angry or repulsed, and lean forward. With the first swipe of my tongue along the enormous head, my eyes roll back with a groan at the salty goodness that is Jagorach. Sandalwood and fire.

Daddy just handed this bad little girl the best lollipop ever.

Chapter 29

Jagorach

The coolness of Kleora's tongue sets me on fire, as does the delighted eagerness in her expression. I had planned for this session to be about discipline. And it partially was. Her backside turned a bright red from my fit of rage, and if she was not a wraith, deep purple bruises would remain for several days. My hurt and disappointment, as well as my anger at her duplicity, saturated the spanking.

I hold most of the blame. If it weren't for my selfish actions, Kleora would have never suffered at the hands of Mogrun. The image of the deep gashes down her chest, the bite mark marring her flawless breast, and his repulsive pecker daring to touch what is mine sent me over the edge.

A scarlet haze of rage filled my vision as I tore the demon apart. The eating of his heart satisfied the beast, and I gloried in the hedonistic ritual. Once I calmed down, the realization my mate's subterfuge continued, which was revealed by Berk mere moments ago, only escalated my anger.

After hours of torture from both Dzun and myself, Berk confessed to the attempted coup, and Kleora's willingness to aid him in assassinating me. Pain shot through my chest and it was all I could do not to show how deeply her betrayal wounded me.

Thank fuck we never mated. The backstabber would possess the power to bring me to my knees. Shit, at her command, I would have gladly laid my neck on the chopping block for Berk.

The sensation of Kleora's mouth gliding over my length shocks me back to the present, and I grip her hair tighter, guiding her up and down. She doesn't protest, in fact, she groans in pleasure at my aggressive fucking of her mouth.

Damn, she's good at this, to be able to take me down her throat without hesitation or gagging. When she eases back, her tongue swirls around the head. My mate is a hellion in the sack. Her deviant needs match my own. When I fear I've gone too far, she begs for more.

I thought for sure she would have screamed her safe word after the first few smacks. Fury rode those hits, and my lack of control appalled me. A Dom must always stay in command when doling out punishment. It should never be in anger.

As soon as I realized I no longer controlled my actions, I took a deep breath and backed off a bit. The spanking needed to hurt; it was not about pleasure. But my mate found it anyway, nearly coming apart when I punished her soaked pussy.

The remembrance has me pumping faster into her mouth, needing the release I have waited so long for from my mate. Her little mewling sounds of bliss have me pulling her hot little mouth off my length with a wet pop. She moans in protest, sticking her tongue out to steal a final lick.

I stand abruptly, forcing her back on her heels, and rip my shirt off over my head. "Remove my jeans." My command is rough, laced with resentment, but heat flares in Kleora's gaze and she doesn't hesitate, reaching up and sliding the waistband down my hips to pool at my feet. I step out of them and toss them to the side with a flick of my ankle to join my shirt.

My mate gazes up my length, her small hands resting on my knees, awaiting my next directive. "Take my balls into your mouth." She immediately rises to her knees and runs her tongue along my tightened sack before gently sucking on them both, continuing to twirl her hot little tongue around and over each one.

Such bliss. My mate, submissive, on her knees, bringing me pleasure. "Fuck, yes. Like that," I groan, brushing her hair from her forehead.

When her tongue ventures lower, I yank on her tresses, forcing her to look up at me. I am not opposed to anal play from my sexual partner, but I am nowhere near done with my perfidious female. "How's your ass, Kleora? Are you ready for round two?"

Her body stiffens, but she nods. "Yes, sir," she whispers.

"Then bend over the bed," I order and step to the side, keeping in contact with her flesh so she remains corporeal, able to feel everything I dished out and what is in store. When she complies, I relish my flaming handprints across her perfect ass.

"Slide your hands up the comforter and keep them there. You move or attempt to rise and the punishment will increase. Do you understand?"

"Yes, sir."

"You remember your safe word?" I think to remind her.

"Beetlejuice," she breathes.

Satisfied, I step over to the nightstand, keeping my fingers on her backside, and reach into the drawer for my belt, the jeweled butt plug, and a bottle of lube. I set the belt on the mattress next to her head and her eyes widen as she understands what the next phase will include. I allow her to contemplate that for a minute.

I press my leg next to hers where they hang off the side of the mattress and lube the plug. She clenches when I caress her seam, parting her cheeks. "Relax, Kleora," I command, and her muscles loosen, allowing me room to work.

I rub the lubed plug over her puckered opening, spreading the moisture before nuzzling the tip inside. My mate moans, arching her back to press against the toy. The diminutive nymph enjoys anal play, but little does she know, after her punishment, she's going to enjoy a thorough fucking in that beautiful ass.

Once I have the plug seated, I reach for the belt and step back. Keeping my toes alongside her foot, I give myself room to swing. Kleora's fingers clutch the blanket, anticipating the coming pain.

"This is for conspiring to have me killed," I say, and snap the belt across her beautiful ass. She gasps and her whole-body tenses, but she doesn't cry out or attempt to rise. "This is for not trusting me." The next slap is harder than the first, showcasing this offense is worse than the first in my mind.

Her cry of pain washes over me and I glory in the sound, rolling my head from side to side in rising lust. She not only deceived me, but she also conspired behind my back with another demon in an attempt to annihilate me. I covet my mate's trust, love, and devotion, above all things.

As I set in, varying the intensity, my need escalates at her gasps and cries, but my heart breaks at the necessity for this discipline, until I glance at the sword tip embedded in the wall.

Would she have handed the weapon she assumed could destroy me over to Berk? Or would she have used it herself? She claimed she had no plans to do so, but then why bring it here? It is true, the sword tip cannot kill me, but it could severely injure me. My skin sizzled upon contact. As an archangel, I would heal, but it would require some time. Time that would weaken me enough for a large contingent of demons to overwhelm me during my healing process.

In Hell, dominance and control are everything. If I were to lose either, even for a moment, my demons would not stop until they crushed me and took control. Life down here would be an endless battle, one after the other, as every power-hungry creature took a shot at the title of king. That could never happen.

By the time I have given a good ten lashings, Kleora is writhing and moaning, lifting her reddened ass for more. Jesus, she is insatiable for pain. Why can she not submit as freely with her trust?

I slow the hits and eye my handiwork. Bright red welts crisscross her plump bottom, distorting the previous handprints. The evidence of her lust glistens between her thighs. One touch from me and the land nymph would fly apart.

I toss the belt on the nightstand and lift Kleora until she's centered on the bed. Next, I grab two pillows and position them under her hips before spreading her legs to make room for my body. Without preamble, knowing she's well lubed with her own juices, I plunge deep into her pussy for the first time.

"Oh, fuck!" she cries out, and white knuckles the comforter.

Her muscles spasm around my shaft as I hold perfectly still, allowing her tight channel to adjust to my size. Sweat beads on my forehead and my muscles quiver with the desire to let loose and pound into her with relentless force. Punish her the way her actions punished me.

The tightness of her sheath is a delicious vice I would gladly endure forever. My body shudders as I fight the desperate urge to move for a full minute before spreading my knees to open her further. With a firm grip on her hip with one hand, I begin a slow pump, gliding my rock-hard length in and out, and matching the rhythm with my thumb on the flat jewel of the plug.

"Jag. Yes," she pants and pushes that delectable ass back for more. I fist her hair, arching her neck and drive faster and harder, gritting my teeth at the exquisite pleasure of her pussy squeezing my cock, milking it for all she's worth. An eruption tightens my sac, but I force it down. I have serious plans for my rebellious girl.

Against my will, my fangs descend, dripping with the venom to mark my woman as mine, to claim her with my bite and bind my soul to hers for all eternity.

A low, frustrated moan vibrates my chest as I pound harder. Do I ever trust her enough to claim her? In her current state, the mark would disappear the second I stopped touching her. Besides, her scheming and plotting with my demons destroyed any chance of dropping my guard and letting her in. And for that, she will endure whatever I dish out until I gain the ability to set her free.

The thought of seeing her at meetings, hearing her laughter, but never being with her drives me insane. A burning desire to punish her more, to scorch tonight into her memory for all eternity, so thoughts of me will ruin her if future partners ever come into play.

Harsh possessive snarls erupt at the notion of anyone else touching her. I eviscerated Mogrun and ate his heart for hurting my mate. How will I be able to stand by and watch another male claim what belongs to me? What God gifted to the Devil.

Fighting to keep my demon rage at bay, I clasp the plug and ease it from her body, slowing my thrusts before eventually withdrawing from her hot, tight sheath.

"No," she whines. "Come back."

The hard slap on her butt stings my palm. Her sharp inhale satisfies the beast somewhat as I lube my pulsing length. "I am far from done with you, my little traitor."

"Jag, please. I...." before she can finish her lie, I ease the head into her well-prepared opening and her words die a quick death as her body tenses.

"Relax, Kleora, or this will hurt," I order with cold menace, gritting my teeth at the perfect stricture her sphincter muscles offer. When the vise eases somewhat, I slide forward, groaning in ecstasy until my balls rest against her scalding ass cheeks.

"Oh God," she mewls, clutching the comforter.

I smack her ass hard. "I told you, my father has no place when you are at my mercy."

A part of me, the bonded demon part, craves to lean down, kiss and nuzzle her neck while laying across her back as I gently pump my hips, but Kleora destroyed the gift of tenderness when she conspired to murder me. So instead, I lean up, fists planted on either side of the pillow, and plow into her ass with wild abandon.

At first, Kleora's muscles stiffen, her grip on the blanket proof the taking hurts. But within seconds her fingers release, flattening on the mattress, and her lower back arches, presenting me with a deeper connection.

"You enjoy being fucked in the ass by your Master?"

"Jagorach," she moans, her forehead pressed into the comforter. "Yes, it feels so good."

The sound of her moaning my name tightens my balls begging for release, but I am still not such a cad I will refuse my woman pleasure. So I reach between her hips and the pillow and gently circle her swollen clit.

"Please," she begs prettily, stroking my beast.

"You fucked me over for the last time, Kleora. Your pleading means nothing. Every inch of this body is mine for the taking. You will regret the day you deceived the Devil."

Her body stills. "So this is about revenge then?"

"It is whatever I want it to be," I bark, continuing to rub her needy clit. "I am your Master, daddy, and jailor all rolled into one."

Her body shudders at my words, her legs stiffening in readiness. "I hate you," she whispers, and my heart aches.

"No, you do not, Kleora. You love the idea of being the Devil's sex slave, submitting to every deviant sexual thought in Lucifer's head. Your body is flush with the idea of calling me Master, obeying every harsh command as I strum your responses like a maestro." She shakes her head, even as her hips press her greedy cunt against my hand. "Say it," I command, sliding two fingers inside, pumping her pussy and her ass at the same time.

"Jag," she breathes, lifting her hips to give me more access but denying me the words.

"Admit your weeping, needy cunt craves whatever depraved experience I grant it, and your lips beg to call me what you most desire," I snarl into her ear. "Say it."

"Yes!" she wails. "All right, yes! Please let me come... Master."

"Your admission sealed your doom. Shatter, Slave. Milk my cock with your perfect little ass."

In seconds, my female detonates. Firm muscles clamp down on my dick and I lift my head, roaring in harmony with her cries of pleasure as I erupt with a release so profound my arm shakes to keep me upright.

My harsh breath fans her neck, ruffles her chestnut tresses, damp with sweat, as I take a moment to recover. I could stay in this warm cocoon forever. Listen to my woman keening in pleasure. But my thoughts soon intrude, squelching the enjoyment and reminding me of my promise the second I learned of her betrayal. To restore Kleora's soul to her body and let her go.

"I am going to ease out, relax your muscles."

"Must you?" she whimpers, reaching back to caress my thigh.

Any other time, I would delight in her responses, crave to hold her in my arms, but my heart is heavy, and my anger bubbles below the surface. If I do not put distance between us, I will break her. I could never live with myself if that happened.

"I am done with you, Priestess," I mutter, my soul fracturing as I head to the bathroom to get cleaned up. Kleora's form shimmers, losing her corporeal form and her ability to feel the effects of my rough treatment. Within moments, her punishment is merely a memory.

When I emerge back into the room, Kleora's curled into a ball, floating mere inches above the bed. She watches me with sorrow as I dress without a word.

"I'm truly sorry, Jagorach. I never meant to hurt you," she whispers. Tears shimmer in the jade depths but never fall, crushing my chest.

"Your actions prove otherwise, Kleora." I harden my heart against her tears. "Besides, as the Devil, I do not possess a heart to damage," I lie. "I will keep my promise. In the next few days, we will restore your life and free you from me and this place."

"As you wish," is all she says before she rolls over, presenting her back to me. I ball my hands into tight fists to keep from going to her and letting the beast take over.

"Be on your knees the next time I visit. Calling you my sex slave was not a threat earlier, but rather a promise. Until we restore your soul, you are mine to do with as I see fit."

She betrayed me. Conspired with my demons to have me killed. I will not soften to her ghostly tears.

Ever.

Chapter 30

Jagorach

"What have you discovered, Troy?" I demand without preamble the second I materialize inside the witch's cabin, three days later, after receiving a text from the male informing me we needed to talk.

My heart and mind warred with going back to my chamber. To Kleora. But my actions sickened me, and I knew if I went back, my hurt and anger would override my common sense again. I refuse to treat my mate no better than a whore, which is exactly what I did.

"It's taken serious research and rare components, but I believe I have the correct spell to restore your woman's soul to her body."

"Reviving her, yes?" I clarify.

"Of course. She will be whole as if nothing ever happened. But I must warn you..." He walks over to the little table under the window where his ingredients for the spell span the surface. "Attached are steep consequences to this kind of black magic. Are you willing to pay the price?"

"It would shock me if there were not," I mutter as Nicole and Logan pop into the cabin. I raise an eyebrow at the vampire queen.

"Mr. Tenebris called us," she shrugs.

"I informed King Darath I perfected the spell to restore the land nymph, but it comes at a price."

"Yes," the vampire Halfling responds with a bitter edge to her tone. "I'm well aware. So, what are the bastards demanding now?"

"I have no clue, my lady. He will reveal the requirements in his own time. I have no authority over what or when it will seek payment, but this spirit will come to you, Lucifer."

"I would expect no less. This is my disaster to undo. Please proceed, Troy. Whatever the cost, I will pay it to restore Kleora's life."

"Recompense might not be from you directly. It may seek restitution from your female."

"What?" My body stills with rage. "Not going to happen. Payment will come from me and me alone."

The witch shrugs. "You might not like it, Darath, but you do not mess around with the Reaper. This is his spell. Are you sure you wish to proceed?"

"I am well acquainted with Dhek Ghemage." An image of the vile creature runs through my mind. That fucker has been after my throne since the beginning. I imagine the skeletal bastard leaped at this offer when he discovered who was behind it.

"Yes, we will proceed," Nicole interjects. "I believe Kleora would agree."

"Very well," Troy sighs. "I should have everything organized in two days. Where do you wish to perform the spell?"

Nicki and I look at each other. "The Vampire Stronghold is at your disposal, Jag."

"I appreciate that, but I would prefer it to go down at my Tucson residence since her body is already there. I will make arrangements for her spirit to join us."

"You can do that?" Logan asks, his eyebrow lifted with curiosity.

"Yes, but apparently Kleora can come and go as she pleases already," I grumble under my breath.

The queen's focus sharpens on me with interest. "Any issues I should be aware of, Darath?"

"Nothing I cannot handle, my lady," I reply with a saccharine grin. At least, I hope it appears sweet. Inside, my black heart is breaking at the thought of Kleora gone from my control forever. From my life.

Yes, my female betrayed me, but it hasn't diminished my sentiments for her duplicitous ass. I crave her bright smile with every fiber of my evil soul. Long to hear her sweet laugh filling my home. Would delight in centuries to educate her in the ways of sexual deviancy. So many more sessions to experience together.

I ache to permit her control over me. My natural tendency is toward sadism, but I also role play. Receiving pain is as gratifying as giving with the right individual. Would the little land nymph be amenable?

I once told her nothing was off the table between us, but with the beast bonding to her more and more, no way in Hades would I allow someone else into our play. I would rip them apart for even daring to cast a heated glance at my female. But there are other ways to enjoy the pleasures of a threesome. Or foursome. Toys. I desire to heighten her passions, her pain receptors, and bring her senses to higher levels of euphoria.

Such fantasies are merely that now—fantasies. After the other night, the second Troy reunites Kleora's soul and body, she will escape to her people and resume her responsibilities as ruler. With the Reaper no doubt demanding my throne, I will lose my mate forever. No one knows the exact location of the Land Nymph Domain. Not even me.

Not yet.

The one bright spot—or endless torture—is I will see her at the Council of Unity meetings unless she withdraws her seat to avoid me. Would she sacrifice the progress she's made for her people to evade coming in contact with me?

"Sabrina has requested, no scratch that, she has demanded she be present for this… whatever this is to restore Kleora," Nicole informs me, focusing my mind. "Are you okay with another nymph being privy to your home's location?"

I shrug. "I am Satan. There is only one being I fear, and He could not give two shits regarding what I do as long as it does not involve His precious humans."

"Wow. Bitter much?" she scoffs.

"Thousands of years' worth, my pregnant Halfling," I state with a hard edge in my tone. "By the way, how is Nox holding up with the pup, Cellica?" A minor flash of guilt burns through me at leaving the vampire to handle the overly sexed Asmodeus alone.

"He claims he's handling it, but every time I speak to him, his voice sounds ragged and stressed. I think the Prince is giving Christoph a real run for his money," she chuckles. "And Liam is about to lose his shit. But let's get Kleora's issue resolved first, shall we? Then you can concentrate on ridding Cellica of the Prince of Hell."

I nod. "Dzun has rounded up most of the other demon escapees, and they are back where they belong, but I cannot promise more will not break out when I bring Kleora forth for the spell. Every time she leaves Hell, she somehow opens a goddamn portal."

"Shit. Well, we will handle those repercussions in two days, I guess."

I nod to the trio. "See you then."

I grab a tumbler of my favorite whiskey and head out to the pool to watch the glorious Tucson sunset. My heart sits like a lead weight in my chest. I crave to go to Kleora, to tell her the news. But every time I think of her, I remember her betrayal and my treatment of her. If I had a human soul, it would shatter into a million fragments.

In reality, I put her in the position to make such a choice. Fury consumed her at the way I manipulated her demise, snatching her chance at an eternity of peace in my father's arms. I shoved her soul into Hell until I could work out a plan to restore the life I stole, so we could be together.

I do not blame her for hating me. If I could hate myself for what I have put her through, I would. But no matter how many times I reassured her, she could not trust me. So she took it upon herself to resolve her own problem.

Can I fault her? She is a highly intelligent, resourceful woman, used to relying on herself to get things done.

Until that moment, at the dark fae castle, we'd dipped our toes in the waters of the lust swirling around us whenever we were in the same room. However, it never went beyond sexual innuendos, sly glances, and fun threats. In my arrogance, I believed I had time to conquer my little mate. No need to rush things. Why not sit back and enjoy the thrill of the chase for a few decades?

Dire circumstances cut our courtship short, and I made a split-second decision. My shriveled heart screamed not to lose the one being destined for me and me alone, even as my mind recognized it was wrong. I have always gone with my gut and damned the consequences, hence the reason I became the King of Hell. My pride and ego ruled that choice.

In my darkest moments, a small fraction of me regrets defying my father. But I have thoroughly enjoyed my life here on earth. Thrilled in conquering the previous ruler of the earth demons and taking over as king. Relished tempting His little pets—the weak but resilient humans—to join the dark side. Taken pleasure whenever and wherever I wanted. I make my own rules and answer to no one.

I would give it all up for a chance to be with Kleora. To have an ordinary life with my female. In a heartbeat, I would turn my back on my duties in Hell if I could. Let someone worthy rule in my stead.

Someone besides the goddamn Reaper.

With Berkonnan and Mogrun dead by my hand, Dzun is the only demon I trust to control and manage my rebellious, power-hungry children. And I would never ask it of him.

It is a moot point, anyway. Kleora and I have no future. There's too much hurt and distrust between us for anything to be salvaged. I should bury myself in my duties when this is over and try to forget her. Procure several lovers to drown my sorrows and disregard what could have been.

I gulp down a big swig and glance up at the sky with disinterest. Tucson sunsets are stunning. The brightness of the reds, oranges, and yellows over the valley is breathtaking. But they pale compared to my mate's beauty.

Will I forever compare everything to Kleora? No female has ever gone toe to toe with my deviant desires and survived. She not only survived, but the nymph thrived. Her exuberance for life, for new experiences, ignites cravings in me I have never dared think about for fear of hurting someone beyond repair. The demonesses I have fucked—used—do not measure up to my petite, pointy-eared beauty. I am ashamed to admit it, but not even my late wife could compare.

Zazzoth preferred gentleness in the bedroom, scorning anything too kinky or outside the norm. But, for a demon, she was an anomaly. Kind. A sweet soul I treated with gentlest caresses, never allowing my beast to show.

Sometimes, sexual frustration gnawed at me. I craved to let loose. Allow my genuine self free rein with the mother of my child. Zazz was not my mate, but she was my wife, and I loved her. Well, as much as the Devil could.

The gods and fate gifted mates, so as Satan, I assumed a one true mate was never in the cards for me. When I courted Zazz and fell in love, I married her, believing adoration would have to suffice.

With Kleora, it is different. It goes beyond conventional love. Our souls are linked. Forged together for all eternity. She is my other half, the part that makes me whole. She seeks my dark ways. Finds pleasure in my deviant behavior and craves the dominant side of my personality. Kleora got off on watching me tear Mogrun apart. Granted, my reaction scared the crap out of her but, it was obvious, her body's responses to the lengths I would go to protect what is mine appealed to her.

Kleora is perfect for me in every way. It is a fucking shame we can never find happiness together.

Chapter 31

Kleora

I've had enough.

I refuse to sit around this chamber, waiting with bated breath for my Master to return like a helpless female. Darath would conjecture it's because I don't trust him, but that's not entirely true. I hope he will do everything in his power to right his wrong and keep his promise. But what if he can't? I require a backup plan—just in case.

Getting on my knees in Satan's bedroom, I press my palms together and do something I've never done before—pray. Actually, I'm calling out to Viessa, hoping the Oracle will hear me and show up.

If Troy fails, I require the one creature who communicates with God on my side. Maybe she can beseech the Almighty to reacquire my soul. Yes, my existence would be over because I have doubts He would restore my life, but perhaps the Big Man will right Darath's wrong.

My mate's rejection hurt me to the core. I'm uncertain the fissure running down the middle of my heart will ever mend. And as much as I got off his degrading words, punishment, and rough taking, an underlying rage tainted the experience. His fury at my betrayal rode his actions. His words. I could've stopped it at any second by employing my safe word, but deep down I got off on his anger, and my soul screamed for redemption for my actions. Darath's discipline offered me the opportunity to show repentance.

What I did—the scheming with Berk behind his back—was erroneous. Even as I performed every task, my inner self balked at the choices I made. Darath's accusations had merit. If I had no intention of going through with Berk's plan, why did I retrieve the sword tip? Did my subconscious want the added insurance? Or was it something deeper? Ugly? Malicious?

I've always been a good person. Killed only in battle. I never hurt someone unless they wronged my people or me. I was confident Heaven was my destination when I perished. Ironically, my insights were spot on.

After my recent actions though, maybe I deserve to rot in Hell. I realized from the start Jagorach was my mate. The only one I would have in this lifetime. But even understanding the magnitude, I still conspired with Berk. Brought back a weapon I assumed would kill my mate. Who does that?

Me, apparently. I'm a horrible person. Despite my subterfuge, I'm on my knees, hoping to convince a deity to help me perform an end-run around Darath as a backup plan in case he and Troy fail. All because I have an irrational fear—based on our last encounter—that Jagorach will cast me out into the depths of Hell if the spell bombs. I endured one week, and it almost broke me.

If circumstances were different between Satan and I, and I could stay with him in this chamber, enjoying our connection and sexual exploits for eternity, I might feel differently. Eventually though, no matter how opulent the cell, I'd go stir crazy living an existence in these rooms alone. But Darath hates me now, and I refused to trust him, so we are at an impasse.

"How may I be of service, Priestess?" Viessa says with a calm demeanor when she appears before me.

Holy shit, it worked! "Oracle, I require your aid."

"So I gathered, my lady."

"Will you bury my body and take my soul to Heaven if Troy's spell flops?"

"I'm sorry, Kleora. That is not up to me."

My lids close for a moment as my heart drops into my gut. "Okay, but you have the ear of God. Right? Perhaps you could speak with Him on my behalf?"

"All I do is honor His wishes, my lady. I'm in no position to steer His actions."

"It was worth a try." I can't help a dejected sigh escaping as the Oracle dashes my hope against the rock wall.

"Have faith in your mate, Kleora. He is a powerful being. I understand you are angry with him for this situation, and rightly so, but believe me when I tell you he is doing everything he can to right this wrong."

"The male loathes me, Vi. It wouldn't matter if I did trust him. He's washed his hands of me."

"Are you sure, Priestess? Anger and hatred mean different things to each individual. If there's one factor I've learned about King Darath throughout this situation, it's that he loves with a deep intensity. He commits without reservation. No matter how furious he may be with you, he'd never allow anything or anyone to harm you." She lays her palm on my shoulder, bringing my body to life. "As you would never hurt him."

"But I plotted against him, Viessa. For my own selfish ends."

"Did you? So, you handed the sword tip over to the demon Berkonnan?"

For Pete's sake. How on earth did she know about that? Oh right, Oracle, stupid. I glance at the tip still embedded in the wall. "No. I didn't."

"Why?" She regards me with her head tilted, the dark straight locks of her bob brushing her shoulder, the ambers watching me with interest.

"I couldn't do it. I refused to hand over a weapon with the power to end my mate's life."

"Exactly, Kleora." She straightens away with a smile, and I shimmer with transparency once more. "You know, Berk never planned to use the tip against the demon king. The blade cannot kill the Devil. You were the sacrificial pawn."

"What do you mean? How could he use me against the King of Hell?"

"Did the demon suggest you mate with Darath?" the Oracle asks.

"Yeah. He did, actually."

"When a male demon completes the bond with his true mate, the link goes beyond the average immortal mating bond. It forces him to grant your deepest desires. If you ordered him to kneel to Berk and hand over the reins of Hell—he would. If you truly desired it. Likewise, if you demanded he rip his heart from his chest, he would. Berk's goals were to restore your life, get you mated with his Master, and then control your thoughts to do his bidding. You were the weapon all along, my lady. The sword was a stall tactic to give him time to get close to you, and King Darath knew it. Hence the reason Berkonnan is now dead."

Darath killed his Lieutenant. What does he have instore for me? "Then why didn't Berk influence me to seduce Jagorach from the beginning?"

"He needed you whole for the mind control to work. A demon cannot influence a wraith. Nor does a spirit have the ability to mate."

Oh, God. No wonder he's never even tried to initiate our bonding. If I were him, I would never grant someone such rule over me. It made what I did so much worse. Even if he'd trusted me, or started to care for me, I dashed those sentiments the second I agreed to that vile demon's schemes.

"How could he ever believe in me again?" I whisper, more to myself than to the Oracle. "I've proven I'm untrustworthy."

She smiles, her expression filled with sorrow. "It might surprise you what love can overcome. Obstacles seeming insurmountable crumble to ash when you have faith."

"I'm not sure either one of us will ever reach such a point after everything that has happened."

"Until you do, you both suffer from the loss."

I snort inwardly. Suffering is my middle name lately.

"I must depart, Kleora. Fate will grant you the opportunity to propose a tremendous sacrifice in order to prove your worthiness to your male and allow the hurt to mend."

"What sacrifice?"

"Your heart will know when the time is right. Take care, Priestess Tanagra."

Great. What else could I offer? He already owns my soul. Not to mention my corpse is currently rotting in his home in Arizona.

That's it. I must get to my body. Maybe by some miracle, I can join my spirit and remains before it's too late. Plus, I'm dying to see where he lives. Wait. Poor choice of words.

Over the course of my imprisonment, I've become pretty proficient at escaping Hell. If I concentrate on Darath, I might appear near him. Of course, I could wind up in Costa Rica, but who doesn't want a tropical vacation? Especially before their death.

Me. The only tropics I desire are the heat of King Darath's exquisite body against my own. Preferably with my actual, living body and not stuck in Hell.

With the threat of this major sacrifice hanging over my head, a future with my mate is slim to none, especially after the way we left things. But hey, I'm a woman. I'll take slim any day.

Chapter 32

Jagorach

"Come peacefully, Mammon. Obey your king, or I will tear you apart," I command, staring into the conflicted gaze of the possessed human shivering in a jail cell.

Irritation rides my shoulders when the demon does not respond. I should be with Kleora, informing her of our plans, not spending precious time collecting a wayward Prince.

The statuesque mortal is strong to fight such a powerful entity as Mammon—another Prince of Hell and the Demon of Greed. Each of the six demons rule different sectors in purgatory. Unfortunately, it appears all of them escaped after Kleora's recent little jaunt to the surface, including Asmodeus, who is currently possessing Cellica.

I did not lie when I told Nicole that Dzun had rounded up most of the demons. This rebellious fiend is the last one.

Who knows when the Prince took control of this human? I glance down at the forged paperwork in my hand—Gemma Christiana. Age twenty-five. Unmarried. Employed as a reporter. No prior record. Not even a speeding ticket. On paper, she's a good girl, but the conniving shit for a joy ride inside her body already forced her to rob a bank in this quaint town of Grand Forks, North Dakota. Within minutes of the crime, the local police hunted her down and tossed her lovely ass in jail to await arraignment.

Dzun is the one who discovered Mammon's location and thank the lava pits, the sheriff in charge is a werewolf from Liam's pack.

I glare at the haggard mortal through the bars of her cell, strung out from fighting the demon playing house within her. Her long golden hair hangs in a tangled mess around her rather striking face. Pain clouds the deep blue eyes, but a fierce determination, I admire, shines through.

I cannot put my finger on it, but there is something different about this mortal. Few could survive a possession from a Prince of Hell. The blonde is not only surviving; she's fighting Mammon tooth and nail. But even as strong as she appears, if I do not evict the Prince soon, she will die.

The sheriff, Drake Silverton, was out of town when the incident happened. So here I stand, my irises covered with dark brown contacts, acting as her lawyer and waiting for the werewolf to show up so we can figure out how to get the mortal into a more secure location to perform the exorcism. Unfortunately, I cannot trace a possessed human.

I sigh with exhaustion at the minutia of details needed to restore this woman's life to normal. It needs to happen without alerting every human who came in contact with her that more is going on here than meets the eye.

"I don't give a rat's ass, Pete," a rough baritone voice barks from the entrance leading into the station house. "I require ten goddamn minutes to speak to the arrestee, her attorney, and look over the evidence. Then you and I will talk."

Two seconds later, the door swings open, and a six-and-a-half-foot, stocky werewolf in jeans, a dirty t-shirt, hiking boots that have seen better days, and a backward ball cap comes striding into the hallway.

"Drake Silverton," he informs me brusquely as I shake his hand. The gray stare is direct and intelligent. "What a damn clusterfuck, King Darath."

I appreciate how the werewolf gets right to the point. "Indeed, sheriff."

"King Scott gave me a SITREP on my way in. How do you wish to proceed with the...." he turns his glower to the mortal. The words die in his throat.

When he offers nothing more, I refocus on him. Maybe the sheriff is slow.

The big man backs up several steps, eyeing the woman like she is a fire-breathing dragon ready to burn him to a crisp instead of a little slip of a human. Granted, a demon-possessed human, but still.

"Are you alright, Sheriff?" I ask.

"Um, yeah. Yes. I'm fine," he replies, shaking his head as if to clear the cobwebs. "What happens to her now?"

The werewolf never takes his scrutiny from Gemma. Not sure if he is aware of it, but his irises flicker from gray to green. A conclusive sign his wolf is fighting for control. Interesting.

"Do you know this woman, Sheriff Silverton?"

"Drake, please," he murmurs absently.

When he offers nothing more, I shrug my shoulders and let it go. My priority is to get Mammon back where he belongs and beeline it to Kleora to prepare for the spell and losing her forever.

The werewolf and I spend the next ten minutes plotting a strategy to bust Gemma out of jail and bring her to Demon headquarters so I can separate the Prince and the human. Hopefully, without harming the mortal. Based on the werewolf's reaction to the woman, she means something to him.

I leave the sheriff to stare at the little bank robber while I assemble his deputies and alter their memories. After several minutes, I have convinced the simple-minded humans they never had a suspect in custody, and the unknown burglar got away.

While under my influence, I call Sebastian to come and deal with the IT end of things. Like wiping any video evidence or paperwork that could implicate the woman. When I discover the bank employees at the time of the robbery are at the station giving their testimonies, I can't believe my luck. With quick efficiency, I wipe any memory of Gemma from their minds and replace it with a faceless image.

When I saunter back into the cell area, the sheriff hasn't moved an inch. The muscled cop—dressed like they pulled him from a river after fishing and camping for days on end—and the human, stare at each other with an unnerving intensity. You know, if those things made me uncomfortable.

"I've taken care of your deputies and the bank employees," I inform the sheriff, whose focus never strays from Gemma. "Sebastian Moretti is getting rid of the computer files. Hand the human over to me now."

Turbulent irises shift to me. "I'm coming with you," he blurts out. "As sheriff, she's my responsibility."

Riiiight. And I'm Little Bo Peep.

"I think it best if you stay here and monitor any issues that might arise. I promise to take good care of the woman and return her to her home." I glance at the paperwork I plan to burn. Devil's Lake, North Dakota… Ironic. They named her hometown after me. I should pay them a visit at some point.

The sheriff glances at the folder clasped in my fingers. "Allow me to take care of that for you," he says and holds out his hand.

Aww. So adorable. The werewolf wants Gemma's address because he knows every piece of information on her is now nonexistent—thanks to Bastian. The wolf definitely has a connection to this woman.

"You realize, once I pull the demon from her, she's merely human. Right?" Immortals and humans do not mix.

Drake inhales a deep breath, like the reality of her mortality pierced his brain. "Yes, but I still want to check in on her from time to time. To make sure there are no lingering side effects."

Lame excuse, but why not? The werewolf will torture himself with something he can never have. A human. Far be it for me to stand in the way of his misery.

I hand over the folder with a grin. As soon as the sheriff unlocks the cell door, I chant a binding spell to keep the demon within the boundaries of the woman's body. The last thing I want is Mammon escaping before I have him secure.

"No!" the Prince shouts, his eerie voice booming off the concrete walls. "Do not make me return, Lucifer. This bitch is sturdy. She can handle my essence."

"The woman is a human, Mammon. No matter how strong, you will eventually kill her." I wrap my fingers around the woman's bicep in a gentle hold.

"Please, help me."

Startled, I stare at the beautiful mortal as she takes control, pleading with me to save her. I observe her with renewed interest.

"You harm her," the sheriff growls at my back. "I don't care who you are. You will suffer."

Earlier, I removed the contacts to manipulate the human minds. Now they brighten with irritation at being threatened, and a soft radiance illuminates the cell.

"You dare threaten me? Over a human?"

"She's more. Can't you feel it?"

Yes, actually, I can. But it surprises me that the young werewolf can as well. "No harm will come to the mortal." I step into the sheriff's space. When the wolf refuses to back down, it earns him a smidgen of my respect. "This I vow, pup."

Drake nods at my declaration. A promise from an immortal is a binding, unbreakable contract.

If I fail, I fear an all-out war with the werewolves.

I shrug. If Troy cannot restore Kleora, the distraction of warfare, to appease the beast, will be just what the doctor ordered.

Kleora's soft voice picks at my conscience. 'Don't let him suffer, Jagorach. Make him forget.'

Goddamn her.

"How old are you, Drake?" I ask through clenched teeth.

"A hundred and fifteen. Why?"

The second his gaze lifts to mine, I snag his mind. "You will not remember coming back to the precinct. Instead, you cut your trip short due to weather and went home."

The sheriff fights my control. His gray irises bounce to the woman. I stride closer, slipping my palm to the side of his neck. Drake jolts at the contact, focusing on me. Damn, his skin feels like a raging furnace.

"According to your deputy, an unknown perp robbed the bank and got away. Do you understand?" The wolf's jaw clenches as he struggles against my influence. I push harder. "Do you understand?"

The tension in the bulky shoulders ease. Drake nods. "Yes. I understand."

I slip the folder from his grasp, even as my snarl of defiance at my mate's influence rumbles in my chest. I loathe her manipulation over my decisions.

"One more thing," I impart with a wicked grin. "On your next vacation, you will feel the urge to go to Devil's Lake. Find the best steakhouse in town for dinner. When a blonde with striking blue eyes walks in and looks at you, seduce her. Do not rest until you have fucked her into the middle of next week."

Take that, Kleora.

Chapter 33

Jagorach

The new possession/holding room is clean and shiny, having never used it yet since moving into our new headquarters. Seeing it, Mammon thrashes against the spelled bindings.

As soon as we left North Dakota and landed at Realm Command Center, the Prince of Hell was having none of it. With no choice, I bound Gemma's wrists with the mystical shackles to contain the demon.

If the sheriff witnessed her shackled, her delicate skin chaffed from the restraints, the wolf would blow a gasket. Maybe I should have left his mind intact and let him accompany us. A violent sparring match with the young pup could have distracted my mind from the coming liberation of my female's soul.

"Where am I?" Gemma croaks. No doubt her throat is raw from Mammon's bellowing to be free.

"Do not worry, human," I reassure, easing her into the iron chair centered in the room. "Soon, you will be home and will remember none of this."

"Where is the sheriff?"

I glance at her in amazement. Not only was the young mortal fighting a Prince, but she was also cognizant enough to recall the surrounding people. This exorcism might be a tad more difficult than I first hoped.

"The sheriff released you into my custody, Gemma. I am going to remove the demon possessing your body."

"It forced me to do horrible things," she whimpers as tears gather in the sapphire depths. "I stole, not caring who I hurt to get what it wanted." Her eyes widen. "Oh, God. I… it made me rob a bank."

"None of that was your fault, and soon you will not even remember what happened."

"I'm a good person," she cries. "Why me?"

The big blue irises beg me for an explanation. Unfortunately, I do not have the answer. Why did Mammon choose this particular human? The wolf was correct. There is something different about the mortal. Did the Prince sense her subdued power percolating below the surface? Does the woman have some cognitive ability that the demon recognized could possess the strength to contain him?

"Are you psychic, Gemma?" I ask.

"No," she responds, surprised by the question. "I'm a reporter for a small local newspaper, nothing more. My fiancé must be out of his mind with worry."

So, she is engaged. Delightful. That piece of information was not in her folder. I would love to witness the sheriff's reaction when he discovers the woman who struck him dumb belongs to another. It should make for an intriguing meeting.

"We will have you home in no time," I reassure her. "Please relax and allow me into your mind." I kneel and secure the shackles to the arms of the chair.

She struggles. "What are you doing?"

"This is for your own protection. The demon inside you is powerful and does not wish to give up your body. He may hurt you in retaliation, and I promised the sheriff I would keep you safe."

At the mention of Drake, the human settles, a resigned but wary expression on her face. "I want to go home," she whispers.

"And you will, but you must trust me for a little while longer. Can you do that, Gemma?" Her full cooperation is paramount for this to work. If she fights me, Mammon could tear her apart.

"What's your name?" she surprises me by asking.

I peer up at her for a second as I continue binding her to the chair. "Jag," I reply. No need to give her my actual name. As the little Valkyrie Alex is fond of saying, 'She would freak the fuck out.'

"Well then, Jag, since I want this damn thing out of me, I guess I have no choice but to trust you."

I grin at her tenacity. "You are resilient, young Gemma. I see now why Mammon picked you to become his vessel."

"Mammon is the demon inside me?"

"Yes. A formidable Prince of Hell." No reason not to tell her the truth. When this is over, she will remember nothing.

"And you're confident you can get the bastard out of me?"

"Yes."

"Then what are you, Jag? Your eyes are red, and you possess the ability to cast out a powerful demon." She watches me, her blue stare clear and direct.

Well, since she asked... "I am Lucifer," I state matter-of-factly, studying her expression.

She snorts but quickly sobers when she realizes I am serious. Her eyes widen, and genuine terror clouds her countenance.

"Do not fear me, little one. I have no interest in your soul."

Most humans assume that when confronted with a demon, we will seek to suck out their souls. And while it is valid for my soldiers of old, nowadays, mortals destroy their lives all by themselves to end up in Hell.

"I don't believe in the Devil," she informs me. "Or God."

A red glow lights up her face, and she gasps. Her eyes, the size of saucers, drop to my mouth as my lethal fangs descend, and she yanks against her bonds when my wings rip through my shirt to fan out into the room.

I would never show her my complete form. It could fracture her delicate mind, but I display enough to prove my point.

"What about now, Gemma?" I ask, using my demonic voice. "Do you believe now?"

"Oh. My. God," she whimpers.

There was a time her fear would have pleased me, ramped up my lust even. I would have played with her terror, forced her to kneel before me, and pledge her undying devotion in order to save her life. But ever since Kleora, those types of antics no longer interest me. The only being to own my passions is the petite land nymph with irises the color of a lush forest.

"Shall we begin?" I ask, putting away the elements of who I am.

"Shit." The woman's breath hiccups and a lone tear slips down her cheek.

I dry the moisture with my thumb. "You have nothing to fear from me, human."

"I never thought I'd need to put my trust in the Devil, but I want this thing out of me. So, yeah, let's do this."

Brave girl. I like her.

When she settles back into the chair, I place my palm on her forehead and lower my lids. Mammon senses my intent and thrashes around, jerking the mortal's wrists against the bonds.

I ignore his futile attempts and chant the ancient spell to exorcise a demon.

"NO!" Mammon bellows as his struggles increase. "Please, Lucifer. Let me have her. She is a perfect match for me."

When I do not respond, he forces the human's body to bow, so I place my other hand on her chest to keep the bastard from breaking her back.

"Wait," he pleads, his voice hellish in his desperation. "I know why this human is different. I can help you."

Even though his comment garnered my attention, I shrug. "Why?"

"Do not cast me into Hell, and I will explain," he bargains.

"Give me more, and I might consider it. But, right now, you offer me nothing."

"She has a connection to the vampire queen."

What the...? Last thing I expected him to say. "Connected how, Mammon?"

"Release me, and I will tell you."

"I could torture you in Hell for the information." I shrug and place my palm back on the human's forehead.

"You know I will never break. I fucking get off to your torment," he moans knowingly. "The more extreme, the better."

Dammit. He is right. Mammon is my age. If there were a true death, he would take it and relish the agony of getting there. The bastard is the Demon of Greed. He salivates for any and all extremes. Like Mogrun, right until I ripped his manhood from his mutilated body.

I call his bluff. "Then let us play, Mammon. You have always had the tightest ass of the six. I will enjoy ordering it ripped to shreds," I lie, sensing his accelerated lust at my words even as he debates his options.

"Fine," the demon grumbles.

What Mammon informs me blows my mind. This vital information ties my destiny tighter to Nicole and the vampires. To all immortals, in fact. Not sure she will jump for joy or skewer my balls with this knowledge.

When Gemma rears up and clamps her mouth over mine, I freeze. Soft lips, along with her tongue, caress the seam of my closed mouth.

I gain my senses and am about to pull away when awareness sweeps over me.

It cannot be.

I jerk back and stare in dismay over the possessed human's head. Fire skirts along Kleora's skin. A burning storm in her livid gaze.

Chapter 34

Kleora

Oh, my God. How could he? Less than a week since our passionate, erotic, boundary-pressing session, and he's already in the arms of another woman, shackled and at his mercy.

Pain explodes in my chest. Fury spreads fire throughout my body, igniting my skin. I don't perceive the intensity of the flames, only the pungent, searing sorrow of his betrayal.

The king stands, his arms outstretched like he wants me to settle down. Calm down? Calm down? I don't even comprehend what that means right now.

"Kleora. It is not what you think."

Of all the asinine things to spew out of his mouth, that's the best he can come up with? It's not what you think? Really?

"Is this a new form of punishment, Darath?" I ask, sarcasm dripping from every syllable, disguising the hurricane of agony underneath. "You couldn't torture me enough physically, so you move on to another?"

"Is that what I did, Kleora? Torture you?" A spark enters his red irises. "Your safe word would have ended it at any time. You know that."

Stop being so damn logical. "What I know is I've discovered you making out with another woman, restrained and ready for you to torment."

"Jag?" the woman murmurs seductively. "Get rid of the bitch so we can continue. My pussy weeps for your cock again."

"Shut up, Mammon," Darath warns with menace.

Oh God. Pain sears my soul.

Deep down, despite what I'm seeing, my heart prayed he had a reasonable explanation for why he had his tongue down another woman's throat. The woman's comments play on repeat through my mind, lighting the fire into a blazing inferno.

"Kleora, let me explain. She..."

I block out everything—his pleading face and the lush lips emitting lies. All I see is the woman's foot reaching out to run along Darath's calf enticingly. A scream builds in my mind. '*How could he? How could he?*' chants through my brain, squashing all else.

I've got to get out of here. If I look at them a second longer, I will kill them both.

"I'm going home," I inform him. "If you discover a way to restore my life before my body disintegrates, I will return." How can I sound so calm when I'm wailing in agony on the inside? "If I do not hear from you in two days, I'll know you failed."

"Do not leave like this, Kleora. Trust me. Give me a chance to explain. I vow it is not what you are imagining."

"He's right," the mortal chuckles, never taking her enamored observation from Darath. "It is so much more. The things he relishes doing to my body satisfy his inner Devil so much more than you ever could. He said as much."

Darath hauls off and backhands the woman across the face. "You will pay for this, Mammon."

The deranged female laughs, spitting blood. "Oh, baby. Yes. You know what I like."

Bile rises in my throat at the level of brutality Darath enjoys. He's been holding back this whole time, giving me little love paddles across my butt when what he truly requires is the kind of violence I will never allow.

I swallow to keep from vomiting across the floor. The fire that ignited across my skin in my rage sputters at his utter betrayal. Defeat slumps my shoulders.

"Peach. You cannot possibly believe this of me?" he states with a quiet intensity that should've alerted me, but the shock spreading throughout my body overshadows everything.

"Like you always say, you're the Devil. *Nothing* is off the table."

"You believe acts of violence against human women is my thing?"

I hear the shock and hurt in his inflection, but I can't reason beyond my own pain. "I don't know what to think!" I yell before conjuring my bow with a bolt already knocked into place. But instead of aiming at my mate, I aim it at the vile human shackled to the chair.

If I can't have him, she certainly will not.

"No!" Darath traces in front of the woman, protecting her from my arrow. "Stop this, Kleora!" he orders, but all I see is the proof he cares enough about this human to shield her. From me.

I refocus my aim on him. "You've hurt me for the last time."

"Kleora." The crimson irises regard me with a penetrating intensity, the muscles tense and ready.

Instead of letting my missile penetrate his heart, giving him a small sample of the giant hole in mine—I disappear.

The instant I materialize in my private chambers in my home realm, I sink to my knees, throw my head back, and roar my agony to the ceiling. Tears burn my eyes but never drop to the floor, and it only increases my suffering.

I've never felt such anguish. The ache in my chest spreads through my soul. I'd rather endure another week in Hell than suffer this one more minute.

Since I can't pound the floor in my translucent state, I wrap my arms around my middle and rock back and forth as my body shakes with dry sobs.

How could he do this? With a human of all things. I had no delusions—or I thought I didn't—regarding Darath's passions. He is a sadist. Enjoys doling out punishment, perpetuating pain, followed closely by pleasure.

Nothing in our experience prepared me for tonight's revelation. He doesn't merely enjoy a swift spanking or flogging. No, he gets off on inflicting violence. It was evident when he backhanded that woman shackled to the chair.

How in God's name did I miss this aspect of him. He never once gave me more than I could handle. Our time together was never about cruelty. It was Dom/sub play. And even though his punishment in the last session hurt—the pain was more emotional than physical. I damaged our fragile bond, and he needed me to understand, to face the consequences of my betrayal. To him. To us.

Looking back, I realize the tender aftercare was absent. The intensity and passion were there in full force, but disconnected in a way he'd never been before. He was cold. Angry.

Underneath, I felt his disappointment, pain, and sadness regarding my lack of faith and trust in him. But maybe I projected my guilt onto him. My emotions became his even though in reality he had none.

How did I misjudge him to such a grievous extent?

By the time my door bursts open, I possess no clue how long I've lain collapsed on my side, hovering over the floor, hugging my knees to my chest as I stare unseeing at the wall. My screams dried up—like my heart.

"Tanagra?"

I recognize my young page's voice somewhere by my feet, but I remain motionless. Nothing matters but the darkness consuming my soul.

"How are you here, my lady?" Liana asks.

I don't even twitch at the tingle sparking when she reaches out to console me, her fingers passing through my shimmering frame. The sensation is microscopic compared to the suffering raging through my body.

Liana gasps, easing back and leaving me blissfully to my misery.

Weeks pass as I lay huddled on the floor until I sense Sabrina's presence in front of me. Okay, it's probably not weeks, more like a day, but in my heart, it seems like a decade. Why hasn't my soul blasted back into Hell? Berk said after an hour I would blink from existence. Was that a lie? Was it Berkonnan who set my timetable and drew me back, and now that he's dead, I'm free to roam the earth?

"My lady. What happened? Did King Darath hurt you?"

Hurt me? He obliterated me.

"You must get up. You haven't moved in two days."

"Leave me be, Sabrina," I mutter.

Time has no meaning. At some point, I should get up, put on my big girl pants and deal with my situation. Later. Right now, if I was alive, my pulverized heart would struggle to beat.

"I cannot, Kleora. The whole of the Demon Realm camps outside our borders."

"What!?" I shriek, vaulting off the floor.

How the hell did he find our domain? For centuries, magic has concealed our region, making it undetectable to humans and immortals alike.

"I've positioned our Walkers in the hidden bunkers to monitor the situation, but it appears the Demon King utilizes a powerful witch. They are attempting to bring down our concealment spell."

Fuck. Fuckity Fuck! How's that for foul language, King Darath? Fury ignites my skin, and Sabrina steps back with a gasp.

"The red-eyed fucker is so dead." Even though my flesh is on fire, my tone drips with ice as I conjure my quiver and bow and prepare to end my mate's cheating ass once and for all.

Chapter 35

Jagorach

After Kleora disappeared, I traced to my Hell chamber. With a sinking heart, I realized she had not returned there. Home meant her home.

"Goddamn it," I growled. Time was of the essence, and I did not have time to track down her hidden region.

The second Sabrina shoved her ultimatum down my throat, I assigned Dzun with the task of locating the mysterious territory. Unfortunately, he was not any closer to finding it.

Fury warred within me, battling the immense hurt working to overtake it. The little hellion misjudged the situation and me. An agonized groan rumbled through my chest at the hurt and betrayal in my mate's smoldering gaze. She genuinely believed me capable of such violence on a woman. Granted, the evidence was damning, but I thought she knew me better.

What must she be going through thinking she submitted to such a vile creature? Self-loathing is no doubt a massive component of her emotions. As well as heartache at my assumed betrayal.

And what about her talent to engulf herself and the surroundings in flames? The first moment I witnessed it, I wondered if Kleora always possessed the ability to conjure fire, or if this was a recent phenomenon since being imprisoned in Hell?

As I shoved my legs into the leather pants, panic settled in my gut. If we did not perform the spell tonight, I feared Kleora would become trapped in Hell for eternity. And while I would still be able to have her with me, the more time she spent down below would ultimately siphon away who she is, and I cannot allow that to happen. I love her too much.

Now, because of her lack of faith in me, she was once again MIA, gallivanting off to God knows where with limited means to find her. The entire task force waits at my Tucson residence to begin the ritual.

Rage rode my spine. Why did she not trust me? Her stubbornness could be her ultimate downfall. I pinched the bridge of my nose and contemplated my next move.

Forced to discover where my wayward mate's home is, I wasted precious hours. Dzun and I searched through every database, known ally or enemy who possessed any knowledge of the Land Nymph Domain. Nothing. Not a goddamn thing.

With a resigned sigh, I punch in Nicole's number.

"Where are you, Jag? We've been waiting for hours," she huffed.

"We have a slight problem."

"Of course we do. Why did I believe events would go smooth for once?"

Without wasting words, I explained what happened, glossing over the demon-possessed human and what I learned from Mammon. That was a story for another time. "Can you connect with her telepathically and inform her the spell is ready to go?" I asked.

"Give me a minute. Although I've never tried to communicate with a soul before," Nicole informed me with an irritated sigh.

I shared her frustration. My impatience grew as I waited to see if Nicki could indeed communicate with my naughty mate. When I get my hands on her, I will beat her ass a bright red that turns the darkest of purples. After I explain the misunderstanding, of course.

"I can't reach her there."

Fuck.

"Is Sabrina with you?" I asked hopefully. "She could discover if Kleora is there and bring her to the house."

"She hasn't arrived yet. Since their home is a secret, she refused to allow any of us to pick her up and teleport her here. Let me find out about her ETA. Hold on."

I clenched my fingers around the phone as my aggravation mounted. It creaked under the pressure as Dzun materialized in front of me. I placed my palm over the mouthpiece. "What now?"

"I might have a lead on the Land Nymph Territory."

I removed my hand. "Nicole," I barked into the phone.

"It appears the bitch is ignoring my calls and texts," she grumbled on the other end.

"Let me call you back." I hung up without waiting for her reply and focused on my commander. "Where?"

He walked over to the bed and unrolled a detailed map of the United States. A large red circle encompassed Northern Georgia. "We believe this is the boundary of their territory. Satellite images show its desolate forest with no roads or structures." He points again several miles outside the circle. "This was the meeting place with the new ruler, Sabrina."

"Why do you suppose this circled area is their Territory?" I asked with a lifted eyebrow and a spark of hope.

"It is the only uninhabited area large enough to conceal a thriving community." He circled the area with his finger. "According to Troy, a cloaking spell protects it, making it invisible to humans and immortals."

"Is it also a protective barrier? Similar to the one over the Vampire Stronghold?" I inquired.

"No. Not that we can tell. The camouflage is their protection. Even once we are inside the shield, we may not be able to see shit. They could be right in front of us, and we wouldn't know it until it was too late."

I would discern if Kleora was nearby. It did not matter how powerful the spell—my soul lit up when she was close.

"Gather the troops, Dzun," I directed, relieved to have a game plan and direction. "It is time to retrieve my disobedient mate."

The second we landed outside the circled area, my mate's presence hit me like a locomotive. I ordered the ten thousand soldiers to spread out and surround the vicinity. I had no desire to start a war with the mysterious nymphs, but her behavior warranted a show of force.

In the middle of a deserted forest, I stand motionless with my arms crossed over my leather-clad chest. My mate needs to understand the severity of this situation and my determination to get her back. She will sit down and listen to what I have to say if I have to strap her to a chair to do it.

"KLEORA!" I bellow, not sure if she can hear me, but I am confident her people have informed her we are here. It is only a matter of time before she shows up. In full combat gear, no doubt. I have lost track of how many times my mate has attempted to kill me.

I cannot sense any nymphs hidden in the forest, but I know they are there. Although they never reveal themselves. Their stealth mode is quite impressive. In this form, I would never suspect a flourishing community lived in front of me. Or lethal warriors hid mere feet from my location. If I transformed into Satan, however, no cloak in the universe would deceive me. I am hoping she has the sense to come to me and it does not come to that.

"Kleora!" I will continue to shout until she shows herself. "Do not make me come in there because I will drag your ass out by your hair, and war will erupt between our people."

A leaf does not rustle. No birds chirp. No creatures scurry. Proof the nymphs occupy and dominate the space before me.

"Is that what you wish, mate!" She cannot possibly desire combat, can she?

"What I want is you out of my life."

I hear the livid voice a second before she appears fifty feet in front of me. Flames engulf her spirit form, dancing along the leather combat attire. The jade irises glow bright, with twin flames flickering in their depths. A blazing arrow is notched and at the ready.

Damn, she is impressive. The Storm Walkers are legendary with their skill and prowess on the battlefield, but that was centuries ago. Besides training, I doubt the land nymphs have experienced war in quite some time.

"Then prepare to be disappointed, mate, because I am not going anywhere," I growl, never moving an inch.

"You no longer control me, King Darath. Go find another willing sap to kidnap and endure your special brand of violence."

"The world could burn. The sky fall, Kleora, but nothing will sever our bond. No matter how much you wish it so."

"I hate you." Her fierce whisper is full of venom.

"So you have stated," I respond with composure, even though my heart is breaking. "Allow me to explain, and if you still want me out of your life, then fine, I will walk away. But only after the spell to rejoin your soul and body is complete." Anguish spirals through my frame, and I tighten my thigh muscles to keep from dropping to my knee and begging for any morsel of her affection.

That will never happen. As the Demon of Pride, my legendary arrogance got me thrown out of Heaven. Yet, in all my millennia, it has not diminished one wit. It will be a cold day in Hell before I drop my defenses and solicit forgiveness for something I did not do.

"You would let me go?" she asks with suspicion.

"Yes." Never. "We have both done things to each other in this quest. I deserve a chance to explain."

"Why the show of strength, then?" she asks, pointing to the legion of demons fanned out among the trees.

"I want you and your people to understand I will do anything to right the wrong I inflicted on your soul. If that means I must take you by force so Troy can perform the spell, then so be it. It is your choice how this plays out."

She hesitates for several long seconds; her face an unreadable mask. "Fine." She lowers the bow. "But only you and Dzun may cross, and no matter the outcome, I want you to vow that you and your troops never reveal this location to anyone. If you do, the Demon Realm will understand genuine terror."

I almost smile at the threat. As lethal as the Storm Walkers are rumored to be, they are no match for me. No species on this planet can defeat Satan.

I appreciate the fact that Kleora is always looking out for her people. It is admirable. "Agreed." I nod, confident once I explain the situation, the land nymph will be back in my arms in record time. Then, we can get this damn spell behind us and move forward—namely, with a thorough spanking.

As Dzun and I cross the threshold, Sabrina rises from the earth where she had been hiding. My commander tenses, eyeing the warrior in her revealing attire with interest. She flicks a brief glance at him before turning her back and walking side by side with her ruler.

Every few feet, I sense another nymph hidden somewhere beneath the ground or above my head, concealed among the branches, but they remain invisible.

After about a mile in, Kleora nods to Sabrina, and she waves her hand. Wood and stone structures appear out of nowhere, dotting the landscape. Some placed high, the trees their foundations, with wooden bridges separating them.

It is like walking onto the set of Robin Hood as he prances alongside his merry men. Civilians step out of their homes as we pass, eyeing Dzun and me with wary curiosity. Their clothes appear handmade and of high quality.

In the distance, vast gardens filled with a rainbow of vegetables and herbs dot an open field. A diverse abundance of fruit and nut trees border the plot, their branches heavy with the coming harvest.

Cotton fields and vineyards cover the hillside on the left as far as the eye can see. Corrals and barns chock-full of pigs, cows, goats, chickens, and horses on the right.

It is impressive how Kleora's people live—utilizing nature in such a balanced way. A give and take. The land provides for their needs, and they protect and nurture the environment, their concealment spell protecting it from outside influence.

The village is peaceful and alluring. I could picture myself chopping wood, butchering a pig for dinner, or cultivating the gardens. Can you imagine the Devil living such a simple way of life? At peace with the world and in tune with nature?

It is comical. And yet, a yearning to do precisely that with my mate by my side burns through my soul.

When we climb the steps to a wrap-around porch attached to a sizable log structure, Kleora halts and indicates we sit in the rockers lining the verandah. I turn to Sabrina instead.

"Could you give us a moment alone? Maybe take Dzun on a tour of the village?"

The warrior narrows her electric blue glare but turns to her ruler for confirmation.

"It's alright, Brina. What King Darath and I have to say should be said in private. I'll summon you if needed."

The fierce Storm Walker pivots and stalks off the porch, not turning to see if Dzun follows.

"Thanks a lot," my commander mutters as he reluctantly trails the evocative female. I'd grin at his discomfort if my situation wasn't so dire.

"You have five minutes, Demon, before I take your head."

Chapter 36

Kleora

Mother Earth. Why is he so damn gorgeous? I force myself not to ogle him from the part of his luscious hair to the gigantic combat boots so I don't leap into his embrace and demand he make me forget everything. Then I remember the woman in restraints and the way her head snapped to the side when he backhanded her hard enough she spat blood.

My insides congeal with disgust and anguish.

The vile but good-looking beast leans against the railing, his fingers gripping the smooth round top. The black leather stretches around his chest, showcasing the perfection of his pectorals. Muscles bulge in his massive arms as he shifts. A warm breeze ruffles the ridiculously gorgeous hair, and the crimson irises study me with such intensity, I fidget in my seat.

Geez, Kleora. You hate him right now. Remember that. He cheated with a human, took his violence out on her. It doesn't matter if he's the only male in your whole life who's made you yearn for wicked, naughty things or made you feel alive when dead.

"Why is it every time we turn around, you are attempting to kill me, female?"

"Maybe because you do such despicable things."

He contemplates my response for several minutes, and my skin crawls with the urge to touch him, to bring my body alive.

"Mammon, the Demon of Greed," he begins, and I breathe a sigh of relief he didn't throw my vile shenanigans in my face, "possessed the woman shackled to the chair. He is a Prince of Hell who escaped because your secret excursions to the surface were opening portals."

I shoot him a sour look. Whoops. He went there. I refuse to let him turn this debacle around on me, or his tight ass is so out of here. I disclose nothing and stare him down.

His lips twitch, but he continues. "I took the human there to perform an exorcism and throw the wayward Prince back where he belongs." He leans forward, and I swallow at the fire in his gaze. "It was the demon who spoke, deceiving you into imagining more was going on, that the encounter was sexual. I assure you, it was not."

"You struck the woman across the face," I remind him. Possessed or not, she was still a fragile human—a victim to a demon.

Boy, do I relate.

"Yes. I should not have done that, but you believed his lies. I saw it in your expression, and he needed to shut the hell up so I could explain myself."

"You were locking lips with her when I arrived, Darath." Yeah, work your sweet ass out of that one.

"No, peach. It was not the human who kissed me. It was Mammon. His style of begging for release and causing mischief."

"The demon kissed you?" I scoff. "You expect me to believe that?"

"Why, Kleora? Were you jealous? Cause if you were, that would constitute a genuine emotion toward me."

Son of a...

I poke his sternum. "Tell me, Darath, would it bother you if I stuck my tongue into another male's mouth?" I ignore the low rumble in his chest. "Would the green-eyed monster rear its head, or would you like it? Are you into sharing? Maybe I should summon one of my previous lovers and we can give it a try."

He grabs my biceps, pivoting to shove my back against the massive log holding up the porch roof. I blink against the brightness of his irises. "Jealousy is too weak and pathetic of an emotion. If you dared touch another, I would strip the muscles from his body and relish in the taste of his heart. Then I would spank your beautiful ass so hard you could not sit down for a week. I. Do. Not. Share."

Oh wow! Okay. Like he decimated Mogrun for hurting me. My ass clenches at the mere thought of another punishment. I'm on board with both scenarios.

Wait. What? No, you're not. Jesus, Kleora.

"Then you know how I feel, Jagorach. I wanted to rip that human apart, limb by limb, for kissing the lips that belong to me."

"Peach," he groans, leaning into me. "You are all I think about every second of every day. No female, mortal, or otherwise, compares to you. I snatched your soul on its way to Heaven to keep you with me. What does that say about my devotion to you? My obsession with you?"

Well, when he explains it so perfectly, in that panty-wetting, deep growly voice, how could I believe otherwise?

"But you've never tried to bond with me. Why?" Viessa revealed I'm his weakness, but I desire to hear it from my mate's lips, to understand his thoughts and reasons.

On many occasions with this virial male, I've sensed the pull of the connection. Relished the primal desire to become one with this unique creature. But has he ever felt the same?

"You are a wraith, Kleora. It would never stick."

"Is that the only reason?" Please, please trust me with the truth, I silently beg.

"Yes."

Ouch. Okay, maybe I deserve that. I must earn his trust. And I will, with a great sacrifice.

"Is the human free of the demon now?" I ask, letting go of my questioning. My husky tone showcases the lust running rampant through my girly bits at his nearness—the sound of his voice.

"No. My mate required my attention first."

Aww, isn't that sweet? He put me above an exorcism.

The heat coming off his body is confusing my brain. Obviously, it wouldn't thrill me to see him go all beastie caveman and torture another to protect me. I snort. That would make me one sick, nature-loving, fire conjuring weirdo.

Which I'm not. At all.

Nor are my insides fluttering at the notion of what type of attention he's referring to. Like loving, kissy-kissy, I'm sorry type of treatment? Or pussy clenching, ass burning kind of attentiveness. Cause this nymph is on board either way.

"How did you find my domain anyway?" I enquire to distract myself from unzipping his jeans and running my tongue along that hard ridge evident in his pants.

"Peach." He grips my chin and lifts my gaze to his. "Have you not learned? I am Lucifer. My abilities and control are endless."

"So," I slide out from the erotic cocoon of his embrace and take several deep breaths of humid air before falling into translucence. "You didn't kiss the girl. You weren't performing sexual acts of violence on the human, and you gathered a huge contingent of your army in order to explain the situation. Is that about right?"

The sexy demon leans against the support with causal grace. His arms cross over his chest, a lopsided, orgasm-inducing grin on his face. "There's nothing I wouldn't do for my woman."

"That's becoming abundantly clear," I mutter, my contemplation falling to the wood planks of the porch. "And what about what I did? Am I forgiven?"

"Fat chance." He has the audacity to scoff.

Anger ignites in my gut as I glare at him. "You expect me to forgive you, but you're unwilling to do the same?" Why am I so quick to fury around this male?

"I did nothing requiring forgiveness." He straightens, stalking toward me, his expression heated. I forget myself and take a step back for every one of his strides forward.

"Are you kidding me?" He can't be serious?

"The incident with the possessed woman was not my fault."

Unbelievable. He truly is the Devil. Answers to no one with no accountability for his actions. Even though in this particular instance, it might be true. But still.

"And what about how you snatched my soul from Heaven? Any responsibility there?" I dispute, hands on my hips.

"It was rash," he shrugs with careless regard. "I admit it, but I do not regret it. Regret is a waste of energy."

I stare, open-mouthed. Rash? It was rash? Understatement of the millennium. My anger morphs into a rage, heating my insides. Without thinking it through, I haul off and slap him across the face. The sting in my palm is satisfying until I peer into the lethal regard of my mate.

Yikes. Probably not a smart move to bitch slap Satan.

Chapter 37

Kleora

His deep angry snarl garners the attention of several nymphs around the area. Two males bravely step forward to protect their queen, but I wave them off. I don't need rescuing. I'm a Storm Walker, for Pete's sake.

"You denied my soul entrance into Heaven. And not just for a little while. For. Fucking. Ever." My finger pokes at his hard chest, punctuating each word. "If your golden boy, Troy, can't pull this off, I'm doomed. You realize that, right? So for you to claim 'it was a little rash,' is a slap in my face."

I pivot, needing some distance, when his large palm grips my nape and spins me back to his chest. I dig my nails into the leather, frozen when his lips brush against mine. Expecting a full-on sexual assault on my body, I'm stunned by his gentleness as he folds me into his warm embrace.

"I did what I did because I need you, mate." His whispered admission in my ear causes shivers to dance along my spine and my hormones to sing their joy in a high falsetto. "Was it selfish? Maybe. But I make no apologies for it. I will never let you go. Ever."

His mouth devours mine, and I'm lost. With this male, all rational thought sinks into the earth. My mind concentrates on one thing and one thing only—his skilled hands on my body.

His kiss is pure dominance without an ounce of regret, matching his words. Darath believes with his whole being, selfish or not, that what he did was for the best. End of story. Period. It allowed us time together to explore our bond and passions. And woo doggie, has he explored my passions.

"Take us to your chambers, Kleora," he demands, suckling my neck in the most delicious way. "Or I will take you right out here in the open for all your people to witness."

Oh, exhibitionism. Kinky.

No. Bad girl, Kleora.

"My lady?" Sabrina's angry tone snags my attention. "Are you all right?"

Darath snarls in frustration but allows me to step back. My legs are rubber, but I clear my throat before facing my commander/temporary leader. "Yes, Brina. Everything is fine." I peer at my mate over my shoulder, needing to get control of this situation. "Please disperse your soldiers, King Darath. I will show up for the spell at the appointed time."

How in holy Hell am I conversing with such calmness when my insides quiver with a blazing inferno?

"No. Time is of the essence. We must leave now," he warns, and tingles race across my nape.

I swivel and face the one individual with the skill to control my body like a pro. He must understand I'm required here. While Sabrina has done an excellent job, my absence left many issues by the wayside. I should make sure she understands every aspect of ruling our people. In case I never make it back.

"No, King Darath. Responsibilities here require my attention first in case the ceremony fails."

"Peach." He grips my bicep hard enough to let me know he means business, but not so harsh it hurts. "You are never leaving my sight. If I must keep you chained to my side, so be it."

My insides clench at the idea of Darath restraining me. Chains, ropes, or handcuffs? Yes, please. Wait. Why was I objecting?

"My lord?" Dzun inquires from behind Sabrina, and her body tenses. "What are your orders?"

"That depends on my little mate's next move," he answers, never taking his intent regard from mine.

Well, this is a pickle. If I insist upon him leaving, the big brute will order his army to storm the compound without a single ounce of guilt. But if I back down, I appear weak in the eyes of my people. Or, option three, I yank the hidden dagger in my boot and stab the sexy beast in the heart. Again.

Yeah. I'm digging the third option.

"King Darath," I pronounce coolly, drawing on my centuries as queen, even though my insides are doing somersaults and cartwheels. "This is not your domain. You and your demons are trespassing on Nymph territory, and I have been generous long enough. Leave, or despite the treaty, I will have you removed by force."

With a snap of my fingers and a quick mental command, my hidden Storm Walkers converge on my location, their bows drawn tight, surrounding my home.

"Sire?" Dzun growls quietly, his irises bright.

Darath's nostrils flare. "Is this how you want to play it, Kleora?" The smooth texture of his tone is beguiling, and I don't detect any fury pulsing from him. Is he amused by my resistance, or is this the calm before the fatal storm? Excitement bubbles at the prospect.

Yup, I'm a masochist for sure.

The seven-foot demon appears to wait patiently for my reply, a cocky grin in place. I'm not foolish. His tense shoulders give him away. So I take a second to peer around. My lethal Storm Walkers stand ready to wreak havoc at my command. Several with murder in their gazes, others with displeasure at the demons' presence. While the rest watch me with hesitant curiosity, waiting to see what their ruler will do in the face of possible war. Will I cower and submit to the Demon King, or will I show my worth?

"This is your last warning, King Darath," I declare with more bravado than I'm feeling, but he gave me no choice. "Don't come into my territory and start pounding your chest, demanding I obey." In front of my people, no less. A hundred percent of the time, I will rise to the challenge. It doesn't matter if I'm merely a wraith.

"So be it," he states. Dzun conjures a deadly curved sword, seizes Sabrina around the waist, and presses the blade into her neck. The events happened so fast, I didn't even perceive the big demon moving, and where did that wicked-looking blade come from?

While I take a mere second to gawk at Dzun holding my commander hostage, Darath bends low and dumps me over his shoulder. What the... I lean up in time to see thousands of demons swarming the area.

"Do not kill anyone unless you have no choice," the asshole declares before shoving open the front door to my abode and striding in with me in tow.

"Kleora!" Sabrina bellows, fury riding her expression.

"Do not engage unless I give the order!" I holler right before the door slams shut. As furious as I am, I do not desire war with the demons. "You son of a bitch," I howl, pummeling his back with my fists. "Put me down. Do you have any idea what you've done?"

The sharp slap on my derriere surprises more than hurts. The thick leather pants protected my flesh. But for how long?

"I warned you, mate, but your stubbornness ruled your decision, and now you will face the consequences."

What on Mother Earth is he talking about? He barged in on my lands with a damn army. How else did he expect me to respond to such a threat? "I said I'd meet you there," I remind him.

"Mmm hmm."

"You're the one who should suffer the consequences, Jag!" I grind out and punch him wherever I can reach, not caring that I'm hurting myself more than him. It feels magnificent.

The demon strides down the hallway, opening and closing doors in search of what I assume is my bedroom. He ignores the hits I continue to rain down. At this rate, my hand will swell and fall off long before he finds his destination.

"Did you believe I would roll over and cower at your display of force? I didn't become the land nymph queen because I am a coward, you infuriating, diabolical, twit," I rant and rave, pounding on him for all I'm worth as the demon opens the last door, discovering my chambers. He's oblivious to my words and hits.

One second I'm hanging over his shoulder—the next, he's dumping me on my bed. Strong fingers grip my ankles, and without a word, he reaches for the zipper of my pants.

"Oh, no, you don't!" I shriek, attempting to slap his hands away, but he growls, pins my wrists above my head with one hand, and undresses my writhing form with the other.

What should have taken seconds takes several minutes as I increase my struggles, making undressing me more difficult. Good. If he hadn't acted like a domineering brute, forcing me to choose between my position of power and his, I might have removed them for him. But because he was once again an overbearing jerk, I'll make damn sure he works for it.

Darath flips me over and lands three hard slaps on my ass as soon as I'm naked. Oh shit, that hurt. I kick my legs and try to roll over. "Stop it, Jag. I mean it."

"Do you?" he answers, and I hear the anger in his tone. "I think you relish your punishments, pushing my buttons to solicit this response."

"Shut up." The comforter muffles my retort, but the original bully heard me and delivers several more smacks. My butt cheeks clench against the sting. Deep down, I realize he's right. I come alive with the pain of his discipline. Love how he dominates me, demanding I obey.

As a ruler, there is no way I will tolerate his aggressive nature outside of the bedroom.

And I'm damn well gonna have that conversation after my lover is done punishing me. So let the colossal beast have his moment. Who am I to deny my mate? Or myself.

Chapter 38

Kleora

"I loathe you," I throw out for good measure as his palm continues its delicious torture, alternating from one cheek to the other. It's all I can do not to raise my ass for more.

"Hate me or not," he utters as if he's in agony. "You will never leave my side. Your rebellious nature overrides your common sense."

Yes. I moan mentally. No, wait. What did he say to me? He can't be serious?

"You jerk." I renew my struggles, even as the fire in my butt spreads right to my clit. "I'm a queen, you pompous ass. I don't need you playing all caveman over me."

"Tell me, Kleora," he rumbles low. "Do you enjoy your spankings?"

"No." I freaking love them.

Another strike, and this one hurt twice as much as the others. "Ow! Goddammit."

"Do not lie to me," he barks. Another resounding slap brings tears to my eyes and floods my core with wetness.

"And you wonder why I fucking try to kill you every chance I get?" I grind out, still in denial.

"It is not because you hate me, peach. It is because of the war within you." His large palm rubs the sting away.

"What in goddess are you talking about?" Distract him, Kleora.

"Deep down where you refuse to examine, you crave my dominance. Your sexual proclivities lean toward masochism. You thrive on pain with pleasure and your cunt weeps from my anger and wicked comments."

Oh no. How is it he understands my inner needs better than I do? "No." I shake my head, squeezing my eyes shut against the lie. "You're wrong."

Darath slaps my ass twice more. "Your pussy tells another story. It drips with your need for more. For what only I can give it."

Shit. How can I keep denying what is so blatantly obvious to him? My face heats with embarrassment. "Fine. I do like it."

"Good girl," he coos, rubbing the sting away. "Do you crave more?"

No way I'm admitting that I indeed want more. Lots more. My body trembles with the need to hear him call me his whore. To spank my pussy into submission. A vision of him forcing me to crawl to him, his collar branding my neck, consumes my thoughts. What the goddess is wrong with me?

Instead of admitting the truth, I grumble, "No." Sure enough, another loud, hard smack. I press my lips together, refusing to humiliate myself by confessing all the shameful things I lust after.

"Oh, Kleora. Are you certain that is your final answer?"

Mother of pearl.

If I lie again, the sadistic fiend will intensify the punishment. Not that I would mind. But if I spew out the truth—that the burn from his strikes makes my clit throb and my insides clench with an impending eruption—I'm admitting a fatal flaw. A weakness.

"Yes, Master. I want more." Sweet Mother. Did that breathy confession come out of my mouth?

"Peach," he groans, kissing my shoulder. "I would gladly grant your every wish." Darath's grip on my wrists disappears. "Get on your hands and knees. My little slave requires a thorough spanking."

I don't hesitate, as eager anticipation flutters through my gut. When his large palm connects with my flesh again, I allow the moan freedom, unable to conceal my need any longer. This is my happy place. Where I find release from whatever shit we've faced every day since my death. My heart is at peace when I'm with my male. We complement each other to perfection.

Do we argue? Heatedly and often. Is he an overbearing, malicious sadist? Yes, but I'm a stubborn, compassionate masochist. We're opposites in every way, but somehow, we work.

"Goddamn, you are beautiful," he moans after delivering a dozen or more smacks. And when Darath's tongue swirls my puckered hole, I nearly detonate, gripping the comforter to control the building storm.

"I relish every single inch of you," Darath groans before flipping me over, spreading my legs and devouring my soaked pussy. He sucks, licks, and nips as deep, hungry groans emanate from his throat.

King Darath eats pussy the same as he faces everything else in his life, with complete and utter devotion, ensuring I receive the greatest pleasure. As the recipient, I revel in the thrill of the ride, waiting with bated breath for the final plunge into nirvana.

Two thick fingers slide inside as my mate gently sucks on my clit with a steady rhythm that soon has me keening low, my muscles tensing.

"That's it, baby. Come for me," he demands before setting back in like he senses how and where his talented mouth will drive me insane. Within seconds, the roller coaster of sensations plunges me over the edge. I'm weightless, soaring, crying out Jag's name and gripping fistfuls of his glorious hair, shamelessly grinding my convulsing sex against his face.

Holy Mother of God. That was beyond intense. I crave more.

I tug on his hair, indicating I desire him on top of me. Darath sheds his leather pants and vest before settling between my thighs. He lifts one leg, planting my ankle on his shoulder. Then, with those scarlet eyes on mine, he enters my wetness with excruciating slowness.

"You are perfect, Kleora. Do you understand me?"

I dig my nails into his chest, glorying in the extreme stretching as he seats his enormous length to the hilt. "Yes, Master."

"I would destroy the world for you, love."

Before I can respond to those passionate words, Darath's hips withdraw and drive forward, filling me with such completeness I cry out, orgasming with the first thrust.

"Fuck, yes, Kleora. Your greedy cunt milks my cock to perfection," he pants.

The demon sets an unrelenting pace, lavishing attention on my aching nipples and breasts until he wraps my legs around his waist and his lips find mine. Instead of his kiss matching the aggressiveness of his hips, the king is gentle. He takes his time exploring every corner and recess, his tongue dueling mine until I moan from the sweet torture and another building eruption.

"Jagorach," I breathe into his mouth. "The things you make me feel. It scares me."

He leans back to peer down at me, his pace slowing. "Never be afraid when you are with me, Kleora. Of yourself or me, but most importantly, of how your body and mind respond."

"But what I enjoy seems so extreme and wrong," I admit, a blush stealing over my cheeks.

"The level you crave is a perfect match for my own. We match, Kleora. I require every dirty and taboo thought in your head. Do you know why?" He waits for the shake of my head before continuing. "Because I feed off of it. The raunchier the better. Shame is a wasted emotion."

I smile. "You say that about a lot of emotions."

"Let us relish every moment and shove the whole bullshit enchilada to the side." Then, to demonstrate, he rises to his knees, altering the angle, hitting the mind-numbing spot with each thrust. "You feel so fucking good."

The momentum of his hips increases, and I lose the train of conversation as my body vibrates, craving what only this demon can offer. When he reaches between us and pinches my clit, I skyrocket, crying out his name. My fingers dig into his thighs as sensations bombard every nerve, lighting them up like an electrical wire.

Darath's groan of release soon follows, and I stare up into the beautiful, heartbreaking face of an angel as he explodes. The irises shine brighter than I've ever seen them, the strong neck arches, and huge lethal fangs glisten with venom in the dim light.

A throbbing begins in the spot between my neck and shoulder, where his bite should be, and a pang of sadness tries to overshadow the joy of this moment. As long as I remain incorporeal, the mark of King Darath will never brand me. Not to mention, Lucifer will never allow another control over his actions.

We may wholly and thoroughly delight in each other, both possessive and jealous, but will we ever experience the psychic experience of bonded mates?

A crack splinters down the middle of my wildly beating heart.

"Jag," I sigh, brushing his long locks from his face. "Will you ever trust me enough to mate with me?" Oh shit. Why in the hell did you ask that, Kleora. Take it back! Take it back!

Darath's body tenses and his expression shuts down. My aching heart shatters.

"Kleora," he moans, pulling from me, and I feel the loss deep in my soul. "We can discuss this later." He rises and snatches up his pants, yanking them on. "Get dressed," he orders, his tone harsh. "We have a spell to perform so you may resume your life."

Resume my life? Why do I feel like that has a double meaning?

I conjure my clothes but remain seated on the bed, needing the support. "What does that mean, exactly?"

"You know what it means. You will live again. Rule your people as before."

The direct, in-your-face demon has difficulty meeting my gaze, and the truth hits me between the eyeballs. After the spell, he's letting me go. Why? It doesn't match up with his possessive, loving words of moments ago. Did he merely tell me what I wanted to hear in order to fuck me?

Humiliation burns a hole in my gut. Without Darath in my life, it stretches into a dim, bland wasteland, with no color or excitement. Yet as a woman of worth. I deserve his bite. I merit a complete mating. Not some fly-by-night, rock-my-world sexual experience. Although that would be icing on the cake.

No. Either he trusts me enough to mate with me, or I cannot continue like this. One, my heart would never survive it, and two, I refuse to subject myself to half measures.

He needs to leave. I can't think when he's near me. "I was serious earlier about needing to wrap things up with Sabrina and my people. I vow I will meet you there in an hour."

He considers me for several moments. No doubt trying to determine if I'm truthful. "Fine. One hour. I will leave Dzun to transport Sabrina when you're ready."

What I observe in his eerie depths destroys me. Grief and sorrow.

He is letting me go.

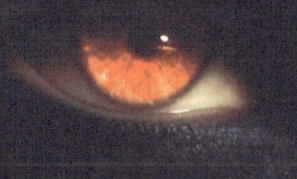

Chapter 39

Jagorach

I sense the second she enters the chamber, but I do not turn. "Where have you been?" My tone is hard. Angry.

After our 'Come to demon' meeting at her place, Kleora completely threw me by bringing up mating. I panicked. With every fiber of my being, I crave that connection with her, to delve into her innermost desires and emotions but the reality is, a bonded mate is never in the cards for Luci.

My only thought was to end the conversation before it went downhill. So I relented, and after forking over the address, I allowed Kleora thirty minutes to wrap her shit up and get to my house.

That was two fucking hours ago. My mind has been going crazy with what my little hellion could cook up now. Did my lack of commitment to mating hurt her enough that she would flee from me and the spell? Or does she have a side deal percolating with another Berk wannabe, another witch? I will rip their goddamn hearts out.

"Preparing for this moment," she says, much to my surprise.

I rotate, my vision feasting on my shimmering mate, her warrior outfit in place. The soft brown leather caresses her transparent frame. "You still do not trust in me or my vow to bring you back?" I bark out a bitter laugh before she can answer. "Of course you do not. That is your M.O., right? Your inability to depend on anyone but yourself?"

"You're correct. I don't trust easily, but neither do you." Her comments pierce my chest.

I push aside my impulsive need to rail at her. Tonight is not about us. It is about restoring her course back to the way it was before I dragged her soul to Hell. "Troy has the spell prepared. Are you ready to resume your life?" She hesitates, and I am taken aback. "Kleora?"

"Yes. Of course. I just... I want..." she swallows, her eyes downcast.

"What, peach? What do you want?" My knees nearly buckle when her head lifts. The lush lips tremble. The erotic jades shimmer with tears that never spill over. "Name it, Kleora, and I will lay it at your feet." My arms ache with the demand to cradle her, kiss away the hurt and anguish in her gaze and forgive... everything.

Am I still furious with her? Yes. Do I trust her enough to complete a mating bond? No. And that breaks my spirit more thoroughly than if she hated me. But, of course, it does not mean I do not prefer her happy. And if it is within my power to transform those tears into smiles, I would cut out my heart to make it happen.

"You, Lucifer. I choose you," she utters brokenly. My entire body stills, but I utter nothing. Instead, I watch her with a wariness that goes bone deep. "I forgive you for snatching my soul because I wouldn't have missed our time together for all the riches of Heaven or my life back."

She takes a tentative step toward me, the emerald irises pleading. For what I am not sure yet, but a spark of something ignited in my chest the second she called me Lucifer in that soft, loving tone. A name that strikes fear in most.

"One day, no matter what happens tonight, I pray you can forgive me for what I've done. You are the light in my darkness, Jagorach. The warmth that thawed my heart and brought me to life, despite everything between us." She swallows. "I love you. You own my soul until I cease to exist. But I understand if you can't trust me, can't get past the duplicity and damage I inflicted."

Every cell in my body is weeping for what could have been, for losing my one true mate. A loss instigated by my actions but sealed by her betrayal. If I were any other creature, and not the King of Hell, I would throw all caution to the wind and gleefully bind this incredible female to my dark soul.

I am the original demon—Lucifer. A fallen archangel with a role to play and his end already written. My inner beast demands I ease her sorrow and help her understand why I must let her go.

"You claim I am the light in your darkness, but I assure you, peach, it is the other way around. You bring me out of the darkness." I brush my knuckles down her cheek, bringing her to life and forcing the tears to fall. "But I cannot forsake who I am or the multitude of responsibilities on my shoulders. You are my greatest weakness, love. Every single minute of every day I will mourn your loss from my life."

"Please, Darath. Don't give up on me. On us."

"I have no choice, baby. The second we bonded, every creature in Hell would use you against me. You would never be safe, and I cannot allow that to happen. Promise me you will live a happy existence among your people, Kleora, away from all this death and destruction."

"Happy?" she asks incredulously. "I can't make such an oath, my love. Without you in my life, I cease to exist. So you might as well cast me back into the bowels of Hell and let the demons have at me because deep in my soul, if you're gone, my essence will rip to shreds."

"Kleora," I grit my teeth against the immense pain permeating my chest. "We can never mate. Not when it would put your life in peril."

"I'm not proposing we mate. As much as it would thrill me to have that connection with you, I understand why you can't take a mate. I respect your decision." She closes the space between us, placing her small hand on my heaving chest. "All I'm asking for is a chance at a relationship. An opportunity to prove to you I'm worthy of your trust and love."

"Kleora." My heart is near bursting with the tumultuous emotions crashing inside me. "It is I who is not worthy of you. To be with me comes at a high cost. We cannot have children. A family. My enemies would use them as leverage against me as my wife and child were. No soul completely bonded to mine will ever enter the gates of Heaven." I grip her shoulders in a bruising hold, hoping the pressure will make her understand the finality of what I am saying. "I will never request that of you."

"Even if I agree?" Sadness marks her question. Deep down, she already knows the answer.

"I refuse to damn you. In the end, Heaven is your destination. That's where you belong."

"You're the Devil. Be selfish. Accept it's my choice."

Oh, how I crave nothing more. But she would come to hate and resent me, and I could not bear it. The second she's reborn, our time together would be marked. Demons, eager for a chance at me, would seek her out, try to control her mind. Others would kidnap her to use as leverage for what they wanted—me. My kingdom. I do not wish her to look over her shoulder, wondering when the next attack will occur in order to be with me. She deserves more. My little peach warrants happiness.

And if we mated, my father would refuse her soul entrance. Hell will not become Kleora's final resting place. Heaven, with my father, is what she deserves.

"Come, Kleora." I hold out my hand. "It is time for you to resume your life." She stares at me for a long moment, and the desire to read her thoughts is a breathing entity in my mind.

When she finally places her palm in mine, relief and sadness pour through me. Sad. What a fucking inadequate word. More like despondent. Miserable. Heartbroken.

Well. As my lovely vampire queen is fond of saying: "Suck it up, buttercup."

You had a brief window of happiness to mourn over for the next century, Jag.

Son of a bitch. I have never been more eager for Armageddon and the end to begin.

Chapter 40

Kleora

A fortuitous numbness spreads through my body as I walk hand in hand with Darath. I hug it close like a long-lost friend, praying it keeps the shattering pain at bay.

The second we walk through the door to our waiting friends, I drop Darath's hand as if his skin scalded my own and move several feet away. The colossal idiot can't forgive or forget. He claims this separation is for my benefit, and maybe a sliver of that is genuine. But I fear the real reason Darath is pushing me away is for his own peace of mind.

The Devil doesn't trust me, and therefore it's easier to let me go than take a risk. Do I think he loves me? If Lucifer is capable of love, then yes, I do. He hasn't come right out and said the words like I stupidly did, but his actions speak louder than any declaration of affection.

I opened my heart to him, and he crushed it beneath his gigantic boot, claiming he's doing it for my benefit. Yeah, and I have a planet for sale at a bargain-basement price. I refuse to fight his belief. He wants to plunge us both into purgatory—I can't stop him.

My priority now is to get my reality back. Afterward... crap, thinking about afterward makes my soul tremble with grief. That word means my life will continue on without the dynamic, commanding presence of my mate, which at this point is unfathomable to me.

"Are you ready, Priestess Tanagra?" Troy asks, and I shiver at the soulless black regard.

My gaze darts to Nicole, the center of our lives. The reason we are all together, fighting for a common goal. Peace for all immortals. She offers a quick smile, rubbing her belly swollen with baby. The prophesied child.

"Are you okay, Kleora?" the vampire queen asks.

I give a jerky nod and scan the rest of the group. Sabrina holds by my side. I know beyond any doubt, she would defend me with her life, slaughter any who would dare to hurt me, even if it meant instigating a war or ending her existence.

Logan Moretti towers beside Nicole, regarding me with interest. I wonder if he's ever seen a wraith before? Next to him are his brother Sebastian and his mate Alex. The big shifter king, Kurtis Ruse, watches me with compassion, his arm draped over his queen, Lucretia.

Another vampire holds steady behind the vampire queen. By the mismatched irises, he must be Nox. I believe he was in the clearing by the cabin, but I remember little about that night. He's a large male, as most Guardians are, and quite beautiful. His watchful countenance shows him to be a warrior through and through.

The powerful Oracle is present with Liam Scott, the werewolf king, and I sag with relief. If things go south, at least Viessa is here to help.

This group of diverse immortals forged a strong friendship in the face of a common quest—fulfilling the prophecy. I'm proud to be considered a member of this task force and the Council of Unity.

Oh, God. I'll have to endure Darath's presence at the meetings. Damn it. How will I sit across the table from him and pretend my world isn't a complete, shattered mess without him in it?

Cross that bridge when you get to it, Kleora. Let's concentrate on getting my life back first.

"Shall we begin?" the witch asks.

"Yes." No! I mentally scream, keeping my gaze off the big male to my left with extreme effort. Instead, I allow the numbness to take over. My heart. My expression. My soul. It's the only way I will survive this.

Along the back wall of the room, splayed out on a raised platform, is my body. It's shocking to see the deteriorated state of my corpse. The skin is gray; the muscles atrophied. Small bald patches adorn my scalp, and my eye sockets sink into my skull.

Darath was spot-on. My time is running out fast. This needs to happen like right now.

"Please lay on the dais over your earthly frame," Troy instructs, and I swallow the anxiety threatening the back of my throat.

When I hesitate, Darath places his warm palm on my lower back. I tilt my head to stare into the crimson regard filled with remorse. "Events will work out as they should, peach," he tries to reassure me.

"No, King Darath," I mutter, the formal title like chalk in my mouth. "Things will never be the same."

His jaw clenches, but he escorts me to the platform. When his scalding grip closes around my waist to hoist me up, I nearly cry out at the exquisite torture of his hands on my body. I bite my lip to keep my emotions from bleeding through.

The second Darath releases me, I sink into the empty, withered shell of my essence, staring at the wood beams crossing the high ceiling. This is it. Don't panic. Don't panic. The chant runs through my mind repeatedly as the crew circles the table.

Troy steps to my head, placing his palms on either side of my body's skull.

"If you hurt her, I will rip out your innards and feed them to Dzun," my demon snarls at the witch.

"Lucifer, we are rejoining her soul with her body. It is going to hurt like hell."

"Thanks for the warning," I mumble.

When Darath reluctantly steps back into the circle between Nicole and Viessa, I take a deep breath and prepare for the worst.

"Brace yourself, Kleora Tanagra," Troy advises before shutting his lids and bringing forth his gray swirling magic.

I slam my lids shut and hold on for dear life, digging my fingers into the table that is somehow solid beneath me. The witch chants, the words growing in volume until they echo throughout the room.

Warm liquid seeps onto my forehead, neck, and chest. I raise my lashes. No, not my skin, my body's skin, but I feel it all the same. Is it working already?

The chant spears through my brain, spinning and building in intensity and volume. After several minutes, my head feels like it's about to explode, and I'm on the brink of screaming, gritting my teeth to keep it inside.

My body hums with every word as if the cells are vibrating and picking up speed through my system.

"Hold on, Kleora!" Darath shouts as the shaking intensifies.

I squeeze my lids tighter and let go of the fear of the unknown. I give myself over to the spell, allowing it to restore my life. The humming increases until my brain is a chaotic jumble. I can't remember who I am or why I'm even here. I let loose a scream.

The suffering has grown bigger than I can manage. Shrieks shoot up my chest and out of my mouth, seeming to go on forever. A pain like no other pain. My mind and body break.

Sobbing.

Screaming.

Agony.

Loneliness forever.

Jagorach… Jagorach… Jagorach.

My spirit rages in a way I've never felt before, overshadowing the complete destruction of grief in my soul.

The Devil. My Lucifer is my… everything, and with this spell, he's lost to me forever.

Rage flows through me, battling the swirling magic, coating my entire frame with dark sorcery and fury.

"She's fighting it," Troy grates out above my head.

"What? How?" Darath asks, a strained quality to his tone.

"No clue. But if she doesn't relax, the spell could do more harm than good."

A gentle touch on my shoulder shakes me to my foundation. "Kleora," the demon whispers near my ear. "Relax, my love."

His endearment eases the rage, and my brain forgets why I'm angry. My love. Yes. I am your love, Jag. The greatest love you will ever know, and you're letting me go. I want to shriek it from the rafters until I'm hoarse.

"That's it, Darath. Release your hand but keep talking to her," Troy commands, and the pain amplifies the second Jagorach releases his hold. I scream.

"Kleora. Listen to my voice, beautiful. Do you recall the night I took you to the Mountain Oyster Club in Tucson? You insisted it was not a date. You always lead me on a merry chase," he chuckles, and I want to weep at the sound.

I remember the upscale western décor of the private club. All I could think about was how much I wanted those incredible lips on my body. The Devil pulled out all the stops that night. He was charming, hilarious, and a wicked flirt. I relive every moment passionately.

Now, I'm lamenting the fact I didn't give in to his charms sooner. I could have enjoyed Darath's special brand of lovemaking for months before my death.

My death. Another jolt of agony fuses with my soul, and I arch my spine at the pain. Holy hell. I'm not sure how much more I can endure. Any second, my brain will shut down.

"Hang on, peach," Darath soothes. "It is almost over."

I shake my head. "Can't," I grit out between screams.

"Yes, you can, and you will. Do it for me, Kleora."

His tone carries that oh so delicious command that I respond to against my will. Even as the cells in my body erupt in agony, my mind clings to our evening in Tucson. I concentrate on every detail of the venue, of Darath, of my emotions. All of it becomes my focus.

That night is my lifeline from purgatory.

Chapter 41

Kleora

S *even months prior*
"Thank you for the lift, Sebastian," I say, stepping from the vampire's embrace to take in my surroundings.

"My pleasure, Priestess," he responds graciously. "If Darath gets out of line, you have my number. Shoot me a text, and I will come to the rescue and kick his ass."

The vampire's wink warms my heart. "I can handle King Darath, Sebastian," I assure him with more conviction than I'm actually experiencing.

"No doubt, my lady," he says before disappearing.

In truth, anytime I'm in the demon's presence, a delicious vibration sets up at the base of my spine. My body feels flushed and achy like I'm coming down with a fever. But since immortals don't get sick, I realize it's lust sparking inside, craving whatever devilish seduction this wicked brute has in mind.

As I skirt the huge bronze cowboy in the middle of the circular drive, I can't help but be impressed by the rustic elegance of the three-story brick structure with its arch entryways. The Mountain Oyster Club gives off a peaceful vibe that is both upscale and homey at the same time.

I adjust the silk shawl; glad I chose it at the last minute. The evening is mild, but the slight breeze has a hint of coolness skating over my exposed shoulders. The spaghetti strap, jade cocktail dress is a land nymph original and retails for $5,000. It's luxurious and silky, brushing against my bare nipples, which only worsens my drive.

As I step to the entrance, my strappy high heels with rubber bottoms—a loan from Jilaya— make no sound on the brick. Nerves jingle in my stomach. Darath wanted to come and get me himself, but I refused. That would classify this as a date, and I'm not ready to claim I'm dating the Devil.

Yet.

The seven-foot fallen angel is my mate. There's no denying that, and one day we will complete our bond, but until then, he'll earn every second.

When I step into the lobby area, the hostess greets me by name, which somewhat surprises me.

"Ms. Tanagra. Right, this way."

I follow the tall, willowy brunette as my gaze bounces everywhere at once. The décor is western-themed, but what catches my eye is the amazing artwork displayed on the walls. Beautiful paintings depicting Tucson's diverse landscape and wildlife. Cowboys on horses either working a ranch or riding through the mountain ranges that surround the beautiful city.

Bronze statues of mountain lions, elk, and deer, along with Indian heritage, adore side tables. And every piece is for sale. This private club must support local artists, showcasing their work for their patrons.

We walk down into an open area with large windows overlooking a magnificent courtyard with a curved step fountain. By the window, they set only one table for dinner, and that's when I realize I'm the only guest in the place. Did Darath rent out the entire restaurant?

The object of my musing ducks through an archway, striding for me with a purpose that sets my heart fluttering. I've never been a shy, simpering fool around the opposite sex, but with Darath, he makes all thoughts rush into the ether, and I struggle to catch my breath.

I stare with longing into the brown eyes. Wait. That's not right. Why are his irises brown instead of the enticing red that liquifies my insides?

"Thank you, Brenda," he says to the brunette. "Give us about thirty minutes before Andy comes to take our order."

"Of course, Mr. Darath."

Oh yes. This is a human establishment with mortal servers, hence the necessity for colored contacts. Kinda hard to explain blood-red irises.

As soon as we are alone, the demon king takes my hand and kisses the inside of my wrist, right over my rapid pulse. "You are stunning, peach."

His compliment warms me. "Thank you, King... I mean Darath." I glance around nervously, making sure no one overheard my blunder.

"Jagorach, please," he requests and pulls out a chair at the table.

"Of course. Jagorach." His name on my lips feels good, and my tense muscles relax. "I have spent little time among... humans over the last few years," I admit quietly, in case their hearing is better than I think.

"The staff here are discreet." He takes the seat next to me instead of across, and the high temperature of his body radiates out, warming my right side. "But they have a strict rule of no cell phone usage inside. So, put it on silent."

"Oh, how oddly refreshing," I exclaim as I reach into my jeweled purse to shut off my phone.

"It distracts from the peaceful atmosphere of the club."

"This is a member-only establishment?" I ask with curiosity.

"Yes. The building itself was built in 1936, but the club opened in 1948."

"I sometimes forget how young the United States is when compared to the likes of Europe and the Middle East."

"Indeed." Darath caresses my fingers lying on the white tablecloth, and a shiver dances along my arm. "You smell delicious, Kleora. I'd love nothing more than to remove your clothes and lay you across this table to feast on you for dinner."

Oh, my! He's bringing his A-game right off the bat.

"Sounds quite scandalous and a sure-fire way to get us arrested." I laugh and am proud my voice doesn't wobble. Inside, my nerves stretch taut, like I've held a drawn bow for hours.

"A bucket list event for certain, peach." His grin is pure wickedness, and dampness rushes my sex. "Sadly, I will have to settle for their wonderful filet."

"How did you become a member here?"

"It helps I possess persuasive powers," he says and hands me the menu.

"Ah, so you cheated," I tease with mock severity.

"I am the Devil, peach. I always cheat."

I laugh. "Good to know, Jagorach. Good to know."

The next few hours were the happiest I'd ever experienced. Darath pulled out all the stops, seducing me with touch, heated stares, and scandalous conversation. In all my years, I'd never enjoyed an evening out more. Among humans, no less.

At the end of the night, as the demon king transported me to my friend's home in Georgia—since I'm required by law to keep the Land Nymph Domain's location secret—so many conflicting emotions electrified me.

I craved King Darath with a fierceness that stunned me, but was also apprehensive about the fact he was the Devil. Not merely the earthly demon ruler, but the King of Hell. Right, wrong, or otherwise, a small part of me, the component infused with a moral compass, had a hard time getting past the element my mate was none other than Lucifer. The archangel who defied God and fell from grace. How could the fates be so cruel as to align me with such a creature?

Before he turned to leave me on Jilaya's doorstep, the sexy brute leaned down and brushed those amazing lips across mine. Tingles scattered the surface, and I couldn't help myself. I gripped his suit jacket, keeping him within reach, and slid my tongue over the fullness before gently biting down.

The king groaned. "Kleora," he breathed into my mouth, his signature scent of sandalwood and fire filling my nostrils.

"Goodnight, Jagorach," I whispered before turning to the door.

"You are enough to bring the Devil to his knees, female."

I grinned at him over my shoulder. "All in due time, King Darath. All in due time."

Chapter 42

Jagorach

"Why is this taking so fucking long?" I bark at Troy. "She cannot take much more."

The glow from my irises filled the dim chamber in an eerie blood red, and my fangs descended with Kleora's first scream of pain. Now, I fight the change with everything I have, but the King of Hell will make an unwanted appearance if the witch does not end her suffering soon.

"It should've worked by now," Troy grits out. Sweat drips down his temples, and his arms shake with the effort to maintain the spell. "She isn't feeling anything. Her mind has escaped elsewhere."

"Not making us feel any better, Tenebris," Nicki grumbles. "Can you do this or not?"

"Maybe we should join hands or something," Alex offers, her concerned contemplation remaining on my mate, who is lying prone on the platform.

"Unless you practice dark magic, it will not help," Troy says.

"I have in the past. What can I do?" I offer. The helplessness drives me crazy.

"Unfortunately, when you touch her, it has the opposite effect on her soul that I require for this spell." His answer pisses me off, but I clench my hands at my side to keep from ripping the witch's throat out.

After another twenty minutes of the black scrutiny flickering, the ancient dialect swirling, and Troy's inky power clouding Kleora's head, the most powerful witch I have ever met calls it quits.

He drops to his knees, exhausted from almost two hours of attempting the impossible. No, goddamnit. I promised Kleora I would make this right. That I would restore her life to her body, and she would live again.

I failed.

A deep, sorrowful roar echoes around the chamber. I realize the sound is coming from me as I fight the change and the immense agony eating away at my black heart. If I were to alter my form in this small room, I could severely injure my friends. Even the shifters are not immune to the power of the Devil's transformation.

A cool hand folds into mine, ceasing my internal struggle in an instant. I glance down in confusion. Viessa, her bright gaze studying me with serious intent, grips my fingers tightly. She controlled Satan.

"How did you do that, Oracle?" I inquire in awe.

"Uncertain, King Darath. But I needed you to calm down, and when we touched, you did."

"Your father, Icarus, was a powerful being, but you, my dear Tri-bred, possess twice his strength. Is there nothing you can do to restore Kleora?"

"I'm sorry, Darath. It is forbidden for an Oracle to go against God's laws."

"Even though I defied him by snatching her soul to begin with?"

"I'm sorry, but I cannot bring her back."

"Icarus brought Nicole back to life," Kurtis argues.

"Yes." She turns to the shifter king. "Queen Giordano lost her unborn child, and my father lost his life because of his defiance. With the prophesied king in the queen's belly, is anyone willing to take that chance again?"

The circle of friends lower their lashes, shaking their heads. As much as they love and adore Kleora, none of them would risk Nicole or her baby to save her.

The Oracle shifts back to me, and dread fills my entire being. I want to slap my hand over her mouth before she utters what I have feared since the second I took Kleora.

"Do not say it," I snarl.

"You must let her go, Jagorach." The sorrow in her expression ramps up my ire. "Allow me to transport her soul to Heaven, and Sabrina to bury her body as she requested so she and her people can find peace."

I peer over at Sabrina. The new ruler of the Land Nymphs scrutinizes every word and move. No doubt she will attack if I do anything she deems unworthy of her friend and former queen.

No way. I cannot let her go. "Bury her body however you see fit," I say, directing my comments to Sabrina. "But her soul stays with me."

"Jagorach," Nicki chimes in, and I swivel to glare at her. She does not back down. In fact, she steps into my personal space. I have always admired her fearlessness, but tonight, it fuels my rage. "You'd prefer your mate's soul to spend an eternity in Hell than gift her a chance at Heaven?"

My fury fizzles as if she doused the flames with a bucket of ice water. Goddamnit. She is right. I said as much to Kleora mere hours ago. What kind of mate would I be if I condemned her for my own selfish reasons? An unworthy one, even if I am the Prince of Pride.

I lower my lids against the pain spreading like cancer throughout my body. This was not how I envisioned it would end. I arrogantly believed the laws of nature would obey my command. That I would restore Kleora's life, and we would discover happiness together. My pride refused to accept any other outcome.

"Luci," Nicki murmurs. "If there was another way to save your mate, I would travel to the ends of the earth to find it. But Kleora's time has run out, and you must do right by her."

"How can you expect such a thing? Would you let Logan go, or would you keep his soul with you and damn the consequences?"

She swallows, her gray focus landing on her warrior for a brief moment. "Well. I'm a damn the consequences kind of girl anyway, so yeah, I'd bind his soul to my own."

"Damn straight you would," Logan growls, and the vampire queen's lips twitch.

"Someone needs to decide, and fast. This spell has sped up the decay in Kleora's body," Troy informs us after having gained his feet. "I can link her spirit to yours."

"Not happening," Sabrina pipes in and takes a stance between Kleora and me. Wrong move, land nymph. "Priestess Tanagra would never want that." Her direct blue stare lands on Viessa. "Take her to Heaven where she belongs, and I will bury her body at home like she wished."

My claws extend, and a deep, angry rumble vibrates up from my chest. Sabrina draws her sword, prepared to fight to the death to honor her friend's desires. But all I see is her standing between me and what is mine.

Logan snatches Nicole from my side, shoving her behind him. "Think this through, Darath," he warns. "You do not want to start a war with the Land Nymphs. Kleora would not want that."

I ignore him. "Get the fuck out of my way, bitch." My voice is the stuff of nightmares. The deepness reverberates around the room, saturated with demonic aggression and fury.

"Jag?"

The soft melody of my mate halts me as effectively as any binding spell. Sabrina wisely steps to the side, and jade irises brimming with tears meet mine.

"It didn't work?" she asks, sitting up away from her body.

"No, baby. It did not." I take a step closer. "I failed you." My previous fury vanishes, replaced by agony so penetrating it amazes me I have not burst into flames.

"You tried. That's all that matters."

"No!" I bark out, making everyone in the room jerk in response. "You do not get to forgive me. Your situation is my fault. I am a selfish, demented bastard who does not deserve your forgiveness."

"Damn straight," Sabrina mutters, earning a glare from Alex.

"Quiet, Brina," Kleora orders, and the warrior lowers her gaze to the floor. My mate glances at her decaying corpse, the circle of friends, and the witch standing behind her. "What are my options?"

"When Sabrina buries your body, I can take your soul to Heaven, Kleora," Viessa offers.

My mate turns her direct scrutiny to mine with a lifted eyebrow. Essentially asking; what do you offer?

"I…"

Wait, Darath. Binding Kleora to Hell is what you want, but is it the best option for your mate?

No. She deserves a chance at happiness. Peace. And she will only find that if I let her go.

"Those are your only options, love," I lie, and every single molecule of my being bursts wide open. I struggle to keep my expression passive as red-hot lava courses through my veins, igniting every pain receptor along the way.

Without my peach, my mate, the love of my life, I do not wish to exist. When her soul ascends past my reach and the warrior buries her body with her people, the time to end my misery cannot arrive soon enough.

Let my vile imps overrun Hell. What do I care if they swarm the human world with their manipulation? My children, if unchecked, will instigate wars, defile countries with immorality, dismantle societies by influencing leaders in authority to control the masses by any means necessary. The United States, as Americans know it now, will cease to exist. Their coveted free, capitalistic society will crumble under the politicians controlled by my power-hungry, greed-fueled demons.

Without Kleora, I could not give a rat's ass what happens. And if I cannot figure a way to annihilate myself, I will join the melee and destroy the fucking world.

"We have another solution." An influx of energy permeates the room as four Watchers materialize to the left of the platform. Their swords of death gleam in the low light, and the inky wings undulate at their backs.

A determined grin spreads across my lips. Well, damn. My brothers have presented me with the perfect opportunity to end my long existence. Once Kleora's soul is resting peacefully in Heaven, I will engage with the fuckwits. They will have no choice but to defend themselves. And a beheading by a Watcher's sword should do the trick.

Chapter 43

Kleora

I ignore the influx of power at the arrival of the Watchers. My sole focus is on Darath. He lied. I opened the door for him to present his option, the one he growled at Nicki when he thought me too incoherent to understand. Did he walk through it so we could be together? No. He slammed it in my face.

Even though I understand his sudden unselfishness, I craved for him to show the self-seeking, arrogant prick who would do anything to keep me by his side. But, instead, he appeared defeated, ready to march away and let me go—for me.

What scares me the most is the crazed light in his beautiful stare. When Dimitri murdered Darath's wife and child, he carefully plotted his revenge, determined to seek retribution. But he never ended his life over their loss. Yes, the demon mourned. I witnessed a glimpse of it when he glanced at the photos I snooped through, but he conquered his grief with thoughts of vengeance.

With me, he has no one to blame but himself. No one to kill, mutilate, or maim. What will my malevolent mate do after I'm gone? His expression breathes death. But for whom? Himself? Humankind?

"The self-righteous assholes showed up in the nick of time," my mate sneers.

"Darath," Nicki admonishes, but the king ignores her, stepping up to Gadriel and shoving him back against his brothers.

"Jagorach. Don't," I plead. What's his plan here? To engage the Watchers and hope they kill him?

"Calm yourself, Lucifer. We can restore your mate," Ezekiel interjects, his palm planted on Darath's chest to keep him at bay.

The Watcher's words freeze the Devil in place. Hell, they arrest everyone in the room.

Viessa grabs Darath's arm, pulling him away from the angels, and miracle of miracles he allows it, but his forceful stare never deviates from his brothers.

"You dare defy the law of God?" she questions, more with curiosity than anger.

The one called Kalaziel glares at Darath. "Yes. Hell needs its king. If Priestess Tanagra's spirit ascends to Heaven, rest assured, the world will suffer the destruction of his wrath. We cannot allow that to happen."

"What do you mean?" I ask. Pretty sure the four fallen angels are about to confirm what I suspected, but I want to hear it from their lips.

"It does not matter," the crazed demon rumbles. "Present your plan, or I will rip your heads from your bodies and dance in your blood."

I gulp in dismay at his daring. This quartet is almost as sacred as the Oracle. One doesn't threaten them without risking their existence. But isn't that my wounded mate's primary goal? If I disappear forever, he will end his life by any means necessary. The reason the Watchers are here—to stop him.

Ezekiel steps forward. His hazel eyes land on Alex, tucked protectively against Sebastian's side, for a brief moment before focusing on Jagorach. "We can unite her soul to her body and then restore the decay."

"Yeah?" Nicki questions with a sneer. Logan keeps her pressed into his front with an arm across her chest. The other hand rests on the hilt of his sword. His eerie emerald irises warn of death to anyone who dares look at his mate wrong. "And what's the toll for such a miracle?"

"Yes. I would like to know that as well." I say, leaping off the table to face whatever comes my way with my shoulders back and my chin high.

"The price does not matter. Do it," Jagorach orders.

"Shut up, Darath," I snarl, surprised by my audacity. Lucretia chokes on a shocked gasp, and Nicki chuckles. My obstinate mate swivels his wicked stare to pin me in place as effectively as a steel rod through my spine. "You may not care about the consequences, but I do. Hear them out. Please."

"I would pay any price to gift your life back, Kleora," he whispers, running his knuckles down my cheek, and I shimmer, coming alive at his touch.

"Would you?" Based on his expression, the scorn in my voice baffles him.

"Lucifer," Ezekiel interrupts the stare-off between my mate and me. "You are correct in assuming that you will pay the cost."

His comment grabs my attention. "What price?"

Viessa informed me I would be the one to make a sacrifice. Not Jagorach.

"You must step down as King of the Demon Realm here on earth and return to Hell to rule. It is where you belong to restore order. God will never allow your death.," Gadriel states, stepping next to Ezekiel.

"Or the destruction of the world before its time," Manakiel adds.

I turn to my mate and poke him in the chest. When his focus shifts to mine, I let him have it with both barrels. "You think I would be fine with you ending your life once I'm gone? Or going on a rampage and destroying everything I hold sacred? After all we've shared over the last few months, did you think I'd be okay with your stupid, asinine plan?"

"Kleora…"

"No," I interrupt. "You don't get to Kleora me. I demand a promise from you, Lucifer."

He doesn't respond. Instead, his jaw clenches, and he lifts an eyebrow in question. Which means I offer no promises, but I'll hear you out to make you happy.

Ugh. Men.

"Vow, that no matter what happens tonight, you make no attempts to end your life. Nor are you allowed to walk away from your responsibilities in Hell and allow your demons to run amok." I pause. Crap, what else could he do? "Oh, and you must vow not to turn your wrath on the humans by incorporating disease, pestilence, or famine."

Darath's lips twitch. "Those were God's tests, love, not mine."

"Oh, well. You know what I mean. Hands off the mortals."

"Are immortals fair game?" he dares to question with a grin.

"No, smartass. Please promise me you will behave, no matter what happens."

The smile dwindles. "That is an agreement I cannot keep, peach." His large, warm hand grips the back of my neck, bringing me flush with his body. Heat infuses my skin, and my sex does a brief flutter, remembering our last session.

Now is not the time to get all hot and bothered. Both our lives hang in the balance. "Please, Jagorach. If my destiny is paradise, do you honestly believe I'll be at peace knowing you're wreaking havoc on the world? Or worse."

"Your fate is not Heaven, young Priestess." Ezekiel's brutal honesty snags our attention.

"Bullshit," Darath snarls. "Her soul's destination was Heaven."

"Your mate has consumed hellfire. She is no longer welcome in God's presence."

I stare at him for several long seconds, trying to process the bomb he dropped in my lap. "Ever?"

"No soul that has touched Hell or mated Lucifer will ever enter the gates, my lady. Your final path is with your mate."

Well, son of a witch's tit. My heart skips a beat at the knowledge God no longer wants me. But wasn't I fighting against going there anyway? My place is with Darath, wherever that might be.

"As I stated, we can restore your life. It is King Darath's future that is about to change."

"How?" I ask, needing more details.

"The Devil must choose a successor for the Demon Realm and step down. The time for Lucifer's journey on earth is over. His sole obligation is Hell."

"For how long?"

"Peach, it does not matter. I knew this day would come." Darath turns to his brothers. "I agree."

"Wait a flippin` minute," I bark, hands on my hips. "I don't agree. You hate it down there. Your only happiness is when you're on the surface."

"That's where you are wrong, love. My only pleasure is with you. There are no limits I would not blast through to protect you. None. I would destroy the foundation of existence if it meant one more moment with you." He nods to the Watchers. "As they are well aware."

Man. There he goes again, saying the perfect thing to distract me. Well. I'm not falling for it. I'm not. At all.

I shake my head. Being close to Darath always sends my mind in one direction. South. I refuse to allow him or my hormones to distract me. "I have a proposition."

"Kleora," Viessa interjects, and I swivel my focus to her. "Are you sure this is what you want to do?"

Freaky Oracle. She already knows what I'm about to propose.

"Do what?" Darath and Nicki inquire at the same time.

"I brokered the deal, Kleora. It is done. You will resume your life," the Devil asserts with a frown.

I turn to the Fallen. "Are you willing to hear me out or not?" I boldly ask, ignoring my enraged mate.

"Yes, my lady," Kalaziel says.

"No. I forbid it." Darath grabs my shoulders, spinning me around and lifting me until we are eye to eye. "You have already sacrificed enough because of me, little one. I refuse whatever stupidity you are about to propose."

Stupidity? How dare he? Irritation rides high, and I almost blurt out, "Fine. Screw you then," but the bonded spirit keeps my rashness down to a simmering glare as I press the blade from my boot against the pulsing vein in his neck. While I would never murder the big stubborn jerk, no matter how infuriated, a squirting jugular would certainly distract him enough I could make my side deal with the Fallen.

"Remember my promise the last time you pointed a weapon at me, Kleora?"

Uh oh. The sexy Dom has come out to play, setting up a pleasant hum in my nether regions. My gaze drops to the lush lips. "An empty threat if you're stuck in Hell," I mutter. The notion is as sobering as a bucket of snow shoved down my pants.

"Enough of these antics!" Gadriel barks before waving his hand over me.

Darath's firm grip on my shoulders slips right through, and I drop to the ground.

"What the fuck?" he hisses in confusion, attempting to latch onto my bicep again, but his fingers glide through my translucent frame. I shiver at the friction.

Red fire pins the Watcher. "That was a mistake, Gadriel."

I jump between the original fallen angel and his brother. Not that I could stop them in my current situation, but a woman's gotta try, right? "Please, hear me out."

"Darath." Nicki's low tone snags everyone's attention as effectively as if she'd shouted. "Either you back off and listen to what Kleora has to say, or we," she waves her hand, indicating the powerful group of immortals in the room, "will hogtie your ass to this table."

"Dude. Don't piss off the pregnant vampire," Liam says, attempting to lighten the mood, but Darath's lips remain compressed in a furious line.

He glances down at me, and I can practically see his mind whirling with what options lay before him. He craves to do right by me. Wants to refuse my chance to bargain with the Watchers because his instincts warn him he won't like what I'm about to propose.

Well, too bad. This is a negotiation, and their first offer sucked balls.

Chapter 44

Jagorach

What is my mate conniving now? "Take the deal, Kleora. They are offering you a chance at life again, to live with and rule your people once more. To be happy."

"Do you honestly believe, after everything we've shared, I could be happy without you, knowing you're miserable, imprisoned, and alone in Hell?"

"You've lived in my chambers for months," I counter with a nonchalant shrug. "It is far from a hardship, my lady."

"It doesn't matter how lavish the accommodation, mate. If you are there against your will, a prison is still a prison," she huffs.

Is that how she felt all this time? Of course, she did, dumbass. She was not there by choice.

My mate nods to Viessa, and confusion creases my brow. The group I had once considered my friends, until this moment, swarm me. Needing an outlet for my frustration, I target the biggest pack member and toss the enormous shifter king across the room. Logan, Bastian, and Nox quickly replace him and pin my arms to the wall. Back on his feet, Kurtis alongside Liam snare my legs while Lucretia and Alex hold my waist.

My roar is deafening. Betrayal and outrage saturate the deep rumbling bellow as I trap Nicole with a vengeful stare. She remained back from the melee, per Logan's orders, no doubt.

"Don't look at me like that, big guy," she smiles ruefully. "You brought this on yourself. I warned you."

I regard the pregnant Halfling. No matter how enraged I may be with this situation, I would never harm the vampire queen or the precious bundle she carries. A quick transformation to my cursed form, and I would be free, but it would injure her and the group working valiantly to save me from myself.

"State your alternative, Priestess. Your friends will not hold him for long," Ezekiel states with an amused glance in my direction.

"I'm proposing you allow King Darath to rule both the Demon Realm and Hell as he has been doing. Quite beautifully, I might add." The crazy nymph is championing me to these morons? Damn. My mate never ceases to surprise me. "In return, you don't have to defy God and restore my soul to my body. I will remain a phantom and aid King Darath in ruling both realms."

"NO!" I bellow and renew my struggles against my so-called friends. They grunt with the strain to keep me in place. "Do not forge such a deal or I will tan your hide beet red, Kleora." The land nymph ruler dares to stick her tongue out at me like a fucking two-year-old.

"God, I love her," Nicole laughs.

"Are you positive?" Gadriel asks with surprise.

"No, she is not certain," I rage. "If any of you permit this idiotic proposal, I will tear you apart. Restore her life."

Why would she agree to remain a ghost when she has the opportunity to live again, to have her life back?

Her determined gleam scares me to death. "Kleora," I plead. "My place has always been in Hell. My time on earth was a further rebellion against my father, which I knew would end one day. So do not strike this bargain with these ball sacks. You have the chance to restore your life."

"You are my life, you absolute moron!" she shouts back, her tiny but lethal fists clenched at her sides. I cease my struggles to gape at the woman before me. Is she giving up her way of life to live as a ghost for me? For Lucifer—the King of Hell? Why?

"As you are mine, peach. Which is why I cannot allow you to do this. By snatching your soul, I condemned you to Hell when your life ends. How can you bid me to shorten your existence in order to be with me now?"

"It's the only course so I can be with you. If I'm alive and you're stuck in Hell, we will never see each other again until I'm dead. Which could be centuries. I... I can't go about my merry way, knowing you're suffering. Miserable. Never able to touch you or kiss you. Hear your laughter. See you smile. As a wraith, we can be together. Do you not want that?"

"Not if it means I deny you the chance to live," I grate out between clenched teeth.

"Oh, for fuck's sake, Darath. Sometimes you are really thick." Nicki throws her hands up in exacerbation. "Do you not get what she's saying? Without you, Luci, she ceases to exist."

"Yeah, what she said." Kleora's head tilts in Nicole's direction. "I'm willing to do whatever it takes to be with you. Can you say the same?"

Can I? I refused to complete the bond with her because I could not trust her. Yet here she is, sacrificing everything to be with me. What else do I want? Kleora is making the ultimate sacrifice. For me. For us. So we can be together.

I wrench my arms, only to discover the pack already eased away. My mind was so caught up in turmoil; I never realized they no longer restrained me. With sure strides, I move to my female and attempt to caress her face. My fingers pass right through.

I growl at my brother for putting this added barrier between us. He waves his hand with a slight nod before stepping back to give us space.

I tug her into my chest, brushing her silky hair behind her pointed ear. "Do you understand the consequences of what you propose? You can never leave Hell. Every time you do, it opens a new portal, and demons escape. A selfish prick I may be, but I would never trap you in Hades for all eternity."

"I might be able to help with that," Viessa pipes in.

"How so, sweetness?" Liam asks, rubbing his hand up and down her arm like he cannot bear not to touch her.

I know the feeling.

"Since King Darath doesn't require a portal to travel into or out of purgatory, the Watchers and I could alter Kleora's spirit in the same way. Then, she could enter and exit as she pleases."

"The Oracle is correct," Ezekiel confirms. "It is possible."

"See," my mate grins. "Problem solved."

"What about your people?" I probe, still not believing she understands everything she is giving up for me.

Sabrina clears her throat. "If you can move about freely, I believe in time our people will accept your ghost form."

Kleora shakes her head. "I would never expect my people to put aside their beliefs so I could continue to be their ruler. Nymphs will never tolerate the fallen archangel as my mate, and you know it. You have done a tremendous job in my absence, Sabrina. The position is yours permanently if you wish to have it."

Tingles of some strange emotion spread across my flesh. If I were anyone else, I would identify it as humility. The Devil humbled? It is laughable.

"You honor me, my lady," the Storm Walker replies with a slight bow.

"Besides, taking on the responsibilities of a demon queen, the Queen of Hell, and Lucifer's mate," she says with a wicked grin up at me. "My time will be stretched pretty thin."

The notion of her ruling by my side sends a thrill jolting through my heart. Then I realize the hole in her scheme, and I squash my excitement.

"Neither my people nor the demons in Hell will accept you as their queen unless we mate fully and you bear my mark."

Kleora's face hardens. "Right. Because you still don't trust me enough to make me yours."

She attempts to wriggle out of my arms, but I tighten my grip. Now that she is back in my embrace, I refuse to let her go. "It is not that, love. You have more than redeemed yourself. I trust you above all others. But the second I take my touch away, the mark will heal and disappear."

"Watchers," the Oracle pipes in again. "Priestess Tanagra offered the greatest sacrifice any being could. Saved you from defying God." Viessa moves to stand next to us, her mate Liam at her back. "Is there a way, in her wraith form, to keep the mating mark, so Darath's people accept her as their own?"

"We are treading new ground here, Oracle. If such an avenue exists, we are unfamiliar with it," Manakiel states with a revered nod to Viessa.

"I may have a solution," Troy offers with a wicked grin.

Of course he does.

I peer down at my incredible woman, a frown marring her forehead. Wait. We should put the brakes on for a damn minute. Events are happening way too fast. I do not think Kleora has grasped the magnitude of what she is proposing. And I need to make damn sure she proceeds with her eyes wide open.

"Can everyone give us a few moments alone, please?" I request, never breaking my gaze from my mate's.

Those who do not teleport, walk out the door. The others disappear.

When we are alone, I grip Kleora's midriff and hoist her up until she wraps her strong legs around my waist and buries her fingers in my hair. Peace invades my system. My female cradled against me is bliss. As the humans are fond of saying, Kleora is my cheerful place. Or is it happy place?

"I crave nothing more than to be with you for all eternity, to have you bear my mark. But not if that means you are unhappy in any way." I bury my face in her neck, inhaling her peach fragrance. "I am so sorry I imprisoned you in Hell. My actions were selfish. Arrogantly believing I could fix it, and everything would be fine."

I lean back to stare into perfect jade. Eyes that captivated me from the first moment I saw them. This female is my life. My mate. The one being in the universe meant for me and me alone. I will never understand why my father granted me a mate, but I have never been one to look a gift horse in the mouth.

"Is this truly what you desire?" I reiterate when she remains quiet. "To stay a wraith in order to be with me, to no longer rule your people or have a seat on the Council? To give up your life?"

Her smile proclaims her answer more profoundly than any words could. A huge weight lifts from my shoulders, and her light, Kleora's pure brightness, enters my soul.

"Brina has proven to be a capable leader with a clear head. She is always welcome to seek my advice, should she require it, and the Council is fortunate to have her. All I ask is you allow Sabrina to bury my body in the land of my people."

"Of course," I reply without hesitation.

"My life is with you, Jagorach. In whatever form. The only time I'm alive is when I'm in your arms. I've discovered things about myself I never imagined in a million years I would enjoy." She laughs, and the melody is like cocaine to this addict's heart. "Enjoy. That is way too mild a word for how you make me feel."

Unable to hold back a second longer, I brush my lips across hers, meaning to convey how much I love, appreciate, and, yes, am humbled by her sacrifice. But like every time before when we touch, my lust rages, my cock swells, and fire slithers over my skin, needing more, craving my mouth on every delectable inch of her.

"Jag," she moans before deepening the kiss. I allow her to take control, holding her tight against me, thriving in her warmth.

She reaches between us and grips my erection, straining against my pants, squeezing and rubbing her palm up and down my length. I moan low, enjoying the friction of the rough material on my throbbing flesh.

In seconds, she rips open the fly and dives inside to wrap her small hand around my hardness. The softness of her skin has my dick jumping with eagerness.

"I love the feel of you, Jag. All hard silkiness ready to offer endless pleasure."

"Hellfire, Kleora. Our friends are waiting in the other room."

She leans back. A devilish glint worthy of a demon queen graces her beautiful face. "It's true, you are quite loud during sex," she giggles, and it is the most pleasurable sound in the world.

"Says the screamer," I counter with a laugh.

"Then make me scream, mate."

As the Devil, I cannot turn my back on a challenge. Not wanting to fuck next to her lifeless body, I pivot and push her against a nearby wall before dropping her to her feet so I can strip off her boots and leather pants. I slide the pretty pink thong down her thighs. With a wink, I pocket the soft material.

Unable to keep my hands from her perfect ass, I clutch and knead the plump, muscular flesh. Kleora moans, wrapping both hands around my straining erection.

"Please, Jag," she pants.

My hips pump, loving the sound of her begging, but a craving for her flavor on my lips overwhelms me. I grip her ass, hoisting her up, and drop to my knees to bury my face in her wet pussy. With the wall and the strength of my palms keeping her aloft, her heels dig into my back, and I relish the pressure as I lick and suck my woman from anus to clit.

"Oh, Jag!" she cries out. Her thighs tremble as they grip my head, and I know she's close.

"Come for me, Kleora." She is the puppet, and I am the master of her pleasure. As a puppeteer, I understand my mate's needs as well or better than she does, so I pierce her swollen bundle with a fang, offering her the pain she seeks while my lips continue to suckle with a steady rhythm.

Her scream fills the room, and I rumble with satisfaction. Not giving two shits that our friends, who are right outside the door, including the Watchers, heard her cries.

Before the last of the tremors ease, I rise and shove into her convulsing pussy with one swift thrust. Bliss. Fucking bliss. To think I almost lost this forever. Lost her.

"Brush your hair to the side, love," I instruct, my fangs low, ready to pierce her flesh and mark her as mine.

Her lust-filled gaze zeros in on my choppers as she pulls her long tresses to one side, exposing her vulnerable neck to the Devil. Such trust humbles me. "This might hurt," I think to warn her.

"I've discovered I'm addicted to your delicious form of pain," she groans, tilting her head more. "Make me yours, Lucifer."

I kidded myself from the start. There was no walking away from Kleora. Not even death could tear us apart. I pull out of her wetness until the head nestles at the opening. "I love you, Kleora. We are one. One heart. One mind. One soul. I am forever at your mercy." My vow echoes through the room right before I strike, plunging my fangs and cock into her at the same time.

I expected her to scream from the agony of my bite, but my perfect mate groans low and clutches my head to her neck, pumping her hips along my length. As I drink down her enchanting essence, everything that is Kleora Tanagra becomes mine. All her memories, her hopes, and dreams, worries and fears—she holds nothing back.

Her absolute love and devotion to me strikes me with awe. No matter how many times I hurt, angered, or disappointed her. In her heart, she stood firm by me. Proof is in the sacrifice she is making in order for us to be together.

Once the mating bond solidifies on my end, I lick the wounds, lapping every drop. I have sunk my fangs into necks before, but usually in the zeal of battle, never to drink their blood. I am not a vampire; blood is not something I enjoy. But Kleora's essence is sweet and tangy. Like her tasty pussy, and I could become addicted to it with ease.

I edge back and pierce my neck with a claw. Kleora dives in, sucking and lapping at the scarlet offering oozing from the wound. As she suckles, tension builds at the base of my shaft, and I pump into her, my balls constricting at the joy and freedom of having my women drink from me.

I have now given Kleora ultimate power over me, and I cannot seem to care. I trust her explicitly. I have seen into her heart and soul, and I have nothing to fear from this courageous female.

Within minutes, the desire to fill her with my seed becomes overwhelming. Her scent surrounds me. Her soft lips nuzzle my neck, and her pussy clamps on my dick in a luscious vise.

When the wound closes, my mate leans her head back against the wall, her regard brimming with tears. I slow my pace. "Am I hurting you, peach?" I question with a frown.

"No. I just… I love you so much, Jagorach." Her petite hands grip my face, her expression fierce. "We are one. One mind. One body. One soul. Now and forever."

"Kleora, my sweet. You have linked your spirit to mine for all eternity. I will spend each day proving you made the perfect choice. You will never want for anything ever again. Your every wish is my command."

"I only have one wish right now, Lucifer."

"Name it, love."

"Make me come with that magical cock."

I roar with laughter and gift my woman what she craves most.

Chapter 45

Kleora

We take forever to come down from the high of bonding sex. Yet even after Darath slides from my body, he continues to hold me. I love when he shows his more vulnerable, loving side. A side I doubt many witnesses.

"Get dressed, peach," he commands, his tone still husky with lust, never taking his hands off of me so the mating mark doesn't vanish. "Let us finish this so I can kick all these assholes out of my house and have my wicked way with you."

Once our clothes are in place, he swoops in for another kiss. The Devil kisses like he fucks—with such intensity, it sizzles in the air, and I'm breathless again by the time he leans back and brushes his thumb across my lower lip.

"Ready?" he asks, and I nod, unable to communicate after that searing kiss.

The bastard smirks before grasping my hand and opening the door. Our friends are nowhere in sight.

"Where did they go?" I ask, twining my fingers with Darath's.

"Traitors are probably snooping around my home," he grumbles in reply.

"Don't be cranky with them, Jagorach. They did what they did to save you from your own stubbornness."

"Your smart mouth is going to turn your ass a delicious red." His robust and husky tone energizes my libido, even though she already had an excellent little workout.

"Is that a threat, King Darath?" I question with mock anger, working to keep the shit-eating grin off my face.

"No, peach. That is a goddamn promise I plan on acting on the first opportunity we get." His Dommie voice spreads tingles over the punctures in my neck as we traverse his home in search of our missing group.

Darath's homestead is stunning and huge. It's done in neutral tans and browns, all masculine and cozy, with large comfortable looking furniture and hardwood floors. But what grabs my attention is the view through the floor-to-ceiling windows in the living room.

Talk about King of the Mountain. His home sits in a crevice high on the side of the northern mountain range surrounding Tucson's desert town. The city landscape glitters like diamonds, and shadows of majestic saguaros dot the terrain. I can't wait to see the view in the daylight.

"Your home is gorgeous, Jag," I breathe, my observation flickering everywhere, taking it all in.

"Our home, love," he corrects, just as the Watcher Manakiel and Sabrina round the corner.

"Permission to take your remains to their final resting place." Sabrina whispers with a bow.

"Oh." Why does my stomach swim with unease? Burying my body is what I've demanded from the very beginning, but the thought of permanently separating from it seems odd.

"You okay, peach?" Darath questions with a concerned frown. No doubt he senses my unease now that we completed our bond.

I squeeze his fingers with reassurance. "Of course. Please proceed, Sabrina. And thank you for always standing by my side, no matter what. I am at your disposal for whatever you may need."

"I may take you up on that regarding the clothing line and contacts."

"Clothing line?" Darath questions with a quirked eyebrow.

I laugh. "I forgot to tell you. Many of the suits in your closet were handmade by my people. It's the backbone of our economy—supplying high-end clothing to the rich and elite. Anonymously, of course."

"Well I will be goddamned," he grins.

"Lucifer," Manakiel barks. "Do not use the Lord's name in vain in my presence."

"You are in my house, Watcher. You can fuck off at any time."

I press my lips together to keep the giggle from escaping at Manakiel's thunderous expression as he grabs Sabrina's wrist and disappears.

"Damn, I love goading that righteous son of a bitch," Darath says with a dark laugh before leading me through an immaculate kitchen to massive sliders that open to the backyard.

And what a backyard. An Olympic size pool with an invisible edge overlooks the sparkling city below. An outdoor kitchen area with a huge TV and living room type seating is on the left under a covered patio. To the right is another deep-seated furniture set, complete with a massive fire pit in the center. Even though the evening temperature is still quite warm, our group circles an inviting blaze, popping and crackling, shooting sparks into the starlit sky.

"Enjoying my home?" Darath frowns as we join the others, easing his enormous frame into a huge wicker rocker before pulling me onto his lap. Contentment fills my soul as I peer around at the immortals I've grown to love over the past couple of years.

Logan reclines on one end of a couch, his pregnant mate sprawled out across his thighs and half the bench with Nox on the other end, her bare feet resting on his lap.

Alex snuggles against Sebastian's chest in another chair as he strokes her hair, conversing quietly with his brother. Lucretia and Kurtis take up the other sofa, her legs bent under her with her head against the shifter's massive torso.

The powerful Oracle has her lithe body draped sideways over Liam's lap, feasting on his neck. The werewolf hugs her to him, soothing his palms up and down her tattooed back, whispering sensual words into her ear. It's erotic and loving, and my body responds to the sexual vibe permeating this group.

The other three Watchers do not join the party. Instead, they hang in the shadows, observing our antics. Just as well. Darath doesn't like them much, anyway.

"We had to escape the sounds booming out of that room before we all engaged in an orgy right then and there," Nicki states in her usual blunt way. "And in my current state, it wouldn't be pretty."

"Your belly filled with my child is the most beautiful thing in the world." Logan's soft rumble is alluring, the fingers running over her stomach, in a loving yet sensual manner, are hypnotic.

A blush heats my cheeks at Nicki's teasing, but Darath chuckles. "The Devil wants what the Devil wants, young Halfling. But my mate appreciates you giving us privacy."

Ha. I do? More like him. But far be it for me to dent his reputation.

"I understand now why you wanted Arizona in the treaty, Darath," Logan says, continuing the hypnotic circling of Nicole's belly. "It is quite stunning. As is your home."

"Thank you, Moretti. You all are welcome anytime. As long as you call first," he adds, and they all laugh.

Troy emerges from the shadows, and I totally forgot he was here. The dude is down and dirty, sexy in an uber-creepy sort of way.

"Shall we make that mark permanent before Viessa and the Watchers do their thing?" He asks, striding to our chair.

"I would be most grateful, Mr. Tenebris," I say, reverting to the diplomacy of a ruler with ease as I sit up and present my neck.

Darath grips my waist, and I sense his ire at Troy touching me. 'Easy, lover,' I whisper in his mind, loving this ability to not only perceive Jagorach's emotions, but communicate telepathically with him.

'Mine.' The possessive growl hardens my nipples, and I'm grateful the thickness of my corset conceals them from my friends.

I wiggle a little when the witch's power heats the skin over the bite to an almost unbearable degree. The stiff erection pressing into my backside inflames me until I'm feverish with desire.

Troy watches me knowingly, and the hotness increases. Is he screwing with me? Somehow escalating the flutters in my nether regions? The dampness saturating my core?

A deep, angry rumble vibrates my back, and Darath's grip tightens to a painful degree as a crimson glow lights up the smirk on the witch's face. The pressure eases.

He was ramping up my passions. The devious fiend. I'm already a sex addict for my demon. I sure as heck don't need an injection of Viagra. Or whatever the female equivalent is to the little blue pill.

Troy steps back, eyeing his handiwork. "Should we test it?"

I nod, attempting to rise, but Darath's grip remains firm. I glance at him over my shoulder. "Jagorach, I'm not going anywhere."

"Stay between my legs," he orders, and tenderness spreads through my chest at his possessiveness. I care little for controlling, overbearing males, and I would never tolerate my mate ordering me about in my day-to-day life. But, sexually, that's a whole other ballgame. I'm on board. Totally.

The second I become translucent, I pivot to Darath and tilt my neck. When he doesn't confirm if it worked, I shift my regard to him. The big male appears at ease. His forearms laying casually along the chair, his massive legs spread in that manly way men sit that's so damn inviting. Like I crave to drop to my knees, pull out his obvious erection and suck and lick until he explodes, not caring we have an audience.

When several more seconds pass, I lift my gaze from the bulge in his pants and meet red fire. Holy shit! The male pride, smug satisfaction, and lust permeating from my mate flood my core with wetness.

"Jagorach," I whisper, transfixed by his fierce expression. "Did it work?"

The Devil grins, and it portrays all his emotions to a tee. "You bear my mark, Kleora. There is no escape. You are mine forever."

My spirit shimmers as my desire ramps up at his possessive declaration, only outshone by my utter happiness at being bonded to this creature for all eternity. "You're at my mercy, Lucifer." My smile spreads with sexual intent.

"Um," Alex interrupts Darath and me eye-fucking each other. "Can you two dial it down a notch or ten? My skin is on fire over here."

"I can resolve that issue for you, Red," Bastian murmurs, rubbing his nose along her neck.

Immortals are inherently sexual beings, stimulated by scent, touch, or visualization. But bonded males are also highly possessive of their females. So while our carnal tension ramps up the group, they would never initiate sex in front of others and risk exposing their mates to other males.

The fact they are still sitting here means they have an urgent matter to discuss before they disappear and screw each other blind. My vagina and I are hoping it happens like yesterday. We demand a lot of Darath's rough, aggressive touches.

I glance over at Nox, the sole occupant without a partner, besides Troy and the Watchers, observing us. His queen's feet rest on his thighs. One arm grips the back of the couch, the other white-knuckles the armrest. By the strained look on his face, he's beyond uncomfortable with the lust permeating our group and itching to get the hell out of here. Especially with his queen's feet in his lap.

"I have a question for Troy," Nicole proclaims from her protected spot between the two vampires, either oblivious to Nox's distress or ignoring it altogether to torture the poor guy. The gray irises pin the dark witch with a hardened glare. "Where is Abigail?"

Troy stiffens. A warm, gentle breeze ruffles through his mahogany locks as his expression shuts down. "She is dead, my lady," he lies without batting an eyelash.

Nicki winces, further proof of his subterfuge.

"You have a history with her, I get it, but she attempted to kill not only me but Liam." Nicole lowers her feet to the ground, slips them into her flats before sitting up straight, a hand on her belly. "Troy, she murdered Icarus, a High Priest Oracle. If I find out you're harboring the criminal, I will make sure you pay dearly for that betrayal. No matter how much you've helped tonight."

"Dead or alive, she is no danger to you, young queen. A vow is a vow."

"Better make damn sure she keeps to the promise, Troy," Logan states with a low, angry rumble.

What vow is he referring to? I glance at Viessa, who's finished her meal and reclines against Liam. Her effortless grace is an illusion. The Oracle watches Troy with interest but doesn't dispute his remarks.

Before Darath arrived at Troy's cabin that night, I spied on the witch before making my presence known. Abigail was indeed in the back bedroom. Well, I assumed it was Abigail. The body on the bed was so charred it was difficult to tell. The only indication it was her was the long, curly blond locks untouched by the destruction of the magic that struck her, and me, down.

Troy stood at the end of the bed. The watchful countenance glittered with power and pain as he focused his dark power in a swirling pattern around her mutilated body, while chanting a spell.

He was attempting to revive her alright, but it appeared either slow going, or he was failing miserably.

I lower my lids in shame as I recall how I offered to help repair her if he aided me. Do I inform the others where she is and what Troy is up to?

Sensing my inner turmoil, Darath grips my waist, breathing life back into my soul before lowering me onto his lap. His hard length presses into my backside, and despite the somber topic, I rub against the enormous cock.

'We struck a bargain with Troy for his help tonight, peach. I will tell you all about it later,' my mate informs me.

"You may be a hundred times my age, but I'm going to offer you a little advice, Troy Tenebris," Nicki states. The irises brighten to emphasize her point. "Unless you wish to be hunted down for the rest of your existence, I suggest you destroy that bitch and walk away."

"You know not what you speak, young Halfling. Abi lost her way. A huge portion of that was my fault, but it was also Icarus's doing. You do not understand the entire story."

"You're right, I don't, but it doesn't excuse her actions or the numerous laws she broke, Troy. But if she comes after anyone I love, I won't stop until she is six feet under for good. This I vow."

A heavy silence saturates the area as we all await Troy's response to the queen's vow. No doubt the witch understands it is not solely the Vampire Nation he will answer to, but the Werewolf Province as well.

Troy bows to the group. "I understand." He turns to my mate. "I left the item we talked about in the kitchen," he says before vanishing.

"He understands?" Kurtis gripes. "What does that mean? He's going to adhere to the vow or take your best shot?"

"I believe it means, fuck you all, I'll do whatever I desire," Lu responds, her expression molten lava.

The witch must care for Abigail a great deal to cultivate such powerful enemies with the shrug of his shoulders. Either that or he's confident in his ability to control his female.

Chapter 46

Kleora

"How are you holding up with Cellica?" Darath asks Nox, tossing another log on the dwindling fire.

"I'm managing," he responds with a quick sideways glance at Cel's big brother glaring at him. "When do you think you can take care of the demon?"

Wait. What did I miss? "What's wrong with Liam's little sister?" I ask.

"She's possessed by a demon," Liam grinds out between clenched teeth, and Viessa rubs his arm to soothe the beast.

"Wait. Is that because of my trips to the surface?" Darath had stated that demons bolted every time I escaped Hell. If one seized the young wolf because of my actions, I'd never forgive myself.

"It was not your fault, peach. You did not know," my mate tries to reassure me, rubbing his heated palm down my back.

"I'm so sorry, Liam," I beseech the werewolf king. "I would never harm your sister intentionally."

"I do not blame you, Priestess," he states, his tone gruff. "But your mate needs to resolve the issue soon."

"The demon seems to go dormant for longer periods of time, so we are coping," Nox says as he rises to his feet. "I should probably head back and check on her."

"I'll be in touch in a few days, Christoph."

Something in Darath's demeanor snags my attention. 'What aren't you telling him, my love?' I inquire mentally.

'Why would you assume such a thing?' he responds, not answering the question. But strong fingers pinch my waist in silent warning, and I recall Nicki hears all internal conversations. So, I wisely shut our dialog down until we are alone.

"I will call later to talk to my sister," Liam warns. Nox offers a jerky nod before disappearing.

"My lady," Ezekiel steps into the firelight. "We must bind your soul to Lucifer's teleporting ability."

Viessa rises with regal grace to her feet as she and the three Watchers surround our chair. Uneasiness settles in the pit of my stomach to be circled by such powerful and divine beings.

"Should I stand?" I ask.

"Unnecessary, Kleora," the Oracle states. "Remain in contact with your mate. Linking to his ability will be easier if you're touching."

Darath draws me to his chest, and I curl up in his embrace, allowing him to shield me from any potential danger. It's an odd sensation to have someone to rely on, and a part of me struggles with the concept.

I've always relied on myself. And I was, and still am, proud of my self-reliance and my strong independence. I didn't require a male to come to my rescue to protect me from the evils of the world. My destiny rested squarely on my shoulders. Confidence reigned supreme with the knowledge I was a woman of power and strength, capable of dealing with whatever life threw my way on my own because I worked my butt off to make it so.

I still am, but now I have a mate to help ease the burden. Someone to turn to if in need. Instead of it feeling like a weakness, it's empowering. We are a team. We have each other's back no matter what, and I wouldn't change it for anything in this world or beyond.

Sharp prickles spread throughout my body. They aren't painful, but rather a bit uncomfortable—similar to an itch you can't scratch, and I bury my face in Darath's neck. His hold tightens. I would endure a ton more if it meant no more demons escaped hell. Cellica's situation is my fault.

A vague memory flashes behind my lids of her and Nox's presence when the first portal opened and Berkonnan came barreling through. In fact, goddess. I attacked Christoph. Oh my, and fire had consumed my body.

I've tried to block that week from my memory. It's a blur of pain and rage, anyway. One I pray I never experience again. With my mate being the King of Hell, I better not, or there will be Hell to pay. Ha!

To distract myself from the odd chanting and the prickling over my skin, I snake my tongue out for a taste of the most wickedly powerful creature in the world. His Satan appearance terrified me at first, but I respect and love it as much as the man holding me with fierce protectiveness, his enormous erection pressing into my hip.

Whether as Lucifer, or Jagorach Darath, I cherish every beautiful inch of him. I crave to experience all he offers in either form.

When the prickling intensifies, I grit my teeth to keep from crying out. An unfamiliar sensation opens in my soul. A firm knowledge of how to transport in and out of Hell and a full array of the complicated labyrinths, imprints on my brain.

The awareness is overwhelming, so I create imaginary boxes in my mind and shove the immense data inside, slamming the lid, and tossing it in a corner when needed to preserve my sanity. It's the only way I can deal with the enormous burden.

Darath kisses my temple. "You are the bravest immortal I have ever met," he whispers in my ear, his warm breath causing a shiver down my spine. "You are my light. My path from the darkness, and I will cherish you all the days of my life."

I tangle my fingers in his hair, unable to respond in kind because of the inferno raging through my soul right now.

"Just a few more minutes, Priestess," Viessa mutters from somewhere behind me.

"Hang in there, Kleora. You've got this." Was that Alex? If anyone would understand the discomfort I'm enduring, it would be the courageous valkyrie. She sacrificed the ability to bear children to be with Sebastian.

"When this is over, demand Luci takes you out for a big, juicy steak," Nicki says. "Actually, that sounds delish. Baby and I are on board with that plan."

"Looks like you are making a late-night run to a restaurant, brother," Bastian chuckles until Alexandria declares she wants one too.

"Dammit," the brothers mutter in unison. "What is the best steakhouse in Tucson, Darath?" Logan grumbles.

"Flemings has a wonderful bone-in ribeye," my mate replies absently, his fingers kneading and rubbing my ass like he's preparing me for something more.

Despite the pain riddling through my bones and muscles, my hormones perk up. More than ready for the next session, as Darath calls them. I bite down on his neck to let him know I'm catching his vibe. He moans in response before gripping a fistful of my hair and yanking my head back to plunder my mouth with his.

When Darath kisses me, the world disappears. I lose focus of my surroundings, and all I care about is how he makes my body sing with awakening.

"Well, I think that's our cue to leave," Kurtis laughs.

"It is done, my lady," Gadriel states as the discomfort dissipates. I groan in relief into Darath's talented mouth.

I'm addicted to pain with pleasure, but only to my mate's kind of pain. My mind and body crave it with an obsession that should scare me but it doesn't.

Jagorach's power pulses over my body and a warm breeze caresses my bare skin. After a minute, I have the foresight to break the kiss and glance around. The patio is deserted. Our friends took off, probably in search of steak, and the Watchers vanished as well.

I peer down. Yup. And I'm naked.

"For the next week," Darath rumbles, cupping my breast before bending down and sucking the hardened nipple into his warm mouth. I arch my neck and clutch him to my chest. Once he's lavished both breasts until the areolas are rigid, achy points, he lifts his head to regale me with his dominant smugness. "You will remain naked, your flesh available and ready at all times."

Before I can respond, he rises with me in his arms and strides to the pool. His hands twist me around to face him, and I encircle his waist with my legs and grip his powerful shoulders.

"Hang on to me, peach."

Yeah, he doesn't even have to ask. I squeeze him into my embrace while he removes his shoes and pants. He grips my ass when I lean back, taking hold of the bottom of his leather vest to pull it up and over his head, tossing it to the side.

"Ready?" he asks, and I nod.

I expected him to walk to the steps and enter the pool. Oh no. Not my mate. He tightens his hold before sprinting and leaping into the air, tucking his legs under my butt. I squeal as we cannonball into the warm water.

I never let go, trusting Darath even as we sink to the bottom. As the bubbles and waves settle, I peer around. We are sitting in the deep end, still wrapped around each other. I gaze at my mate, praying my breath doesn't give out, and the big brute grins, bubbles escaping his mouth. I can't help but smile back, adoring this side of him. The playful, fun-loving aspect that startles me every time.

When my lungs burn, I tap his shoulder and point to the surface. He shakes his head, the long, dark locks floating around his face, and my brow furrows. Instead, he leans in and captures my lips.

Warm breath enters my mouth, and I inhale, capturing his exhale. Once he's assured I'm no longer at risk of drowning, the pressure on my lips changes. The kiss softens, explores. I press my chest to his, needing the feel of his flesh against mine.

Instead of bringing me closer, Darath pushes me away, and I'm confused by the change. He shoves me out of his lap and let's go. At first, I panic, ready to head to the surface, but then I realize I'm insentient without him touching me. Floating with the water, almost like I'm part of it.

Without a solid body of bone, muscles, or lungs, there's no need to hold my breath because I don't breathe. My eyes widen in wonder, and I move through the water, never displacing the liquid.

Unable to breathe underwater, Darath springs to the surface and leans his back against the edge. Down here, I have a bird's-eye view of his impressive package. The male seems perpetually hard in my presence, and I love it.

Like a stealthy cougar on the hunt, I slink through the water and plot my next course of action. If I touch him, I'll animate, needing to hold my breath again, but maybe I could suck him off until my lungs burn and then let go for a second or two and then get back at it. I could torture the Devil for hours.

I peer up through the surface and notice my mate watching me with curiosity. 'Hang on to the edge, lover, 'cause I'm about to take you over it.'

I grip the base of his shaft, and he jerks in response, but I don't give him time to stop me before I press my lips around the engorged head, pumping my hand in rhythm with my mouth. I keep at it as long as possible before my lungs force me to let go.

When I glance up, the shimmery sight through the water captivates me. Darath's arms extend out along the edge of the pool, his head dips back in ecstasy. The bright moon and glittering stars are a perfect watery backdrop.

I did that. I'm pleasuring Lucifer in a way he's never experienced before, and pride swells in my chest. Then, needing to offer more, I devour him again, setting a tempo. I lick, stroke, and suck for as long as my lungs will allow, before backing off for a couple of seconds, and then diving back in. Soon Darath's hips buck to my cadence, and his knuckles whiten from his fierce grip on the edge.

When I sense he's close, I release him for a brief moment to ensure I have enough breath to last through his orgasm. The minute his glorious cock is in my mouth, I grasp his tightened sack with one hand, caressing and swirling his balls. The king spreads his legs, his feet braced wide along the inside edge of the pool's bottom. I slip a finger past his balls and press the pad against his anus, swirling the puckered opening while I increase my pace with my mouth.

Within seconds, the muscled thighs stiffen. His fist grips my hair as his warm, salty cum shoots down my throat, and I push my finger past the restriction, finding the soft spot to drive him insane.

I hear his muffled "Hellfire," as he vigorously fucks my mouth.

When my lungs are near bursting, I'm forced to let go. Only this time, I stay in contact with his body, sliding up his abs and torso until my head breaks through the surface. I gulp in a lungful of blessed air and smile at my mate, gazing at me in awe.

"That's a first for the Devil," he grins, cradling me to his chest.

"One of the many perks of being mated to a wraith."

Chapter 47

Kleora

My comment, said in jest, produces the opposite effect—the Devil sobers. I frown up at him, gliding my palms over the silky, wet surface of his massive chest.

"I would gift you the moon if I could," he declares, brushing dripping hair from my neck to contemplate his mark. "As powerful as I am, I failed to offer my mate the one thing she craved. Life."

"You're wrong, Lucifer. You granted so much more. An existence I never dreamed I wanted. I died in that castle, and if it weren't for your stubborn determination, we wouldn't have this. Us. An eternity to enjoy each other." I grip his face between my palms. "If you lament your decision, then you regret us."

"Never. I could never regret having a single moment with you." His arms tighten around my waist. "I look forward to my future for the first time in thousands of years. A future spending every second of each day proving to you how much you mean to me."

"Can I see it?" I whisper.

"See what, peach?"

"Your true form." He stiffens. Uncertainty consumes the gaze searching mine. "Please, Jagorach."

He contemplates me for a long moment, and I fear he's going to deny my request. When he finally offers a quick nod, excitement spirals through me.

"You should resume your translucency until after the shift," he instructs. I release my hold, floating back a couple of feet, eager to observe the transformation.

His body morphs, and the surrounding water expands out like it's clearing a path for royalty. His muscles bulk up, and the bony protrusions jut through his flesh at the shoulders and elbows. The golden skin darkens to an inky black, and the long, luxurious hair vanishes, showcasing a smooth, rounded head. Two horns, thick as tree trunks, curve over his skull.

It's the wings that really grab my attention, and a memory flashes through my brain of their warmth, folding around me in a protective manner. I'm not sure when that occurred, but I'm fascinated by their stark, lethal appearance.

When the transformation is complete, I glide back over, needing to touch and be touched by this version of him. Irises as bright as a male cardinal, watch me with apprehension. Is the Devil afraid I will reject this part of him?

Never. No matter what form he holds.

My hand trembles as I reach out, like I'm afraid the apprehensive beast will take flight at the slightest provocation. The second my fingers caress his broad, muscular chest, his body jerks as if no one's ever caressed him in this configuration before.

"Kleora." The low demonic voice sends chills down my spine, but I ease closer until my breasts brush the hardness of his abs.

With a tight grip on his shoulders, careful to avoid the sharp protrusions, I wrap my legs around his waist to hold myself above the water. I stare in wonder at the malicious beauty of his wings, drumming up the courage to touch them.

Will he allow it? I sense his anxiety and the last thing I want is to make him uncomfortable, but I can't help myself. The second my fingertips graze the leathery surface they flutter and I squeal with delight. The Devil tilts his head, examining every nuance and fluctuation of my face. It's eerie if I'm honest, but in truth, they escalate my pulse and quicken my breath.

Like I clearly picture him taking me mid-flight, the wings flapping in cadence with his... I glance down into the water... oh my, his enormous cock.

"Are you turned on by my Devil appearance?" The stunned expression says it all. I'm saddened this being has lived thousands of years, and no one ever expressed how breathtaking this side of him is. Yes, he's intimidating and downright terrifying, but apparently, that's my type.

"Lucifer, you are magnificent," I breathe, running my fingers along the horns on his skull.

His cock jerks, tapping the back of my ass in the water, and a shudder runs through him. Hmm. It appears the impressive tusks are an erogenous zone... Interesting.

"Allow me to switch back, and I will fuck you properly," he says, his crimson stare devouring my flesh.

"No," I state simply, and he frowns.

Before he can rebuff my advance, I reach down and bring his raging erection between us, right over my sex, and glide my aching folds along its length. I groan at the exquisite friction of water and steel.

"I crave the Devil between my thighs tonight. As your mate, you cannot deny me of my deepest desire." Using the bond against him is wrong, and based on his growl, my ass will suffer the consequences later. But I don't care. The wraith wants what the wraith wants.

"I cannot hold back in this form, Kleora," he grates out, the demonic tone deepening.

"Silly beast, who said anything about holding back. Didn't you once tell me you were going to fuck me senseless?"

I'm startled when the mighty wings whoosh, raising us above the pool with ease. Several of the daybed cushions float through the air to land on the flagstone next to the edge of the pool.

Darath lowers me to the makeshift bed, and I'm near delirious with lust. His big beautiful length kept up the titillating slide across my pussy, now soaked with my own juices within minutes of exiting the water.

I blink in amazement at this demonic creature between my thighs, his black wings spread out above us like a sunshade. Or, in this case, a moon shade. I reach up and grip both horns, and the beast bucks at the contact. Instead of bringing him to me, I push him downward, needing that talented tongue, doing those clever things to make me scream.

The Devil grins, and my insides spasm. It's wicked and demonic. "Hang on, peach, and do not let go," he orders before diving in with gusto. His wings flutter as he devours my sex. Licking, sucking, pinching, and biting like a... well, like a crazed demon.

Claw-tipped hands shove my knees up to my shoulders as he sets in, tonguing my anus before biting my ass cheek. The slight pain clenches my insides, and I crave more. With my fists still gripping his smooth horns, I guide his mouth to the spot that aches for him.

Darath latches on to my clit, sucking and flicking the swollen bundle with a swift vibration that has me crying out in record time. Before the tremors ease, my mate pierces my flesh with a fang and devours me until my entire body vibrates with the need to detonate.

"Come, peach." The low guttural command has my muscles tensing, and when he sucks my clit deep, I lose it, coming apart until blackness dances at the edge of my vision.

"Jag. Fuck."

The Devil chuckles, sliding up my body, and I release the death grip on his horns. "That's next."

In a millisecond, he has me flipped over on all fours, and his enormous dick plunges into my sopping flesh. I cry out, my muscles objecting to the painful stretch of his new size. A fire erupts in my belly, spreading with the force of a volcano. Darath stills.

After several seconds of him not thrusting into the eager wraith, I push my ass back, letting him know I'm more than ready.

"Stop, Kleora, or I will split you in two. Your fire ignites my lust to a punishing degree."

Split me in two? I might combust if he doesn't start thrusting. And what does he mean by fire? I lift my lids and peer down my body. Sure enough, I'm engulfed in Hellfire. It quivers along my skin in the most pleasurable places and I buck my hips at the exquisiteness. "Please, Lucifer," I beg. "I can take it."

"I love the sound of your begging as much as your screams," he growls before easing out and plunging deep once more, not caring the flames engulf us both.

Mother Earth. He wasn't kidding. I think he's rearranging my uterus. I'd have half a mind to tell him to go slow, but the demon picks up his pace, fucking me hard and fast, and I can't seem to care. The pain soon turns to soul-shattering pleasure. I clutch the cushions, somehow unsinged by our passionate combustion, and do what any woman in my position would do—hold on for dear life and enjoy the heck out of being thoroughly taken from behind while engulfed in flames.

'Cause ya know, that's normal.

Darath's enormous body hovers over me, and a black claw-tipped hand snakes across my chest to encircle my throat. He wrenches my head to the side and, without warning, pierces my flesh in the same spot as before.

I fight against the excruciating pain radiating through my neck and shoulder, but the demon clamps down harder, and I have no choice but to submit. Rough snarls vibrate along my skin as he pounds deep, and an ache builds in my core. I foresee this orgasm being the most intense one to date.

Darath pulls me up against him until we are both kneeling, and at this angle, he grazes that perfect spot with every thrust. I grip his thighs, digging my nails into his muscle, and a low rumble of approval vibrates around the fangs embedded in my trapezius muscle.

The view of the sparkling city through the flames can't compare to the magnitude of this moment with my mate. I was born for him, and he for me. I never would've guessed in a million years I would end up with Lucifer. But we don't choose our destiny. The gods or fate decided for us.

When the enormous leathery wings cocoon me in their warmth and protection, dousing the flames, I scream my release. Every molecule in my body flies apart, my soul soars above us. He was right; he ripped me in two, but oh, what a way to go.

Within seconds, Darath releases my neck and roars my name. His arms banded around my middle. The wings tremble and pulse with each pump of his hips as his scalding seed fills my womb.

Holy mackerel, I fucked the Devil... and I liked it.

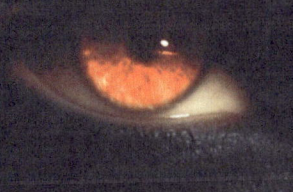

Chapter 48

Jagorach

I observe with tenderness my mate in my arms, sound asleep. This past week has been the happiest I have ever been. I shut down any distractions from the Demon Realm, instructing Dzun to handle it, and appointed a new general in Hell.

Tomorrow I head over to Nox's cabin to take care of my little Prince of Hell issue. Then it's off to the Vampire Stronghold to discuss with Nicole the information I gleaned from Mammon.

If what he said is true, the Princes will be useful in the prosperity of the supernatural world. Speaking of which, I should check in on Gemma and see how she is fairing after her ordeal with the Demon of Greed.

At some point, someone should inform the human of her importance, but there is no need to traumatize the frail creature too soon. It is wise to give her time to get over her possession before we blast her mind with the realization that monsters do, in fact, exist and live right next door.

Kleora moans in her sleep, and I refocus on her naked form sprawled across my chest. A frown mars her perfect features, her little fist clenched under her chin. A nightmare, perhaps? That will not do.

I attempt to reach out mentally to ease her mind, but she bolts upright, a piercing cry escaping her lips.

"Hey," I soothe, scooting back against the headboard and folding her in my embrace. "It was only a nightmare, peach. You are safe."

Her fingers clutch my chest, the remnants of her dream lingering in her trembling frame. I open my senses and am startled by the terror racing through her mind.

"Kleora." I rub her back, loving the sensation of her silky skin. "Tell me about your dream." She shakes her head, clutching tighter, and the Devil rises in my chest, ready to eviscerate anything that dares to hurt our female. Physically or mentally.

It still astounds me that she demanded I take her in my demonic form the first night. Not one individual on this planet, including my late wife, had ever asked the Devil to appear. For a good reason. When I shift, I am held within the grip of extreme emotion—Namely rage. Those who typically gaze upon Lucifer, it is the last sight they ever see.

"I... I relived my time trapped in Hell," she admits before burying her face in my neck. "I never want to endure that again."

My arms tighten, and my heart stops at the reminder of my failure. One of many regarding Kleora. How easily the fiends could have taken her from me forever. The fact she survived a week and can still communicate in complete sentences is a testament to her mental strength and endurance. It is no wonder nightmares plague her sleep.

"I vow you will never step foot in Hell again, love."

"I don't mind your chambers." She peeks up at me, and I drown in the jade depths. "And as long as you are by my side, I can endure anything to help serve as queen."

How I worship this creature. She is willing to go back to where I imprisoned her, the origin of her nightmares, to be near me. "No, Kleora. I forbid it. You will wait for me here while I take care of business in Hell. Is that clear?"

She leans back with a raised eyebrow. "Look here, Jagorach. You don't get to dictate where, when, who, or what. I'm your partner, not your sex slave. Well, I wouldn't mind being your sex slave in the bedroom, but anywhere else—not happening."

"Is that so?" I reply in mock anger. "Does my mate require another reminder of who controls her body?"

The visual of her strapped to the spanking bench last night, her bottom bright red from the paddle, the evidence of her utter enjoyment glistening on the inside of her thighs, hardens my cock to painful proportions.

"Yes, Master," she grins with excitement, and I laugh at the absolute rightness of my mate.

"How about I let you have control tonight?" I offer. The excited gleam in her expression tightens my balls.

"How about right now," she says with an eagerness that would worry me if I were anyone else.

Before I can respond, frantic knocking on the bedroom door tenses my muscles. Who in the hell could that be? I sent everyone home. Kleora and I are the only ones in the house... at least we were until a few seconds ago.

"Get dressed, peach," I mutter, setting her on the floor. The second she is translucent; she conjures up a pair of cutoff shorts and a black tank top.

"Jag?" a familiar masculine voice beseeches through the door. "I know you're in there. I can hear your heartbeat. Open up, I need your help."

"Oh boy," Kleora winces. "This can't be good."

"Indeed." Why would the young vampire come to me and not Nicole or Logan? I summon my own outfit before swinging open the door. I am startled by the harassed appearance of the Guardian as he strides into our bedroom, his fingers raking through his hair in agitation, and by the looks of it, not for the first time.

"What troubles you, Christoph?"

He glances at Kleora. "Hey, Kleora," he waves lamely.

"How can we help you, Nox?" my mate questions, concern softening her regard.

"It's Cellica," he says, snagging my full attention.

"What about her?"

"She's gone. I came back to the cabin after the night of the spell, and the house was deserted." He focuses on me. "I've searched everywhere I can think of, but it's like she vanished into thin air. Liam is gonna kill me."

"She has been missing for an entire week, and you are only coming to me now?" Irritation rides my voice. Hellfire, what was he thinking?

"I didn't want to alert anyone. I'm a tracker. I hoped I would locate her and bring her to you."

"Christoph," Kleora reprimands. "We must inform the others and organize a search party."

His shoulders drop in defeat. "I guess I imagined you could pinpoint the demon inside her, and I could retrieve my... the pain in the ass pup."

"You do realize which demon lives in Cellica, right?" I demand, slipping socks and shoes on my feet while Kleora searches the room for her flip-flops. Why she does not conjure them is perplexing, and any other time I would tease her about it, but with Liam's little sister missing with Asmodeus riding shotgun, I refrain.

My question stops Nox's frantic pacing. "No. Who?" he asks with a new wariness.

"His name is Asmodeus. He is the most powerful Prince of Hell, besides me, of course."

"You said it was a demon of lust, not a goddamn Prince of Hell."

I cast him a sour look. "Does no one understand how shit works down there?" Not expecting an answer, I snatch my phone off the nightstand and shoot a text to Nicole. Something the Guardian should have done a week ago. The vampire queen, not to mention the werewolf king, will be all kinds of pissed at Nox.

"Fuck. Fuck. Fuck," he hisses, realizing how deep in shit he sunk himself. "I don't care what happens to me. My priority is Cellica." His broad shoulders stiffen, and determination hardens.

"She is all our priority now, Nox," I murmur as my phone dings with a text. "Well, it appears the gang is getting together at your cabin for your funeral in ten minutes."

"Great," Christoph mutters. "Sorry to barge in on you like this. You're right. I should have gone to my queen first."

"I usually am, young vamp."

He offers a lame smile. "See you in ten." The defeated tone has me biting my lip to keep a grin at bay.

As soon as his image dissipates, I turn to my female. "This is about to get soap opera epic, peach. Dress up."

She laughs. "You're incorrigible."

Chapter 49

Kleora

Darath insisted we arrive early to be front and center when Nicole and Liam ream Nox a new one. His words, not mine. I snicker. The creature thrives on the drama of others, but secretly I kinda do too. As long as it's not my drama and no one gets hurt.

While we wait for the others to appear, I admire Nox's secluded getaway. From the outside, the cabin appears rustic, blending in with the surrounding forest. However, the inside takes on an entirely different form. It's the ultimate bachelor pad, complete with foosball and pool tables in the living room.

In the corner is a well-stocked bar with draft beer on tap. On tap. Like a regular bar would. The floors are hardwood, the appliances stainless steel, but the furniture is colorful bean bags and a couple of gaming chairs set in front of the biggest TV I've ever seen.

An enormous stone fireplace sits in the other corner, with almost a cord of wood stacked next to it. Jesus. That's a lot of timber to maintain inside the house. Doesn't he worry about termites or carpenter ants? I'm going to have to discuss wood safety with the boy. Keep it outside and only bring in what you can burn in a few days.

My gaze roams over my striking mate as he jokes with Nox by the bar, no doubt working to ease the vampire's anxiety. Tonight, he went with black slacks, showcasing the scrumptious ass I'm jonesing to spank since the second he mentioned it. The red silk, long-sleeved dress shirt matches his eyes and highlights his powerful physique.

Over the last week, after Darath introduced me to his playroom—like a real authentic sexual dungeon—he's trained my body, soaring it to reach heights of ecstasy I never imagined.

My thoughts flashback to the spanking bench he'd strapped me to the other night, and my insides flutter. A part of me, buried deep in the nether regions of my mind, lives a speckle of shame. The extreme measures I enjoy should scare the ever-living crap out of me. Should I seek therapy or something?

According to my illicit mate, my sexual appetite for pain is perfection, but that's because he gets off on inflicting it. So maybe it's time to have a private word with Sebastian and get his opinion. After all, he is the resident expert on all things BDSM…

He might give me a few pointers on how best to handle my mate when he's on the receiving end. Does Darath relish the degree of pain I do? What if he requires more? Would I enjoy inflicting a high level of suffering on my male?

I glance up, and my mate's heated stare bores into me. 'Thinking about our role reversal later tonight, peach?'

'Actually, yes,' I respond. 'I wondered about your level of pain tolerance?'

His sexy growl rolls around in my head, making my girly bits sit up and take notice. 'Nothing you could dish out would be too extreme, Kleora. You will discover I love receiving as much as giving. But if you find you are uncomfortable in any way being the one in control, I am perfectly happy being the only Master in the bedroom.'

Wow. Why is it every time he says the word, Master, my entire body clenches with need? And we should not be having this internal conversation with Nox two feet away. I hope we resolve this issue pronto. One, so Cellica is safe, and two, so Darath and I can be alone in the playroom.

'I'm eager to brighten your bottom red, Lucifer,' I declare with a saucy grin.

The Devil's irises illuminate.

"You guys mind keeping the sex vibes down to a minimum," Nox mutters, stepping behind the bar to refill Darath's whiskey. "I've had my fill over the last several weeks."

"Why do you have a full bar in your house when you only consume blood?" I ask with interest, attempting to ignore the fire in my mate's gaze.

"I entertain a lot, and not all my friends are vampires," he shrugs, handing Darath a tumbler of amber liquid.

Logan and Nicole materialize next to the fireplace, and the queen's furious regard zeros in on Nox. I almost feel sorry for the Guardian until I remember Cellica disappeared a week ago.

Even though Nicki appears livid, she says nothing. Instead, leans against her mate's sculpted torso and rubs her belly. The Halfling looks ready to pop that kid out any second.

Please, God, not yet. I have plans for my man tonight.

Nox leaves the bar and heads straight for his queen, dropping to one knee in front of her with his head bowed. "Forgive me, my queen, for not coming to you first with this issue."

"You mean last week," she scolds, her eyebrow arched in irritation.

"Yes, my lady. I assumed I would find her, but she has evaded me."

"How is that possible, Nox?" Logan asks. "You are a goddamn tracker, for fuck's sake."

Christoph rises to his feet to face his former commander. Brave. "I do not know," he admits in a low whisper as Kurtis and Lucretia enter the room.

The second Bastian and Alex arrive, Christoph stiffens but turns to his superior. The male he should've gone to with this problem first. Nox is second in command and answers directly to Sebastian.

"I'll spare us all from having to hear the story more than once and wait for Liam to get here, but when the werewolf finishes with you, Nox, you will answer for this insolence."

I shiver at the ice coating Bastian's tone and notice a similar response in Alex. Although the way her heated regard flickers with silver, I imagine she's feeling a different emotion entirely.

Hmm. Interesting. Maybe I should pick her brain instead of Sebastian's. I wonder if he allows her control?

"Yes, sir." Nox's jaw clenches, no doubt regretting his decision to deal with Cellica by himself.

As soon as Liam and Viessa appear, a definite charge fills the room. Liam is beside himself with rage. His whiskey irises flash with the blue of his wolf, and before anyone can blink, the werewolf king slams his fist into Nox's nose.

The vampire stumbles back several steps but remains upright, straightening to meet his friend for more. The werewolf loses it, knocking Christoph off his feet before straddling him and pummeling his face.

"Where… is… she?" Liam bellows in-between blows.

Nox doesn't protect himself or retaliate. He knows better. The king is on the edge, and if the vampire even hinted he might fight back, the beast would appear, and it would be all over.

'Do something, Jag,' I mentally plead, surprised no one else has stepped forward.

'Would you like some popcorn, love?'

'Are you serious right now?' I'd laugh at the devilment on his face if Nox wasn't my prevalent worry.

Nicole nods to Bastian and Kurtis. They advance, grabbing hold of Liam's arms and hauling him off the bleeding vampire.

"I will kill you if your stupidity hurts my sister, Nox. Do you hear me?" he snarls, the beast heavy in his tone.

Christoph climbs to his feet. Blood coats his face, but the swelling and cuts from the wolf's fists heal in an instant. "Yes. I would welcome death if something happened to her… because of me." He grabs the dishtowel Lucretia holds out for him and clears away the crimson staining his nose and cheeks.

Sebastian steps forward. "Tell us what transpired and leave out nothing."

"There's not much to communicate. I came home from the night of the spell, and she'd broken through the restraints, demolished the room, and vanished."

"Is it possible she was taken?" Logan asks.

"If true, Asmodeus has them bedded already," Darath offers with a straight face, and I want to smack the back of his head. He is so not helping.

Blue and green light up the living room as a low, menacing snarl bursts from Christoph's chest. "Anyone who dares touch her will suffer for days before I rip their throats out."

Nicki steps between Nox and an advancing Liam. "Enough," she barks, halting the wolf in his tracks. "If we have a snowball's chance in Hell of finding your sister, we require everyone, including my disobedient Guardian."

"Um," I clear my throat and step forward. "I'm the most mobile, seeing as I am able to travel anywhere, even if I haven't been there. So I could search a lot faster."

"Unless you can track her, peach, it would be like attempting to find a needle in a field of haystacks." Darath plants his big palm on my shoulder, bringing me to life. "I have a couple of obedient hellhounds I use for hunting wayward demons. Never one who was possessing an immortal, but it is worth a try."

"Thank you, Darath," Sebastian says, unrolling a map across the pool table. We all gather around. "In the meantime, Nox is the best tracker the Vampire Nation has, so we will begin a perimeter sweep." He circles the area around the cabin and then proceeds to make larger circles out until he's covered the U.S. and Canada with ever-expanding rings. "We move outward until one of us senses her. Do not intercept. You hear me, Liam?" He directs his sapphire glare at the king. "Relay the info to Darath so he can extract the Prince."

"Once I have Asmodeus contained, it is essential the little wolf ingests vampire blood to recover," my mate announces. Nicole glances at him with a shrewd expression.

What is the Devil playing at now? I reach back and pinch his thigh. I'm dying to question his motives, but since Nicki can hear our mental conversations, I keep my thoughts to myself until later.

"Not yours, Nox," Liam rumbles, and Christoph's jaw hardens.

"Whoever is closest, Liam," Logan interjects. "Do not be a narrow-minded ass."

"Why do you object to Christoph, regarding Cellica, wolf?" Darath inquires with curiosity. I'd also love to know the answer.

"Cellica isn't immortal yet," King Scott barks. "She's a child compared to Nox's century and a half of life."

"Logan is like a hundred times my age," Nicki smirks. "Some girls like way older men."

"Careful, baby," the warrior purrs. "Or I will demonstrate what this old man can do."

"Look at King Darath and I," I add. "He robbed the cradle, so to speak. I'm merely four hundred to his couple of millennia. So, I'm sorry to say, King Scott, but age as the argument is pretty weak."

"She's my baby sister," the wolf rumbles. "And I'm well aware of Nox's reputation with females."

Ah. Interesting. Nox is a player.

"Nothing is going on between us," Nox says, and I catch Nicki's wince out of the corner of my eye. "You're right. She is a child and not my type."

"Then why so possessive, Vampire?" Darath probes, and we all wait, needing the answer as much as Liam.

"I... She's my best friend's sister. If something happens to her on my watch, I'd never forgive myself."

Lame. As excuses go anyway.

"Christoph, if this Prince hurt Cel, you won't have time for remorse. You'll be dead." Liam's livid growl is downright scary, but Nox doesn't back down. Instead, he nods his agreement. Like he'd welcome his friend's retribution.

"Can we please focus on the task at hand and finish with all this drama?" Kurtis huffs with irritation.

"Before we disperse," Darath interrupts, "we have another problem."

Chapter 50

Jagorach

"Seriously?" Nicki grumbles. "Is it possible to have one problem at a fucking time? Or better yet—no problems."

"I second that sentiment," Lucretia says with an exaggerated eye roll.

"It is more of a logistics nightmare than a real issue," my helpful mate offers, and I grin down at her.

"Spit it out, Darath," Sebastian orders, his arm once again draped across Alex's shoulders. "We should head out before Cellica's trail grows any colder."

"Our first problem lies with the timing of Cellica's transformation into immortality. If Asmodeus possesses her during the change, the Prince will bind with her soul and no amount of magic in the universe can remove him."

"What!?" Liam and Nox exclaim at the same time.

"Why are we just hearing about this now, Luci?" Nicki asks, glaring daggers at me.

"A Prince of Hell has never possessed an immortal before, and certainly never a werewolf before transition. The cowards prefer humans."

"Why?" Kleora asks.

"For a Prince, or any demon for that matter, a human's soul is like crack to a junkie. Their essence contains something an immortal doesn't."

"And what is that?" Alex questions with interest.

"Mortality. To feed off and slowly kill a human brings power to the demon, and the more souls they have under their belts, the higher they rank in Hell."

"So a demon possessing an immortal cannot kill it?" Logan asks.

"Correct. Hence the reason Dzun and I had to do a little research on the matter. But never fear, my friends. We discovered it will be a symbiotic binding. According to my commander, if she transitions before I can remove Asmodeus, the little wolf can still resume her normal life. However, every full moon, the demon will take control and unless Cellica is mated, Asmodeus will force her to satisfy his raging lust with whoever is around."

"Well, that's just fucking great," Liam grumbles in frustration.

"And if she's mated?" Nox asks.

"Then her mate will enjoy the effects of the Demon of Lust," I announce, my grin spreading.

"Then it's even more important we find her asap," Sebastian interjects.

"Indeed," I respond before continuing my little raid of issues. "Remember when Nicki's mother informed us about rare human women who could breed with immortals? Breeders, she called them and said they needed to be identified." When they all nod, I continue. "Well, I found one..."

"What?" Nicki exclaims, straightening away from Logan. "First off, how did you find her, and second, how do you know she's a Breeder? Was she wearing a goddamn sign?"

Before focusing on the pregnant Halfling, I glance sideways at my mate, knowing she will bear the responsibility for what I am about to reveal. "Dzun found the Breeder female when he was searching for another Prince who escaped."

As expected, Kleora stiffens next to me, and I sense the guilt radiating from her in waves. I squeeze her shoulder, hoping it reassures her enough until we are alone.

"Mammon, the Demon of Greed," I resume, "latched onto the female because he sensed there was something different about her. After being near her, I perceived her uniqueness as well."

"Unique in what way?" Lucretia inquires.

"She was still a Homo sapiens but different. Like a weak kinetic field surrounded her body. She fought the beast, able to take control for long periods. Which is unheard of for a human possessed by a Prince. He did not want to relinquish his prize. He could feed on her soul and not worry about damaging the body and needing to seek another for quite some time. They are not only cowardly, but lazy as well."

"Are you saying we somehow use the Princes to help us find the Breeders?" Lucretia asks, fascination evident in her expression.

"We could." I hesitate, wanting to make damn sure they understand the complexity of the situation. "Handling a demon soldier is one thing, but controlling a Prince is an entirely different set of issues."

"Did you cast the one out of the human?" Logan inquiries.

"Yes. But it took some time. He fought tooth and nail. It surprised me the ritual did not kill her. Another aspect of being a Breeder, perhaps."

"Do you believe you can control them enough to help us find more of these enhanced women?" Nicki questions with a raised eyebrow. "The ability for an immortal to breed with a human is life-altering for our species. More so for the vampires than any other."

"I could. If, and that is a big if, we offer the greedy bastards the right incentive."

"What kind of incentive?" Liam pipes in, his arms crossed over his chest.

"That will depend on the demon. We may have to negotiate different terms for each one."

"Great," Kleora mutters. "Because demon bargains always go as planned."

An image of Mogrun molesting my precious mate spikes my rage. In tune with my emotions, she senses my inner battle and leans into my side to offer reassurances that, despite what happened, she is fine. I tamp down on the aggression and concentrate on the matter at hand.

"Viessa." Nicole turns to the Oracle standing with regal grace next to Liam. Even though the deity is almost six feet, the werewolf's bulky form makes her appear petite. "Have you received any insight or visions to help with locating these enhanced women?"

"No, my lady. I will increase my daily meditation and see if it helps."

"I believe the human, Gemma, the one possessed by Mammon, feels a connection to an immortal already." My revelation draws all eyes.

"Who?" Logan questions.

"A werewolf." I swivel to Scott, keeping Kleora tucked against my side. The feel of her body next to mine soothes me. "The Sheriff, Drake Silverton, had an immediate reaction to Gemma. His wolf was distressed about letting her go."

Liam grins. "Well, if anyone deserves a mate, enhanced human or not, it's Drake. That wolf has been through Hell, strode through the fire, and came out the other side with his demons in tow. A mate might be what he needs to overcome his past."

"Unfortunately, his reaction forced me to wipe his memory of her, but I planted a seed to ensure they meet again."

"Darath," Nicki snags my attention. "Work on the safest way to utilize the Princes. If we can employ their bloodhound abilities to locate the Breeders, it's a win-win all around. But for right now, let's concentrate on finding Cellica and getting rid of her extra baggage before her transformation."

"Of course," I reply.

"Kurtis and Lu, search the first two quadrants." Sebastian steps up to the circled map. "Liam and Viessa, take the next two. Alex and I will hunt in the last. Everyone, employ as many of your troops as you can spare in this pursuit. Darath and Kleora will comb the full area with the hellhounds."

"Where do you want us?" Nicki queries, examining the plan.

"You, my love, will be safe at home, where I can watch over you," Logan states, his tone brokering obedience.

The spitfire Halfling slowly pivots to face her mate. "Is that so?" she asks, her expression surprisingly friendly, which is a dead giveaway to the anger boiling beneath.

Nicole is as stubborn and reckless as she is beautiful. Goody, more drama. Where's my damn popcorn?

Chapter 51

Kleora

"Fight me on this, Nicole, and I will tie you to the bed until you give birth to my son." The hard edge in Moretti's tone has everyone holding their breath, watching the warrior's green irises glint with steely determination.

Nicki regards her mate with her head tilted. The tension in the room is palpable. Will she defy Logan or realize his harsh tone is the fear talking? Live births for vampires are rare. If the mother makes it full-term, the baby is either stillborn, or the mother dies during childbirth. The fact she's made it this far in her pregnancy is a miracle in itself.

Finally, after a full minute, she waddles up to the angry vampire. "Our son, and you're right. I'm sorry."

Logan's shoulders visibly relax as he enfolds his mate and queen in his arms. "Tonight is the last time you will teleport. No more until after our Lucian is born."

"Agreed. And for the record, I'm still not sold on the name Lucian," she responds, nuzzling her face in his chest.

Well. I think I've seen everything. Nicki, not only backing down but being rational for once. I glance up at Darath and almost laugh at the disappointment creasing his brow. My mate thrives on drama and chaos.

'It appears our playtime will have to wait until we locate Cellica, and she's demon-free,' I confess my regret to Darath, despite Nicole being a secret voyeur to our conversation.

Lucifer squeezes my hand, peering down at me. His eyebrows dance up and down with wicked intent before he turns to the group. "Kleora and I will head out and deploy the hellhounds," he announces. Nicki shoots me a smirk.

"Keep us posted, and we will do the same," Liam says before we disappear.

The second we land in our bedroom, the giant demon kisses my cheek with the promise he'll return shortly after he speaks with Dzun and releases the hounds.

I shudder at the notion of what the dogs of Hell look like.

Not one to twiddle my thumbs, I conjure a sexy dominatrix outfit, all black leather and spandex, and head to the playroom to prepare. Depending on how quickly the beasts locate the young werewolf, we're limited on time, so I want everything set and ready.

Five minutes later, I'm standing in a room filled with more sex apparatuses than I know what to do with. The closest encounter I've had with being in sexual control was shoving a male onto my bed and climbing on top.

Darath said nothing was off-limits, as long as it only included the two of us. What would he enjoy? A spanking? With a belt, flogger, or whip? Would he relish a little anal play? Or should I tie him up and give him pleasurable torture until he begs for release?

Damn my inexperience in this area.

I can't wimp out. It's not like I can do a Google search since I cannot hold a phone or type on a keyboard without touching my mate. Right now, this wraith thing is a real hindrance. I have to make sure I'm touching Darath at all times in order to even pick up a whip.

I wander through the chamber, examining the gigantic bed with black satin sheets and tall, intricate posts at all four corners. The spanking bench, an X-looking apparatus, and chains with cuffs hanging from the ceiling on wide rails that run in a crisscross pattern the length of the ceiling.

Hmm. Do you shackle your lover to the rails and then move them about from one station to the next? Darath and I must spend more time here so I can figure all this out. My stomach clenches with desire, craving to experience everything in this place at the hands of my accomplished mate. We've merely explored the tip of the iceberg of possibilities in this room.

You need a game plan, Kleora.

Right. Focus. I walk over to the bed and notice leather cuffs dangling from the tops of the posts. They hang at the perfect height for Darath. A delicious idea unfolds in my brain, and I rush to the display table holding the various toys. I mentally choose the ones I want, since I can't pick them up before wandering to the alcove, showcasing the tools of pain hanging neatly in a row.

Excitement, along with nervous energy, bubbles in my gut even as a torrid fire spreads through my center. With our mental connection, since we're mated, I will discern Darath's emotions. Whether he's enjoying it or wants more or less. My first priority? Discovering his safe word... if he has one.

"Wish I could read your mind right now."

Darath's low rumble has me pivoting to the door where the big sexy brute is leaning against the frame with his arms crossed, a smirk firmly in place.

"No need," I reply. "You're about to find out."

"I am all a-tingle with anticipation, peach."

Is he messing with me? Sometimes it's hard to determine if he's serious or not.

"Do you have a safe word, King Darath?" I ask, strutting toward him, my hips swinging as seductively as I can muster in my four-inch heels. He grunts, the devilish scrutiny taking a leisurely journey down my frame and back again. By the time the ruby irises pin mine, I'm breathless.

"As a matter of fact, I do." He straightens, and I notice something glint in his hand. "But first, I have a gift for you. I meant to give it to you earlier, but we got distracted, and your... condition gives me an excuse to always touch you."

In two strides, he's within six inches, and I inhale his intoxicating scent. Darath clasps my nape, and in an instant, I'm flesh and bone. Desire whooshes through me like a flash flood.

Cool metal clicks in place around my neck. Darath smiles with male pride before gripping one of my hands and pivoting me to face a large mirror on the wall.

My eyes widen at the wide silver collar with strange symbols on the surface. I graze my fingertips across the smooth surface with wonder.

"It's beautiful, Jag. And as much as I adore being collared by you, I won't be able to wear it unless you're touching me."

He drops my hand and steps back, and for a split second, I believe he's angry. My gaze snaps to his. Instead of ire, amusement lifts his lips.

"Look again, love," he says, nodding to me in the mirror.

I peer back at my reflection. Holy cow! His skin isn't in contact with mine, and yet I'm still corporeal. I lift my arms and gaze in amazement at the clarity of my skin before turning to Darath.

"How? What?" I stare at my mate for an explanation for this wonderful development.

"I had Troy spell the cuff with my blood. So anytime you are wearing it, you will remain sentient. A little workaround I devised if things didn't go as planned. Likewise, it is a symbol of your rank, my queen." His proud grin has me laughing with delight.

Not only did my man present me with the perfect gift, but he's thwarting the angelic dickheads who believe they are doing God's work. And maybe they are, who knows. But oh my goddess, I'm alive. Tears threaten. The collar is Lucifer's equivalent of a crown, and I couldn't cherish it more.

"I don't know how or when you created this, and I don't care. All I know is I love you, Jagorach," I declare, grabbing his shirt and pulling him down to meld my lips to his. The second my tongue glides across the seam, the big demon moans low, hauls me against his torso, and takes control, plundering my mouth with breathtaking skill.

He lifts me, and I wrap my legs around his fit waist, gripping fistfuls of his gorgeous hair. Within seconds, I'm lost in the desire burning through my body, shamelessly grinding my aching sex against the rock-hard abs.

A whimper escapes when he pulls back. "I adore you, Kleora. You are my life, my reason to exist, and mine for all eternity. I would destroy worlds for you, disembowel anyone who dared touch what belongs to me, and dance in their blood."

Well, doesn't that make a girl's heart pitter-patter? "And eat their hearts?" I question with a teasing grin.

"If you wished it, yes. I would grant you my kingdom if you demanded it."

The seriousness in his regard fades my smile. "The only thing I demand of you, Lucifer, is your love and touch. Nothing else matters."

"You possessed those the second I laid eyes on you," he admits before sliding me down his chest. Once he's sure I'm steady on my feet, he lowers to his knees in front of me, and my breath catches. "You own me. Heart. Body. Soul. Tonight, I submit to your will." His grin is pure Devil. "Have your wicked way with me, peach, before our duties call us away."

Nervous butterflies dance in my stomach as I step back and examine the absolute masculine beauty of my mate. Yes, he craves violence, and chaos, and has a mischievous streak a mile wide I adore. But he's also loyal, possessive, loving, and a damn skilled lover who offers me the level of pain and pleasure my body requires.

I never thought I would fall madly in love with Lucifer in this life or the next. But here I am, rocking it, as Jilaya would say.

We still have so much to accomplish and overcome. Nicole must survive the delivery of the prophesied vampire king. Abigail is in the wind with Troy as her protector. And Cellica has disappeared, possessed by a Prince of Hell.

But no matter the obstacles in our path, Darath and I, along with our pack of friends, will fight tooth and nail to fulfill the prophecy and protect each other. An immortal couldn't ask for a more glorious task or a better network of loyal comrades.

With a grin, I shove aside my apprehensions of the future and set forth on showing my incredible mate how much I worship every single magnificent inch of the Devil himself.

THE END

Also By

A.R. Vagnetti

Storm Series – A Complete Paranormal Romance Series

Forsaken Storm
Forgotten Storm
Forbidden Storm
Fiery Storm
Fractured Storm
Fatal Storm
Final Storm... The Conclusion

Coming Soon

Immortal Breeder Series – A Storm Series Spin-Off

Gemma's Fate
Calista's Destiny
Willow's Doom
Layla's Future

Keystone Series – A Dark Fantasy Romance

Diamond Key
Emerald Key
Sapphire Key
Ruby Key

Talk To me, Stormster

Thank you, dear readers, for continuing to love the Storm Series! Stay tuned for **Final Storm**, the last book in the series, featuring Christoph Nox and Cellica Scott!

If you loved Fatal Storm or any of the books in the Storm Series, please consider reviewing it or recommending it to a friend—your reviews help indie authors so much.

Let's Connect: Join the Stormster Club! You will get exclusive previews, book recommendations, and news on upcoming releases. A.R. loves to connect with readers.

Stormster Club Sign Up at my website: www.arvagnetti.com
Email: ar@arvagnetti.com
Please Follow A.R. on:
BookBub – Goodreads – TikTok – Instagram – Facebook – Pintcrest – Twitter

Acknowledgments

It takes a squad!

Writing a book is a team effort. We'd like to think the author sits at their computers and, poof, a full-length novel happens. But, unfortunately, the reality is I couldn't do what I do without the assistance of some very special people.

My husband. Bless his soul for putting up with my long hours at the computer—all my ranting and raving over software, design, and the dreaded marketing. But, most importantly, for making an effort to follow my ramblings.

My editor, Haley Willens. Thank you, thank you, thank you for being the grammatical genius I am not. You took my gibberish and created something magical.

My betas. Dawn, Paul, Mia, and Jodi. You were tough on me this time, but I greatly appreciate it because you made the story more in-depth and cohesive. You guys are my rock.

Thanks go to my Street Team. You are the last eyes before publication, and your reviews mean the absolute world to me. I read them over and over again.

And let's not forget the gorgeous cover by Les at German Creative. Your creative talent is awe-inspiring, and every book gets better and better.

Most importantly, I would like to express my undying gratitude to my loyal and faithful readers. My Stormsters! Thank you for not only picking up my books, but reading them, loving them, reviewing them, and coming back for more. Without you and your love of spicy paranormal romance, I wouldn't be an author.

So rest assured, dear reader, the Storm series is all your fault.

About The Author

A.R. Vagnetti is an American writer who grew up in the scalding Tucson desert. Her debut novel, Forgotten Storm, is the first book in her Storm series and won the Top 20 Best Indie Books of 2019, among other awards throughout the series.

She does her best writing while camping, traveling, and on the beautiful shores of Lake Huron, where she is now blessed to spend her summers away from the Arizona heat.

A.R. loves to transport readers into a fantastical world of paranormal romance where bold Alpha males will sacrifice anything for the strong, deeply scared, kick-ass females they love.

Made in the USA
Columbia, SC
07 February 2024